THE WAR WITHIN

A Novel

H. A. PELL

This book is a work of fiction. All incidents and dialogue, and all characters except for some well-known historical figures, are products of the author's imagination and are not to be construed as real. Where real-life historical figures appear, the situations, incidents, and dialogues concerning those persons are entirely fictional and are not intended to depict actual events or to change the entirely fictional nature of the work. In all other respects, any resemblance to actual persons, living or dead, events, or locales is entirely coincidental.

HICKORY HILL
CABIN BOOKS™

Manufactured in the United States of America.
Cover by Vila Design.

*For my wife, Teresa, with my love and gratitude.
This novel would not have been possible without
your help and support.*

"[T]he final—and most important—thing you should know about these JTTFs: They are working 24/7/365 to protect you, your families, and your communities from terrorist attack."

HTTPS://WWW.FBI.GOV/INVESTIGATE/TERRORISM/JOINT-TERRORISM-TASK-FORCES

PROLOGUE

May 2005. Near Baghdad.

Jack saw a flash of light and heard the explosion less than a second later. Seventy-five meters ahead a Humvee flew through the air like a toy truck hurled by an angry child. It tilted in mid-air, the shattered hulk landing on the driver's side with its underbelly exposed to rounds coming from the east side of the road.

Inside the Humvee, Specialist Marvin Robbins, nineteen years old, looked down at what was left of his lower body. As he died he wondered how he had gotten to the quarry back home in Georgia, on a moonless night, diving into the dark water below. Another soldier, Specialist Ricky Daniels, was wedged inside, pinned under one of the seatbacks with his leg bent in two directions.

Staff Sergeant Jerrod Cramer, who had been manning the Humvee's M240 machine gun, lay sprawled alongside the vehicle. One of his legs was pinned beneath it, flattened into the thick dust of the roadbed. The other leg lay some yards away, fully detached, as if a mannequin had hopped away leaving it behind.

Jack saw the Humvee taking enemy fire and screamed, "Move! Move! Move!" into his headset. Private First Class Isaiah Johnson, his driver, had stopped their Humvee in the middle of the road. He stared ahead, frozen in terror. The sound coming from their own M240 confirmed that Sergeant

First Class Sam Jacobsen had fixed on targets. The Humvee finally sprang into motion, performing a perilous ballet as it sharply turned and went over a rise, wheels coming off the ground. It slammed back on all fours and sped toward a high spot at the rear of the smoking Humvee.

Jack saw Cramer struggling to remove his right foot from underneath the vehicle. He had tied his bandana around his left thigh, just above where the jagged thigh bone exited into space. The IED hadn't set off the vehicle's fuel tank, but the enemy rounds were about to finish the job. The fuel tank was the Achilles Heel of the vehicle, and the Army knew it; fire suppression panels were being tested for installation. Too late.

Jack knew they had little time. Cramer would be shot—or more likely incinerated when the tank exploded. He yelled, "Go left!" They swung by the downed Humvee and with Jacobsen providing cover, Jack leapt out of the moving vehicle. He rolled, and his momentum carried him toward Cramer and the burning Humvee.

Crawling along a shallow depression, Jack heard the snapping sound of bullets flying over his head. His goggles and the bandana he wore across the bottom of his face had come off. Dust caked around his nostrils and his vision blurred as he crawled toward the vehicle. He felt a sharp pain on one of his legs but continued to crawl to the Humvee.

Laying on his back, with his knees up, he saw that the right pant leg of his uniform was torn away on the outside of his thigh. He placed both feet on the Humvee's roof and pushed. He managed to push the vehicle slightly from its position. Cramer pushed both hands down into the roadbed and pulled his crushed leg from beneath the vehicle. Jack released the pressure and the Humvee rocked but remained resting on its side.

Smoke began to fill the inside of the Humvee and Daniels' screams of "*Help!*" were all that Jack could hear over the gunfire. Daniels was still pinned inside as flames began to lick the perimeter of the fuel tanks. Jack peered through the opening in the roof and saw Robbins, whose entire lower half was blown away. Dead.

Daniels reached up for Jack, screaming from the heat and flames that were beginning to engulf him. Gagging and exposing himself to enemy fire, Jack reached in and grabbed the shoulder strap of Daniels' protective vest. He pulled with all the strength he could muster, and Daniels tumbled out on top of him.

Jack had no recollection of what occurred next. An explosion. The smell of burning flesh . . .

* * * *

AT the field hospital, when the mist dissipated from his brain, Jack felt excruciating pain. The medic quickly hooked up another bag with morphine and he floated off into unconsciousness. Two days later he was flown to Germany, first to Ramstein Air Base and then transferred to the medical center in Landstuhl.

The explosion had slammed Jack to the ground, with Cramer's full weight on top of him. The broken ribs would knit together without problem. The edge of a broken bone exiting Jack's left forearm had left a crescent-shaped laceration. Adjacent to it would be a scar line, a permanent reminder of the metal plate and screws imbedded below. The pain he had felt while crawling toward the Humvee came from a bullet piercing the outer portion of his thigh.

The burning flesh that he had smelled before losing consciousness had been his own right leg. Skin grafts started at his knee and ended in a circle around his calf where his boot had prevented the flames from spreading. His leg would be scarred but he would have full use of it.

* * * *

THE recommendation packet for the award of the Silver Star included witness statements that Captain Jackson Thomas had hoisted Cramer on his back and was dragging Daniels away from the Humvee when it exploded, flipping and landing ablaze on its roof. Acting under fire and without concern for his personal safety, Jack had saved two lives. Ironic because Jack had sworn he would never join the military and follow in his father's footsteps.

CHAPTER 1 – A Choice

As Jack was being awarded the Silver Star, newly-promoted Brigadier General Maxwell Thomas was sitting in his office. Six weeks before, he had been assigned to the U.S. Army John F. Kennedy Special Warfare Center and School at Fort Bragg, North Carolina. General Thomas had graduated first in his class at West Point. The West Point ring on his hand was massive and carried the motto "Duty, Honor, Country" that had been adopted by the Academy in 1898.

The general was a large man at six feet four and two hundred and thirty pounds, molded into a rock-solid physique. He had slate gray eyes with rugged, leading-man features. He kept his hair cut in the "high and tight" style, shaved close on the sides and a shade longer on top. Known as "Supermax" to his troops, it was legend that even kryptonite would have no effect on him. He had been in the thick of combat on several occasions and was riding in a Humvee that was destroyed by an IED. He walked away with a slight wound just off his right eyebrow, the thin scar adding to his aura of invincibility.

He met an eighteen-year-old Irish-Italian beauty named

Roberta O'Reilly when he was a newly-commissioned second lieutenant stationed at Fort Bragg. Lieutenant Thomas promised Roberta that he would marry her when he returned from his second tour of duty in Viet Nam.

When Captain Max Thomas returned to Fort Bragg in 1975, he wore his first Silver Star medal for heroism. He had assumed command in the field when his company commander was killed and, while exposed to enemy fire, saved his company from decimation by the enemy. He made good on his promise to marry Roberta.

The first child born to Captain and Mrs. Thomas was an eight-pound, five-ounce boy. Thomas decided that his son would be named Jackson Jonathan Thomas, the full name of General Thomas Jonathan "Stonewall" Jackson in reverse order. His expectations for Jack were clear from the moment he was born.

When Jack was in high school Max contacted the Superintendent of West Point, a former classmate. He suggested that the football coach might want to recruit Jack as a potential team member. Jack was an All-State player and was heavily recruited by major universities around the country.

He was eligible for admission to West Point as the child of a career military member; his father's status as a West Point graduate would also carry great weight. In addition, Max had secured an agreement by the U.S. congressman in his district for a nominating letter. Jack had no intention of going to West Point; he completed the admission application only to appease his father.

* * * *

JACK had just gotten home after football practice during the fall of his senior year of high school. His father was home on leave from the Balkans and was working on an after-action report in the home office near the front door of their two-story home. Jack was hot, tired, and not in the mood for any discussions with his father. He closed the front door, called out "Hey Dad," and headed up the stairs.

"Hey Jack." Jack heard the beckoning tone and stopped on the stairs.

"Sir?"

"Got a sec?"

"Kind of tired, Dad. Can we talk later? Got a lot of homework," Jack said as he continued up the stairs.

"How about I get some pizza delivered and we talk over dinner?"

"Okay, Dad," Jack said from the top of the stairs, resignation in his voice.

He knew that his father wanted to talk about West Point. They would be hearing from the admissions committee in a few months. He could hear him say, again, about how he had all the qualities that would make him a great leader, and how "this nation needed great leaders."

Jack had seen first-hand what it meant to devote your life to the military and the sacrifices that were made—not only by the soldier but also by the family. When it came time to choose a college Jack could only think about his mother. She had been left when she needed his father the most because he was a "great leader" and had put "this nation's needs" before hers. Jack was determined that he wouldn't put his own family through that kind of hell and he couldn't forgive his father for what he had done.

He received the appointment letter to West Point the same day he received the letter of acceptance to the University of North Carolina at Chapel Hill. He immediately wrote a letter declining the appointment, knowing that another person who wanted to attend would now have that opportunity.

Jack's interests were in a much different direction. He was fascinated by the business world. He admired Warren Buffet, the wealthiest man in America—not for his wealth but because of his business acumen and how he lived his life, humbly, without ostentation and the accumulation of material possessions. Buffet was also a philanthropist and wanted to leave the world a better place, something that was important to Jack as well.

For Jack, it was the taking of an idea, building a company, and contributing to the welfare of his community that was exciting. Maybe his father was right. He was a leader, but it was in the business world that he wanted to exercise that leadership. He would gain the loyalty and respect from employees based on his management style and his respect for them as employees—not by forced order and discipline. He wouldn't always be gone on some "mission" with a chance he wouldn't come home. He would always be there for his family.

* * * *

WHEN Jack was an undergraduate he decided to attend law school, believing that a law degree would be helpful to him in a business career. He applied for and was accepted at UNC's law school. On the first day, in his Criminal Law class, he met Pam Sorensen.

For many men, finding and marrying the girl of their dreams is a process. There's the initial attraction based on physical characteristics. Conversation ensues, and then discovery that the young lady that fate has placed in their path also provides the deep abiding friendship sought in a lifelong companion. To the surprise and amazement of many who are lucky enough to progress to this point, this woman also seems to find them equally captivating. As time goes by, mutual infatuation matures and molds itself into something more solid and lasting. A true relationship of caring and mutual respect and deep understanding. When Jack met Pam, none of this happened.

By the end of the first week of classes, Pam had moved into Jack's apartment. The romance had been instantaneous and with all the subtlety of a tornado ripping across the Oklahoma landscape. The attraction and connection and deep level of understanding was immediate and at a level neither had imagined was possible. It was as if that long-sought after puzzle piece, the one that seemed to be missing from the box, had suddenly jumped into its designated spot to complete the puzzle, joining the brilliant sunrise to its vast supporting ocean below.

Pam's Scandinavian ancestry was revealed in a beautiful woman with long, natural blonde hair and fair complexion. People she met for the first time, judging merely by appearance, would invariably underestimate her intelligence. Pam had attended Duke University on a full scholarship, graduating Phi Beta Kappa with a degree in English literature. It had been a surprise to her professors—some were aghast—that she would be attending law school and not pursuing her doctorate in English. They would have been even more surprised to find out that she wanted to be a criminal prosecutor.

Pam's desire to work in the criminal justice system was the result of a personal and tragic experience. James "Big Jim" Sorensen had been a North Carolina Highway Patrolman. Pam was twelve years old the night he had been called out to help find a man who had murdered an elderly couple who lived near the interstate. He had just gotten off duty and was about to put Pam to bed, as he always did, when he got the call. The man had stolen the couple's car and was last seen on I-95 heading south near where the Sorensens lived. Trooper Sorensen went out on the call and never came back.

Pam heard the words at the funeral. The high speed chase. The heroism of her father. But she couldn't accept that it was her Dad that they were talking about. She pushed her face into the blackness of her mother's dress, wanting it to be a dream. She would wake up and he would be there at her bedside, reading her stories, and laughing at the silly "knock-knock" jokes that she would tell him. But even at age twelve, she knew that the evil in the world had found her, and as much as she pressed against her mother for protection, it wouldn't let her go.

* * * *

IT was a summer Saturday morning. They were about to become third-year law students. Pam decided that it was time to talk to Jack about an issue lurking in the background of their relationship. "Jack, I think there's something we should discuss."

"You're not . . . ?"

She knew by his tone of voice that he was joking, and she gave him one of her "I'm serious" looks.

"Okay, sorry, I'm listening."

"I know that you're interested in a business career. There's no guarantee that you'll find the position you want here or even in North Carolina. You could end up anywhere." Jack knew that Pam was an only child and that she was very close to her mother, who was a widow. He knew, or thought he did, what she was going to say.

"I've never told you the complete story about my father." Tears welled in her eyes. I told you he died in the line of duty, but I didn't tell you about the man who killed him. At the time of the murders of the elderly couple, he had only recently been released from prison. He had been released early because he had a plea deal on a charge of assault with intent to commit murder. Instead of a ten-year sentence, he got only three." She wiped her eyes where tears had begun to roll down her cheeks.

"He should have received a lengthy sentence for his prior crime. If justice had been done, three innocent people would still be alive. I hadn't always wanted to be a lawyer. But then I realized that I could help protect others . . . ." Her voice trailed off. Jack put his arms around her and pulled her close.

She spoke with her head against his chest. "I've decided to be a prosecutor, Jack. And I know that my mother needs me here, so I'll be looking for a job in this area of North Carolina."

"And so will I," said Jack.

He knew that Pam's mother depended on her for help. Whenever her mother was ill, Pam would make the two-hour trip to care for her. He also knew from his own experience how important it was to be there for your family in time of need. He was prepared to remain in North Carolina. One month later, everything changed.

CHAPTER 2 – Little John

Major Max Thomas had reached back to the Revolutionary War to name his second son, born two years after Jack. He would be called John Thomas, after the Major General of the same name who had led the siege against Boston and forced the evacuation and retreat of the British. During the French and Indian War, then Colonel Thomas had led a division that captured Montreal. There was no doubt that Max Thomas expected both of his sons to be military leaders.

When he was a child, no one would predict that this John Thomas would become a leader of men. He was smaller than most of the boys his age and extremely shy. It had not taken long before the call of "hey, here comes little John" on the playground would evolve into a nickname.

Little John would always be picked last when the boys divided up into teams for football, basketball, or baseball, except when big brother Jack was a team captain. Even at a young age, Jack was recognized by the other children as a leader, and the star of every sports team he played on.

It only took one boy to bully Little John when Jack wasn't around. Once Jack found out who had pushed John down on the playground, retribution was swift. From that day on, everyone knew you didn't mess with Jack's little brother.

It was Jack who gave his brother his nickname. Tired of hearing the other kids use the name "Little John," Jack began using the initials "J.T." and made it a point that the others should use it as well.

Although Jack was two grades ahead of J.T. in school the difference in their intellectual abilities was insignificant. What John lacked in size and weight he more than made up for in I.Q. And where Jack would get an occasional "B" in a course due to his involvement on a sports team, J.T. would absorb the material and receive perfect marks.

With Max deployed for lengthy periods J.T. could express himself in ways that he knew his father wouldn't approve, but that his mother allowed. She wanted her sons to express their individuality. She allowed J.T. to wear his hair long and his "school clothes" generally consisted of jeans and a T-shirt.

With his black-framed glasses and his perfect GPA, J.T. was considered a nerd by some but still very much accepted by another group of students with whom he fit right in. Unfortunately, J.T.'s ability to succeed in school without much effort would result in a turn of events that would impact not just his life but Jack's life as well.

CHAPTER 3 – Call of Duty

It was a September morning in 2001. Jack did exceptionally well during his first two years at the law school. He was on the Dean's List every term and was selected for the Law Review. Now in his third and final year of law school, he was at the top of his class and could be selective as to which law firm or corporation he would join.

He was about to leave the student lounge for a 9 a.m. class when the room suddenly went quiet. All eyes went to the wall-mounted television. There had been an explosion at the World Trade Center in New York.

American Airlines Flight 11 had been hijacked by terrorists and had crashed into the North Tower of the World Trade Center at 8:46 a.m. At 9:03 a.m. other hijackers crashed United Flight 175 into the South Tower. The newscaster reported that American Airlines Flight 77 crashed into the western façade of the Pentagon.

As the coverage went on through the morning, the students stayed glued to the television and classes were cancelled. It was later reported that after the crew and passengers of United Airlines Flight 93 learned of the other hijackings and attacks, they attempted to take back control of their own hijacked flight. The plane crashed into a field in

Somerset County, Pennsylvania. In the end, almost three thousand people were murdered and six thousand were wounded.

It was that September morning that changed Jack; seeing the United States under attack, one that shattered thousands of lives, brought things into focus. As a child, Jack stood with his mother and brother in the crowd of families who watched as family members marched off to fight some unknown and unseen enemy. Other times his father had left in the middle of the night, unable to say where and how long he would be gone. But on that September morning, Jack finally saw the face of the enemy, the face of evil. It had become real. The "call of duty," answered so many times by his father, was now calling him.

The United States' response to 9/11 would be called the War on Terror and Jack's response would change his life in ways that he couldn't have imagined only a week before. He enlisted in the Army on September 12, 2001, with orders to Officer Candidate School after completion of basic training. Answering the call of duty meant leaving law school—and the woman he loved—but he wouldn't walk away and leave it to others to protect the country and its freedoms.

Jack completed basic training at Fort Jackson, South Carolina, and graduated first in his class at Officer Candidate School at Fort Benning, Georgia. Following his commission as a Second Lieutenant, he completed the Airborne and Ranger schools. He served one tour in Afghanistan, where he was injured in a chopper crash. His injuries had not been severe and after recovery he was re-assigned to Iraq. He received an early promotion to Captain and was given a company command.

By the summer of 2005, Jack had been shot, suffered serious burns, and had saved the lives of two men under his command. He had been awarded the Silver Star, the Bronze Star for Valor, and two Purple Hearts. Despite his rejection of his father's efforts for him to pursue a military career he was on his way to advancement into the general officer ranks—if he decided to remain in the Army.

CHAPTER 4 – A Career Decision

The Army transferred Jack from Germany to the VA Hospital in Durham, North Carolina. He had just returned from physical therapy when a slender young man with a pony tail and a spiderweb tattoo on his elbow peeked around the half-closed door to his hospital room.

"Hey. Heard there was some war hero in this room."

"J.T.!" Jack tried to get up too quickly to hug his little brother and grimaced in pain. J.T. rushed over and put his hand on Jack's shoulder.

"Nope, you're not getting up for me. Just lie there." As J.T. turned a chair in the room so he could face Jack it struck him that this might be the first time in his life that he could help Jack in some way—instead of Jack taking care of him.

Jack read his mind and smiled. "It's about time you got here. I'm counting on you to spring me out of this place. How about we head over to Chapel Hill for some steaks and a few beers?"

"Not a chance. They probably have you on a special diet and I don't want to be responsible for a relapse."

"Yeah, special diet. The food's so special I asked the

nurse if I could get a box of M.R.E.'s sent up here."

"M.R.E.'s?"

"Meals ready to eat—field rations."

"Oh, yeah. Still hard for me to get over the fact that you went into the Army after—" J.T. stopped suddenly. "You know what I mean."

Jack was silent. He recalled the image of his father coming into their room in the early morning hours in his camouflage uniform. Kissing them on the forehead and telling them good-bye. He would tell them that he would be back soon, but they knew that might not happen.

From their second-floor bedroom window, they would see him leave in his pickup truck. Jack would peer through the curtains, following the taillights in the darkness until the truck disappeared around the corner. The sounds of his mother's soft crying as he went by her bedroom door floated in the back of his mind . . .

"I know. Not something I thought would happen either."

J.T. remembered the day a sedan came slowly up the street. It was the middle of the day in family housing. Men in dress uniforms in a sedan coming down your street only meant one thing. He began to cry as the sedan slowed down near the house—but then it continued to the Denson's house, two doors down. It stopped and the two men in uniform got out to deliver their message of death. He had run to his mother's bedside and buried his head in her side.

J.T. changed the subject. "So, what's next?"

"Not sure. My obligation is up. I can return to active duty, or there's something else I've been thinking about. I can get out and finish law school."

Jack's grandfather had established an educational trust

fund for his grandchildren. The fund paid Jack's tuition and living expenses for his first two years of law school. He now had veteran educational benefits for tuition and could use the trust fund for living expenses. He had also accumulated a large sum of tax-free money during his two combat tours.

"Makes sense," said J.T. "You've only got one year left, assuming they will give you credit for your first two years after you've been away so long."

"I checked. As a returning veteran, I can start next month where I left off, as a third-year student."

* * * *

AS Jack neared graduation from law school, he had several options for employment. While in Iraq, he had spoken with a captain in the Judge Advocate General's Corps who was assigned to one of the Special Forces groups. He could return to the Army as a JAG officer and combine a military and legal career.

He also knew that with his law school resume, he could leave the service and do what he had planned to do before enlisting—join a law firm or begin a career in business. Large corporations were recruiting and hiring military officers who had proven leadership qualities. His law degree gave him an advantage over the competition.

Early in his final semester of law school, Jack saw a poster on the school bulletin board that would fix the course of his future. The Federal Bureau of Investigation would have representatives at the school to provide students with information on careers with the agency. He noted that one division of the FBI focused on counterterrorism.

At the FBI informational meeting he learned that the FBI's counterterrorism efforts included identifying those in America who would join with foreigners to commit terrorist acts overseas or fight alongside terrorist groups against U.S. soldiers. The agents also explained that the agency had the important mission of identifying and stopping home-grown violent extremists planning attacks against the U.S.

A Special Agent explained that the FBI's Joint Terrorism Task Force, the JTTF, was composed of small cells of locally based investigators, analysts, linguists, SWAT experts, and specialists from dozens of U.S. law enforcement and intelligence agencies; the task forces were in over one hundred cities nationwide. They had broken up terrorist cells from Northern Virginia to Oregon, foiled attacks on Fort Dix, on JFK Airport, and on both military and civilian targets in Los Angeles.

What stuck with Jack, even years later, were the agent's comments about counterterrorism investigations in the U.S. The JTTF was always involved in the investigations, and that stopping terrorism was the number one priority of the FBI. Jack thought about the September morning when the country had come under attack. There was no longer just a war against terrorism being fought overseas. There were terrorists waging a war within the United States. After leaving the meeting with the FBI agents at the law school, he filled out his application to join the FBI.

* * * *

MONTHS later, when Jack graduated from law school, he had several offers of employment. One offer was an associate position with the largest law firm in North Carolina. Another was from a large corporation with multi-million-dollar contracts with the federal government to provide military weaponry.

He had also talked with a recruiter about the Army's Judge Advocate General's Corps. The Army had guaranteed him a slot at Fort Bragg with the U.S. Army Special Operations Command after completion of the JAG Basic Course in Charlottesville. He would retain his rank of Captain.

He had heard nothing from the FBI.

CHAPTER 5 – A Snake

It was a Saturday, the day after Jack's graduation from law school. He woke up at 5:30 a.m. and got ready for his normal run and workout. It was almost two hours until sunrise. He reached over to turn on the small lamp by his bedside. Cones of light escaped from the top and bottom of the shade creating curves of light on the dark wall behind the lamp.

He reached down and felt the outside of his thigh. The scar from the bullet was like a furrow left in a newly plowed field. He pulled his knee up and saw that the scars that had covered his knee and shin had begun to lose some of their color and look more natural. The donor site had been on his upper thigh and the area had healed without complications.

The plastic surgeon who did the grafting had warned Jack about the risk of infection. But things went better than expected and the doctors later told him that he had been "lucky." He would recover with full function of his limbs and the scars would fade. *Not all the scars*, thought Jack. *We might still be together today.* He went out the front door and jogged toward his downtown gym.

Jack didn't work out at the type of fitness club typically found in a suburban shopping center, designed to appeal to the masses. Housewives worried about their spreading hips. Students believing that they could stay in shape by walking on a treadmill for twenty minutes, while continuing to eat pizza and drink beer. Middle-aged professionals, mainly men, who could no longer see their shoes when looking down. Treadmills, elliptical machines, and stationary bicycles stretched from wall-to-wall. Perhaps, over in the corner, there would be a rack or two of dumbbells and a single bench press station, generally empty.

Jack worked out as he had when he played football—with weights. Where he went there were a few bicycles and treadmills for cardio and recuperation from injuries, but resistance training was key for size and strength.

The bench press stations were not machines; they were benches with a bar perched over it on metal stands. There were dumbbell sets lining the walls. Metal triangles with pipes jutting out and spearing circular weights of all sizes.

Perhaps the biggest difference was the sounds. Resistance training meant grunts and the expulsion of air when the bars went up. Workout partners shouting encouragement. The sound of the exertion required to reach personal limits and then going slightly beyond.

The name of the gym was simple and to the point. The Weight Room. It was designed to gain inches not lose them. The front of the gym, running along the street, was completely glass. The bottom three feet had been painted green from the inside. The name of the gym was written on the glass in block letters, green outlined in black, and stretched the entire length of the gym. Instead of using "O's" in the word "Room," there were black weight plates, with the number "100" printed along the inner circumference of the plates.

Jack pushed open the door and entered. There was only one other lifter in the room and he was a giant. Jack was just under six feet two. He was at least four inches shorter than the man on the other side of the room. The man's chest and arms were huge, but he had a narrow waist with a washboard of muscle covering his abdomen. His legs were like tree trunks with clearly-defined quadriceps.

The giant was wearing a lifter's tank top shirt. The narrow straps over his shoulders exposed most of his back. Jack, who had seen a lot of big men in locker rooms, couldn't recall any that were as wide across the back. The upper back muscles stretching from the spine to the armpits were like featherless wings. With his dark hair and beard he could have played Samson in any stage production.

He was facing Jack, pulling down on a bar hooked to a cable that wound around a pulley. The pin was set at the bottom of the stack of weights which was being lifted with ease. Jack could not help but stare at what was reflected in the mirror on the back wall.

On the giant's shoulder, a snake with open mouth peered with red eyes. Its head was positioned with a bend between it and the rest of its body, giving the impression that it was about to strike, or perhaps strike again. Drops of blood dripped from the snake's fangs.

An artist with great skill had labored for hours on this human canvas. The snake's skin had all the texture and variety of the subtle colors of an actual snake; it was shaded in tones of green, gold, and black and possessed an iridescent sheen. The body stretched down and coiled twice around a sword's blade on the inside of his forearm.

As the giant pulled the bar down, the snake seemed to

writhe. It swelled in size as the muscles in his arm expanded. The scales looked three-dimensional, and it looked as if the snake might rise off the skin's surface and slither away. There were some words written in script in a foreign language above the serpent's head. Jack couldn't make out all the words, but he had an idea what they might say.

Jack was already warmed up from his run and started his routine for the day. Saturdays meant upper body work, starting with biceps and triceps. He pulled the thirty-pound dumbbells from the rack for a warm-up set and would then increase the weight for the next set.

As he finished his first set he heard a deep voice with a southern drawl. "Hey man, can I get a spot?" Jack turned. The giant was sitting on the bench press bench, straddling it, and about to get under a barbell loaded with six hundred pounds.

"Sure." Jack walked over to the head of the bench and waited.

The giant tightened the leather belt around his mid-section, then laid back, supine on the bench, with his feet flat on the floor. As he reached up to grasp the bar, Jack could see that his well-worn lifting gloves were huge and must have been custom made. Where the finger sleeves stopped just above the knuckles the leather was stretched thin and the stitching was frayed. The back of each glove was embossed with a sword and crossed arrows.

Jack cupped both of his hands under the bar, between the giant's hands, keeping his back straight and knees slightly bent. He knew that it would take all his strength to stop the bar from crashing down if the bar slipped—or if one of the giant's muscles burst under the strain. He recalled the agony of a lineman on his college team who was going for a personal best on the bench press. One of the pectoral muscles in his chest detached from the bone and rolled up in his chest.

The giant took a few deep breaths, pushed the bar off its perch above and lowered it down to his chest. In the next instant it exploded upward. All the giant's upper body muscles were in play, with his back slightly arched until his elbows were straight, but only for an instant. He lowered the bar and repeated the process a second time, a third, then three more times, each time with a grunt followed by an explosion of air from his huge chest.

He finally nestled the bar back onto the metal cradles on the top of the stands. He slid out and up to a sitting position with an agility inconsistent with his massive size. Looking over his shoulder, he said "Thanks, man, 'preciate it."

Jack stuck out his hand. "No problem, name's Jack."

The giant enveloped Jack's hand with a hand the size of a catcher's mitt. With a straight face, he said, "Poindexter." He then broke into a huge laugh at Jack's reaction. "Naw, man, just kiddin.' Name's Mike and thanks for the spot."

Jack broke into a grin. Mike continued to chuckle as he turned to go to the water fountain. Jack read the words above the snake's head that he knew would be there after seeing the gloves: "De oppresso liber," the motto of the U.S. Army Special Forces. The Special Forces emblem of a vertical sword with intersecting crossed arrows was well-known to anyone in the Army's Special Operations Command—a command that included Jack's former unit, the 75th Ranger Regiment.

As Jack went back to the dumbbell rack he looked in the mirror and saw Mike was coming over towards him. He turned around.

"When were you in Landstuhl?"

Jack was a little startled at first but then put together that Mike must have noticed his injuries. *Guess the burns and scar are a dead giveaway.* "Last year."

"Saw the work on your arm and the leg burns. Probably a Humvee fire," Mike said in a subdued voice.

Jack nodded. "Yeah, that's right. I was with the 75th." He glanced down at Mike's gloves, and asked, "Which group?" Jack said, referring to Mike's Special Forces group number.

"Third."

"Still don't get the SF's relaxed grooming standards," Jack said, shaking his head. "When the Rangers go to long hair and beards, I'll know things have really gone to hell."

"Yeah, we are known as a different breed." He hesitated, then said, "I heard from some operators I know that some Rangers got in some heavy shit last year. Your unit?"

"Yeah."

"Well, sorry to hear that."

Mike knew that there had been fatalities. He was thinking about one of his own team members who had been killed by a "friendly" villager with a bomb strapped to his chest. It was like losing a member of his family.

"So, what brings you here? I thought all you SF guys climbed mountains when you had some time off," Jack said, half in jest.

"Yeah, did that first," Mike countered, grinning. "Had some leave and I'm here visiting my sister. You out for good?"

"Well, I just finished law school and I'm thinking about getting back in, this time as a JAG. I've also got an application in with the FBI. Or maybe just hanging it up and going civilian."

"Are you shittin' me? You goin' from Rangers to an office?"

Jack laughed. "If I go back in, they're going to assign me to an SF group as their JAG, so I may be seeing you in the future." As explained to Jack, the SF groups had assigned JAG officers who advise the Group Commanders on international law, rules of engagement, and prisoner of war issues but they also prosecute green berets at courts-martial for violations of the Uniform Code of Military Justice.

"Well, you won't see me in court," Mike said with a laugh. "I'm divorced and there's no way I want to be near a lawyer any time soon—or ever!" Jack knew that the divorce rate for SF was extremely high. He knew from his own childhood about how little can be told to family members about missions. The stress on a marriage was always there.

"We're not all so bad. How about we get together for a beer, and I'll even buy to show you that not all lawyers are out to take your money."

"Sure. I'm pretty flexible right now," said Mike.

"There's a bar and grill just around the corner from here that's pretty good," said Jack. "Why don't I meet you there later? That is, unless there is a woman somewhere in the picture. It's a Saturday and I don't want to mess up a date."

"Well, no woman, but there is this guy—" Mike stopped and roared with laughter at the look on Jack's face. "Man, you are so easy! What I was really thinking was that you might have some lady lawyer friends that would want to come along."

There was a friendly rivalry between the Rangers and Special Forces soldiers. Jack would get the last word. "Well, yeah, but not sure you're their type. They prefer good-looking, intelligent men. And you are SF."

"Okay, Ranger. Just point the way and I'll show you tonight whose type I am."

CHAPTER 6 – A Recruitment

Jack pushed open the door to the bar and grill. It was a Saturday night, and there was a crowd standing around the hostess desk. He saw that Mike was in a booth in the corner of the room and walked over. "I see you've gotten a head start," Jack said, motioning at the beer in front of Mike.

"Yeah, I was thinking I would get the party started without you," Mike said with a smile. Jack sat down and ordered a beer from the waitress who had followed him over to the booth.

"Listen, Jack, I have somewhat of a confession to make. I'm not with the Third Group anymore—but the part about the divorce was true. The time I was away did a number on my married life, so I decided to try a different career path. I'm a Special Agent with the FBI. I'm just coming from an undercover assignment."

"The FBI knows my workout schedule and your being in the Weight Room was part of the application process?"

"As to knowing your schedule, the answer is 'yes.' And as to the application process, technically, 'no,' it's not part of the application—that part is over. I just wanted a chance to see for myself if you would be a good candidate for a special team within the FBI. Congratulations, you've been selected to join the agency, assuming you get through the Academy, which I don't think will present any difficulties for you."

Jack sat back and tried to process what he had just been told. Joining the FBI was now a reality. "Thanks, I know that a lot of good candidates are considered. I wasn't certain—"

"And that's exactly why I wanted to talk to you before you knew you were in. I didn't want you to know that I was FBI, so I played it undercover. I've known guys like you who have incredible records but want everyone to know how great they are. You downplayed your combat action and your own injuries. I'm looking for people who are mission-oriented and don't care who gets the credit."

"Mike, I'm still getting used to the idea of becoming an FBI agent. A special team?"

Mike sat back. "I'm a Special Agent, but I'm also on a SWAT team. You hit several qualifications for entry as a special agent and your law degree puts you ahead of the game. So, I'm here for two reasons. The first one is that I am the FBI's designated closer. We don't want you to be lured away by some law firm where you would make a ton of money and be really unhappy." Mike grinned, but he knew that guys like Jack, who had military service and been involved with special operations were not necessarily out to make a lot of money as their primary occupational goal.

Jack had already considered whether he could sit in a law office all day, every day, in some high-rise. He would be working long hours and having to keep track of his time, minute by minute.

"Yeah, I'd considered that and that's why I was looking at the JAG Corps."

"I'm not going to disrespect the Army's JAG officers.

They do a great job. But they don't do hands-on investigation of crimes. They're still in the office most of the time and they're also subject to overseas deployment. I might be wrong, but I was thinking you were ready to settle down. Maybe start a family."

Jack knew that once you were in the uniform, there were no guarantees where you might end up, or for how long, regardless of your duty position. He thought back again to his own family life and the months his father was away. He saw what it ended up doing to his family. Although J.T. still harbored a deep resentment against his father, Jack began seeing things differently after the attack on the World Trade Center. He remembered leaving Pam and knew the hurt he must have inflicted.

"Okay, what's the second reason you're here?"

"To recruit you for one of our SWAT teams. In two years you can volunteer. Our HR department sends me applications of potential volunteers. You are exactly the type of person we need for SWAT. You're a proven leader. Can definitely see you leading one of our field office teams, and even an enhanced team."

"Enhanced team?"

Mike smiled. "Let's just say that the agency has put together some larger SWAT teams for major operations in cities across the country. The official line is that there are more incidents for response and a 'more target rich environment for terrorists and criminals.' The agency's description, not mine. The enhanced SWAT teams are probably one of the most elite tactical law enforcement units out there. We only recruit the best."

"You're on an enhanced team?"

"Yeah, been on one for several years." He smiled. "I guess the FBI must be like the Army and makes mistakes every so often with personnel assignments. I was promoted to team lead for the Washington D.C. area team last month."

Jack could see that Mike was humble about his work. Up to that point he had only said that he was "on a SWAT team." It wasn't until he asked that Mike had told him that he was an enhanced team leader. "Well," said Jack as he raised his beer mug, "congrats on the promotion."

Mike nodded and raised his glass. "You don't need to slow down on the beer tonight. See that young man trying to pick-up that good-looking lady over there?" He pointed to a nearby table where an athletic-looking black man in jeans and a button-down collared shirt was handing a drink to a young lady.

"He's a Special Agent who lost a bet with me on the World Cup. He seriously thought the Nigerian team would advance further than the U.S. team. He's got designated driver duty tonight. His name is Kalu Adeniyi."

After another hour of discussion, Jack made his decision. He would accept the invitation to attend the FBI Academy, and he was interested in volunteering for the SWAT team down the line. He already knew that he wanted to do counterterrorism work, and Mike had explained the different branches of the counterterrorism division.

Kalu walked over to the table. "Kalu, this is Jack Thomas, our newest FBI recruit."

"Pleasure to meet you, sir." His voice was soft, with a lilting Nigerian accent. Jack sensed right away that he was prior military.

"You too, Kalu, and please just call me Jack."

Kalu turned to Mike and said, "You know, it just might have worked out for me. See that young lady over there?" He turned and smiled at the young lady at the table where he had been sitting. She smiled back at Kalu. He turned back to Mike. "I told her what I was doing, and she told me that she needs someone to drive her home too. I'm coming back here after I drop you both off."

CHAPTER 7 – Ready to Roll

Four years later.

Special Agent Jack Thomas looked over his notes. Move out time was in thirty minutes. He had seen action as a SWAT team member over the past two years, and the agency had recently promoted him to Special Agent in Charge of the Charlotte field office SWAT team.

Unlike the FBI's Hostage Rescue Team, the SWAT team members were not full-time tactical officers. During non-mission hours, they performed their normal duties in several different divisions, including criminal investigations, counterterrorism, and cybercrime.

The SWAT team was using the Army National Guard armory in Fayetteville for its staging area. Jack turned to Tom Coughlin, the Special Agent that headed the FBI's satellite office in Fayetteville. They had heard the starting up of the rotors on the Black Hawk that was sitting out on the tarmac outside the armory. He smiled and said, "Nice to get what you ask for."

They would be operating in a rural area. Because of wooded areas which could cover escape routes, Jack had requested aerial surveillance. The Regional SWAT team leadership was only too happy to provide it. The team pilots needed night-flying hours.

"Yeah," said Coughlin, "we can definitely use some eye-in-the-sky capability."

The SWAT team members had already suited up with flame resistant military issue uniforms and gloves, Kevlar helmets, night-vision goggles, standard military issue bulletproof vests, and gas masks. Each man wore a Springfield .45 caliber handgun as their sidearm and carried an H & K G3A3 battle rifle. Extra ammunition was carried in the vest and because the rural terrain, they wore knee pads and hiking/climbing boots.

The team's two snipers were using the Remington 700 Long Action .308, the same weapon as the Army's M24 Sniper Weapon System. While in the military, both agents had confirmed kills in Iraq and Afghanistan. They would be conducting the assault in a rural area and it was crucial that the snipers were placed in an overwatch position. Jack had positioned them on the eastern and western boundaries, and they were already in place.

"Okay, listen up," said Jack, and the men, who had been making final equipment checks, gathered in a loose semi-circle around him. The armory had a large and open concrete floor area with a metal roof that arched thirty feet above their heads. The interior of the armory was dimly lit; the dark glass of the locked offices, which lined both sides of the drill hall floor, reflected the images of the assembled men.

"Childs, when we off-load you'll lead your team to the front door. We'll provide cover with the Bison as long as possible."

Steve Childs was twenty-seven years old and had enlisted in the Army at age eighteen. After Airborne and Ranger training, he completed the Special Forces qualification course. He had been constantly deployed as an SF team member and decided that if he was ever going to have a normal family life he would have to leave special ops. His head was shaved, revealing a long scar along his temple. A bullet had left a permanent reminder that life or death is sometimes a matter of inches.

Jack turned towards Kalu Adeniyi. "Hey, Kalu, how's the Bison?"

Kalu had been performing pre-operation checks on the Bison armored personnel carrier. The Bison was an all-terrain vehicle with eight wheels. Powered by a 275-horsepower engine, it could move at high speeds carrying eight soldiers. A 7.62 machine gun was mounted over the commander's hatch.

"She's ready to roll, sir," he said.

"Can't break you of that 'sir' habit, can I?" said Jack, smiling.

"Nah, sir," said Kalu, with a wide grin.

At age ten, Kalu had come to the United States from Nigeria with his father, mother, and older sister. He served with the Army's Fourth Infantry Division, and was an expert driving every type of wheeled or track vehicle in the Army's inventory. He had also been on the Army Martial Arts team. His father had passed away when Kalu was deployed overseas, and when he learned that his mother was critically ill, he decided to leave the Army to spend as much time with her as possible.

Kalu went back to school and received a Bachelor of Science in Computer Science. He joined the FBI under the Tactical Recruitment Program and after working two years in the Cyber Crimes Division he volunteered for the Tactical

Mobility Team. He was experienced in delivering tactical personnel to areas of operation and in pursuit and tracking operations. Jack was glad to have him for the mission.

The team conducting the assault loaded into the Bison. All team members carried ballistic shields with Childs designated as the off-load team leader. Jack sat in the commander's seat behind Kalu. The night periscope had been put into place so that Jack would be able to observe from within the Bison.

Jack made a final check on both the command net and the assault team net radio channels. The chopper pilot, also a combat veteran, gave Jack an affirmative response on the check. He would be looped into the command channel during the operation.

Jack looked at his watch and turned to Coughlin. "Okay, Tom, let's roll."

* * * *

MANUEL Ortega pushed the off button on the television remote. The white farmhouse was quiet, except for the snoring coming from one of the back bedrooms. The house was on a twenty-acre vegetable farm outside of Fayetteville. It had been built more than a hundred yards from the two-lane road that ran by the farm, at the apex of a circular driveway that wrapped around a half-acre pond.

Ortega's mother was pregnant with him when she was smuggled into the U.S., along with her own mother and brother. He was born in McAllen, Texas, thereby affording him U.S. citizenship. His citizenship status had been helpful to his business dealings through the years. His business was thriving, and he expected to crack the seven-figure mark before the end of the year.

The snoring from the back bedroom was coming from one of his drug mules. He and the woman sleeping next to him had just returned from Texas after driving for twenty-four straight hours. They left with forty thousand dollars in cash and returned with a large quantity of cocaine. The drugs had been transported from Honduras, through Guatemala and Mexico, and then smuggled across the border.

Agents had tracked their mini-van from North Carolina all the way to the Mexican border. After receiving a tip coming from Texas, a joint operation was put into effect by the field offices between North Carolina and Texas. The plan was to let the exchange happen then follow the van back to North Carolina. They would make sure the drugs got back to Ortega's farm before they made the arrest.

The FBI didn't know that the drugs were already being prepared for transit off the farm. One of Ortega's men, Sanchez, would be leaving for New York with the cocaine within the hour.

The mini-van had been driven into the barn immediately upon its arrival. There was a chance that someone had tipped off the DEA that drugs were being transported to the farm. Usually someone that had been busted and was anxious to make a deal. A snitch who would give up someone in the chain to avoid a lengthy prison sentence—and risk being killed in retribution while serving their sentence. The mini-van had been bought for this one trip and Ortega had already planned to get rid of it the next day.

* * * *

THE Bison rolled down the state road leading out of Fayetteville toward the Ortega farm. Jack was in the commander's seat behind Kalu, and the eight team members sat cramped inside the back compartment, four on a side. Jack thought back to that night, more than four years ago, when Mike Bronson had convinced him that the FBI would be the right choice. *He was right . . . Can't imagine working fifty-plus hours a week in an office . . .*

The Academy had been a challenge, but as in college and in military training courses, he had graduated at the top of his class. He had volunteered for the SWAT team when he was eligible.

When the SWAT team leader in Charlotte went to the Denver office to head its enhanced SWAT team, Jack was promoted to the team leader position. It was a quick rise, but the promotion had been based on merit, and none of the other SWAT team members were resentful. His military background and experience, as well as his outstanding performance as a SWAT team member, had elevated him to the position. He was recognized for his judgment and leadership by his superiors as well as his fellow agents.

Mike had turned out to be both a mentor and a friend. He was still at the D.C. office, and they would get together when he was at Quantico or the FLETC, the Federal Law Enforcement Training Center that was run by the Department of Homeland Security. *Wouldn't be here tonight if it wasn't for Mike,* thought Jack.

He looked out the center periscope. The regular M17 day scope had been replaced by a passive night periscope. Fortunately, the drug delivery to Ortega had coincided with a new moon. The darkness would prevent normal observation for a good distance. With the night-vision goggles, there would be more than enough ambient light for the team members to make out figures in the darkness around the house, and to have the advantage after making entry.

Federal warrants for search and arrest had been secured. Jack would announce the warrants by loudspeaker before engaging. Although it would be hard to mistake the FBI in an armored personnel carrier for a burglar, Jack could imagine a defense lawyer claiming that the homeowner had the right to protect his property from intruders.

They were a quarter-mile from the farm when Jack received a report from one of the sniper teams. The team had infiltrated to the tree line running down the farm boundary several hours before.

"Charlie Six, this is Sierra One. Got some activity. Looks like someone is getting ready to leave the property. Lights are on and a car trunk lid is up. Over."

"Roger, Sierra One," said Jack. "How many tangos? Over."

"Just one. Looks like a mule is getting ready to leave. Over."

Jack had a decision to make. Surprise and overwhelming force were key in any mission. If they made their approach before the vehicle left, they would lose the element of surprise. They could wait and let the car leave; local law enforcement had barricaded the roads, but they had no idea when the car would leave. The driver could be packing the vehicle first, then getting some sleep for a departure after daylight.

"Sierra One, this is Charlie Six."

"This is Sierra One, over."

"Keep an eye on the house. Report back in five mikes if

nothing changes. If the car moves out or the house goes dark, let me know. Over."

"Roger that."

"Did you copy, Sierra Two?"

"Roger," said the other sniper, who had been observing Ortega's house from the woods on the other side of the property.

Jack spoke to the men in the Bison. "Team Alpha, we're going to pull off the road for five mikes. May be a vehicle coming from the farm. We don't need him calling Ortega and letting him know that he saw the FBI headed his way."

In the back of the Bison, Childs groaned. He never liked riding cooped up in the back of any vehicle—much less a Bison while in full gear. Childs keyed his mike and asked, "Do we get overtime for this?"

Jack just grinned and shook his head. "Yeah, be sure to do all the paperwork and get that to me." He paused and then keyed his mike again. "We may have to be a little more proactive on the front end of this. If they know we're coming in, I don't plan to stop and cut the lock on the gate. We'll let Kalu do his thing and drive right through it."

In the front seat, it was Kalu's turn to smile. He hadn't taken the Bison through a barred gate yet. He might get the chance to drive it through the front door.

Jack knew from surveillance that a three-board fence ran along the road fronting the property and metal gates closed off each driveway opening at night. The farm had been observed at night. The agents had discovered that when a vehicle turned in to the driveway floodlights were activated. Jack assumed that an alarm system was also in place to notify the house occupants of any vehicles entering.

Sanchez had finished packing. The cocaine had been removed from a secret compartment in the mini-van, put into air-tight containers, and then stuffed into the deflated spare tire. The tire was installed on a wheel rim using a tire-changer in the barn, inflated, and then placed in the compartment under the floor of the car trunk.

It would take at least forty-eight hours before the drug vapors could permeate the surrounding materials so that a drug detection dog could alert to the cocaine. Sanchez would be in New York by then. He put his suitcase and some wrapped gifts in the trunk; his sister lived in the city and his nephew's birthday was coming up.

"Charlie Six, this is Sierra One, over."

"Go, Sierra One."

"Tango still inside. He put a tire into the trunk. Probably has the coke in it. Trunk now closed and he's inside with the lights on. Over."

"Roger. We can't sit here any longer. We've got a bird in the air who's been circling. We're headed in."

"Roger, out."

"Black Hawk One," said Jack, "this is Charlie Six. You read me? Over."

"This is Black Hawk One, read you Lima Charlie, over." Jack heard the chopper's rotor blades in the background on his headset.

"Entering in one mike. Be on my six. If I start firing at an elevated target, the rounds might go through. I don't want to be the first agent to shoot down his own chopper."

The pilot chuckled and said, "Yeah, that would probably ruin my day. I'll be behind your firing point. Headed in now." He adjusted his night-vision goggles, broke his circle pattern and flew straight towards the farm.

"Sierra One, Sierra Two, this is Charlie Six. Lights out." Both snipers acknowledged receipt of the command.

Sanchez was headed out to the car when the Bison came growling out of the dark. It pushed through the metal gate, snapping the chain and bending the iron bars. The gate slammed open, the clanging of metal barely heard over the roar of the turbo-diesel engine.

As the Bison came up the drive, Jack announced the warrants over the loudspeaker and for all occupants to immediately exit. He had just finished when the Bison rolled onto the pressure plate buried in the gravel driveway.

The alarms went off, but the flood lights didn't come on. The Bison remained shrouded in the darkness. The snipers had exploded the flood lightbulbs on Jack's command. Glass had rained down from the poles as the Bison had breached the gate.

Sanchez had been opening the door of the car when the Bison came through the gate. He made the final mistake of his life by pulling out his gun and firing a round. The sniper's rule of engagement was that if any gunfire came from any occupant and he had a shot, he should take it. He didn't miss.

Sanchez had turned slightly, and the round hit him center mass. He went down in a heap by the side of the car, a large dark circle spreading on his white shirt.

"This is Sierra One. One tango down in yard by car."

As the Bison moved up the drive, automatic weapons began firing from the farmhouse. Rounds began thudding into the Bison and skipping off its angled nose.

"Kalu, time to off-load," Jack said calmly into his mike.

"Roger that," said Kalu, and he brought the Bison to a

halt. Through the periscope, Jack could see muzzle flashes coming from two top windows of the house. "Alpha Six, exit as planned and give me a go ahead when all ready."

"Roger," said Childs, the Alpha team leader. The back door opened, and Childs and the other three agents came out, keeping low behind the Bison and with their ballistic shields up. Twenty second later, Childs keyed his mike.

"All set, Charlie Six."

"Roger," said Jack. "Move out, Kalu." As planned, Kalu started the Bison moving towards the farm house at a slow walking pace, Childs and the other agents crouched behind it with their shields up. They were now thirty yards from the house. Rounds still were clanging off the Bison when Jack popped the hatch and reached up for the 7.62 machine gun that was mounted above the hatch. He heard the Black Hawk behind him.

"Black Hawk One, if you can paint the front with the Nightsun, do it now."

"Roger," was the response from the pilot and three seconds later, the SX-16 Nightsun searchlight, mounted beneath the Black Hawk, came on. The high-intensity beam was pointed directly into the windows of the house. Anyone looking out the windows would be temporarily blinded.

When the searchlight came on, Jack fired multiple rounds from the 7.62 machine gun, raking the house between the two windows. Jack had been concerned about using the machine gun and had checked for any homes in the land behind the farmhouse. There was only forest land behind the planted fields, broken only by a line of utility towers.

Broken glass and wood splinters flew off the face of the house. With Jack providing covering fire, Childs and the other

Alpha Team members quick walked behind their shields to the front door. They went up the steps and took up positions on each side of the door. Only sporadic fire now came from a second-floor window.

Jack was about to give Childs the go ahead to breach the front door of the farm house when the agents on the porch heard a loud "whoosh" coming from the interior. Flames immediately appeared in the bottom floor windows and lit up the porch area. Smoke began seeping from beneath the door and from the windows.

The team quickly cleared the porch and Childs keyed his mike. "They've set fire to the house. No way that fire could have gotten that big that fast from a round hitting something. Heard a shot inside."

A diversion, Jack thought. *No need to burn down the house to destroy whatever coke was inside.* "Send a man around each side. They may be headed towards the woods. Black Hawk One, circle around and light up the fields behind the house and the wood line. Copy?"

"Ten-four." The Black Hawk sliced through the air to the back of the property, scanning the fields with the search light. "Got a man and a woman standing out in the back with their hands up."

"Roger," said Jack. "Childs, you copy?"

"Roger," said Childs. "We've got them in sight."

Jack switched to the command channel. "Foxtrot Delta, this is Charlie Six."

"This is Foxtrot Delta, over." Fire Captain Jessie Hamilton, a Marine Corps veteran, was with the Fayetteville Fire Department. A fire truck was parked on the road, less than a quarter-mile away. There were also two ambulances and a rescue team standing by.

The Sheriff's office had already closed off the section of road that ran by the farm, detouring vehicles from the area. There were deputy sheriffs in vehicles posted on all roads leading away from the farm, including the one that could be accessed by foot through the woods on the back side of the property.

"We've got a house fire. Bring the truck up to the gate. We haven't cleared it yet. Will give you the go ahead when it's confirmed clear. Want to make sure there's no more incoming rounds."

"Roger that," said Hamilton. He ordered the fire trucks to be pulled as close to the house as possible but still out of any potential lines of fire.

When the alarm went off, the man and woman that had been sleeping in the back room scrambled out of bed and rushed to the front window. Seeing the Bison in the front, they ran out the back door. Once in the glare of the Nightsun spotlight, they knew that running was useless. They threw up their hands.

In addition to Ortega, the other person in the house was Morales, his bodyguard. Morales had been with Ortega for many years and had been loyal to him. Ortega had tested him not long after he had brought him into his inner circle. He had another gang member from Texas offer Morales a large sum of money if he would look the other way when he came to kill Ortega. Morales had agreed but then told Ortega about the plot. He asked Ortega if he should play along and then kill the man. He had been with Ortega ever since.

At the sound of the gate crashing, Ortega and Morales had grabbed two of the automatic weapons from a downstairs closet. Ortega realized that there was only one way out, but they needed some time. They ran up the stairs and began firing from the upper floor windows.

Ortega had started in the drug trade by using tunnels to smuggle drugs across the U.S.-Mexico border. One tunnel he had used, from Tijuana to San Diego, was over eight hundred yards long.

Immediately after taking possession of the property, Ortega brought in workers from Mexico who were experienced in digging tunnels. They began by cutting a trap door in the floor of a downstairs closet. The men worked in the crawl space beneath the house, taking out the excavated soil and spreading it on the fields behind the house. The tunnel would be used only for an emergency escape and Ortega checked it every few weeks to ensure that there were no cave-ins. The tunnel exited at the edge of the woods. A tractor shed was built over the opening and the trap door was covered with a bale of hay. The men then returned to Mexico. They were never seen again.

As the Bison approached the front of the house, Ortega yelled to Morales to continue to fire rounds from the upper window to slow the FBI down. Morales was the only other person who knew about the tunnel. Ortega had already briefed him on how they would escape. He kept a five-gallon gas tank and a flare gun in the closet to create a fire and delay entry into the house. The fire would burn rapidly and destroy the house—as well as any evidence of an escape route.

Ortega quickly spread the gas along the front wall of the house, dousing the couch and bottoms of the drapes. "Keep firing!" he yelled. He lit the flare and tossed it onto the couch. Fire erupted and quickly climbed up the drapes. Smoke began curling across the ceiling as Ortega darted to the closet and opened the trap door. "Okay, let's go!"

The fire at the front of the house was intense. Jack had confirmed that no one else had exited from the rear of the house. "Foxtrot Delta, need you up here now. This might be a rescue mission."

There was the immediate sound of a siren and the fire truck came roaring up the drive. Hamilton, the fire captain, knew that the previous owners of the property had installed a standpipe adjacent to the pond to draw water in case of a fire. A fireman jumped off the truck, connected the pump house with the standpipe, and the truck rolled forward towards the fire. Within thirty seconds of Jack's call, a thick stream of water was being directed into the flames.

"Charlie Six, this is Sierra Two, over." It was the sniper team on the edge of the property near the farm house. The voice was low, and Jack could just make it out on his headset.

"This is Charlie Six, over."

"I'm hearing some activity north of my position. No agents there?"

"Negative, Sierra Two. Keep your position and watch for anyone coming in your direction. Heading your way now." Kalu had heard Jack and immediately gunned the turbo-diesel. The Bison churned around the side of the farmhouse towards the rear of the property.

"Childs, take charge of the mop-up here," said Jack. "I'm headed to the woods. Could be that some of them made it out."

"Got it covered," said Childs.

Jack called to the chopper. "Black Hawk One, need you to light up the woods northwest of the farmhouse."

"Roger that." The Black Hawk swung around, and the searchlight beam cut through the darkness, illuminating the pine forest. The light rays filtered through the tree trunks and branches, creating spots of light and shadow on the thick pine needle floor of the woods.

"Charlie Six, this is Black Hawk One, saw something northwest of the shed."

"Roger. Kalu, head straight for the utility easement and then cut west." Jack took a quick look at the map of the area surrounding the farm and saw a row of homes lining a country road on the western edge of the forest.

Above the roar of the engine, Kalu acknowledged and headed towards the line of utility towers that ran along the northern border of the property. The Bison moved like its namesake, a beast cutting through the long rows of crops illuminated by its headlights. Streams of dirt and parts of plants spewed out behind its rear wheels. The Bison cleared the field and cut left, moving rapidly along the cleared easement under the utility towers.

"Charlie Six, this is Black Hawk One. Last saw a tango to your south about one hundred meters."

"Roger," said Jack. Through the periscope, Jack saw where the search light was pointing down into the forest. "Kalu, this is where I get out. Continue slow along this utility line. Keep giving warnings over the loudspeaker. I want whoever is out there to hear where you are."

"Roger that," said Kalu as he brought the Bison to a halt. Jack scrambled out of the Bison, hit the ground and moved into the woods towards the last spotting. "Black Hawk One, move to the south of your last sighting and scan the road." The Bison was trolling the northern boundary and the chopper was to the south. Back to the east, the farm was covered with agents. Jack was hunting. The tango would head west, away from the sounds of the chopper and the Bison.

"Roger." The chopper moved off and Jack could see the searchlight re-directing to the road to the south.

Jack switched to the command channel. "This is Charlie Six. Need all law enforcement on roads on western boundary to be on the lookout for anyone exiting the wood line." The sheriff's department acknowledged and called additional deputies to the scene.

Jack flipped down his night-vision goggles and moved into the woods. He crouched down, took several steps, then stopped and listened. The image before his eyes was in various shades of green. The light intensity faded as he peered into the distant darkness. He circled around so that he was east of the last sighting of whoever had escaped.

He removed his headset and the sounds of humming insects and crickets filled his ears. He carefully moved through the woods, stopped and then scanned the area ahead through his night vision goggles. Suddenly, fifty meters ahead, he saw what looked like a hump-backed animal rising off the forest floor. A man with a backpack came into view, moving away from him. Jack slowly pulled his Springfield .45 from his holster.

Jack waited to make sure the man was alone then weaved through the trees in case he turned and fired. Jack was no more than twenty-five meters away when the man went into a clearing. Jack knew that there were several houses along the road to the west. *He'll break in and take a hostage.*

Jack went to a kneeling firing position with the laser pointer directly on the man's back. "FBI!! Hands in the air!!"

Ortega froze. Jack saw the gun in his right hand. "Just toss it and you'll live to see a prison cell."

Ortega could tell that the voice was directly behind him. He slowly turned around and looked down at the red dot, now centered on his chest. He had not yet raised his hands.

"My friend," he said, "I have enough in this backpack to make us both rich men."

Jack rose up and walked forward. He kept his .45 aimed squarely on center mass. "Last chance. Toss the gun or you're a dead man."

"Okay, okay, I'll put it down," said Ortega. He began crouching as if he was going to put the gun on the ground. Instead, he began to straighten his arm. Jack squeezed the trigger, milliseconds before Ortega's gun fired.

CHAPTER 8 – An Invitation

The next day at the Fayetteville FBI office, Tom Coughlin and Childs gave Jack a run down on what happened while Jack, according to Childs, "was having fun in the woods." The fire department had been able to get into the house and found an unconscious man with a gunshot wound to the abdomen. They identified him as Oscar Morales, a gang member and Ortega's bodyguard.

Because Ortega had bent down in the forest, Jack's round had struck him in the upper right shoulder. Ortega's body twisted from the impact of the .45 caliber bullet, and the round he fired went into the dirt. He fell to the ground and the gun fell out of his hand. Jack had kicked the gun away and called for medical assistance.

Ortega and Morales were in rooms at the hospital, each with one wrist handcuffed to the hospital bed. In Ortega's case, it was his left wrist. Jack's round had severed a nerve and he had no feeling in his right arm.

"Morales was royally pissed off when he finally gained consciousness," said Childs. "At the hospital, he told us how Ortega had planned an escape through a tunnel. There were still fire department officials at the site, so we radioed that information to them. Sure enough, there was a tunnel from the house over to the tractor shed."

Coughlin said, "Turns out that Morales didn't know that he was part of Ortega's escape plan. Morales is a similar size and build as Ortega. With a major fire, and a burnt corpse, positive identification may have been impossible. Doubtful that even the bullet wound would have been discovered. If the house collapsed, the escape tunnel entrance probably wouldn't have been discovered. We would think that Ortega had died in the fire, and he would actually be somewhere in Mexico."

Childs said, "Ortega torched the place and got in the escape hatch. When Morales came down, he shot him. That was the shot we heard when we were on the porch. Guess it's too bad for Ortega that the fire department was on the scene and able to put the fire out before it burned the house down—with Morales in it."

Jack laughed. "I guess we better keep both their hospital rooms well-guarded. You know Ortega will try to get the word out to eliminate Morales, and Morales may want pay-back for being shot and left to burn."

He looked down at the evidence report from the previous night. "Well, the spare in Sanchez' car was full of cocaine and there were two kilos of coke in Ortega's backpack. Guess the State could also prosecute on arson and attempted murder, but with the life without parole he'll get in federal court, probably not necessary."

Coughlin's desk phone rang, and he picked it up. "Yes, he's right here. Hold on. Jack, it's Mike Bronson." He handed Jack the phone.

"Hey Mike."

"Hey Jack. Heard you're not too busy down there in Carolina."

"Oh, yeah. Nothing much going on here." Jack knew that Mike, an enhanced SWAT team leader, was aware of all SWAT missions nationwide. He would be reviewing Jack's after-action report.

"Well, seems like there may be something brewing your way. The JTTF headquarters would like the pleasure of your company here."

"I accept, as if I had a choice. Where and when?"

"Next Monday morning, at 0900 hours. The meeting will be at the Department of Homeland Security. Homeland's providing most of the intel on an upcoming operation. You'll be meeting with Special Agent Morris. The chief of the Counterterrorism Division, Mack MacCauley, wants you to brief him here after your meeting at DHS. I'll be in the office Monday morning, so let's do lunch after you're done."

"Sounds great." Jack wondered why an FBI agent would be working over at Homeland Security but knew that agencies sometimes transferred people based upon specific needs. "So, what else can you tell me about the meeting? You know how I love coming up to headquarters in the dark."

"Don't know much, but I will be curious how your meeting with Special Agent Morris goes."

CHAPTER 9 – Into the Cave

Somewhere in the mountainous region between Pakistan and Afghanistan.

Abdul Mohammed Al Mahmoud pushed back the blackout curtain that hung over the mouth of the cave. Once inside, he saw that this was not the cavern containing the leaders. It was only the entrance to a tunnel leading into the interior of the mountain. As his eyes adjusted to the semi-darkness, he made out the curve of the rock that formed the tunnel's ceiling. Some thirty feet down the tunnel, he saw a vertical sliver of light.

The guard at the entrance took Mahmoud's weapon and frisked him. He had been vetted by an al Qaeda leader, but alliances sometimes shifted. The best policy was a complete prohibition of weapons in the presence of the Mullah. The guard turned and placed Mahmoud's AK-47 on a blanket behind him where it joined several others. Daggers of different sizes and shapes were lined up on a second blanket. The guard jerked his head towards the tunnel and Mahmoud continued toward the second curtain.

The tunnel began to narrow. Although only five feet seven inches tall, Mahmoud had to crouch slightly to avoid the rocks jutting from the tunnel's roof. The floor was fairly level, but rocks randomly poked out from the coarse soil.

The light was dim. It was difficult to distinguish shadows from the objects which cast them. He carefully made his way. He was about to be entrusted with an important mission and would look like a fool if he tripped and fell.

A youth, perhaps no more than fourteen years old, stood by the second curtain. The dusky light revealed that his left pants leg was tied in a knot below his knee.

As Mahmoud stepped closer, he could see that the boy's face was scarred on one side. It looked like it had been pressed on a frying pan and then released, minus pieces of flesh. One eye was covered over with a mound of scars. Tufts of hair stuck out from his scalp, like corn field stubble after harvesting. A makeshift crutch, made from a staff with rags wrapped around its top, was tucked under his left shoulder. Not long before, the boy had used the staff to herd sheep.

The boy's presence was evidence of the personnel assignment system. He could not operate in the field, but his presence as a guard allowed another able-bodied soldier to engage the enemy directly. His AK-47 was ready. If there was an attack at the mouth of the cave, he would fire his weapon until his ammunition was gone. He had no cover. He would die, but his shots would alert those within the command post inside, and they would have time to seal the entrance with pre-positioned explosives. He would gladly die a martyr, either shot by the enemy or buried alive by his own people.

As Mahmoud approached the inner curtain, the boy leveled his rifle at him. Mahmoud avoided the side of the curtain closest to the boy. The boy turned his head as Mahmoud passed by, keeping his one eye and the rifle barrel focused on him. Mahmoud pulled back the curtain, ducked his head, and entered the inner cavern. What he saw surprised him.

The tunnel suddenly widened into a large cavern that was nearly forty feet wide by sixty feet long. It was a natural cavern, with the rock now almost thirty feet above his head. He stared at the volume of weapons in the cavern. Its entire length contained arms and munitions stacked higher than Mahmoud's head. Boxes of assault rifles, grenade launchers, and anti-tank rounds that were used to make IED's. Stacked boxes of field rations, many with U.S. markings. Enough weapons and supplies to outfit a thousand-man army.

Banks of truck batteries were stored away from the ammunition and weapons and were used to power the ventilation fans that hung from crude metal frames. The floor was covered with rugs, and groups of men sat huddled together on them. Some were talking in low voices, watching intently as one of the group drew his finger in a line across the rug. A plan was being made for an assault on a nearby outpost, Mahmoud imagined. Or perhaps this was the direction of an enemy convoy.

As he walked by, the men stopped what they were doing and stared. He was a stranger and wasn't to be trusted until he had proven himself loyal to the cause.

Mahmoud didn't notice a small indentation in the far wall of the cavern. There was a slight rise in the floor of the cavern to a ledge. Behind a large jutting portion of the cavern was a narrow opening that sloped upward and formed the mouth of a tunnel. It was only large enough for one person at a time to crawl through and exited into a ravine on the opposite side of the mountain from where Mahmoud had entered. Thick brush obscured its location from aerial observation. If the tunnel leading into the cavern was destroyed, this was the way out.

Access to the ravine would require helicopters, and troops would have to descend by rope to get into the area. They would be easily picked off by other fighters who kept a constant vigil from an elevated position tucked beneath a rocky ledge on the other side of the ravine. By the time the Americans figured out that they had escaped into the ravine, their intended targets would have melted into the mountainous terrain.

A man with a black turban and thick beard, leaving little of his face exposed, came up to Mahmoud. Mahmoud spoke first. "As-salamu 'alaykum."

"Wa' 'alaykumu as-salam." The Taliban fighter motioned Mahmoud to an area further back in the cave, where Mullah Omar Mohammed, the Taliban leader, was holding a council. Some were his lieutenants, and others were al Qaeda.

Although Omar had never met Mahmoud, he already knew that he had been born in Columbus, Ohio, and that Abdul Mohammed Al Mahmoud was not his birth name.

CHAPTER 10 – Home-Grown

Abdul Mohammed Al Mahmoud's real name was Peter Mahmoud. His father, Adel Mohammed Mahmoud, had been born in Amman, Jordan, to a wealthy family. Adel had been a brilliant student and his father decided that Adel would attend college in the United States. Adel left Amman to attend Ohio State University, where he majored in engineering. He had intended to return to Jordan after graduation, but he met Rebecca Smith, a nursing student, and all that changed.

Becky had been brought up in a Christian home but when she left for college, she left behind the Christian perspective on sexual activity before marriage. She met a strikingly handsome Jordanian, Adel, at the school's student union. They began "dating," the jargon for having a relationship that included sex.

When Becky became pregnant, she told her parents that she and Adel were getting married—and that she was expecting. Her parents had hoped that Becky would marry a Christian but realized that now this was not an option. They were firmly against abortion. While they were quietly upset that Adel was a Muslim, she told them that he wasn't religious, and she certainly wasn't. As the father of their grandchild-to-be, he would be accepted as part of the family.

As for Adel, he decided that it would be better to tell his parents that Becky was a Christian than tell them that she was an atheist. Adel's father was respected in the Christian community in Amman. He believed that Muslims and Christians could peacefully coexist.

Becky's first child had dark skin, dark hair and brown eyes. He was a small baby, at only six pounds and one ounce, and was the proverbial "spitting image" of his father. Adel's plan to return to Jordan had long been discarded. He knew that his son, and any future children, would grow up in America.

Although he had been warmly welcomed by the community, he knew that his children might well be subject to prejudice because of the color of their skin and their heritage. Adel thought that perhaps giving his son a Christian first name, Peter, would help. He was wrong.

Peter Mahmoud was an intelligent boy, which made matters worse. His elementary school years were not too bad. It was when his parents moved to Cleveland that things got rough. He was bullied because he was small and smarter than his classmates. He was taunted as a "raghead."

Peter dreaded the bus ride to school. The bus driver could do nothing to stop the bullying that took place at the back of his bus. When the situation began interfering with Peter's studies, Adel enrolled him into a private school. All students wore uniforms, and there was a strong focus on academics. Peter thrived in the school and made excellent scores.

* * * *

PETER Mahmoud began his journey to becoming a radical extremist on September 11, 2001. It was as if the terrorist attacks were a switch—one that turned subliminal prejudice into overt bigotry. On his way home, he was beaten by a group of older students. He told his father that his cut and swollen lip had occurred when he fell on the athletic field. His father saw his torn clothing and looked sadly at him but could say nothing. He knew that the events of that day would make life hard on his son—and on him.

Peter began looking at his life through a different lens. He was an outsider. He would never be treated like an American child. He began to study Islam and came to believe that the Muslims were the only people who would ever accept him. He began to study the Koran.

Peter asked his father if he could visit family in Jordan during his summer vacations. He went to Amman and stayed with his uncle and cousins. He began studying Arabic. By the time he was fifteen, he had a conversational knowledge of the language.

Although Peter's grandfather was conciliatory to the Christian population, his uncle had rebelled against such thinking. His uncle took him to a mosque where he heard talk of how the West was waging a war of aggression against Islam, in much the same way that it did during the Crusades. He was impressionable. He heard how "the perverted values of the non-Muslims had even invaded the Muslim societies." *My own father is not observant of his faith anymore,* thought Peter. *We have a Christmas tree in our house every year.*

Peter began reading radical tracts on the internet. He listened to the inflammatory rhetoric from those that would have their form of Islam spread over the rest of the world. By the time he started college, he was a practicing Muslim with extremist beliefs.

He now believed that Sharia was divine law, and that it was to be literally translated and applied in the modern world. He viewed all secular governments as corrupt and that they should be destroyed. In his mind, a worldwide government adhering to the principles of Islam must be established. It might take decades, but in time he believed it would happen. He had become radicalized to the extreme Islamic fundamentalist cause.

Mahmoud applied for admission and was accepted as a student at North Carolina State University in Raleigh. He was fascinated by how things were built and decided to become a mechanical engineer. He would graduate and then go back to his "true" homeland.

He began attending a mosque in Raleigh and continued to travel to Jordan during the summer months. He now spoke in the same way as his uncle and cousins. The Western culture was a perversion and would be brought down one day.

Without Mahmoud's knowledge, while he was in Jordan, he had drawn the scrutiny of an al Qaeda operative. Reports were made. The al Qaeda leadership believed that if this American was dedicated to the cause, then he could become a weapon to strike the Americans in their own land. A meeting with a local al Qaeda leader was arranged when he was in Amman after his sophomore year.

The al Qaeda leader made further arrangements for Mahmoud to meet with Mullah Omar, the Taliban leader. On Mahmoud's next trip to Jordan he was secreted out of Amman to the isolated mountain hideout on the Afghanistan/Pakistan border to receive instructions from Mullah Omar.

Omar told Mahmoud that there were other Americans that were loyal to their cause and there was an important mission to accomplish—with his help and help from the other Americans. He told Mahmoud that the leader of the Americans was a great man who had fought with the mujahideen and would be in charge of the mission.

Peter Mahmoud, college student, returned to the U.S. after his meeting with Mullah Omar as a jihadi with a mission that Omar said, "would make the 9/11 destruction and deaths seem to have been only a small victory."

CHAPTER 11 – Homeland Security

Jack entered the Department of Homeland Security building for his meeting. He recalled Mike telling him the meeting was with Special Agent Morris. *I'll have to ask him how an FBI agent ended up at Homeland Security.*

He showed his credentials to the security guard. Security was tight, as would be expected. His FBI credentials allowed him to retain his Glock 22, .40 caliber service weapon. He walked to the bank of elevators across the lobby. It was a typical D.C. government building. Marble floors, large wooden planters, and the normal assortment of framed photographs of government leaders lined the walls.

Before the meeting, Jack had reviewed the organizational structure and mission of the DHS. The Office of Intelligence and Analysis provided law enforcement, including the Joint Terrorism Task Force, with predictive intelligence on potential terror attacks in the U.S. Jack entered the elevator and pushed the button for the fourth floor.

When Jack stepped off the elevator, he saw a reception area immediately ahead. Couches and synthetic-leather chairs were arrayed around a low, glass-topped table. The reception desk was directly in front of a highly polished wood wall. Mounted on the wall was the seal of the Department, an eagle in a circular blue field clutching an olive branch in one claw and arrows in the other. In the shield before the eagle was a dark blue sky with twenty-two stars, representing the original twenty-two agencies and bureaus that formed the Department of Homeland Security.

Behind the desk sat a young woman with her long dark brown hair pulled back and held with a clip. She wore stylish, black-framed glasses. The name plate on her desk read "Mary Sullivan." As Jack approached, she looked up from a file.

"Good Morning, Ms. Sullivan, I'm—"

"Special Agent Jackson Thomas," Mary said, smiling.

"I'd probably ask you how you would know that, but I am in the Office of Intelligence and Analysis."

"Oh, yes, we know all about you, but if you would like to leave one of your business cards with me, I will include it in the file."

Jack took out one of his cards and Mary took it using her left hand, with the back of her hand up, so that Jack could see that there was no ring on her third finger. She smiled again and said, "I'll let Special Agent Morris know you're here." Jack thanked her and sat in one of the chairs across from the reception desk. He was fifteen minutes early for his appointment, so he was prepared to wait.

At ten minutes before his scheduled appointment time, Jack heard the sound of high heels coming from the hallway to the right of Mary's desk. A woman wearing a navy-blue suit with a white blouse entered the reception area. Her skirt came to just above the knee, and sheer stockings revealed the toned legs of an athlete. *Dancer or ice skater*, thought Jack, before realizing that he was staring. He glanced up and saw that her hair was cut short, with a layered look, revealing a face that could only be described as beautiful. Not cute. Not good-looking. Beautiful.

Her suit was fitted, revealing a figure that could place her on the cover of a certain sports magazine's swimsuit edition. *Fashion model . . . maybe they're doing an ad to recruit female agents,* thought Jack, not making the connection with his appointment. But when she walked directly towards him, he recovered and quickly got to his feet. She stopped in front of him and stuck out her hand.

"Special Agent Thomas, I presume," she said with a smile. She was accustomed to seeing a momentary look of surprise when meeting male agents who didn't know that they were meeting with a female agent.

Jack saw a woman with a flawless complexion, wearing red lipstick that accentuated the fullness of her lips. Her smile was captivating; it had that genuine "girl next door" quality. As he reached forward and took her hand, he caught the fresh scent of her perfume.

"Yes, nice to meet you, and please call me Jack." He had not expected to meet a female FBI agent this morning, especially not one that looked like Special Agent Morris.

"Well, nice to meet you Jack. I'm Katherine Morris, but my nickname is Kat, and that's what they call me around here. If someone asked for Katherine, I wouldn't know who they were looking for." She turned to the receptionist, "Mary, we'll be down in the conference room if anyone from the Chief's office is looking for me."

She turned and as they walked down the hall, she thought, *what a handsome guy . . . carries himself with confidence . . . probably ex-military.*

They reached a glass-walled conference room. There

were eight chairs around a dark wood table. A video screen was bracketed to the wall about halfway up and a small video camera was mounted on top of the screen.

There were two folders on the table, in front of the middle chairs on each side. Kat Morris sat down in the chair closest to the door, and as Jack crossed around to the other side of the table and as he pulled out his chair, he said, "I was curious. You're a Special Agent?"

She decided to tease him. She laughed and said, "You're surprised that I'm a Special Agent?"

"No, no, no," he almost stuttered. "I didn't mean it that way. I just didn't think any FBI personnel were at DHS." He hoped that she didn't think he was underestimating her. He was feeling something he hadn't felt in a long time. He wanted to impress this woman.

"Well, Jack, right again. I'm not FBI. I'm Secret Service."

Jack had forgotten that the Secret Service was a component agency of the DHS, and their agents were also titled Special Agents. "Sorry—not that there's anything wrong with being with the Secret Service," he said, and smiled.

She now felt a little guilty. She said, "Nothing to be sorry about, even if you had known I was Secret Service. The Secret Service doesn't ordinarily fill slots within HSI, Homeland Security Investigations, so I could see how you might be confused. I should have set that straight right away when we met."

"No problem, but I'm curious again. You said that Secret Service doesn't usually fill slots here?"

"As you probably already know, the Office of Intelligence and Analysis has a primary mission to share threat and intelligence information with state and local law enforcement, as well as other federal agencies. In addition to our normal partnership with the Joint Terrorism Task Force, the Secretary created a liaison position in the Homeland Threats Division who will join with the JTTF on the operational level."

She saw that he was genuinely interested, so she went on. "I volunteered to come over from Secret Service to fill that slot. So, I am the liaison for counterterrorism operations from the HTD and will be representing the DHS for JTTF operations."

It was Jack's turn. "I see you've got all the acronyms straight, so that's a good start."

"Ouch!" Kat said, but with a grin. "But I guess I deserved that. Now we're even." She smiled again and opened the folder, ready to go to work. Before she began, she looked over at Jack. He was following her lead looking down at the folder.

"Are you prior military? Some of what I will go over deals with the situation in Iraq and Afghanistan."

Jack looked up. "Yes, I was Army and spent some time in Afghanistan and Iraq a few years back."

There was something in his tone, and in his eyes, that made Kat believe there was much more that he could have said but didn't. Jack's reluctance to talk about his time in the Army made her even more curious about him.

Without looking at her notes, Kat began to give Jack the background. "After 9/11, and the U.S. invasion of Afghanistan in October 2001, the Taliban regrouped into Pakistan." As Jack looked across the table, he thought, *an extremely attractive and intelligent woman. With a sense of humor.*

"Prior to the September 11 attacks, Osama bin-Laden pledged an oath of loyalty to the Taliban leader, Mullah Omar Mohammed. He called on all Muslims to support the Taliban.

Omar escaped to Pakistan when the Taliban were driven from power in December of 2001. As leader of al Qaeda, it was a message that the attack on the Taliban was an attack on al Qaeda as well. Since 2003, the Taliban insurgency has been gaining strength under Omar. Since 2009, the Taliban have been resurgent throughout Afghanistan.

"The Taliban now appear to be planning something that may be bringing the battle here, with al Qaeda's assistance. We've received some highly classified intelligence from the CIA."

Jack glanced down at the summary in the folder, noting more detailed information was contained within the report. He realized that Kat was giving him the basics; he would read the report later and get back to her with any questions. "I would assume that some of what you are about to tell me won't be in this folder."

Kat nodded, and said, "That's right. We want to keep a lid on this whole operation. We are seeing something that we haven't seen before. The leaders of the Taliban and al Qaeda planning a major attack in the United States. We also believe that there is a cell of home-grown terrorists involved. Americans who have taken up the extreme Islamic fundamentalist cause."

"Do we know where they are in the process?"

"That's the problem. We aren't sure when, or exactly how, the attack might take place. When Timothy McVeigh bombed the Murrah Building in Oklahoma City in '95, it was all done with a rental truck and materials available to the public. There were one hundred and sixty-eight fatalities, including nineteen children.

"When that Army major killed thirteen people at Ft.

Hood, we found out that he tried to contact al Qaeda before the attack, but there's nothing to show that he was anything other than a lone-wolf terrorist. If home-grown terrorists can inflict such damage, we believe a terrorist with help from al Qaeda could kill many more."

"I haven't heard anything about the Taliban being involved in terrorist plots here," said Jack. "Have there been any foiled plots that the public isn't aware of?"

"Not to date, but an attack here, in response to the U.S. presence in Afghanistan, would be a major recruitment and propaganda tool for the Taliban. They would show that even as the U.S. is in their country, they can strike back within our borders. They need al Qaeda's network to pull off an attack on the U.S. mainland. We don't have a specific city as the location of the terror cell, but the intel points to North Carolina."

* * * *

WHEN they had finished discussing the file, Jack said, "Mind if I ask you a personal question?"

Kat smiled. "Well, it depends, but I guess I won't know until you ask. Are you one of the FBI agents that has a law degree?" She was glad that he hadn't just stood up and thanked her for meeting with him.

"Guilty," said Jack.

She smiled and said, "Then I'll just lodge an objection if the question is out of bounds."

"How did you end up in the Secret Service?"

"Well, counselor, I see nothing objectionable about that question." She was teasing Jack again, but he didn't mind. He was intrigued by this Secret Service agent. He hadn't dated anyone for a while, and perhaps he would ask her out after the meeting. "If I do tell you that, I'll need to go into some of my family history."

"I'd love to hear it."

Kat thought about it. Her family history was personal, and she had always felt that it made her the person she was. But there was something about this man. She wanted him to know about her.

"Well, it's kind of a long story. Remember, you asked for it."

"I have a lunch appointment—but I'll gladly break that."

"Okay, but after I'm done, I expect some background in return."

"You got it," said Jack. They had gone beyond simple flirtation to something more. It had only been a few hours, but they both sensed it.

"Both of my great-grandfathers served in World War One. My grandmother on my mother's side was two months pregnant when her husband, Henry Dawson, shipped out to the Pacific during World War Two. He was with the 3rd Marine Division at Iwo Jima. He never returned, one of the thousands of Marines killed in action."

"He left with his wife two months pregnant?" Jack thought about how hard that must have been for her grandfather.

"He didn't know she was pregnant. She knew that it would only make him worry more while he was gone. She knew he couldn't be there for the birth."

"So, he never knew that he was going to be a father." Jack wondered whether it would have been better if he had known that there would be a child born if he didn't survive.

"You're wondering whether it would have been better for him to have known." She said it as a simple statement, without any question or doubt in her voice as to what Jack was thinking. "My grandmother had to make a choice. She believed that if he had known, it would have been worse. She knew he would think that if he didn't return, it would be more difficult for her to remarry—more difficult for her to find a husband—and he would be carrying that concern the whole time he was over there. She decided not to tell him."

"I see," said Jack. He thought about his own mother's sacrifices when his father was deployed.

"Sure you want to hear all this?"

"I'm very interested. We have something in common. I'm from a military family, but you'll have to hear about that sometime later." His implication that he wanted to see her again wasn't lost on Kat.

"Well, here goes. My other grandfather, his name was Harold Smith, was with the 4th Infantry Division when it landed on Utah Beach."

"Normandy."

"Yes, and his unit, the 22nd Infantry Regiment, helped liberate Paris. He told me stories about how he and Ernest Hemingway used to hang out together. Hemingway attached himself to the 22nd and wrote about the unit as it went from Paris through Belgium into Germany." She thought back about how many times she had asked him questions; he would always give her sound and common-sense advice.

"Grandpa Harry made the military his career. He also served in the Korean War as a battalion commander. My father, Preston Smith, didn't want to join the military and follow in his father's footsteps."

Jack just smiled and recalled how he had been adamant that he wasn't going into the military. *Her last name is different. No ring . . . married and divorced? Kept her married name?*

"But he did, right?"

"Yes. He graduated from William & Mary in May of 1969 with an accounting degree. The summer after graduation, he married my mother—the baby that my other grandmother didn't tell her husband about when he went to the Pacific. My Dad passed the Certified Public Accountant exam and was hired by a major accounting firm in Richmond, but that wouldn't last.

"On December 1, 1969, the first draft lottery was held. Dad was born on Valentine's Day, and my mother had always loved the fact that she could celebrate my Dad's birthday on such a special day. Well, on that first lottery, anyone with a February 14th birthday got a lottery number of four. There was no deferment based on marriage. Married men were considered in the same status as single men if they married after 1965.

"Dad knew that he was likely to be drafted the following year, so he enlisted with the option of attending Officer Candidate School at Ft. Benning."

"Really," said Jack. "And I suppose he was in 50th Company, right?" Jack remembered the day he had arrived for OCS at Ft. Benning and his assignment to the 50th.

"Yes," said Kat, with some surprise.

"Sorry, didn't mean to interrupt. So, what happened after he graduated?"

"Well, my mother moved in with my grandmother. Grandma knew that it would be unbearable for my mother, who had never known her own father, to lose her husband. She wanted my mother to be with her while my Dad was serving in Viet Nam. That's where they were sending everyone graduating out of OCS.

"Dad did survive the war—but not without sacrifice. On his second tour of duty in Viet Nam, he was seriously wounded. He had already been awarded a Bronze Star for valor and a Purple Heart. He returned home from his second tour with a second award of each but less his left arm. He had shrapnel wounds to his left side. They had to amputate his arm and reconstruct his hip. After recovering, he went to law school on the G.I. Bill. With his background in accounting, he became a very successful tax attorney here in D.C. Still practices."

"So, you decided to do public service and follow in the family footsteps," said Jack.

"I was graduating from high school when Grandpa Harry died." She remembered what had been said at the church service; Harold Smith exemplified what was to be known as the "Greatest Generation." In her college history courses, she learned that many of the children in that generation—some as young as ten years old—had helped their families survive the Depression by working long hours. And then the world was imperiled by a madman. She had always wondered what it would have been like back then. Millions of young men and women had joined the fight in the military services, and as factory workers, nurses, and civilian volunteers.

Kat grew quiet, then said, "You enlisted after 9/11, didn't you?"

"How could you possibly know that?"

"I don't know, Jack. You did say you served in both Iraq

and Afghanistan. Somehow, I just knew. I was in my third year of law school on 9/11. I had thought about going into the JAG Corps when I graduated, but my father convinced me not to go into the military. He told me to give private practice a try first. Guess he was worried about his daughter being in uniform during wartime.

"I graduated from Georgetown Law and was recruited and hired by a large D.C. criminal defense firm. It was an opportunity to get directly into the courtroom. Of course, the partners handled the high level, white-collar crimes heard in federal court. I got the mid-level drug traffickers who had enough money to hire us."

"So, you defended drug dealers?"

"Innocent until proven guilty—which most were and ended up in prison. Most of the time it was me going to the prosecutor and trying to cut the best deal that I could. I lasted two years and then decided it wasn't for me. I still wanted to go into public service, so I applied to the Secret Service. After training, I requested assignment to the protective services division and my request was approved. I had a pipe dream that I would be assigned to help guard the President, before I found out that it was a detail for much more senior agents.

"I saw that there was an opening for a temporary replacement, a female, for the detail protecting the Vice-President's wife and children. I was probably a little junior for that, but I was in the right place at the right time."

She stopped abruptly, recalling the White House award ceremony where she had met Captain David Morris. His Special Forces unit was receiving a Presidential Unit Citation for a highly dangerous and successful operation. Her eyes began to moisten. Jack sensed a sudden change in her demeanor.

Kat decided that she needed to change the subject. "Why are you interested in my background?"

Jack said, "Just interested in how someone ended up with the Secret Service."

"Just interested? And not because we will be working together?"

Jack's face must have shown his surprise. "Looks like you know something I don't."

"No one told you that I'm going to be on the counterterrorism task force that you're heading?"

* * * *

A MONTH after Colonel Harold Smith's funeral, Kat had returned to the small church cemetery, built on former pasture land in Loudoun County, Virginia. Across the landscape, the promise of flowers from the Spring rains had been fully realized. The open fields surrounding the church were adorned with wild yellow Indigo, their petal spires reaching up through the field grasses.

As she walked toward the spreading oak that shielded his grave from the summer sun, she saw that a tombstone had been erected at the head of the gravesite. A simple epitaph had been cut into the gray marble face of the stone: "Deeds, Not Words." The motto of the 22nd Infantry. *Grandpa Harry's last advice,* thought Kat.

CHAPTER 12 – Engraved In Stone

Kat Morris walked with Jack to the elevator after the briefing in the DHS conference room. After Jack left, Kat walked by the reception desk on her way back to her office.

"Uh, Special Agent Morris, intelligence report needed," said Mary. She tilted her head down, looked over the top of her glasses, and raised her eyebrows.

"What?" Kat feigned ignorance as to what Mary was suggesting.

"Are you kidding me? When that guy walked in the door, I almost lost it. I thought he must be a movie star playing the part of an FBI agent. My gosh, do they get any better looking than that? And his build, and the way he moved—"

"Okay, okay, calm down, Mary. All I know, at this point, is that he's from the Charlotte field office, he's on their SWAT team, he served in the Army, and he's the team leader of the JTTF that I'll be on."

"Oh, I see. So that means you'll be, uh, *liaising* with him?"

Kat just gave Mary an "I don't know what you mean" look, smiled, and walked back to her office. The name plate on the door of her new office had been installed the day before. It was black plastic, with white letters engraved into the surface.

The last place that she had seen the name "Morris" engraved had been at Arlington National Cemetery—on her husband's tombstone.

* * * *

CAPTAIN David Morris' Special Forces unit was operating in Afghanistan. He had been to Iraq and Afghanistan before, and told Kat that he had to leave again. She knew not to ask where he was going or how long he would be gone. He couldn't tell her. All he would say was the standard "don't worry, I'll be fine."

It was only a week after he left that the knock came on her door. Two soldiers in dress uniform and the "we regret to inform you" speech. It was over a year and a half since the funeral, and her friends had suggested that she just give it a try. Go out with someone. Just have dinner and see how it goes.

Mary had set her up with a Secret Service agent and they had gone to a restaurant in Georgetown. She broke out in tears when the agent, who was also prior service, was talking about his military experience. All she could do was to compare him to David. He took her home before they had finished dinner.

When she had sat down with Jack earlier, there had been something new. He seemed, in many ways, like David, but interesting in different ways. She knew that it was unfair to use David as a yardstick—unfair to other men, as well as to herself.

But she also knew her assignment to the task force would likely preclude any kind of dating or relationship. Jack would be focused on his duties as task force leader and would follow the fraternization policy in the military. *Dating relationships are strictly prohibited between superiors and subordinates. Not the military, but he'll follow the rule for the same reasons.*

CHAPTER 13 – Strictly Professional

Jack returned to the FBI headquarters after leaving Homeland Security and went directly to the Counterterrorism Division. He was fuming—as angry as he had ever been over an agency issue.

He looked at Mack MacCauley, the Division Chief, on the other side of the desk. MacCauley had been with the agency for twenty-five years and was called "Mack" by superiors and subordinates alike.

"Mack, I looked like an idiot over there! They have a Secret Service agent as the liaison for counterterrorism operations that knows more about our agency business than I do."

"Okay, Jack, calm down. The Director must have talked to the Secretary of HS about it. The Secretary must have told his staff and it got down to this Special Agent Morris. What did he tell you?"

"It's Special Agent Katherine Morris. She told me that I'm heading the task force and she's on it. I prefer telling people they are on my team instead of them telling me."

"Okay, well, I'll take the hit on that one. I think the

higher-ups wanted to make sure you were going to be the designated task force leader. They saw that you were junior in years of service and wanted to confirm that you had the qualifying prior experience. The okay just came down. I thought this Special Agent Morris was just going to give you the intelligence report. I was going to tell you about the task force leader position when you got over here."

Jack had calmed down and realized that the agency was giving him an opportunity that not many agents with his time in service were given. "Not a problem, Mack. I appreciate the chance."

Mack looked at a file on his desk. "We're working with the Cyber Investigative Joint Task Force to get you as much information as we can. When are you headed back to Charlotte?"

"I've got a flight leaving Dulles this evening, so I'll be in the office in the morning."

"Okay. Understand you're going to see Mike Bronson before you leave?"

"Yes. I'm meeting him for lunch."

"Well, tell him that I said hello. And you might ask him about this Special Agent Morris. He knows some guys over at Secret Service from doing enhanced SWAT training. If they need any SWAT assistance at the White House, that's who they call. He said that he had heard about Special Agent Morris before, but he didn't tell me anything about her being a female agent."

Jack flashed back to his phone call with Mike when he was in the Fayetteville office. Mike had told him about his appointment with "Special Agent Morris." *He didn't tell me that it was not only a meeting with a female, but an incredibly attractive one—*

the type of information that Mike would normally have given me.

* * * *

THE restaurant was just a short walk down Pennsylvania Avenue from the FBI Headquarters. The late summer D.C. heat had kicked in, so Jack took off his coat, loosened his tie, and rolled up his shirt sleeves. But his mind wasn't on the heat.

He got to the restaurant at just about the same time as Mike Bronson. He was coming from the other direction and, at his size, he was not mistaken as part of the usual lunchtime crowd. Most tourists thought he must be with the Washington Redskins.

"It's great to see you here in the big city," said Mike. Charlotte was the second largest city in the Southeast, just behind Jacksonville, Florida, and a national and international financial center. It was also the major banking center of the Southeast—only New York City had more banking resources—but Mike liked to chide Jack as coming up from the rural South when he came to D.C.

"Yeah," said Jack, "we just got our indoor plumbing at the Charlotte office. You can check it out next time you're down in the boondocks." They quickly ordered, and Jack waited, thinking about how he would bring up the subject.

"Great job on the Ortega raid," said Mike. "I knew that when I first talked to you in the Weight Room that you would make a great SWAT team leader."

"Well, you know it's a team effort. We've got a great group there." Jack paused. "I have a question for you."

"Shoot."

"The meeting at DHS, you know, the one that got me up here to the big city. Looks like I'm heading a task force and a certain Secret Service agent will be on it—Special Agent Katherine Morris, you know, the one you said I was going to meet at DHS, is the one who told me. Did you know that I was going to be made a task force leader?"

"Absolutely not. Just about the meeting with Special Agent Morris. I must confess that I had, uh, heard about her." He grinned and looked up at the ceiling, and then back at Jack, rubbed his chin and said in an innocent voice, "And, well, yeah, I did hear that she's not a bad-looking woman—"

"Yeah, you might have *at least* clued me in on that. In the reception room she walked right up to me and I was, let's just say, a little surprised." He recalled what Mike had said on the phone when he was in Fayetteville. "I believe you said you wanted to know how the meeting with 'Special Agent Morris' went?"

Mike just smiled and said, "I thought it would be better if you just made your own judgment about her." Mike had heard about Kat's meltdown from the Secret Service agent who had gone out to dinner with her. *Better he didn't hear about that from me.*

"You dating anyone now? What about the old flame from law school? Did you look her up?"

"Pam. Yeah, when I was back during a tour. She's married."

"Well, sorry to hear that."

"That's okay—not meant to be anyway. I met a girl when I was back in law school finishing up, but that lasted only until she got a job in Atlanta. Then there was the fitness instructor—"

"Okay, I get it. Although, as far as any potential romance, you're probably disqualified. I believe she would be looking for an intelligent individual, Mr. Ranger. You guys do look for enemy fire to jump in front of, so I'm told."

Jack laughed. "I'm heading a task force and she's on it. So, looks like this will be strictly professional. That's as far as it can go."

"Speaking of that, looks like you may have me hanging around. I just got my orders to head down to the boondocks in a few days. Looking forward to seeing the new plumbing facilities."

CHAPTER 14 – Extra Eyes

Jack picked up Mike at the Charlotte airport two days later. They drove to the FBI's field office headquarters, located in a downtown federal office building.

When they got off the elevator on the sixth floor, they greeted the young man who sat in an enclosed booth on the opposite side of the hallway. The top half of the booth was bullet-proof glass and a metal drawer, much like one at a drive-through bank, opened just below the bottom edge of the glass. The agents produced their ID, a requirement for all agents, even if they were stationed at the field office.

The man touched a button located on the underside of his desk and a buzzing sound emanated from the door at the end of hall. The door's surface was hardened steel with stamped graining that gave it the appearance of wood. In the corner above and to the left of the door was a small square of glass. A video camera recorded everyone coming off the elevator.

After entering the door, they were in a formal reception area. A tall and attractive woman in a black dress got up from behind the desk and came out to meet them. The name plate on her desk said "Sarah." No last name.

"Right this way gentlemen." She led them down a

corridor to a conference room.

As Sarah was passing by, Mike looked at Jack and raised his eyebrows. As he passed her at the doorway going in to the conference room, he said, "Thank you, Sarah."

"You are very welcome, Mr. Bronson."

After the door was closed, Mike said, "Well, she knows my name. That's a start."

"That's only because I warned her about you," Jack said.

The conference room had glass panels along one wall, providing an expansive view of the Charlotte skyline. A large table took up most of the room. At the head of the table sat Carl Roberts, a twenty-year veteran of the agency, who was the Special Agent in Charge of the Charlotte office. Several other agents already sat at the table.

"Good afternoon, gentlemen," said Roberts. "Have a seat. This will be brief. The name of this mission is Operation Homefront. Our intel from the CIA and Homeland Security has revealed information from sources overseas and in the U.S. that al Qaeda is working with the Taliban to plan and execute one or more terrorist attacks in the U.S. The focus is in Eastern North Carolina and the resident office in Raleigh oversees the coordinating activities for the task force. The actual headquarters site for the task force will be located at the National Guard facility located at the Raleigh-Durham airport.

"Special Agent Thomas is the designated task force leader. Headquarters has detailed Special Agent Bronson from the D.C. office to the task force as we may need to utilize the D.C. enhanced SWAT team in support of the task force. The task force will be augmented by Special Agent Morris from Homeland Security." Mike looked over at Jack and smiled. *Knows I was impressed by her,* thought Jack. *Guess there's no harm in calling her . . .*

"In addition, there will also be a civilian contractor joining the task force who has been working for the CIA in Afghanistan."

Mike looked over at Jack and said, "I've worked with this contractor before. When I was told about this mission, I asked HQ if he could be pulled in. He's got a special skill set which I believe could be very useful."

"Sounds great," said Jack. He was glad to have Mike on the team but began to wonder if Mike's involvement was something more. *Headquarters wants a set of eyes on the task force and specifically on me. Guess they want to make sure that a "junior" agent can handle this assignment. How this goes could affect my career with the agency—one way or the other.*

CHAPTER 15 – When Hell Freezes Over

Jack received his orders on Tuesday. He and Mike would fly to Raleigh on the following Friday. He had put out that all task force members would meet at 0900 hours on Monday morning.

On Thursday night his phone rang. He thought it was Mike, but it was a woman's voice on the line.

"Hi, Jack. This is Kat Morris."

"Hi. Was going to call you. Are you reading my mind?"

"Hmmm, let me see. Yes. You were going to ask me if I was free for lunch on Saturday. I'm flying out tomorrow."

Jack smiled. "Amazing." She had gotten her orders and would be in Raleigh. He wondered whether there was anything else about the task force that she knew and he didn't.

"You probably know that a certain large individual will be with me?"

"Oh, absolutely. We have a mole over there at the FBI."

"I can almost believe that."

"I've got my government vehicle. I've heard about Special Agent Bronson. Plenty of room, even for him."

Jack gave her the details of where they were staying, they

said their good-byes and he hung up. As he finished packing, he realized he hadn't felt this way since the first time he met Pam.

* * * *

AFTER the chopper crash during his first tour, he spent several weeks in the U.S. He hadn't been seriously injured but he was ordered back to Fort Benning for observation and recovery. While there, he decided to try to locate Pam. He looked through the N.C. Bar directory, believing that she would practice law close to home. When he couldn't find her name, it hit him that perhaps she was no longer Pam Sorensen.

He knew that each law school graduating class kept a directory. Graduates would update their contact information by sending it to the law school. It was a good way to make referrals as the attorney's place of business and practice area were also listed. He called the administrative office at the law school and told the woman answering the phone that he had been a student there, was in the military, and was trying to locate a classmate.

"You said '2002' as the graduating class?"

"Yes, that's right."

"Well, there's no Pam Sorensen listed—but there is a listing for a 'Pamela S. Richardson.' Hold on a sec. There's also an Andrew Richardson. Maybe they got married. You want that number?"

Andy Richardson. Jack remembered him well. Very smart. Played lacrosse at Duke undergrad. "No, that's okay. Appreciate your help." He thought about calling and congratulating her but decided there was no point to it.

* * * *

AT noon on Saturday, Kat pulled up to the downtown Raleigh hotel in a black, late model Mercedes Benz. Jack and Mike came out of the lobby and got in. Jack sat in the front seat. Kat was dressed informally as they all had agreed. She wore little makeup, and was wearing jeans, a knit top, and sandals—but was still striking.

Mike said, "Really nice to meet you, Kat. I called Jack about the appointment at your office. Hope this guy wasn't too rough on you in your meeting."

Kat laughed and said, "Yeah, he downright insulted me when we first met. Didn't think I could possibly be a Special Agent."

"Well, I think that we got over that hurdle," said Jack, playing along. "When I met Mike the first time, I was thinking the same thing about him."

As they turned onto the road leading by N.C. State University, Mike said, "No one would ever mistake this for a government-purchased vehicle."

"You're right, you won't find this model in most standard government motor pools. It was free, courtesy of the federal forfeiture act. Belonged to a drug kingpin. He survived an ambush by a rival, so it's outfitted for high security and has some special features. Because it was used for his interstate cocaine distribution ring we got to keep it. Of course, I put up a big fight about having to drive the Mercedes."

"I'll bet you did," said Mike.

When they arrived at the restaurant, the hostess took them to a private table at the back of the restaurant; Jack had called ahead and requested the table. As Kat was about to sit down, Jack began to pull out her chair for her. It was a reflex for Jack. He had always done it for Pam, and she had always appreciated it. But he knew that some women saw things differently.

He was about to remove his hand from the chair when Kat said, "Thank you, Jack," and she stood for a moment longer to allow him to continue. "And in case you were wondering, I'm not one of those women who gets offended by male courtesy." She smiled and looked at Mike. "I'm sure Jack just beat you to it, right Mike?"

"Oh, absolutely! I'm all about male courtesy," Mike said, with a straight face.

During lunch Kat asked them how the DHS could improve intelligence support to the FBI's counterterrorism division. Talk also turned to how both Jack and Mike ended up with the FBI. Jack downplayed his time with the Rangers, his tours in Iraq and Afghanistan, as well as any mention of being injured.

Mike could see that Kat was genuinely interested in Jack's military background. Based on what he had heard, he was a little surprised. He was glad he hadn't volunteered any information about Kat before Jack met her; he saw the attraction and maybe that, and the passage of time, had made a difference. "Don't let Mr. Humility here fool you. Jack risked his life to save two soldiers and received the Silver Star—in addition to a couple of Purple Hearts."

"Not sure this is something we need to talk about," said Jack, looking over at Mike. "Or I'll have to start talking about some of your exploits."

Mike just shook his head quickly to warn Jack not to go there. It was legend that Mike had silently entered a house in

Iraq where suicide vests were being assembled. With one hand he had grabbed and crushed a terrorist's windpipe—silencing him before he could alert the others.

Jack turned to Kat and said, "Mike was a football star at Notre Dame and several NFL teams wanted to sign him. It was big news when he turned down a pro career to go into the Army."

"Yeah, and I almost didn't get into SF because of my size. I was at the limit for height and weight, and had to drop thirty pounds, which wasn't that hard by the time I got through training."

The waitress came up to ask if they would like any dessert. They all declined. Jack asked for the check.

"Already taken care of by your friend here," she said, smiling and nodding toward Kat.

Jack and Mike turned to Kat and started to protest. She said, "What? Can't stand a little female courtesy?" Jack and Mike laughed and jumped up to pull out her chair. "Thank you, gentlemen," she said, and they all walked out to the parking lot.

After Kat dropped them off back at their hotel, Mike turned to Jack. "So, when are you going to ask her out?"

"Ask who?"

"C'mon, Jack. I just sat at lunch with the two of you. I can see it a mile away. If you aren't interested in Kat, and vice versa, then my radar needs a major overhaul."

"Look, Mike, I would be lying if I didn't say I was interested. I mean, who wouldn't be? There's just some things right now that wouldn't make it possible."

"Like?"

"I'm leading the task force. You know the fraternization

policy. And sometimes this kind of relationship turns into a sexual harassment claim."

Mike laughed. "Hey, you're the lawyer. Even I know that there's no policy against dating someone from a different federal department. She's not FBI, and she's not even DOJ. And it's not harassment if it's consensual, right?"

"Well, that works until later, when someone breaks it off. It then becomes harassment. As long as we're in a senior-subordinate relationship—"

"I know, I know, it's the military thing. Well, maybe it will work out for you down the line."

"What makes you think Kat would even be interested in me?" Jack didn't think he had mistaken the signals, but he was curious if Mike had picked up on anything.

"Boy, are you blind or something? I see the way she looks at you."

"Well, let's see how things go. And speaking of asking someone out, guess you struck out with Sarah at the front desk?"

"Hey, so Sarah didn't think it was appropriate for her to give me her phone number right then. That doesn't mean she won't give it to me at some other time."

"Yeah, like when Hell freezes over."

CHAPTER 16 – The Hangar

Jack had picked up a government sedan from the motor pool at the federal building. On Monday morning he and Mike drove from the hotel to Wade Avenue and then merged onto I-40. He joined the traffic heading west towards the Research Triangle Park and took the Raleigh-Durham Airport Boulevard exit.

After entering the airport grounds, they turned off onto a side road and drove for another half mile until reaching a manned guard gate. Ten-foot high fencing extended from each side of the gate and barbed wire ran along the angled brackets at the top. Looming thirty meters behind the fence were the hangars belonging to the National Guard's aviation unit. The unit flew both attack and support helicopters.

They showed their ID's to the guard and entered the parking area. Jack saw an Apache attack helicopter on the tarmac near the hangars. He recalled that when he was south of Bagdad, Apaches flew into a heavy barrage of anti-aircraft gunfire to engage some of the Republican Guard's Russian-built T-72 tanks, the most advanced equipment that the Iraqis had in their military arsenal.

Jack had coordinated with the Raleigh FBI office and the N.C. National Guard to use hangar space for the joint task force. He drove into an open door at the end of the hangar and saw a black Mercedes parked inside.

Mike looked at his watch. It was 8:15 a.m. "Looks like Homeland Security is here early."

"Yeah," said Jack. "I have no doubt that she's already pulled in all the available intel from her office this morning. Very impressive."

Mike smiled and looked over at Jack. "Yes, that would be my evaluation, in every way."

They walked to where an eight-foot high partition wall had been placed at a ninety-degree angle to the hangar wall. It was one of the sides of an enclosed area of approximately fifty feet by fifty feet. A panel had been pushed back about four feet from the hangar wall to allow access to the area inside the partition walls. Along the hangar wall were rectangular tables with grey tops and metal legs. Several computer screens were spaced along the wall, with the computers and keyboards lined up on the tables beneath the screens.

A large whiteboard in a rolling frame stood near one of the partition walls. Next to the whiteboard was another long gray table surrounded by gray metal folding chairs. A table with several white bakery boxes, with doughnuts, pastry, and bagels had been placed in the corner. There were two large coffeemakers plugged into an extension cord. Several glass pitchers with juice sat in ice-filled tubs.

"Nice," said Mike.

"Thanks go to the Raleigh office," said Jack.

Mike nodded over towards other side of the partitioned area. "There's the contractor."

A young man stood by the white board with a marker in his hand. He looked like he hadn't shaved for a few days, but it was a sparse beard, with bare spots where the facial hair refused to grow. He was wearing jeans and a black T-shirt with the relativity equation on the front. His glasses had black frames and thick lenses. His name was Eric Teilberg.

CHAPTER 17 – The Savant

Eric Teilberg was born in Hampton, Virginia, the youngest of three children. Eric's father was an electrician who worked as a civil service employee on the Navy base and his mother was a school teacher.

At age two, doctors diagnosed Eric as autistic. His parents took the news in stride. They were determined to treat Eric in the same way as his older brother and sister. They would soon discover that the world wouldn't treat Eric in the same way as his siblings, or like most other children in the world.

The Teilbergs bought many different toys for Eric, but he preferred playing with the plastic interconnecting pieces that could be joined together to build things. One day, his mother noticed something strange about the plastic pieces on the floor. None were connected, but there were several piles containing progressively larger numbers of blocks in each pile.

She counted the pieces in each group. The first group had two pieces. Next to that group was a group of four, then eight, then sixteen pieces. It was extremely rare for a three-year-old to use one-to-one counting to determine the number of items in a collection. Eric was counting at age three and exhibiting multiplication skills. By age seven he was multiplying a series of two and three-digit numbers in his head. At eight, he was reciting the prime numbers in sequence from one to ninety-nine thousand, nine hundred and ninety-one.

At age ten Eric was tested by a university professor doing research on children and adults with extraordinary mental faculties. The value of pi, the ratio of the circumference of a circle to its diameter, is an irrational number and continues infinitely without repeating. After a single viewing of the value of pi out to one thousand decimal places, Eric stated the numbers in correct sequence. Eric was diagnosed as having "Savant Syndrome."

Approximately one in ten persons with autism has some special skill at varying degrees. Eric, however, was an autistic savant with an unusually wide range of skills, placing him in a very small group of savants world-wide. He was able to memorize numbers and word sequences, do instantaneous calculation of numbers, and able to recall map or graphical detail after a single viewing.

In addition to his other abilities, Eric had a very unusual language talent, even among those diagnosed with savant syndrome. The skills exhibited by savants are usually right brain hemisphere as far as type, which are non-symbolic and direct perception skills. The augmented abilities usually result from right side compensation due to trauma, injury, or illness that affects the left hemisphere of the brain.

It is the left hemisphere type skills that tend toward logic skills and language specialties. Although there was no doubt that Eric had prodigious "right side" capabilities, he could also, with intense study of a language text, dictionary, and tutoring with a native speaker, acquire fluency in a foreign language—in a matter of weeks. He spoke six languages by age thirteen, an ability that would also figure into his future employment.

*   *   *   *

AS a pre-teen, Eric remained somewhat detached from others. He would become agitated when introduced into new settings or environments which disrupted his normal routine. Gradually, as he entered his early teenage years, he became better able to engage with others in social settings. He learned to look at people when they spoke to him and to respond with some type of statement—even if the person wasn't asking him a direct question. Eric was deemed a "high-functioning" autistic savant.

Eric could have gone directly to college, but his parents believed that thirteen years of age was just too young to be on a college campus. He went to the local high school and graduated in two years. In addition to the required courses for graduation, he took accelerated math and physics courses offered by the nearby community college. He also taught himself a new kind of language. In a matter of weeks, he learned several computer programming languages and began to code his own programs.

He quickly found that available computer programs failed to utilize fully the massive amount of open data on the internet. Eric's programs tapped into and analyzed millions of bits of under-utilized information, including scientific data from research being done in the fields of biology and physics.

Eric received attention from the national medical research community for his program which tracked the deterioration rates caused by cancer in different types of body cells, and the correlation of those rates to gender and ethnicity. As with any mathematical formula he had ever solved, and the numerical sequence of the decimal places of pi, he could recite every line of code he had ever written, forward or backward.

After Eric's graduation from high school, at age fifteen, his parents felt that with supervision he could attend college. He was awarded a full academic scholarship to the University of Virginia. Due to his taking advanced college courses while in high school, Eric completed a double major in Applied Mathematics and Classical Literature in two and a half years. While at UVA, he also served as a teaching assistant in advanced Ancient Greek and Latin studies.

At age seventeen, Eric applied for and was admitted to the Ph.D. program in Applied Mathematics and Statistics at Duke University. His primary motivation for attending Duke was the presence of the Statistical and Applied Mathematical Sciences Institute at the nearby Research Triangle Park. Known as "SAMSI," the institute's mission is "to forge a synthesis of the statistical sciences and the applied mathematical sciences with disciplinary science to confront the very hardest and most important data- and model-driven scientific challenges."

It was at SAMSI where Eric first came to the attention of a postdoctoral fellow who, in addition to doing research, was a surreptitious "talent" recruiter for a U.S. government agency. Eric was brought into the agency for special projects, although the agency kept him on the books as a contractor and not an employee.

* * * *

BEFORE arriving in Raleigh, Eric had been on assignment in Afghanistan. At first, the soldiers had good-naturedly called him "E.T." These were his initials but were being used to equate Eric to the short, large-eyed extraterrestrial of Hollywood movie fame. They considered Eric's skill set as something out of science fiction.

The movie had been one of Eric's favorites as a child. However, he believed that he bore no resemblance to the main character and was put off by the nickname. When members of the team asked for his help to save them time in doing assignments, he told them he didn't respond to anything other than "Eric." They started calling him "Eric."

When the call came from D.C., he had been pulled out of Afghanistan by chopper, put on a jet, and eighteen hours later deplaned at the Raleigh-Durham airport. A dark gray sedan had picked him up at the arrivals curbside and driven him to the aviation hangar.

As Eric left the sedan, the driver called out the window, "Nice meeting you, E.T." Eric just laughed. He instantly knew that his buddies in Afghanistan had sent a message to the driver to deliver a parting joke. *I sure will miss those guys.*

CHAPTER 18 – Operation Homefront

Mike had worked with Eric in D.C. and he was very familiar with his extraordinary abilities. When Mack MacCauley told him about the mission he immediately looked for Eric's work location. Finding that Eric was in Afghanistan, he contacted some operators there. They told him they were winding up a mission and that Eric could probably break away and head back to the States.

Jack walked over and held out his hand as the young man held out his. He was perhaps a head shorter than Jack. As Jack shook hands with Eric, Mike said, "Jack, this is Dr. Teilberg, but we just call him Eric. I think you'll find that he has some very special skills."

"Nice meeting you, Eric. If there's anything you need, just let me know. I'm assuming you have already met Special Agent Morris," Jack said, looking over to Kat.

"Yes, and you can call her Kat," said Eric, in a serious tone. "She told me that everyone calls her that, so it's okay."

Jack smiled and said, "Yes, I've heard that. I'll remember to call her that."

Jack moved over to the conference table and the others took seats around the table. "First of all, we can thank the N.C. National Guard for the operations space. We told them that we are working on a major interdiction effort and that we may need to coordinate with the Guard's aviation unit at some point. The Guard was glad to give us some space here, which also allows us to rapidly access commercial air transportation from the airport.

"We'll be having more members of the task force here later today, but I wanted to give you some classified information that we've received from the CIA and NSA. We believe that a nation sponsoring terrorist activities may be accessing some local law enforcement communication networks. Our computer security analysts haven't found any compromised networks here, but D.C. decided that we should compartmentalize some information."

Eric said, "We have connection to the NSANet, so we're separated from the public Internet. This will allow us to access TS classified information and NSA's systems and databases."

"That's good to know," said Jack. "From the classified briefing that I received on this operation, we will definitely need that access. We are at a turning point in Afghanistan. After all these years we are still in combat mode, and we are still sustaining casualties. But we've had some recent successes that have caused the Taliban to initiate a new strategy.

"We have intercepted information that the Taliban, with the help of al Qaeda, is planning an attack here in the United States. There are vague references to a major explosion that is being compared to the attack on 9/11. The traffic also suggests that there are already agents in this country that will be executing this plan.

"This strategy may well backfire. We will do whatever we can to stop this attack, but if it happens, we would probably see the same type of post-9/11 response. More troops and a major escalation of force. But the Taliban seem to believe that the propaganda value outweighs that risk. According to our analysts, they believe that a strike here in the U.S. would create a major influx of recruits.

"Russia was in Afghanistan for ten years in the '80s. Millions fled Afghanistan, mainly into Pakistan. The Taliban want to keep us bogged down in a war. One that our people think can't be won. It's the loss of political will that will lose this war."

Mike said, "I guess that was the story of Viet Nam. Before my time, but the veterans I know, to a man, say that the politicians lost that war. We didn't lose any major battles."

Kat said, "The longer the Taliban hold out, drawing troops in and inflicting casualties, the greater the chances that the U.S. will withdraw its support."

"I heard the same," said Jack. "This may be part of a war strategy overseas, but our mission is to stop a terrorist attack here in the U.S. And what we do know from intercepted communications is that if the attack is successful there will be thousands of casualties."

CHAPTER 19 – The Hitchhiker

The hitchhiker saw two men in the dark blue, extended cab pickup truck that had pulled over on the side of the interstate entrance ramp. It had the look of a work truck. The tires were rimmed in dried mud, and there were splatters on the fenders. The camper top was dinghy white and the glass was tinted.

"Hop in."

The driver was a large man, with long dark hair and a full beard. The passenger, the driver's younger brother, was smaller, and his hair and beard were light brown. They had been on the road for two hours, looking for the right person. The sun was setting, and they were about to turn around and head home. They were east of Winston-Salem, heading west, when they finally found him.

The hitchhiker got into the back seat of the truck. He was about the same age, height and weight as the man in the front passenger seat. Light brown hair and beard.

"Thanks for the lift," said Robert Alan Haislip, not realizing that this was a ride that he shouldn't have taken.

"Where you headed?" The driver had pulled back up onto the interstate. Mahmoud had brought them the message. It was their father who had devised the plan. "Make sure he is traveling a great distance."

"As far west as you want to take me. Headed to LA."

"So, no wheels?"

"Naw, had this old Pontiac, but the damn transmission went. My card is maxed out so here I am, ridin' on my thumb. Stayin' on the road."

"Yeah, saw your bedroll under your pack. We're going to Fort Smith, so you're welcome to ride. That'll get you through Arkansas. Got family out West?"

"Yeah. Got a younger sister. We ain't seen each other for a while. Figure I'll just surprise her and show up at her door. I've had it with small town Virginia. Gonna' stay in California. I'm goin' to get a job, live by the beach somewhere and kick back."

"No family here?"

"My mom passed last year. Ain't talked to my dad in years. Had a run-in with him and moved out."

"Six-pack in the cooler. Grab as many as you want."

Haislip couldn't believe his luck. He stuck his hand in the cooler and pulled a can off the plastic ring. The beer was ice cold. He drank one down and then another. He was halfway through a third when his eyes got heavy. He hadn't had much sleep since leaving Culpeper, the small town in Virginia where he had been working as a grill cook. He dozed off with his head leaning against the side window.

The driver turned the rear-view mirror to bring Haislip into view. Not an exact resemblance to his brother but sunglasses and a hat would help with that. Satisfied, he looked ahead and saw a sign for a rural road exit one mile ahead. No gas stations. No restaurants. Just an exit onto a two-lane country road. He slowed, took the exit, and turned onto the road.

Deep woods lined both sides of the road. He drove on for a quarter of a mile, then slowed when he spotted a break in the wood line. He turned onto a gravel road that had been carved through the forest. It was early evening and the sparse moonlight that had outlined the truck on the open road had disappeared. The truck became lost in the shadows. Haislip stirred and opened his eyes.

"Gotta' take a leak," said the driver. He turned in his seat and said over his shoulder, "Not stopping again for a while. If you need to go, best go here." The driver got out, went around to Haislip's side of the car, and stood a few feet away, with his back to the truck. He recalled his father's last words before they had left. Make sure he's out of the truck.

Haislip pushed open the door and got out. He was unsteady and put his hand against the truck. "Man, dark out here." His last words.

The brother in the front seat had gotten out of the truck. He wrapped his arm around Haislip's throat from behind in a chokehold. He leaned back, bracing himself against the truck, and Haislip had to come up on his toes. His hands went reflexively to his throat to pull away the arm choking him.

The driver had turned around when his brother had applied the choke hold. He pulled a military combat knife from the sheath attached to his belt. Haislip's eyes went wide in terror. The knife sliced upward under his rib cage, piercing Haislip's heart.

Haislip was dead before he was laid on the ground. They went through his pockets and found a cell phone and a slim leather wallet. As instructed, they immediately crushed the phone with a hammer, removed the battery, and tossed it into the woods. Inside the wallet were a driver's license, a credit card, and twenty-seven dollars. They also found a business card from a car salesman with some phone numbers scribbled on the back. A folded up pay stub from a restaurant in Culpeper, Virginia. A scrap of paper with a phone number and address in Pacoima, California.

They swung the tailgate down and opened the back glass of the camper top. A tarp had been spread on the truck bed. They put Haislip's body on the tarp, folded it over, tossed in his backpack, and then shut the tailgate and top. The stop had taken less than ninety seconds.

They headed back east on the interstate and stopped at a convenience store, parking on the side of the store to avoid any video cameras. The younger brother put the remaining beer cans, still on their plastic ring holder, and the empty cans into a plastic bag. They didn't drink alcohol. He tossed the bag into a trash barrel and got back into the truck.

The driver took out the wallet. He pulled the driver's license out and read the name. Robert Alan Haislip. Haislip might be Robbie, Bob, or even Bobby, to his family and to those who knew him. He would be just Robert to them.

He turned to his brother and held up the license. He looked at the photograph and then over to his brother. "Close enough."

* * * *

WHEN the men got home, their father went through the backpack. It contained Haislip's life possessions. There was a worn picture of a white-haired woman standing in front of a Christmas tree. A watch that was engraved with Haislip's initials and high school graduation date. There was a manila envelope filled with old birthday cards tucked into a side zippered compartment. But it was a folded piece of plain white paper that was of most interest. He unfolded the paper and looked at the reverse side.

"Surely we are being guided in this effort." It was a copy of Haislip's tax return from the previous year. At the top was his social security number.

He copied the information from the watch, the names from the cards, and all the information from the tax return onto a single sheet of paper. He took the photograph, cards, and tax return and burned them in the fireplace. He later put the ashes in a garbage bag that went to the county dumpsters. The initials and date on the watch were removed with a bench grinder and it went with the other garbage into the dumpster.

Three days after the Hendricks brothers picked up Haislip, a cashier's check for the balance due on the credit card in his wallet arrived at the central U.S. Post Office mail handling facility located in Jacksonville, Florida. Mahmoud had used a printer to put the address for the credit card company on the envelope.

Cash purchases had already been made but not all the necessary purchases would be made with cash. It would arouse suspicion. There were other purchases that would require the use of a credit card.

* * * *

MAHMOUD left his apartment and went down the stairwell to his Mazda Tribute that was parked on the street. He drove west, then turned onto the beltway entry ramp and merged into the morning traffic. He took the U.S. 1 South exit and headed southwest.

He had done his research on a library computer terminal. As an engineering student, he had a genuine interest in the methods and materials used in the construction of a nuclear reactor.

The construction of the nuclear plant had taken one-half million yards of concrete, enough to build a four-lane, seventy-five-mile-long interstate highway. The reactor vessel had an inside diameter of fourteen feet, and a wall made of eight-inch-thick carbon steel. The container structure walls were made of four-and-a-half-feet-thick concrete, with a five-eighth-inch-thick steel liner. However, Mahmoud's interest went beyond that of the typical engineering student.

In a website dedicated to halting the use of nuclear power, he found the official complaints that concerned groups had filed with the Nuclear Regulatory Commission about security at the plant. Intruder detection equipment inoperable. Security rule breaches involving private contractors working at the plant. Haphazard inspections of vehicles entering the plant. Plant officials ignoring a fire alarm that rang for hours before it was turned off.

It was a nice summer morning. The heat had yet to build across the Piedmont, so Mahmoud drove with the windows down.

He didn't believe in luck. He was convinced that he was being assisted by a great force. Many engineering students had requested to participate on a tour of the plant being held that day. There was a very limited number of spots, and each student who applied for the tour was given a number. A random drawing had been held to pick twelve students for the tour, and his number was the first one selected. A sign.

It was still early. Sunlight glanced off the metal roofs of the barns dotting the countryside. Shadows from utility poles angled across the road. To the south, above the pine forest, a singular white cloud stood out against the Carolina blue sky. The cloud was vertically aligned, with a curved shape. It moved like a woman undulating with the light breeze flowing across the Piedmont.

However, the bottom of the cloud was not balanced upon some airy platform. It emanated from the massive, 523-foot tall concrete cooling tower of the Shearon Harris nuclear power plant, just twenty miles from downtown Raleigh.

CHAPTER 20 – Person County

The next Friday, Mahmoud drove northwest on Highway 70, heading out of Raleigh towards Durham. He had met the others on a few occasions, but today's meeting would be at a new location. He didn't make the turn that would take him into the city of Durham. He took the road which led north of the city into rural Person County.

The car lots and convenience stores were left behind. Small, wood-frame homes with faded and peeling paint appeared on the sides of the road. Pick-up trucks occupied the driveways. Some were parked on cracked concrete and others rested on patches of crushed rock from which grass and weeds jutted out. Mobile homes flaunted satellite dishes.

A confederate battle flag, the "Stars and Bars," hung proudly from the side of a double-wide. Small log tobacco barns sat on crumbling rock foundations, the skeletons of a now defunct tobacco industry that had once flourished in the area. An above ground pool sat forlornly against a deck with its curved metal side split open, exposing the algae-covered blue plastic lining.

Mahmoud slowed to make sure he didn't miss the narrow two-lane asphalt road which wound through the open farmland. He found the road, continued another half-mile, then turned onto an unpaved road flanked by field fencing.

As he drove, he scanned the fence line, getting close to his destination. Livestock fed on the pasture behind the fencing. In the distance, crops were ready for harvesting. A silo, several barns, a tractor shed, and large rolls of hay could be seen from the roadway. This wasn't just acreage. It was a working farm.

He saw the opening in the fence ahead, where a driveway intersected the road at a ninety-degree angle. On each side of the drive, where it met the roadway, there were brick pillars with black metal and glass lamp fixtures mounted on top. The drive ran into the property then disappeared into a grove of trees.

Mahmoud left the bright sunlight and entered the shade cast by the trees. Ahead, on a small rise, he saw a two-story, white wood-frame farmhouse, bracketed by hardwood trees. A large front porch wrapped around the house. Shrubs encircled the base of the porch.

There was nothing remarkable about the house, other than it was modest compared to some of the other large, brick homes that wealthy professionals who worked in Durham had built to "get out of the city." As he neared the house, he saw a narrow drive of crushed rock. He had been told to follow the drive and go behind the house. After making the turn he saw the large barn, fifty yards behind the main house.

An area next to the barn was enclosed with fencing. Rabbit hutches and hen houses sat at the back of the enclosure. A fish pond lay beyond the barn, with a small dock of uneven boards reaching from pond's edge thirty yards into the water. A garden had been fenced on the other side of the barn. The fencing kept out the deer that were plentiful in the area.

Mahmoud parked the SUV next to a dark blue pickup truck that sat on a concrete pad in front of the barn. He got out and started towards the barn. The doors were closed but before he could reach them one side swung out several feet. A large man wearing a black Army gas mask came out through the opening. Mahmoud stepped back several feet.

"As-salamu 'alaykum," said Mahmoud.

Frankie Hendricks removed his mask. "Wa 'alaykumu as-salam." He towered above Mahmoud. His Italian heritage was apparent. Long and raven black hair, parted in the middle. A full black beard framed his face, which had an olive complexion. He was seemingly out-of-place; he would more likely be stepping out of a bar in Little Italy, New York—not a barn in North Carolina.

A screen door slammed at the back of the house and Mahmoud turned around. Two men were walking towards the barn. Johnny Lee was an inch or so shorter than his older brother. His hair and beard were brown, not as dark as Frankie's. He didn't have Frankie's olive complexion; it was naturally light but had darkened with a farmer's tan. He resembled their father, Calvin, who walked beside him, wearing bib overalls and work boots.

Calvin Hendricks was a tall man with a muscular build. His hair and beard were gray, with tinges of yellow revealing that he had once been blond. Absent the gray hair he could be mistaken for someone twenty years younger.

If Hendricks had been born at an earlier time, then perhaps Shakespeare would have been referring to him when he said that the eyes are the window to your soul. When Mahmoud met Cal, the first thing he noticed were his blue eyes. They seem to possess both a calm and a fury, like the sky just before an approaching storm. But there was something else. To Mahmoud, they were more like searchlights than windows, able to look inside his own soul, revealing the unsaid and demanding the truth.

He walked toward Mahmoud with a slight limp. A souvenir from a Russian bullet.

CHAPTER 21 – The News

Calvin Hendricks had been born and raised on the Person County farm, along with an older brother, Benjamin, and a younger sister, Jane. His father, Johnny Lee Hendricks, was a White supremacist and a virulent anti-communist. His mother had died of cervical cancer when he was ten years old.

Johnny Lee Hendricks had fought the Germans in Europe. He was angered beyond measure when Roosevelt "cozied up" to Stalin, and Russia ended up with "a bunch a' commie countries." As time went by, the senior Hendricks grew more and more disenchanted with the "fedral guvmint," sticking its nose into state business, including who attended which schools in the South.

Cal had been a bright student in school. His grades were above average in high school, but he started hanging around with the wrong crowd. He began drinking with his buddies and cutting classes. Suspensions followed.

His father told him that he could just work on the farm if he wasn't going to school. But Cal had other ideas. He was restless, and when his best friend enlisted in the Army, Cal decided that he would do the same. His father knew that meant he would be going to Viet Nam and called him a "dang fool."

Cal was assigned to the Fourth Infantry Division, was wounded in combat, and received a Purple Heart. After recovery, he served a second tour of duty and then redeployed to Fort Carson, Colorado.

In Colorado Springs, Cal met Sophia Rosetti, a dark-haired beauty of Italian descent. Sophie was a waitress at an off-post bar and he began spending his off-duty time at one of her tables. A romance ensued, and she moved into Cal's off-post apartment.

One day she broke the news to Cal that she was expecting. Although Colorado was the first state to legalize abortion, she had been brought up in the Catholic faith. She told Cal that she was going to have the baby. If they got married, as she suggested, then the government would pay for all their health care costs and Cal would get additional money for both his quarters and food.

Cal was perplexed. Sophie had never mentioned being Catholic, and she had not stepped a foot into a church in the six months he had known her. Marriage wasn't on his mind when she moved in, and he definitely wasn't thinking about children. But Cal felt a moral obligation to do "the right thing." Besides, the Army would make him pay child support anyway, so why not get the additional money for quarters and food.

Cal's parents were Southern Baptists and he had been baptized as a child. Sophie got the approval needed by the local Catholic bishop to marry a baptized non-Catholic Christian. They were married in a Catholic Church two weeks later.

Cal wanted to name the baby Johnny Lee, after his father,

who was killed in a tractor accident when Cal was in Viet Nam. Sophie, however, was adamant that the baby be named Francis Rosetti Hendricks. She idolized Frank Sinatra and using her family name was important to her. Frankie had the dark hair and complexion of the Rosetti family and, as a nine-pound seven-ounce birth weight foretold, the size of the Hendricks family.

Frankie was three months old when Cal began to wonder whether he had made a mistake. He began going out again with his old drinking buddies. At a downtown bar he ran into an old girlfriend. They started talking and one thing led to another.

Sophie had basically shut down at home and he wondered whether she had just found a way to quit working. She had gotten pregnant and married a soldier who had a steady paycheck. While pregnant, she had put on a lot of weight and had shown no signs of getting her figure back. She got up long after Cal reported for duty on post and sat home all day, usually in her bathrobe. As far as he could tell, she watched the TV soap operas unless she had to go to the grocery store. He felt trapped.

Cal went to the personnel section at his battalion and put in for Ranger School. He would attend the three-week airborne school at Fort Benning, and then the two-month Ranger school. He also requested a permanent change of duty station to Fort Bragg. He longed to be back home in the South. Sophie and the baby could stay in Colorado Springs and move to Fayetteville later.

When Cal told Sophie his plans, she went ballistic. Her immediate response was to shout, "So you want to get away from me and the baby! You're never around when I need help with Frankie. I'm the one who gets up in the middle of the night, every night, when he cries. I'm here all day with him while you're out doing who knows what!"

Cal had heard it all before and it was part of the reason he had signed up for training across the country. What he hadn't heard came next.

"And perhaps you'd like to know that we're going to have another baby!" Sophie burst into tears, got up off the couch, ran into the bedroom and slammed the door. Cal stood in the middle of the living room in a state of shock.

He had waited six weeks after Frankie was born and, although Sophie was not terribly responsive, she had capitulated. She had assured him that she had been fitted with a diaphragm. Cal didn't realize that even if fitted correctly, a diaphragm was not always effective and condom use was recommended. This was all news to Cal.

Chapter 22 – Soldier of Fortune

Fort Bragg, N.C.

Cal left Sophie and Frankie and completed his training. He lived on-post at Fort Bragg and began enjoying the life he had known before Sophie came along. He decided that perhaps she was better off now that she was with her mother in Arizona.

Sophie's father had been an alcoholic who was killed in a single car accident when Sophie was sixteen. Marie Rosetti, Sophie's mother, also had a drinking problem, but had been on the wagon since her husband's death. She was helping Sophie with Frankie, and Cal was relying on her to help with the new baby. Cal sent a check to Sophie every month. In the military failure to support your family could result in punitive action, including loss of pay.

Cal began working on getting an equivalency diploma for high school. The command had told him that any further promotion in the Army depended on it. He was due to re-enlist in six months. Without the diploma he might not be able to re-enlist.

He had absorbed his father's attitude about the federal government. He didn't see any connection between the military and Washington, a place filled with politicians whom he deemed "a bunch of crooks." Even the President had been part of a scheme to break into a place called Watergate, and then had to resign and get out of town when he got caught. They had screwed up in Viet Nam and didn't let the military win the war. The commies were taking over so "what the hell were we doing over there anyway."

Events then occurred which made Cal's obtaining his equivalency diploma a moot point. A little too much beer at a strip joint. A girl who was another soldier's date. Some fisticuffs resulting in a close encounter with the local police and then the military police. The next day Cal's name showed up on the blotter report, a daily listing provided to the chain of command showing all law enforcement activities in the past twenty-four hours.

The arrest wouldn't result in a court-martial. His C.O., the unit commanding officer, decided that some administrative action was the appropriate disposition. He told Cal that he would consider his entire record in reaching a decision.

Cal was still waiting to hear what his punishment would be when he picked up a magazine in the day room of his barracks. He read a story that would change his life.

A magazine with stories about "soldiers of fortune" had a feature story about something called the Rhodesian Bush War. Communist-backed guerillas were fighting the Rhodesian security forces in a civil war. Cal read about how ex-U.S. military soldiers, officer and enlisted, were joining up with the Rhodesian security forces. Several ads were designed specifically to recruit Viet Nam veterans. "Do you love being a soldier? Adventure awaits you as a member of the Rhodesian security forces."

Cal thought that this war in Africa would let him live the soldier life and fight, in his mind, a worthy cause: protect the ruling [white minority] government from the communist-backed [black] guerillas. He had grown bored with the daily peacetime training calendar that had activities far removed from what really happened in a combat zone.

There was a constant stream of BS from the command, including additional training classes that had nothing to do with his job. Now he probably was going to get busted a rank, which meant a pay cut. *What a crock of shit.*

CHAPTER 23 – Decision Made

The next day, Cal was called into the C.O.'s office. He stopped at attention in front of the commander's desk and saluted. "SGT Hendricks reporting as ordered." The C.O. looked up and returned the salute.

"At ease, Sergeant." He closed Cal's personnel file and leaned back in his chair. "Sergeant Hendricks, you have served this country in wartime. I'm not going to initiate proceedings which could result in you receiving less than an Honorable Discharge."

"Thank you, sir."

"Well, you may not want to thank me after I tell you my decision. I have several options, but I think the most logical option at this point is to bar you from re-enlisting. You haven't made satisfactory progress on obtaining your equivalency diploma, and this limits your continued progression in the NCO ranks."

He looked down at Cal's file. "This bar fight is not the first disturbance in the civilian community on your record." Cal flinched and recalled the drunk and disorderly charge a little over four months before that had been dismissed. He and some buddies from his unit had gone a little too far in celebrating at a sports bar after a Super Bowl.

"I would ask for another chance, sir. It won't happen again."

"Sergeant, this action does give you another chance. It does not prevent you from seeking enlistment in the future. Get your diploma and start taking some community college courses. Stay out of trouble and chances are that you will be able to re-enlist. This all-volunteer Army needs soldiers like you, but I must take some action. You can appeal this decision . . . ."

The rest of what his C.O. told him was lost. He was thinking about the soldier he had punched. He was a high-ranking NCO in the 82nd Airborne. He doubted he would even be standing there if it had been some Private. Now the Army was giving him the shaft.

"Is there anything you would like to add?"

"No, sir."

"Sergeant, you're dismissed." Cal saluted and left the office with a new plan.

CHAPTER 24 – Johnny Lee

While Cal was making his plans to join the Rhodesian security forces, Sophie had been seeing doctors at the Army hospital at Fort Huachuca. The doctors were concerned about her weight and the pregnancy. She had become clinically obese and had developed several associated medical problems, including gestational diabetes, high blood pressure, and signs of damage to her kidneys. Perhaps most significantly, she had been diagnosed with a heart condition, cardiomyopathy, a weakening of the heart muscle.

Although not due to deliver for another month, Sophie began experiencing the onset of contractions. Her mother took her to the hospital and she was admitted.

Cal knew nothing about her health condition. They rarely talked, and he just continued to send her money every month. She said she would let him know when the baby was going to be born in case he wanted to come to the hospital, although she wasn't sure he would take the leave time to come out to Arizona.

A week after Cal had been told about the bar to re-enlistment, he was told again to report to the commander's office. This time there was another officer sitting in one of the chairs in front of the desk. After reporting, his C.O. told him to take a seat in the other chair.

"Sergeant Hendricks, I have some news that I never like to give. At zero-two-four-five hours this morning, your wife, Sophia Rosetti Hendricks, passed away at the hospital at Fort Huachuca, Arizona. It was a cardiac arrest that occurred just after the birth of your son. Everything possible was done to try to save her life, but all attempts were unsuccessful. On behalf of this command, the United States Army, and the United States of America, I want to extend our sincere condolences to you."

The other officer, Major Howard Harris, was a clinical psychologist with the Medical Service Corps. He had been watching Cal closely as the commander had informed him that his wife had died in childbirth.

Soldiers who heard news like he had just received had many different responses. Some became so filled with grief and stress that they suffered a catatonic episode. Others switched back and forth from grief to outrage at the military for "letting it happen," seeking a cause upon which to place blame. There were those who almost expected to hear this kind of news—fulfilling their own expectations of tragedy that seemed to haunt their lives. It was SGT Hendricks' response that caused the psychologist to raise his eyebrows.

"No, that's not true," he said, in the same way as if someone had just told him that the earth was flat. "Is this some kind of joke?"

He couldn't believe what he was hearing had really happened. It wasn't that he didn't care for Sophie, for Frankie, or about having another baby. It was just that they existed in another reality from his. She would always be there to take care of Frankie and the baby that was coming. And he would be able to continue with his life as he wanted to live it. Her dying was not even remotely in the mental picture that he had painted.

His mind drifted to the first time she had set down a beer in front of him. "Is there anything else I can do for you?" He was sure she meant it in a way other than to bring him something else to drink. *But things had changed. She had changed and so had he—in ways that neither one could have thought would happen . . . they had been in love . . .*

"Are you okay, Sergeant Hendricks?" Cal had drifted away in thought. He looked up.

"You said, 'the birth of your son.'"

"Yes. The doctors delivered the baby by Caesarian section," said Major Harris. He was a little underweight because of premature birth, but he's healthy and without problems. He's in the neonatal intensive care unit as a precaution—"

"Johnny Lee Hendricks. That's his name!" Cal was now agitated and loud. He stabbed the air with his finger, forgetting for the moment that he was talking to his superiors. "They need to put that on the crib or whatever they've got him in!" He looked at Major Harris and his voice softened. "What happens now?"

"I'm here to help you any way that I can. I've been appointed as the Survival Assistance Officer, and can help you with any arrangements, get forms filled out for benefits, and arrange for your transportation. Your file states that Mrs. Hendricks, and your son Francis—"

"Frankie," Cal said, staring straight ahead. His voice was hoarse, and he whispered, "His name is Frankie."

"Yes, uh, I was just going by the official Army file listing dependents. Mrs. Hendricks and Frankie were staying with your mother-in-law, Marie Rosetti. We have your appointment form listing Ms. Rosetti as a designated caretaker for Franc—, uh, Frankie, but she doesn't have authority for custody or guardianship of Johnny Lee."

It then struck Cal that he was expected, as the children's father, to go to Arizona and pick them up or do something with them. "I need to call some of my family about this."

He knew that Marie would take care of both children, but his sister Janie had talked about adopting. Janie and her husband couldn't have children of their own. She had married a guy she met in high school that had done well as a real estate salesman. They lived in a large house outside of Durham, not far from the Hendricks family farm in Person County. *Maybe they could take care of them for me.*

CHAPTER 25 – Off the Wagon

One week after the birth of Johnny Lee, Marie Rosetti herself settled the question of who would care for the children. Cal had flown out with Janie, his sister, to attend the funeral. He was going to tell Marie that his sister and her husband were going to care for Frankie and Johnny Lee. *She will probably put up a fight about it,* thought Cal.

When he was at the hospital Marie showed up, somewhat disheveled. The makeup she had applied to her face was not done with a steady hand. She was completely unhinged by her daughter's death and had fallen off the wagon hard.

She pushed through the doors from the waiting room and saw Cal, wearing his Class A green uniform, looking through the nursery room glass at Johnny Lee. The baby had been moved out of the Neonatal Unit to the hospital's general nursery room.

"You sonova' bitch!" Her words were slurred. She walked unsteadily down the hallway towards Cal. "Wha' the hell you doin' here?! You gotta' lotta' nerve comin' here—"

A nurse grabbed Marie by her coat sleeve, forcibly turned her around and took her back out through the large double doors into the waiting area. Her curses grew fainter as the doors closed behind her. Marie was well known to the hospital staff. She had been staying at the hospital, night and day, after Sophie had been admitted.

The staff also knew about Cal. Marie had told them how Sophie's husband had abandoned her and the baby. It was Marie who was in the waiting room when her daughter was brought into the delivery room to have the baby. And it was Marie, not Cal, who was there when the doctors came out and told her that her daughter, her only child, was dead.

The transfer of custody had not been an issue at the hospital. Cal had made the appropriate changes in his military records, appointing Janie and her husband, Greg, as caretakers of both of his children in case of his absence. Hospital records were updated to show that only Cal and Jane Johnson were authorized to visit Johnny Lee and to take custody upon his release from the hospital.

Cal had received assistance from the local JAG office in obtaining a court order to pick up Frankie. Getting the order had not been difficult.

It had been raining the night that Marie went to the hospital in a drunken state. The combination of nighttime driving in the rain, Marie's emotional state after seeing Cal, and the alcohol—especially the alcohol—were just too much. After being escorted from the hospital, the nurse attempted to call a cab to take Marie home. Before the nurse could alert a police officer at the hospital, Marie left and drove out of the hospital lot.

When she got to an intersection several blocks from the hospital, she failed to notice that the car in front of her was stopped for a red light. She tried to brake but it was too late, and she slid into the car.

She was confused when flashing blue lights appeared in

front of her. She had expected to see lights in her rear-view mirror. A police officer exited the car, walked back to her car, and politely asked her to exit her vehicle. He smelled the alcohol and pointed the flashlight beam into her face. The officer asked a few questions and put on the handcuffs.

The report to the Family Services Division of the State's Social Services Department was completed by the time the Department opened at 8 a.m. A review of Marie's driving record showed a history of alcohol abuse. She had already attended an alcohol abuse program.

At an emergency hearing, the judge found that Marie had exhibited reckless behavior by driving while intoxicated. Cal had parental rights and had not abandoned his wife and child. He was on active duty in the armed forces and had dutifully sent money to support them.

Frankie, who had been picked up by the social services and was in the custody of a foster home, was released to Cal. After a week, the hospital doctor authorized Johnny Lee's release from the hospital. Cal, Janie, Frankie, and baby Johnny Lee flew back to North Carolina.

Marie would never see her grandchildren again.

CHAPTER 26 – Rhodesia

After Cal joined the Rhodesian security forces, he became a member of the "Crippled Eagles," a group of American mercenaries and expatriates that met informally during the Bush War. They considered themselves to have been abandoned by the U.S. government, hence the name. Cal was perhaps one of the more outspoken members of the group. *I put my life on the line in Viet Nam, and when it came time for the government to support me, they kicked me out.*

In Cal's mind, politics had now invaded the military. It had become as corrupt as the politicians who were, as Cal liked to say, "taxing the working man and giving it away to the lazy colored folk," although Cal would vehemently deny that he was a racist. He drew a sharp line of distinction between the blacks who served with him in Viet Nam and those who rioted in the streets or got welfare checks.

In 1979, the Bush War was winding down, and negotiations were set for December in London between the warring parties. Cal saw the handwriting on the wall and returned to North Carolina in early December 1979. Although he had been barred from re-enlisting, he was still an honorably discharged Viet Nam war veteran, and had a passport bearing entry and exit stamps from South Africa.

He went back to the Person County farm where his older brother, Ben, had taken over after their father's death. He would help on the farm until he could figure out his next move. Frankie was now five years old, and Johnny Lee was three.

Janie and Greg brought up the subject of legal adoption with Cal. He thought about it, but now that he was back, he couldn't see how he could give his sons to someone else. They would start calling Greg "Dad" and all that.

Janie told Cal that they would continue to care for the boys, whatever he decided, but that they couldn't leave their home and community to come live on the farm. If they were going to care for the boys, then Cal would have to visit at their place and they could come out to the farm on weekends.

It was during this time, around Christmas, 1979, that a chain of events began that would result decades later in Cal, Frankie, Johnny Lee, and Peter Mahmoud concluding their noon prayers at the farm in Person County.

CHAPTER 27 – A New War

January 1980. Person County, N.C.

Russian paratroopers landed in Kabul, Afghanistan, on Christmas, 1979. The government, under Prime Minister Hazifullah Amin, was fighting a civil war against fundamentalist Muslims. The Russians claimed that they had been invited into Afghanistan to fight terrorists and were there to support a legitimate government. Thousands of Muslims joined the mujahideen, who had declared a jihad, or holy war, on Amin's supporters, including the Russians.

Not long after the Russians began their campaign against the mujahideen, a pickup truck pulled up to the Hendricks' farmhouse. The two men who exited the truck may have been dressed like farmers, but the closest they had ever been to a real farm was when they drove past them along the way from the CIA's headquarters in Langley to Dulles Airport.

The U.S. government had a file on every American that joined the Rhodesian security forces. It had an interest in a specific Viet Nam veteran who had shown a penchant for participating in foreign wars.

Government policy was based on the premise that the "enemy of our enemy is our friend." The Cold War had been roaring along. There was an opportunity to stop Russian aggression and gain valuable intelligence on Russian military tactics and equipment.

The U.S. government could not be seen overtly providing aid in a civil war between the legitimate government of Afghanistan and a religious faction inside the country. The U.S. government needed a covert operative who would funnel weapons, including the surface-to-air missiles known as SAMs, to take out Russian helicopters and support planes—and who would train the mujahideen how to use them.

*   *   *   *

CAL sat at his kitchen table and listened. *So, these guys are government, but not the government that has to kiss the public's ass,* thought Cal. *They want Cal Hendricks to fight the communists—no, they need me because the politicians in D.C. don't have the guts to go in since they fucked it up so bad in 'Nam.*

Cal looked at the two men across the table, and said, "How can I be sure I won't get hung out to dry over there?"

"You won't be on your own. We have other operatives in-country. Native Afghanis who have trained in the U.S. and who have direct communication capabilities with our people in the region.

"This is, uh, classified, but we already have been providing a certain amount of U.S. dollars to some of the tribal chiefs to assist them in obtaining weapons from other nations. These are nations that can more readily supply small arms and other military equipment to the mujahideen. We need confirmation that the weapons we are providing are getting through and that these Muslims know how to use them."

There was something about the tone of the CIA man's

voice when he was talking about "these Muslims." If Cal had been a little more sophisticated at that time he might have realized that this "part" of the government had little concern for the mujahideen or the Muslim people in general. It was about stopping the Russians from expanding their communist ideology in that region of the world, and that was enough for Cal—except for one other thing.

Cal took a pen from the kitchen drawer, wrote a number on a napkin, and put it on the table in front of the two men. "Put this in my bank account every month and you've got a deal."

The number Cal wrote was three times his monthly salary when he had been kicked out of the Army. He didn't know about politics, but he knew that if the government was giving big bucks to these tribal soldiers, they had plenty that they could give to him.

Cal instinctively realized that the U.S. government would disavow him if he was discovered by the Russians. He would be nothing more than a mercenary who had left Rhodesia for the next war—which happened to be true. What Cal didn't realize was that the government would have paid him three times what he had written on the napkin.

CHAPTER 28 – A Wedding

January 1980-June 1984. Afghanistan.

After some refresher training, Cal parachuted into a remote area of Afghanistan. He linked up with the mujahideen and soon became a trusted ally. He ate, slept, and fought with the jihadi warriors. There was mutual respect between the mujahideen and Cal based on their possession of military and survival skills.

Growing out of Cal's respect for the mujahideen was a curiosity about their religion. They prayed before battle and were ferocious warriors. He began to receive instruction in the ways of Islam from the mujahideen.

Cal had never been religious growing up, but it seemed to him that the basic concepts of what he had been told as a child and what these Muslim warriors believed were not so different. One God. Angels. Holy books. Adam, Abraham, Moses, David. Even recognition of Jesus, although not God as a Trinity, a concept which Cal had always wrestled with. And a belief in a day of Judgment when it was decided whether you spent eternity in Heaven or Hell.

His life depended on the mujahideen, and they trusted him the same way. He dressed like them. He learned to speak their language. Except for the light color of his beard and the color of his eyes, he would have been physically indistinguishable from the mountain warriors.

He had been with the mujahideen for more than two years when he first met Mohammed Omar. Omar had gone from Afghanistan to Pakistan in the late 70's to study at a seminary for Sunni Muslims. He later moved to Kandahar province and joined the fight against the Russians in the early 80's.

It was just prior to an ambush of a Russian convoy. Cal was on a ridge with a sniper rifle in an over-watch position while a group of mujahideen placed explosive devices along a roadway below. Unbeknownst to Cal, a group of Soviet scouts, a small unit sent ahead to check for possible enemy, had traversed the ridge and gotten behind his position.

As Cal was focused on the dust rising in the distance from the movement of the Russian vehicles, there was a burst of gunfire behind him. He flattened himself into the rocks and brush, wondering if the next shots would be the last sounds he heard.

Instead, he heard someone say in Pashto, "Praise Allah. It was not your day to die." He turned and saw a tall man, in mujahideen garb, looking down at him. He raised up and followed the motion of the man's arm to a group of rocks behind him. Two dead Russians soldiers were lying on the ground. Omar had saved his life and they became close friends.

Cal now prayed fervently to Allah as he went into battle. He soon had a reputation as a brilliant tactician and was renowned for his bravery. The years went by and he had become one of them. A jihadi.

* * * *

IN a remote region of Afghanistan, a religious marriage ceremony called a Nikah was performed. There would be a marriage contract between the man with the golden beard, now called Atal, meaning hero or leader in Pashto, and Banafsha, the daughter of a tribal chief. Mohammed Omar was an honored guest.

Some four months after the wedding, Cal was wounded in the leg by a Russian bullet. The CIA had both Cal and Banafsha airlifted by helicopter out of the mountains to an air field in Pakistan. They were then flown to the military hospital in Germany.

While recuperating, Cal had prayed for guidance as to his future. With his conversion to Islam, he now understood that family was important to a happy life. He had two sons whom he had neglected, and it was a grave sin to "despoil orphans." *Have I not made my sons orphans by abandoning them? Have I not stolen or robbed them of something of immeasurable value—the comfort of their own father?*

He would seek forgiveness from Allah and would be the father to his sons that he was meant to be. *They will now have a father and a mother who will reveal the pillars of Islam to them, and they will grow up as Muslims.*

CHAPTER 29 – A Funeral

April 1984. Durham, N.C.

Eight months before Cal returned from Afghanistan, Jane discovered that Greg had been seeing another woman, a divorcee who had received a very large property settlement from her ex-husband. It had begun when he was showing her homes for sale.

One day, after he had shown her several homes, he suggested that they break for lunch. She suggested they go to her apartment. Then, one late afternoon, they met at an unfurnished listed home and took advantage of the empty master bedroom floor. She bought the house, and Greg visited on a regular basis to make sure that she was happy with her new purchase.

Three months later, the police showed up at Greg's house. Janie answered the door. They told her that they had a warrant for Greg's arrest. He had been embezzling money from the company's escrow account to pay for escapades with his girlfriend.

Greg was sentenced to two years in prison. They spent all their savings on Greg's attorney's fees, and Janie couldn't make the payments on their large suburban home on her schoolteacher's salary. The bank was threatening foreclosure.

The real estate market was slow, and she couldn't sell the house. It looked like she would lose everything.

* * * *

JANIE called her older brother, Ben, who had been running the family farm since their father had died.

"Hey, Janie. How's my little sister?"

"Well, actually, Ben, things are not going too well. But you don't sound so well yourself?" He sounded like he had a cold when he answered the phone. She heard him cough.

"Oh, I'm fine, just coming down with one of those nasty summer colds."

Ben Hendricks was forty-five years old and had never married. As the years went by, Janie had sensed that Ben was homosexual, but he had never confided in her. He was fourteen years older than she, so she really had not known him well as she was growing up. She understood that if he had wanted her to know he would have discussed it with her—and maybe he would at some point.

Ben had been ill since that Spring. He had been putting off testing but finally went to a clinic. The AIDS virus had first appeared in the U.S. in 1981, only three years before. Every day the news seemed to report thousands of new cases and growing fatality rates.

"I need to get out there and make you some soup."

"Well that would be great, but what's going on with you?"

"Ben, I should have told you before this. Greg got into big trouble and was sentenced to prison." She began sobbing on the phone.

"Janie, I'm so sorry. You know that I always had my

doubts about him but always accepted him as part of the family."

On the other end, Janie had stopped crying and wiped her nose. She said, "Well, you won't have to worry about that any more. I've filed for divorce."

"I know that will be rough on you. You still have those boys. You know how much I care about my nephews."

"I know. I've always been grateful to you for helping with Frankie and Johnny Lee. They love coming out to the farm to see their Uncle Ben."

Ben started to laugh, which suddenly turned into several rapid coughs. He cleared his throat and said, "I believe they came out to see the animals, not me."

"Well, maybe both," said Janie. Ben always had a way of cheering her up. "But what I was calling about was to ask you for a little help on something."

"Janie, you know that anything I can do for you, I'll do it."

"Well, the house has to be sold, and right now I just can't—" She broke down again into sobs. The stress and anxiety of how she was going to deal with the loss of income, selling the house and moving was too much for her to handle.

"Janie, Janie, you don't have to worry about that house. It was too big for what you needed anyway. I don't know why Greg bought it. Probably just to impress other folks.

"You bring the boys out here this weekend. While they feed the chickens, you and I will do some talking. I'll help you pay that mortgage until it's sold. You and the boys can stay here until you decide what you want to do. Buy or rent another house, or just stay here.

"If you want to pay me back someday, I might even let

you, but let's just say that I have more money now than I thought I would ever have, and I need to put it to good use—and that's helping you get through this. I'll even let you make me some soup. How about it?"

Janie had calmed down and wiped her tears away. "Ben, I love you."

"I love you too, Janie."

* * * *

BEN'S health continued to decline. Janie cared for him until he died in late 1984, one of the 5,596 deaths from AIDS that year. Cal was still recovering in Pakistan and missed Ben's funeral.

The farm had been left to Ben, Cal, and Jane in equal shares. Ben left everything in his estate to Cal and Jane, making them co-owners of the farm. Ben had invested his money wisely over the years. Janie and Cal each received almost three hundred fifty thousand dollars when the estate was settled.

CHAPTER 30 – A Baby Boy

In January 1985, Cal returned to the family farm in Person County with his new bride. Janie barely recognized him.

He was only thirty-two years old, but there were strands of gray woven through his long blonde hair. His beard was thick and full, and turning gray. His eyes seemed to have changed. They were the same dark blue but the intensity that she had seen when he had come back from Rhodesia was gone. They now had the peace and calm of a mountain lake. Perhaps an even more striking change was in Cal's manner of speaking. There was a significant softening of his accent—as well as in his temperament. He spoke in a deliberate and measured way. Janie was startled by the changes. He was a different man.

The CIA had made good on its promises. Banafsha received permanent resident status and Cal would receive Veterans benefits, including a disability pension. His pay for his time in Afghanistan was considered duty in a combat zone and therefore tax-free—as was his inheritance from Ben's estate. Cal had more than a half-million dollars in cash. He withdrew most of it from his deposit account and put it in a safety deposit box.

Cal strictly followed Muslim dietary laws, eating only

foods that were "halal" or lawful. He immediately had the workers, whom Ben had hired many years before, take the hogs off the property. He also directed them to remove all the soil where the hogs had been kept.

The workers were Christian men and Cal thanked them for their service. He then told them that they would not be needed any longer. He asked the imam at the Durham mosque if there were any men who attended that were looking for farm work. He was given several names, and after interviewing them, he chose two. He also hired the wife of one of the men to help Banafsha with domestic chores.

Cal told Janie that the boys would now be living with him, and that Banafsha was Frankie and Johnny Lee's mother. He expressed his gratitude to her for all she had done and would allow her to come visit them.

Janie immediately went to a lawyer about gaining custody of the children. The lawyer told her that she had no real possibility of keeping custody. Before Cal left, government attorneys had prepared a custodial agreement that she and Greg had signed. It was specific to them as a married couple, provided them with temporary custody only, and waived any custody claims. Greg and Janie were now divorced, and Greg was in prison.

Janie decided that she would not try to fight for custody. If she lost, and it appeared likely that she would, she had no doubt that Cal would make it difficult for her to visit the boys. She sold her half of the farm to Cal for one hundred thousand dollars, knowing that it would eventually go to the boys and stay in the Hendricks family.

Jane also decided that it was the time to do what she should have done long ago. She filled out the applications for adoption and underwent the background check. She was more than financially qualified and had sterling references. Six months later she brought home a baby boy. A child of her own. She named him Benjamin.

CHAPTER 31 – Indoctrination

Cal removed the boys from public school. He had made inquiries with the education departments at colleges in North Carolina and Virginia for graduating students with certain qualifications. He wished to speak to Afghani or Pakistani students, or those whose parents were from that region, who would like to work as a full-time home tutor. The colleges were more than happy to help minority students find jobs.

He was given the contact information for several graduates, but only one young woman met the most important qualification. She had emigrated with her family from Balochistan, Pakistan, at age ten. She was fluent in both Pashto and English.

When Cal interviewed her, she told him that she had been looking for a position in the public schools but would become a home tutor if the salary was reasonable. Cal told her that he would offer her twenty percent more than a starting teacher's salary in North Carolina's public-school system. Her work schedule would be from 9 a.m. to 4 p.m., from Sunday through Thursday.

There was one condition that was non-negotiable. She would be required to wear traditional Muslim woman's garb when at the farm. She accepted and, as part of the agreement, she gave English lessons to Banafsha. Cal's attorney ensured that all the appropriate tax and social security forms were prepared and filed with the IRS.

In addition to a general education, Cal arranged for the boys to receive formal instruction about Islam and the Muslim faith. He hired a Muslim graduate student in Duke's doctoral program in religious studies. The student came on Fridays, the holy day of the week, while Cal was at the mosque in Durham. This was a short-term home madrassa or religious school for the boys until they were more versed in the faith. After a period of instruction by the graduate student, he would begin taking them to the madrassa that was near the mosque.

At first the boys resisted. They missed their Aunt Janie. No hot dogs or bacon, and no ham and cheese sandwiches. They were used to watching TV at home, not studying and doing farm chores. Aunt Janie and Uncle Greg had only made them go to church on Easter and Christmas. Now they had madrassa every week and had to study a different kind of bible, called the Koran. The boys soon understood that Cal was their real father and that they were to do what they were told. If they didn't, they were punished. No bargaining, no second chances.

As the months went by, the boys had a change of attitude. They wanted to please their father and their mother, Banafsha. They did their schoolwork and chores and looked forward to the day when they would attend the mosque with their father and the other men.

When the boys became teenagers, Cal began giving them military-style training, including marksmanship and hand-to-hand combat. They learned how to move through the woods and hunt deer. They went on camping trips in the mountains and learned survival skills.

They hungered for their father's stories about Rhodesia, and the fighting alongside the other Muslim men in Afghanistan against the communists. They told each other that one day they would also join the fight against the enemies of Islam.

CHAPTER 32 – Omar

In 1994, a late model pickup truck turned off the road and onto Cal's driveway. Inside were two men dressed in jeans, T-shirts, and boots. Cal had been out on the porch and watched the truck as it came up the driveway. He knew they were CIA before the truck had rolled to a stop. He walked out to the truck.

"Good afternoon," said Cal. "Why are you here? Did I forget something over there and you came to bring it back to me?"

The agents laughed. "No," said the driver, "you got everything you took, and more." They knew that Cal had put away quite a haul of tax-free cash.

The passenger said, "We're looking for information. After the Soviets left in '89, and the Najibullah communists were overthrown two years ago, there was a lot of in-fighting between the mujahideen tribesmen."

Cal had already heard this information through Banafsha's communication with her family members. One of her brothers was in the process of emigrating to the U.S.

"Yes, I have heard."

"Someone you may have known, a mujahideen named Omar Mohammed, is now a very important person to us. We have information that Omar has organized a small group of madrassa students, recruiting them in Afghanistan and in Afghan refugee camps in Pakistan. Looks like we have the beginnings of another civil war between the old warlords and this group led by Omar."

"It has been more than ten years. I am not sure I would even remember this man. Is there a description?"

"I think you would remember him. He's very tall, even by U.S. standards. He supposedly was an outstanding marksman, at least at one time. He lost an eye, but that happened in the late 80's, after you left. We thought perhaps you might also know that as well."

They stopped and looked at Cal closely for a reaction. They thought Cal knew exactly whom they were talking about. They had information that Cal had delivered weapons to Omar's commander.

"Ah, yes, I do recall someone, tall, who was very expert with the rocket launcher." Cal wasn't sure why the CIA was interested. They could be lining up to support the warlord faction against Omar. He saw no reason to deny that he knew of Omar. Perhaps it was the best way to find out why the CIA was asking questions.

"This Omar has steadily increased his forces to the point that they are a definite threat to acquire and control territory. We believe that Kandahar may be on the short list. We are looking for any information. We'd like to better understand his thinking and learning what may be his long-term goals in the region.

"We thought that since you may have been with him in combat, you might be able to provide some information that we might not obtain from other sources."

Cal remained silent, considering the words of the agents. *Other sources meaning undercover operatives—spies. The U.S. will never be a friend of Islam. After the Russians withdrew from Afghanistan, the U.S. had done nothing to prevent the communists from taking control. The U.S. only supported the mujahideen to stop Russian aggression and now it supports the Israelis against the Arab Muslims in Palestine.*

"If we are speaking of the same person, I can tell you that he is a brave and courageous man. He is a man of faith who would give his life for his brothers. He was much respected by all those who knew him and there are many who will follow him into battle. Other than that, there is nothing I can tell you."

The agent in the passenger's seat turned off the recorder that he had activated by pressing his elbow down on his armrest. "Thanks. We may check back with you at some point."

Cal had determined that he would not provide any information to the men, but said, "I will be glad to help if I can. But tell me, this group led by Omar. Do they have a name?"

The agent driving the truck started the engine. The agent in the passenger seat had pushed the window button to close the window before turning on the air-conditioner. He took his hand off the button so that the window stopped halfway up.

"Yeah, they're called the Taliban."

* * * *

IN 1996, Cal told Frankie and Johnny Lee to come into the living room after dinner. The Taliban had now become a force in Afghanistan. Cal thought the time was right to explain what was happening to the boys, who were now young men.

He told them about Mullah Omar Mohammed and about the Taliban. They knew from their knowledge of Pashto that "Taliban" meant "students." They had been students at a madrassa as had Omar's original followers.

"Mullah Omar has taken Kabul and is now in control of a great part of the country. But the Russians and Iranians are helping the Tajiks in the north fight against them. This 'Northern Alliance' is killing our people. Innocent people."

"What can we do to help?" asked Frankie. "You fought the Russians. You fought with the mujahideen and now they are fighting again. We should go there and fight these Tajiks."

"My son, we have gotten word from your grandfather. He and your uncles are fighting with Omar, and alongside thousands of the refugees coming back from Pakistan to Afghanistan. Al Qaeda soldiers are coming from all the Arab countries. The al Qaeda leader, Osama bin Laden, has called for all in al Qaeda to come fight against these invaders."

"What will the United States do?" asked Johnny Lee. "Will they help this Northern Alliance? Will the United States help the people trying to kill our family?" He was looking toward the kitchen, where Banafsha was washing the dishes from their meal.

"I am not sure," said Cal. "But I can tell you this. I have received word that for now, we are to remain where we are. We should not draw any attention to ourselves as Muslims. We can still go to the mosque on Fridays but be careful when you are delivering crops or picking up equipment or supplies.

"Do not get into discussions about Afghanistan and the Middle East. Never speak of the mujahideen. I have been told that we may be needed one day. But we will not be needed to fight the invaders overseas. We will be needed here in America."

CHAPTER 33 – 9/11

September 11, 2001. Person County, N.C.

It was just after noon prayers. Cal, Frankie, and Johnny Lee had been out since 5:30 a.m. It had been a late year for corn, and they were just finishing up the harvest.

Frankie and Johnny Lee were now in their twenties and both were married. The imam at the mosque had helped arrange meetings between them and the daughters of others attending the mosque. Cal and Banafsha, and the parents of the women, had also met and discussed who would be best suited to marry their sons. The women whom were chosen had given their consent.

Cal had not needed any additional farm help since his sons had gotten their high school diplomas and began working on the farm. Their wives prepared lunches for them to take to the fields. The three men would stop work, say their noontime prayers, and then eat in the shade of one of the large oaks at the edge of the woods. They would then continue to work until mid-afternoon.

Cal was on a tractor when he saw Banafsha in the distance, frantically waving for him to come in. She and the other women had been out since early that morning gathering potatoes and had returned to the farmhouse at noon.

Before they began the scrubbing process, Banafsha had turned on the radio. Cal had installed a short-wave radio system, and it was tuned to a station in Pakistan. The farmhouse had one television and Cal would only allow it to be on for the nightly national news.

Banafsha could not believe what she had just heard. There had been an attack in New York City.

* * * *

AFTER the attacks on 9/11, the U.S. sent its demand to Omar that Osama bin Laden be extradited to the U.S. to stand trial for the attack. Omar's official position was that the U.S. needed to provide evidence of bin Laden's involvement in the 9/11 attacks. If evidence was presented, then the Taliban would turn bin Laden over to a third country. However, it was the widely-held belief that Omar would never turn over bin Laden.

The U.S. began its bombing campaign in early October 2001, and the U.S. sent Special Forces soldiers to assist the Northern Alliance and other anti-Taliban soldiers. U.S. ground troops arrived later in the month.

By mid-November the Taliban had been driven from most of its stronghold cities, including Kabul. In November, Cal and Banafsha listened to a BBC interview with Omar, who was in Kandahar. During the interview, Omar said that the situation in Afghanistan "is related to a bigger cause—the destruction of America."

Banafsha had heard nothing from her family for many months. She knew that her father, uncle, and older brothers were all fighting in Afghanistan against the Northern Alliance and its ally, the United States. Her younger brother had emigrated to the U.S. and was living in northern Virginia.

Banafsha's brother had established contact with someone in Pakistan who was providing him with information but had not contacted them with any news over the past month. Finally, in January of 2002, her brother called and told Cal that Omar had left Kandahar and was hiding somewhere in Pakistan. The Afghan military, which was led by former leaders of the Alliance, had tracked Osama bin Laden to the Tora Bora cave complex southeast of Kabul, but bin Laden had escaped.

Osama bin Laden had made good on his pledge of loyalty to Omar and had been recruiting al Qaeda affiliates in Arab countries to take up arms against the Americans, in much the same way as he had recruited fighters to battle the Northern Alliance. Battles were sporadic over the next few years, but began escalating in 2005, and had continued since then.

The call, the one that Banafsha knew might come, finally did. It was Banafsha's younger brother. She listened for a moment and then broke down in tears. American Special Forces soldiers had discovered a supply area and kept watch until a unit of Taliban fighters arrived there. The Americans had covered the avenues of escape and it was a massacre.

Banafsha's father, uncle, and two of her brothers were dead. Her eldest brother had been one of the few able to escape. She handed the phone to Cal and lay with her face in a pillow, sobbing. On the other end, Cal's brother-in-law handed the phone to someone who spoke in broken English.

"We are sending someone to you. He is an American by birth, but he is a jihadi. We are depending on you to be the leader of a mission and this other American has some special knowledge and skills that will be very useful to you. With your help, we will strike a blow that will be felt across America and the world."

CHAPTER 34 – Atal

Frankie and Johnny Lee had come back to the farm from the mosque. They told Cal that a young Arab man wanted to speak with him. He had told them that it was important. The man said that he would be back the following Friday.

Cal had been apprehensive. He had not felt well that morning and had told Frankie and Johnny Lee to go into Durham without him. Now his sons were saying that some stranger at the mosque wanted to speak to him.

Cal had been expecting to hear from someone but knew that the CIA had infiltrated mosques after 9/11. *They are waging war against Islam in Afghanistan and infiltrating our places of worship in this country.* Perhaps the CIA had been listening to the call from his brother-in-law and it was an undercover agent that had approached his sons.

Frankie then told his father something that the man, named Mahmoud, had told him outside the mosque. He told Frankie that he had a message for "Atal" from Omar. Cal had never told anyone his Pashto name. Only Banafsha would know that name and she would never talk to a stranger. The next Friday Cal met Mahmoud at the mosque.

Mahmoud told Cal the plan that had been given to him. He showed him the information he had gathered, as well as the pictures he had taken on his tour of the nuclear power plant. Although Omar had picked the target, Mahmoud repeated what he had been told to say:

"You, Atal, are to make the final decision as to the target. If you believe that there is little chance of a success with this target, or that a different target would better meet the objective, then the target should be changed."

The objective was to strike such a severe blow that it would create a powerful recruiting tool. The Taliban would show that the war was being brought to the U.S. and would not just be fought on Afghanistan's soil. The Taliban would be planning assaults contemporaneously with the strike here in the U.S. With continued military support from Pakistan, it could take back much, if not all, of the territory it had lost.

After Mahmoud left, Cal began analyzing how they might attack the nuclear plant. It soon became clear to him that it would be difficult, if not impossible, to cause the type of damage to the nuclear plant that would meet the objective. Certainly, they would be able to enter the facility, but even a large truck bomb would have little effect on the structure itself.

There was another possibility. A gathering that occurred every year. A strike at that location would not only cut off the head of the snake but would cripple it for many years. Cal believed that the U.S. public would not stand for another protracted war like Viet Nam. Russia had been bogged down in Afghanistan for ten years and then had to withdraw. The blow would show that the U.S. aggression and its killing of Muslims in their own lands would have a response. The war would be brought within America's own borders.

Cal believed that it was his destiny and his fate to carry out the mission. *Nothing exists outside of His Will. I was rejected by the government and put out of the U.S. military so that I could train in Rhodesia. If I had not been, then the CIA would not have sent me to Afghanistan where my eyes would be opened.*

I was placed alongside Omar in battle and I was brought back here to raise my sons for Jihad. And now I will be in battle again with Omar. It is His Will and what He does not Will does not happen.

CHAPTER 35 – The Exchange

Rock Creek Park, Washington D.C.

Mahmoud did exactly as he had been instructed; he purchased a specific brand, size, and color backpack at a big box discount store. He packed it with some T-shirts until it was full. He bought a baseball cap with the logo of the Washington Redskins, and a pair of reading glasses—to be thrown away immediately after accomplishing the mission.

He left Raleigh very early in the morning. He had his instructions about where and at what time he was to be in Washington D.C. at Rock Creek Park. He had been given an answer to a question.

After parking his car, he walked quickly to the pre-arranged location, took off his backpack, and sat down on the end of a nearby bench. He put the backpack on the ground, pulled out a small paperback from the top of the pack, and tried to read.

A tall black man wearing khaki pants, a checked shirt, and jogging shoes slowed down on the walking path. He walked toward the bench where Mahmoud sat and placed the walking stick that he had been using next to the end of the bench, angled against the seatback.

He was carrying a backpack on his shoulder by one strap.

He slipped it off and slung it down onto the bench. He then sat down and took a sandwich from the zippered pocket on the front flap.

When the man stopped at the bench, Mahmoud had been surprised, and then concerned that this man would interfere with the plan. But he noticed that the backpack that the man had placed on the bench was of the same type and color as his own.

The man asked Mahmoud, "Do you know when this Rock Creek Park became a National Park?" Mahmoud could not place the man's accent. Perhaps somewhere in Africa.

"Yes," said Mahmoud, "it became a National Park in 1895. It was the fourth National Park." The man understood this to be the correct response, although it was factually, and purposefully, incorrect. Rock Creek had become the third National Park in 1890, when President Harrison signed the act of Congress establishing the Park.

Cal had been told not to look directly at the man who would sit next to him. This was for his own protection. If information was sought from him later, he would be unable to identify the facial features of the man, regardless of how much "pressure" might be applied.

Mahmoud's backpack was still on the ground. He pushed it with his foot in the man's direction. He then slipped his arm through the shoulder strap of the pack the man has set on the bench, got up and walked away toward his car. He did not look back. Inside the pack was twenty thousand dollars in cash.

*   *   *   *

WHEN Mahmoud returned to Raleigh, he began purchasing what he needed for the next phase of the operation. He bought a Canon camera and a new laptop. He also bought a plane ticket.

He had been disappointed when Hendricks told him that destruction of the nuclear plant would not be feasible. But when Hendricks told him of the new target, he was excited by the possibility of utilizing his engineering knowledge as part of the mission. He would be an important part in striking the blow.

CHAPTER 36 – Busted

Fall, 1999. Raleigh, N.C.

During high school, J.T. had experimented with controlled substances, although nothing that interfered with his ability to achieve a high academic standing. If physical education had not been a graded subject, he would have been valedictorian of his graduating class.

As J.T. entered his sophomore year at college, he became a little more adventuresome. The trust fund was great for paying for school, but it didn't help get him to Florida, or even Myrtle Beach, on spring break. His father had made it clear to him:

"If you want extra money, you need to get a part-time job. You're making good grades without a whole lot of studying, so you must have a lot of time on your hands. And what about a summer job? You can get a job for the summer and save it for travel. Work is not a four-letter word, son." *Yeah, yeah,* thought J.T. *Well, there are easier ways to make a few bucks.*

A friend of his, Jimmy Hubbard, an agriculture major whose family farmed in Eastern North Carolina, was the source. He brought the baggie of mushrooms to the campus following a weekend at the family's farm. He showed the baggie to J.T. in their dorm room. "Know what these are?"

"Looks like mushrooms in a plastic baggie."

"Yep, that's exactly what they are. Mushrooms. But," he said, pausing for effect, "these are magic mushrooms."

"So, these are the ones that can get you high?" J.T. had heard about such a thing but had never actually seen them. He was somewhat skeptical as they looked like ordinary mushrooms. He also knew that some mushrooms were poisonous.

"High as a kite. He took another long swig on his beer. "You can eat 'em straight, put 'em in brownies, make tea with 'em. Best high ever an' safer than alcohol," said Jimmy as he drained the rest of the beer.

"Where'd you get them?"

"Best thing 'bout it!" Jimmy was gleeful now, as he had almost been waiting for J.T. to ask him that very question. "Don't cost a penny! They grow in cow shit!" He now had a triumphant look, which was somewhat comical as he also was feeling the effect of having chugged the beer. He reached down for another. "We got some pasture land where we keep cows. Best time to check out the cow patties is in the morning. You can find 'em in the woods, but 'round here, seems like most of them are the bad kind."

It seemed harmless at the time. Pot was getting expensive. Sell a little of the magic mushrooms to some friends at school. Make a little money to go to the beach. Why work at the college cafeteria washing dishes? I can just spread some joy to my fellow classmates and make some cash at the same time.

It all fell apart when the psilocybin in the mushrooms had a somewhat startling effect on a coed during her biology class. Liz Templeton, who was active in her church and had never smoked a cigarette—much less any illegal substance—had been somehow paired in a dorm room with Cindy MacRae, a bleached-blond party girl.

Cindy had told Liz that they needed to keep their food separate in the refrigerator. As Cindy had put it, "keep your hands off my stuff, pulleeeze."

Liz had come back to the room from morning classes to grab something to eat. Cindy had no more classes that day and was in town at the tanning salon. Liz usually had cans of a carbonated lemon-lime drink in their refrigerator but saw that she had forgotten to restock.

She took a small blue spiraled notebook out of her purse and jotted "soda" down on her shopping list. She looked again in the refrigerator and saw a bottle of what appeared to be iced tea in the back corner. The bottle was labeled as a cola drink, but it looked like Cindy must have made some iced tea and was using the bottle to keep it in. Liz knew that Cindy had been specific about her food, but she didn't think she would mind if Liz had a little bit of her iced tea. She got out a paper cup.

When Liz's parents got the call from the hospital, they were immediately terror struck. Had she been in a car accident? "No," said the doctor on the other end of line, she just seemed to have had some type of nervous breakdown. "Did she have a history of mental illness? How about prescription medications? Any history of daytime hallucinations? Drug use?"

No, no, no, and certainly not their daughter, she would never do drugs! The doctor told her parents that whatever it was seemed to be wearing off and that she was now resting comfortably. Her parents had no explanation why she would have screamed that the mice the students were dissecting were still alive and making noises!

Several hours later, when asked what she had eaten that day, she mentioned the tuna sandwich she had made at lunchtime. She then confessed that she had drank "only a little" of her roommate's iced tea that had been in the cola bottle in their fridge. The doctor and the nurse exchanged knowing glances. They had seen many students in the E.R. over the years. Sometimes it was brownies, sometimes it was tea.

Cindy had just finished painting her toenails chartreuse when the knock came on the door. "Hold on a sec!" She still had on her bikini from her trip to the tanning salon. She thought about putting on a T-shirt, but it might be that gorgeous guy from her English class. He said he might drop by to help her study that "lengthy" book they were reading, Moby Dick. Cindy opened the door and there stood a uniformed campus police officer. She immediately told the officer where she got the mushrooms.

Since Cindy was not a dealer she could enter a pre-trial intervention program with drug and alcohol abuse classes. If she completed the program, which included community service, the charges would be dismissed.

J.T. was not so fortunate. In the eyes of law enforcement, he was a dealer, and a message needed to be sent to any student who was providing other students with a controlled substance.

The police acted quickly, before word of the events of the afternoon might filter back to J.T. A young narcotics squad police officer with long hair, a beard, and dressed like a student, came to his door that same night. He said his name was Jason and that he was looking "to score some mushrooms." He told J.T. that he got his name from his girlfriend, Cindy. Jimmy had warned him not to sell to anyone he didn't know from his classes but when Cindy's name was mentioned, he forgot all about the warning.

Jason pulled out cash and J.T. retrieved a baggie from his own refrigerator and handed it over to Jason. Jason handed over the cash. J.T. had just uttered the words "pleasure doing business with you" when Jason showed his badge and told him that he was under arrest. Jason reached under his shirttail and pulled out handcuffs that were in a case on his gun belt. He snapped the handcuffs on J.T. and read him his rights.

* * * *

THE phone rang late that night at the Thomas home in Fayetteville. "Hello," said Aunt Gina, in a groggy voice.

"Uh, Aunt Gina, this is J.T. I'm, uh, in a little bit of trouble. I'm calling from the jail in Raleigh." He was both embarrassed and angry. He was angry at himself because Aunt Gina was the last person in the world whom he would want to disappoint. She had been his "mom" for almost half his life. He was the "baby" of the family and he always felt that he had a special connection to Aunt Gina—more than Jack did.

After J.T. explained everything, Aunt Gina told him not to worry. She would be there in the morning, after the banks had opened, to pay for the bail bond. He told her that the police had isolated him in a separate holding area, so that he wouldn't have to spend the night with other inmates. He begged her not to tell his father. "I don't want him to know and I certainly don't want any of his help on this. Besides, I'm sure he's much too busy to get involved," he said, with sarcasm in his voice.

Aunt Gina knew why J.T. held a deep resentment against his father. She had tried several times to talk to him about it and even suggested counseling. J.T. had refused.

She didn't see the same level of resentment in Jack because he had internalized his feelings about his father's decision; he didn't display any of the outward signs of hostility that J.T. exhibited. She could only see that Jack just rejected his father's attempts to direct him into the military. She assumed that he just felt that going into the military meant that you would be choosing that life—and the sacrifices that come along with it.

Max was deployed, and he hadn't been able to tell Gina where he was or when he would be back. Aunt Gina told J.T. that since she couldn't tell his father what had happened, it would be just between her and him for now.

The next morning Aunt Gina withdrew one thousand dollars in cash from her savings account. The bail bondsman put up the rest and would keep the thousand dollars as his fee. On the way to the car J.T. swore that he would pay back every cent. Aunt Gina just gave him a hug, smiled, and said, "Let's go home."

CHAPTER 37 – A Diagnosis

April-December 1989. Ft. Bragg, N.C.

Since the early 1980's, the 7th Special Forces Group had been operating in Central America. Max would bring back gifts for Roberta and the boys from places like El Salvador and Honduras. They were glad for their mother when their father was home. She seemed so much happier.

During a period when Max was in Panama, Roberta began experiencing some pain in her upper back, between her shoulder blades. She also felt some numbness and tingling in her arms and thought that perhaps it was a bulging disk. Or maybe it was a sprain from lifting some furniture. She recalled that Max had something similar happen after lifting weights.

She exercised regularly, so she tried resting for a week. She noticed that it was more difficult to take her rings off every night before she washed her face and to put them back on in the morning.

When Max was able to call, he told her that it looked like he would be in Panama for a while. He couldn't give her any more details. He told her not to worry about anything she might hear. She decided not to mention the pain, thinking that more rest would help. Besides, her husband shouldn't be worrying about her when it sounded like he might be involved in something major.

One morning while showering she felt a swelling under her left armpit. She called the clinic on post and explained her symptoms. The nurse asked her if she could call her right back. Minutes later, the nurse called back and told her that she had an appointment at Womack Army Medical Center the following morning. She said that the on-call doctor, after hearing her symptoms, wanted her to undergo an immediate round of testing.

Roberta thought about asking her best friend, Sheri Godwin, for help with the boys. Sheri's husband was also in the 7th SF Group, and she and Sheri were members of the Family Support Group. The members helped spouses of deployed military members, doing anything from home repairs to babysitting, or just being there in a time of need. She decided to just tell Sheri that she had a physical the next day and asked her if she could pick up the boys from school.

* * * *

ROBERTA dropped off the boys at school the next morning and went directly to the hospital. Testing took the entire day and included a mammogram, chest x-rays, bone and CT scans, an MRI, and a biopsy.

A nurse called her the following week. Roberta and her husband needed to come in to speak with the doctor—that afternoon. From the tone of the nurse's voice, Roberta knew. A chill went down her spine. She had no idea when Max might be back in-country. She decided to try to contact him after she spoke to the doctors.

Roberta's heart sunk when she found out that her

appointment was with Dr. Warren Hester. Colonel Hester was the head of the Oncology Department at Womack. He was a highly respected doctor in both the military and civilian medical communities. Seeing a senior military doctor under these circumstances meant bad news.

Dr. Hester quickly got up from his desk when she came into his office. He came around the desk and adjusted the two chairs facing his desk so that they faced each other. After he had helped seat Roberta, he sat down across from her.

"Mrs. Thomas, I hoped that your husband could be here with you. I understand that he is in an operational status in Central America. I have immediate access to the Southern Command headquarters, and can arrange a call to him right now if—"

"That won't be necessary," said Roberta, cutting him off and locking her eyes with his. "I know that he is probably involved in something very important and now is not the time to interfere with his . . . focus."

"As you wish," he said with some concern, knowing that what he was about to tell her was not something that she should be dealing with alone.

"I am so sorry to have to tell you that it is breast cancer. And it is a highly aggressive form. It has already metastasized—spread to other parts of your body. Your chart shows that your last mammogram was ten months ago. Unfortunately, the accuracy of a mammogram detecting breast cancer is not one hundred percent. Some fifteen percent of mammograms fail to detect breast cancer." He paused and waited.

Her worst fears realized, Roberta calmly said, "Go on."

"The presence of a tumor may, as it did in your case,

manifest itself in ways that are not so typical. A tumor may be situated so that it causes pain in the rib cage or back. The tingling in your arms, the numbness, and the swelling of your hands are signs of lymphedema. The lymphatic system can, and has in your case, spread the cancer. You have some identifiable cancer cells in your lungs, as well as in the bones of your arms." He paused again.

Roberta eyes began to tear. She was thinking of her two young sons. "How much time do I have?"

"Well, I wouldn't jump there—"

"Dr. Hester," she began, with a forthrightness that surprised him, "please don't tell me that there's a very good chance that I will survive this when that isn't the case. If you are certain that this cancer has spread to the point that it cannot be cured, then I have the right to know that—and to know that now," she said, again looking straight at the doctor.

Dr. Hester took a deep breath and let it out. "There are some ongoing studies on the five-year survival rate for women who are diagnosed with Stage Four breast cancer. These are recent, so I can't be precise with a number. Based on the literature I have reviewed, there's somewhere between five and ten percent of women diagnosed with Stage Four breast cancer who survive at least five years. This means, of course, that some survive longer."

"And at least ninety percent don't live as many as five years, perhaps some dying within months, correct?"

"Mrs. Thomas, I am not going to get into specific predictions in your case. What I am telling you is that with appropriate treatment there is still a chance, albeit a slim one, that you can survive this."

"Appropriate treatment?"

"There has been some spreading to the lymph nodes in the breast and near the neck. The tumor is still at a size where we will be able to operate. We need to quickly schedule the mastectomy. After that, chemotherapy to stop or slow the growth of cancer cells, and radiation therapy to kill bone cancer cells."

This time Dr. Hester stopped, and looked directly at Roberta. "And you want to know what the effects will be," he said, already sensing what Roberta was about to ask him.

She nodded, and he continued. "The mastectomy could result in the loss of nerve function due to the incision, with resulting numbness. There may be some sensitivity due to the irritation to nerve endings. There is always the risk of infection, but this is something that can be managed without too much difficulty. Chemotherapy and radiation will attack healthy cells as well as cancer cells. You may experience loss of appetite, nausea, vomiting, weight loss, diarrhea, and hair loss."

As Dr. Hester spoke, Roberta's mind filled with images of Jack and John as babies, then toddlers, and now young boys. She pictured a day when they each would meet someone and fall in love. They would marry and then have children of their own. But she knew that she wouldn't be there. She thought about herself in her own wedding dress, with the dashing Max Thomas at her side. She was so much in love with him—and still was.

"Mrs. Thomas?" He had seen that look before. A patient confronted with their own mortality in a sudden way. He wished that he didn't have to interrupt her thoughts, but time was now of the essence.

"I was asking you about setting a date for the surgery.

This is something that really needs to happen quickly. I know that you will want your husband to get back here as soon as possible."

"Yes, yes, doctor," she managed with a faint voice. "I'll speak with him and call back in as soon as possible." Dr. Hester leaned forward and placed his right hand gently on top of her left hand, which was resting on the arm of her chair.

"I know that you are thinking about many things that may have nothing to do with actually fighting the odds. We will do everything medically possible to get you through this. I know you have a husband and two children who—"

"Dr. Hester, by the ring you are wearing, I see that you are married. Do you have any children?" He leaned back, not sure of where the discussion was heading, but knew that it was important to listen.

"Yes, Carlene and I have been married nineteen years and have three children, two girls and a boy."

"And were they all born while you were in the Army?"

"Yes, I was in the Army-funded medical school program. My wife was a nurse at the hospital where I did my residency."

Roberta had turned her head slightly to gaze out the window behind Dr. Hester's desk. She noticed a family photograph on top of the credenza beneath the window. She turned back and looked at Dr. Hester with somewhat of a quizzical look on her face. "Were you with your wife when they were born?"

Hester knew now where she was heading. Military spouses suffer great sacrifices in their personal lives, especially those married to special operations soldiers. A call in the middle of the night and "Honey, I've got to go, don't worry."

Operational security required complete absence of

communication for extended periods of time. No husband there to share birthday parties, school plays, and band concerts. In the middle of the night, the three-year-old is sick and crying, and the six-month-old baby has a one-hundred-three-degree temperature. All the responsibility of taking care of the children, doing the home repairs, and paying the bills. The car won't start, and the kids are screaming in the back seat, and the stress of not knowing whether her husband will come home safely.

"Mrs. Thomas, I can arrange to have your husband back here within forty-eight hours."

"Doctor, I met my husband when I was eighteen years old. My father served in WWII but left the service to start a business in Fayetteville. I didn't know what it was like to have a father in the military, to be uprooted every few years, to attend different schools, and to have an absentee parent.

"Max was a lieutenant when we were engaged. When he said he had orders to Viet Nam, you can imagine how I felt. He told me that we would marry when he returned. I later realized he said that because he knew he might not return. He did not want me to be a widow at such a young age."

She paused and again looked out through the window. "I love my husband, and I know that he loves me. But I also know that when we did marry, I wasn't his first love. He loves this country and has placed his service to it above all else. Above me. Above his children."

She stopped as the tears had welled up in her eyes. As she reached down for a tissue from her purse, her tears dropped softly on the carpet. She wiped her eyes. A calm seemed to come over her.

"Doctor, I don't want you to arrange his return just yet.

I know what must be done. But I would like you to do something for me."

"Just tell me, and I can assure you that I will do everything I can."

"Can you find out what he is doing? Of course, I understand that certain things are classified, but there are probably some things that could be relayed to me that wouldn't impact national security. If you can let me know, and then I can tell you about having him back home quickly. I would expect that you will be honest with me about his current duties."

"I'll make the inquiry this afternoon and contact you as soon as I hear back. I may not be able to give you specific mission information, but I should be able to give you a general idea of what he's doing. I do believe that in an emergency he would be able to return as soon as possible."

Roberta said, "In the meantime, I do want to schedule the surgery and any treatment that you believe is appropriate. I'll do everything I can to be with my children for as long as possible."

CHAPTER 38 – Sacrifice

December 20, 1989. Fort Bragg, N.C.

The phone rang in the Thomas home. The boys were home on their Christmas school break. It was Sheri. "Have you heard yet?"

"Heard what?"

"We've invaded Panama! We're at war! It's called Operation Just Cause and they're going after Noriega."

Roberta's heart sank. Dr. Hester had told her that he would call her no later than noon that day with news on Max's situation. She didn't need to speak with him now. She knew that the 7th Group was in Panama, and that Max would be one of the first to engage the Panamanian Defense Forces, even before any regular troops reached the ground.

The Special Forces teams would be destroying communications sites and making impassible those access routes needed to defend strategic locations. They would be providing targeting information for bombs. The missions were both dangerous and crucial to the success of the invasion. They would be in harm's way, limiting the potential deaths and casualties for soldiers that were part of the invading force.

Roberta asked Sheri about Frank, her husband. She told her that Frank had packed some things and had been staying on post somewhere for the past week. He had told her that he might be going somewhere but, as usual, couldn't tell her exactly where or when. She now assumed that he had been in the staging area by Pope Air Force Base, which was adjacent to Fort Bragg. Once briefed and with their gear assembled, no one left the hangar area.

Roberta knew there was no way that her husband could leave his command in time of war. His troops looked to him to lead them and to use his experience and judgment to put their lives in the least amount of jeopardy, and still complete the mission.

She also knew that Max was being groomed for higher rank and command. He was on track to become a general officer. His actions now could very well cement the future of his Army career. She wouldn't put him in the position of choosing her over his command, especially when there was nothing he could do but stand by and watch her receive treatment.

* * * *

FIVE days later the phone rang at the Thomas home early in the morning. As soon as the receiver was picked up, a bellowed "Ho Ho Ho, Merry Christmas!" came from the receiver. There was an echo in the radio-telephone transmission from Panama. The call sounded like it might really be coming from the North Pole.

"And Merry Christmas to you, Max," said Sheri. "This is Sheri. I'm here for a few days."

"Oh. While Frank's here, you're staying with Roberta. Really appreciate your doing that. Is Roberta up?"

"Uh," Sheri hesitated, not quite sure if she would say the right thing. "Roberta told me to tell you that she had to have some surgery done, but not to worry. She's at the hospital for a couple of days. I'm staying here watching the kids. They're out of school on vacation."

There was silence on the other end and a tightening in Max's chest. No one just had "some surgery" done at Christmas if it wasn't serious. And he knew that if she had contacted him earlier, then she would have been asking him to come home in the middle of a critical mission. "How is she?"

Sheri's mind raced. Roberta had told her specifically what to say, but before she could get the words out, she broke down, sobbing, "Max, you need . . . to . . . come home." She wiped her eyes, composed herself, and told Max that Roberta wasn't in any immediate danger, but that Roberta had told her to tell him to contact Colonel Hester at Womack, and then to call her at the hospital.

Colonel Hester gave Max a complete briefing on Roberta's condition. She was three days post-surgery. It had gone well. They had removed a major tumor and there were no signs of infection. Her vital signs were good. They were waiting for her to recover from the surgery before beginning chemotherapy. Hester had served as a young doctor in Viet Nam and he knew what Max must be going through.

"We're at a stopping point until she recovers from the surgical trauma. Her body needs time to heal from the surgery. However, it is important that we start chemotherapy no more than thirty days after surgery. It will greatly increase her chances"—he was going to say, "of survival," but stopped.

The major combat operations in Panama had ended on

December 24th. When Max spoke to Roberta following his call to Colonel Hester she sounded well. She cheerfully told him that she was completely recovering from the surgery, and she would be going home that day. Sheri was coming to pick her up and they would be having Christmas dinner with the kids that afternoon at the house. There was "no need" now for him to leave his command in the middle of things there just to come home and sit around the house.

On New Year's Eve, Max walked into the house in Fayetteville. He had caught a ride on a C-130 back to Fort Bragg. He stayed the night and caught the return flight to Panama early on New Year's Day.

When Max came back from Panama two weeks later, he and Roberta called Jack and J.T. into Max's office. Max told them that "Mom is sick" and would be having some treatment. She might look a little different during the treatment, but they shouldn't worry. Roberta hugged them both and told them the same thing. Jack saw the tears streaming down his mother's face. His father's eyes were wet. *Dad never cries! Why are they so sad if everything is okay?*

* * * *

SIX months later, Iraq began massing troops on the border of Kuwait. On August 2, 1990, Iraq invaded Kuwait and the United States responded with Operation Desert Shield and Operation Desert Storm.

Max Thomas was re-assigned to the 5th Special Forces Group. He was given the mission to provide liaison and conduct Foreign Internal Defense (FID) operations with the Pan-Arab force. The Pan-Arab force included the Saudi

Arabian land forces, the Egyptian forces, the Syrian forces, the Kuwait forces, and other member nations of the Gulf Coast Coalition. The SF teams would conduct training in calling for close air support, staff planning, combined operations, armored and mechanized warfare, and basic civil affairs.

At the beginning of August, Max had come to Roberta with orders in hand for Fort Campbell. His orders had an arrival date in mid-August and then deployment to Saudi Arabia later in the month. He told her that he could submit a compassionate action request and reassignment. She just smiled.

"Max, don't be ridiculous. What are you going to do? Sit by my chair all day? Drive me to the hospital and back?"

"But—"

"Max, I'm not trying for martyrdom here. You need to go because I fell in love with the man you are." Tears welled up in her eyes. "I may be here another five years or another month. But if I have to live knowing that you threw away something which you were meant to do in this world, I couldn't live with myself—no matter how long I live."

Roberta held back the tears and her voice became calm. "The country needs you. It may be because of you, and the decisions that you will make, that soldiers will live to come home to their wives and children." She wiped away the tears that had begun rolling down her cheeks. "You should go. I'll keep up the fight here—"

"And how do you think I will be able to live with myself?"

The question was more than rhetorical. Max was defeated. He knew that if he did stay he would be the martyr. He put his arms around her and sobbed. In that moment, he realized that it was Roberta who was the stronger one—

stronger than "Supermax" who had led men into combat.

Max deployed to Saudi Arabia the same day that Roberta was receiving her regular chemotherapy treatment. Her cancer was deemed incurable. The focus now was on her surviving with the greatest quality of life. She knew that there was nothing that Max could do except what he had been called to do. Serve his country.

CHAPTER 39 – Last Rites

As Special Forces troops combed the Iraqi desert looking for SCUD missile launchers, Roberta became progressively weaker. To Jack and J.T., their father had gone away when their mother needed him the most.

Jack asked his mother why "Dad wasn't there to help take care of her." She did the best she could do to convince him that their father was needed where he was, but he couldn't understand why other people were more important than their own mother.

Regina de Luca, Roberta's aunt on her mother's side, was only eight years older than Roberta. Aunt Gina had not married, and she treated her great nephews as if they were her own children. When Roberta became too weak to care for the boys herself, Aunt Gina moved into the home.

When Roberta got weaker, she decided to receive palliative care at home. A private nurse came every eight hours to check on the drip that had been placed in her arm, and Gina was with her around the clock.

In early October, the leaves began to turn color. A mottled brilliance of red, gold, orange, and yellow had rolled down into the Piedmont from the mountains. The hardwood trees, masked throughout the summer months by the constant green of the pine forests, had announced their presence in a grand way.

But the brilliance was gone now. The leaves had faded when the temperatures dipped and dropped away as the winter winds blew.

The doctors told Max and Roberta that three to six months were left. But there was a sudden turn in Roberta's condition. The forecast that Roberta had months to live would prove to be inaccurate.

Gina had fed the boys breakfast and made sure that they had their coats on before they went to the school bus stop. She had just put the last dish into the dishwasher when the nurse came into the kitchen, placed her hand on Gina's shoulder, and said, "It's time."

Gina reached behind her back, undid her apron, and placed it on a kitchen chair. She walked up the stairs to the bedroom and pushed open the partially closed door. She had been able to speak with Roberta the night before, but now it appeared that Roberta had lost consciousness.

Roberta was on her back with her eyes closed. Her mouth was slightly open, and the pattern of her breathing was different than the night before when the priest had come and administered the Last Rites. Her breathing was labored, as if there wasn't enough oxygen in the room.

Gina crossed herself and knelt by the side of the bed. She took Roberta's hand in her own and prayed. She spoke softly to Roberta, although not certain whether she could hear or understand what she was saying.

She told Roberta that she loved her. That she would soon be free of all pain, and in the presence of the Lord. She told her of her love for the children, and that she would care for them the rest of her life as if they were her own. It was then that Gina felt the slightest of pressure from the hand that she held. Not long after, Roberta's suffering was over.

CHAPTER 40 – Mellow

January 2000. Raleigh, N.C.

He had explained the options but the college student, caught red-handed dealing hallucinogenic drugs, didn't really understand that he was going to jail. "It's your call J.T. Based on this judge, getting six months and doing your time in the county jail is probably the best you can expect. If you agree, I'll make that offer to the Assistant D.A. in return for a guilty plea."

J.T. looked across the table at his appointed attorney. The conference room at the Public Defender's Office was cramped. The gray metal table had a vinyl surfacing that had seen better days. It was beginning to peel up at one of the corners. The grained surface had scratches from file folders with metal clips being slid across its surface.

Mark Shapiro was J.T.'s public defender. He was twenty-six years old and had graduated from UNC's law school the year before. He sat across from J.T. in one of the six gray metal chairs arrayed around the table. The chairs had vinyl padded seats and backs. Yellow foam was beginning to squeeze out through the cracks in the seats. The legislature had been cutting the budget and had used a machete when it came to the PD's office. Providing resources for criminals was not high on the list of priorities for the politicians.

"I thought that mushrooms were kind of like pot," said J.T. "I mean, you can just pick them, and you can even smoke them like marijuana."

He had been shocked when his lawyer told him that where marijuana was a Schedule Six controlled substance, the lowest category, hallucinogenic mushrooms were Schedule One controlled substances—the same as heroin! He had been charged not only with possession and distribution, but also with manufacturing a controlled substance, a much higher felony on the state's sentencing grid.

"If you don't deal on this, the State is going to go for the max on these charges. The law gives the judge a lot of discretion. You could get almost two years active time, which would mean Central Prison. As a first offender, the court could also give you intensive probation, but that's not likely. First of all, you were distributing a hallucinogenic drug to college students. On campus!"

"You mean hallucinogenic like LSD?"

"Exactly," said Shapiro. "There was a serious incident involving a student on LSD just last year. It really put the spotlight on these kinds of drugs—"

"But a mushroom high is mellow, not anything like acid."

"Look, I know that, and you know that, but the word 'hallucinogenic' is all that it takes to put fear in the community about what is going on at the college." He paused and then gave J.T. the real reason that he might be looking at some serious time.

"Your big problem is named The Honorable Samuel J. Ackerman. He's the equivalent of the hanging judge in the Old West. Extremely tough on drug offenders." Shapiro knew that the Asst. D.A. would probably not agree to six months. He would insist on a longer sentence that would put J.T. into the State prison system.

"If this had been a smaller amount, of say—marijuana, and only a possession charge, you would probably be looking at a short term probationary sentence. But I can tell you that he is death on distribution and especially on dealers."

J.T. blanched when he heard the term "dealers." He had never considered himself a drug dealer. He was just making a little cash and providing some people with a pleasant high. He could be going to prison. *Maybe I should call Dad,* J.T. thought. *No, I'm not going to give him the satisfaction of me crawling to him now that I'm in trouble. He wasn't there for Mom. I'd rather go to prison.*

CHAPTER 41 – Ms. Burnett

Wake County Courthouse, Raleigh, N.C.

A voice from the other side of the world said, "Good Morning, this is Lieutenant Colonel Maxwell Thomas. I would like to speak to the presiding judge in the John Thomas case, please." The tone was direct and respectful.

The judge's assistant, JoAnn Burnett, asked, "can you tell me the nature of your call?"

"Yes, ma'am. I'm John Thomas's father. I was informed that he has a pending trial date. I would appreciate the opportunity to speak with the judge. My current assignment prevents me from traveling on the trial date. I'd like to request a continuance."

"Colonel Thomas, I'm afraid that you can't speak directly to the judge. Your son has an assigned attorney. Please hold and I'll give you his contact information." She pulled the copy of the court file from her desk drawer and opened it. "His name is Mark Shapiro." She gave Max Thomas the Public Defender's Office number and suggested he get in touch with Mr. Shapiro as soon as possible.

After she hung up, she glanced through the Thomas case court file. She walked over to Judge Ackerman's office door, which was open, with the file in her hands. He was sitting at his desk, reviewing jury instructions. "Mind if I interrupt for a minute?" She went in and closed the door. A minute later, she came out without the file.

* * * *

JOANN Burnett was bright, efficient, and very good with people. After high school she attended the local community college and received a paralegal degree. There were no paralegal jobs available at the time, so she responded to an ad for a legal secretary with the Court Administrator's office.

A year after she started working, a prized position as an administrative assistant to a newly elected judge, Samuel Ackerman, came open. She interviewed with Judge Ackerman and he was impressed that she had a paralegal degree. She got the job.

Ten years later Judge Ackerman was designated as the Senior Superior Court Judge and JoAnn Burnett assumed the additional administrative responsibilities that came with that position. Ms. Burnett handled all administrative matters for the Judge, as well as supervising the entire legal secretarial staff.

Ms. Burnett's official job title was Principal Administrative Assistant for the Court, but the attorneys who appeared before Judge Ackerman knew that she wielded additional power that did not appear on her job description. Woe be it to the attorney who got on the wrong side of Ms. Burnett. She had the judge's ear and could make life difficult in ways that an attorney would never see coming.

The phone rang on her desk. "This is JoAnn Burnett. How can I help you?" It was Charles Askew, an Asst. D.A.

After reviewing the file, Judge Ackerman told her to contact the counsel in the case. She had called the prosecutor's office earlier that morning and left a message for Askew to return her call. He immediately called her when he received the message.

"The judge was wondering if the State and the defense expected to reach a plea agreement in the Thomas case," said Ms. Burnett.

Askew was puzzled. This was new. He'd never gotten a call from the judge asking about a settlement. He usually just called the judge's office when a plea deal had been reached.

"Well, we're, uh, still in the negotiation stage." Askew thought there might be an offer out, but he had a lot of cases.

"Would the State like to meet with defense counsel in the judge's chambers?" She knew that Askew would say "yes" before she asked but did not want it to appear as if the judge was requiring the conference.

"Yes, that would be fine. Shall I contact the defense counsel?" He couldn't remember who the counsel was off the top of his head.

"Yes, please. He can see you and Mr. Shapiro next week, on Friday, at noon. How does that sound?"

Askew thought, *she knows I didn't recall the defense counsel. Saving me the trouble of looking him up*. "That would be fine. I'll speak with Mr. Shapiro right away."

She knew that both counsel would agree to that time. There were no court proceedings scheduled on Fridays. No attorney would tell a judge that they have a lunch date and couldn't make it to an in-chambers meeting.

"Okay, see you both then." She said goodbye and hung up the phone. She had thought that the judge might have a special interest in this case involving this student dealing hallucinogenic mushrooms on campus—and she was right.

CHAPTER 42 – The Axe Man

Assistant D.A. Askew and Public Defender Shapiro sat in the chairs in front of Judge Ackerman's large mahogany desk. Judge Ackerman had used personal funds to purchase the desk and chair, the credenza behind the chair, the leather couch, and the leather side chairs on the other side of the room.

Anchoring one end of the credenza was a two-foot tall statute of "Blind Justice," the woman with the eternally worn blindfold, finding justice on the scales held out before her. The State and U.S. flags flanked the credenza. The high-backed leather desk chair behind the desk was empty.

Askew and Shapiro had arrived at ten minutes before the hour. Judge Ackerman had been given the name the "Axe Man" because he had been known to drop the axe on both defendants and counsel.

There was a legendary story about a Charlotte attorney who was thirty minutes late to court. He had rushed in and said that there had been a massive tie-up on the interstate. He had left early but had been stuck in traffic. Judge Ackerman began his cross-examination: "Now counsel, do you regularly travel from your office in Charlotte to Raleigh?"

"Yes, your Honor."

"And you were aware that there are traffic jams on the interstate almost every weekday morning?"

"Yes, your Honor, but I left two hours earlier than I would usually—"

"And wouldn't you agree that the smart and prudent thing to have done would have been to stay in a hotel here in Raleigh last night so that you wouldn't have missed your court time, or wasted this court's time?" The judge stopped, looked down from the bench at the counsel over the glasses that were perched on the end of his nose.

"Yes, your Honor," said the attorney with resignation in his voice. He paid a two-hundred-dollar fine for contempt of court and was never late to court again, nor were any of the other counsel who appeared in Judge Ackerman's court.

At two minutes before noon, Judge Ackerman, in his judge's robe, swept in through the side door of his office from the courtroom next door. Askew and Shapiro popped up out of their chairs. "Sit, sit," said the judge.

The judge took off his robe and hung it on the rack standing in the corner of the room. A navy-blue suit coat hung on a coat hanger. He was wearing a starched white shirt, navy suit pants, and a bright yellow tie. At age sixty-two, Sam Ackerman worked out every morning, ate a healthy diet, and had a plus-two handicap on the golf course. He also played number one singles on the judges' tennis team in their annual charity tennis tournament against the local Bar attorneys.

He sat down in his chair and opened the manila file folder that JoAnn Burnett had placed on his desk. The charge sheet that was attached with a two-hole fastener on the left side of the folder.

"Hmmm. A manufacturing charge. Possession and

distribution. Schedule One controlled substance. He looked up at the defense counsel, Mark Shapiro. "Counselor, I have a pretty good idea where the State will be on this case. Should I expect a jury trial on this?"

Shapiro was in a bind. There was no plausible defense. A plea of "not guilty" would result in the court dropping the hammer when the jury came back with findings of guilty on all counts. J.T. had not agreed to plead guilty yet, despite all of Shapiro's efforts.

"Well, Your Honor, I'm dealing with a nineteen-year-old college student who has never been in any trouble before." Shapiro was new as a lawyer, but he had learned that the sooner he could get any mitigation evidence before the court, the better.

"Yes, I'm aware of that."

The judge looked over to the right side of the file folder. "I assumed that neither of you would have objected to the court having the State probation office do a P.S.I."

Askew and Shapiro looked at each other, and then back to the judge. They both assured the judge that they certainly had no objection to the court having had a pre-sentence investigation report completed. The P.S.I. was normally done after a finding of guilt, and prior to a sentencing hearing. It was usually completed in cases involving prison sentences but could also be useful for intermediate sentences involving rehabilitation programs.

The judge looked at Askew. Chuck Askew had practiced before him for the past three years. He was a tough prosecutor, who would undoubtedly rise in the ranks of the District Attorney's Office. "Chuck, do you really think this case warrants a manufacturing charge?"

The prosecutor was somewhat taken aback. He hadn't studied the file or done any significant research. A new assistant had prepared the charges. It had seemed like a cut-and-dried drug case. But good trial lawyers think quickly on their feet.

"Yes, your Honor. The defendant took the raw material, processed it, and then packaged it in a different form for sale."

"And you have some case law that supports your argument? Taking an organic substance, cutting it up, drying it, and putting it in a plastic baggie constitutes manufacturing as intended by the State legislature in enacting the applicable statute?" The judge raised his eyebrows in punctuation.

"Well, not at this time, your Honor," was all that Askew could manage.

Judge Ackerman wasn't letting Mark Shapiro off the hook. It was time to deliver an important message. "Mark, and I hope it's okay if I call you Mark?"

"Certainly, your Honor."

"I know that you haven't been in practice too long. I was wondering about whether you would be filing a motion to dismiss this charge?" It was less a question and more like a two-by-four board to the side of Shapiro's head.

The judge said, "To prove a manufacturing charge, the State must prove possession and the intent to manufacture. A good example would be where a defendant is found in possession of pseudoephedrine and the equipment to make methamphetamine. Or marijuana seeds, indoor grow lamps, and hydroponic equipment." He paused and looked down at the file.

"Now, I understand from the file where these mushrooms were originally 'harvested.' He looked up at

Askew. "Unless the State is going to argue that the defendant had arranged for pasture cows to manufacture the growing medium for these mushrooms, I don't believe that this charge will, uh, stick." The judge smiled. "Pardon the word choice in light of the growing medium involved."

Shapiro was elated, even though he had been chastised for missing the legal issue. Perhaps the court would keep the confinement to six months and his client would serve his time in the county jail.

The judge continued, "If the defense submits a motion to dismiss this charge, the court would grant it." He looked at Shapiro. "If not, the court would dismiss it on its own motion."

"Yes, your Honor," was now all that Shapiro could manage. He began to breathe a little easier, but when the Judge began speaking again, he thought he could hear the sound of prison doors slamming shut on his client.

Judge Ackerman looked first at Askew and then at Shapiro. "This is a serious matter. The distribution of a hallucinogenic, whether on a college campus or in society in general, can have grave consequences. Unless serious consequences are attached to such conduct, I'm afraid that there will be little deterrence to this type of activity."

Oh my gosh, thought Shapiro, *I have got to get J.T. to agree to some kind of deal. If he goes to trial, he is going to get hammered.* Shapiro's thoughts were broken up by words that neither he—nor Askew—expected.

"I've reviewed the defendant's background. If the defendant decides to plead guilty to a possession and delivery charge, then I would be inclined to impose an intermediate sentence. However, I'm not pressuring him to do so and will confirm on the record that he would be waiving his right to a trial knowingly, intelligently, and voluntarily after consultation with counsel."

Under the state's sentencing scheme, an intermediate sentence meant that the defendant would not receive an active sentence, either in county jail or prison. The defendant would get to walk out of the courtroom instead of being led out the side door by the bailiff and into confinement.

"I'm assuming if the defendant pleads guilty, his suspension from campus will become an expulsion from the university. With a drug distribution felony on his record, he will have a difficult time finding a university that will admit him." Shapiro nodded his head, thinking that someone with J.T.'s intelligence would have a tough time finding any fulfilling employment in the future. A check in the felony conviction box on an employment application eliminated most white-collar jobs. Even blue-collar work was hard to find as a convicted felon.

"If the defendant pleads guilty, it will serve as an example to other students and hopefully change the attitude about these so-called magic mushrooms. There's nothing magic about hallucinations.

"In addition to intensive supervision while on probation, I would include an order for drug treatment for the defendant. The P.S.I shows that he comes from a good family but had some tragic circumstances occur in his youth. He's a smart young man and if he can just get away from drug use, he may still have a bright future and overcome what will be a serious handicap, at least in the short term. If the State and the defendant should agree on a plea deal for a year of supervised probation, the court is likely to impose that sentence.

"I want to reiterate that I have no preconceived notion as to whether this defendant is guilty of any of these charges. He is innocent until proven guilty by the State. If he decides to go to trial, he will get a fair and impartial hearing on the remaining charges."

Askew was speechless. A judge had wide discretion on lower level drug felonies, but Judge Ackerman generally imposed some active time, in some cases less than six months to keep the defendant in the county jail instead of the prison system. *Perhaps he was annoyed by the manufacturing charge,* thought Askew. *Ackerman was tough, but fair, and maybe he thought the State was piling on. Sending me a message.*

Askew had no obligation to make an agreement on behalf of the State of the type the court had mentioned. However, the reality was that if the State didn't deal Judge Ackerman would still be the sentencing authority. Askew knew that he would be wasting his time and, worse than that, he would have to appear in front of Judge Ackerman in the future on other cases. *Well,* thought Askew, *this case will soon be off my trial calendar.*

Shapiro was able to quickly suppress the jubilation that he was feeling. He knew that the other public defenders would be crowding around him back at the office, wanting to know how in the world he had gotten his client off on probation in a drug distribution case—in front of "The Axe Man" no less!

"Your Honor, I will discuss that with my client, and with the State, as soon as possible."

Askew had regained his equilibrium. "Yes, your Honor. I'm certain we can come up with an agreement that would do justice in this case."

Judge Ackerman got up out of his seat and the two

lawyers immediately stood up, understanding that the meeting was over. The judge came around his desk and walked out with them into the outer office, shook their hands and thanked them for coming by. After they had left, he came over to JoAnn's desk. "Thanks, JoAnn," he said, and went back into his office.

JoAnn made a call to the number Max Thomas had given her when he had called.

"Hello," said Aunt Gina.

"Hello, is this Ms. de Luca?"

"Yes, it is. Who's calling?"

"This is JoAnn Burnett from Judge Ackerman's office. I just thought you should know that Mr. Shapiro may be trying to get in touch with Mr. Thomas."

When the judge got back into his office after seeing the two attorneys out, he called his college roommate, Keith Palmer. Palmer had retired as a Brigadier General and was living in Boca Raton.

"So, you ready to go next month?"

Palmer had tickets to the Army-Navy game. He and his wife were going to Raleigh. The two men would then head up to the game while their wives would enjoy some shopping time without the men around.

"You better believe it. I'm thinking we crush Navy this year."

"Yeah, I'm thinking the same," said Judge Ackerman. "Hey, you remember 'Mad Max' Thomas?"

"Hell, yes. Probably best defensive end we ever had. Too bad he wasn't there a few years earlier, we could have seen him play. Why do you ask?"

"Oh, no reason. Just thinking about some of the guys

who played for us in the past." Ackerman twisted the West Point class ring back and forth on his finger as he spoke, a subconscious habit.

"Got to run. I have some afternoon business to attend to. See you next month." Ackerman put on his coat and left the office. It was Friday afternoon and with no court scheduled he still had time for a quick lunch and eighteen holes.

* * * *

IT was Aunt Gina who had contacted the Special Forces Command and told them that she needed to contact Lieutenant Colonel Thomas due to a family emergency. She knew that J.T. didn't want his father to know about his case but contacting him was the right thing to do. She had been entrusted with J.T.'s care and even though he was technically an adult, she still felt responsible. He was in trouble and needed his father's help—even if he wouldn't admit it.

CHAPTER 43 – A Degree

After J.T.'s expulsion from college, he moved back to the family home in Fayetteville. His probation officer had been a short and wiry man named Tom Berkshire. Berkshire had been an MP with the 18th Airborne Corps and retired at age thirty-eight after a twenty-year career. He had spent two decades enforcing the law, and now he liked to say that he had the opportunity to help rehabilitate offenders.

Berkshire was known for his pleasant and outgoing demeanor, but anyone who assumed that they could take advantage of him, whether because of his size or his manner, would be making a serious mistake. Berkshire was a black belt in Kung Fu and had continued his development in advanced katas and weapons.

J.T. was impressed with Tom Berkshire, and Berkshire was impressed by J.T.'s willingness to do everything required of him during his probationary period. He didn't complain or seek any slack from him, not that Berkshire would have given it. It was Berkshire who had arranged for J.T. to work at a brick manufacturing plant.

North Carolina had been the leading producer of brick in the nation after World War II. Although it was no longer first in the nation, it maintained enough capacity to supply brick to most of the Eastern U.S. Sanford, a short drive from Fayetteville to the south and from Raleigh to the north, was one of the state's principal brick-producing areas.

Berkshire had an Army buddy, Ralph Jordan, who was in charge of inventory control and distribution at the brick plant just north of Sanford. Jordan had been the senior logistics NCO in Berkshire's last unit and retired six months after Berkshire.

Berkshire called Jordan and told him about J.T. "He's a bright kid who made a stupid mistake that he is now paying for. His Dad is SF and you know how hard that is on a family. His mother died when he was young, which is no excuse, but I have to believe that it had something to do with this situation."

Jordan said, "Well, I could use someone right now. I was just given a new computer program and it's a little complicated. They also have me pulling some extra duty here on the materials ordering side of the operation. I'm guessing someone of his age would be able to understand how this new program works, then train me," he said with a chuckle. "When can he start?"

J.T. moved to Sanford, and it was not long before he was proficient in his work at the plant. He contributed some innovative ideas to ensure accuracy in inventory control and to reduce shipping costs.

He was a hard worker on and off the job. A local community college had accepted all his freshman credits and he completed his Associate of Arts degree by taking classes at night. He found out that his criminal record didn't bother universities offering on-line education courses from admitting him as a student. He received a bachelor's degree in Systems

Management with a 4.0 average.

The trustee of the O'Reilly Trust Fund had determined that he had been "admitted as a student and was working toward a degree at an accredited institution" as to his night classes at the community college and his on-line courses. The fund paid for all his tuition costs, travel costs to the community college, as well as all expenses for the two trips to California for proctored final exams for the on-line courses.

J.T. received his bachelor's degree in the mail and had it framed. He hung it over the computer located in the second bedroom of his apartment. The room was his office, where he could do any overflow work instead of staying late at the plant. It was a night that he did stay late at the plant that would bring him trouble.

CHAPTER 44 – Blue Lights

It was Sunday afternoon. J.T. had called Jack that morning, wanting to talk. He asked Jack if he could come down to Sanford. Jack didn't like the sound of J.T.'s voice.

Jack turned right onto U.S. 1 and continued southwest towards Sanford, leaving the nuclear power plant in his rear-view mirror. He crossed over the Haw River and saw the exit for the Jordan Lake Dam. The Dam is on the east side of the southern tip of Jordan Lake, a reservoir constructed by the Army Corps of Engineers in 1982.

Loved going out on the boat with J.T. . . . crappie and bass fishing. Jack laughed out loud, recalling the time J.T. had gotten a strong hit, stood up to step over the cooler, slipped and went into the lake, rod and all. *Maybe they could do a little fishing . . .*

Jack pulled into an apartment complex a mile off the highway. The buildings were three stories high and brick, as were most of the buildings in the area. He climbed the stairs to the second story, knocked once on J.T.'s door, and entered. He had an immediate sense of gloom.

All the window blinds were closed. The drapes over the sliding glass doors that led out to the small deck were drawn to the center, with a quarter-inch gap. A thin pane of sunlight came through the narrow opening, bisecting the room. Jack could see small particles of dust floating up on the sheet of light, swirling in the air current from a slowly rotating ceiling fan.

J.T. was sitting on the couch, bent forward, with his face down and cradled in his hands. He had kept his hair long, wearing it in ponytail while at work. It now hung loose, covering both his hands as well as his face. His bosses at the plant had given him a hard time at first for having long hair, but as time passed, they saw J.T. the individual. His long hair was not a lifestyle statement.

Jack looked down at J.T., who had stayed on the couch with his hands on his knees. His eyes were red.

"I'm in trouble, Jack."

Jack looked down and saw "Little John" again, on the playground, with the hurt look of an eight-year-old that had been bullied by a gang of prepubescent children. Jack walked around the coffee table in front of the couch. J.T. followed Jack with his eyes as he went to the back of the apartment. He reached up and pulled the drapes open on the back wall with a force that almost took down the curtain rod.

Sunlight flooded the room. Dirty dishes were piled in the kitchen sink. Letters and junk mail were spread over the kitchen table. An open pizza box sat on the kitchen counter. Dark grease spots on the brown cardboard surrounded a lone slice of pizza. The cheese on the slice had hardened and flies were taking off and landing on it like jets on an aircraft carrier.

Jack closed the box and stuffed it into the garbage. He got down a can of ground coffee, a filter, and loaded the coffee maker with water. After he had the coffee brewing, he turned around and said, "O.K., what's up J.T.?"

"I'm up on a drug charge," J.T. said. "They found some

pot in my truck." He looked up directly into Jack's eyes. "I swear it wasn't mine!" Jack knew J.T. was telling the truth. If it had been his pot, he wouldn't have called him. J.T. wouldn't lie to him.

Jack's training, both military and legal, took over. "Okay, first thing we do is straighten up this place. It's a pig sty, and no one can do their thinking in a pig sty—except maybe a pig but that doesn't count."

He thought he saw a small smile start on J.T.'s face and his eyes brightened a bit—what he'd been looking for. They did the dishes as a team, Jack rinsing and J.T. stacking the dishes in the dishwasher. Jack saw the precision in how the dishes were placed, and said, "Looks like you've learned something useful from stacking bricks at the plant."

"Funny. Actually, I did design the rack system for equipment storage, and the layout of the yard for efficient forklift loading avenues and . . . ." He stopped mid-sentence and looked at Jack with a bleak expression on his face. "I'm about to lose it all, Jack. The job and any future I might have had with the company."

Jack grabbed a pen out of a coffee cup on the countertop next to the refrigerator. "Got some paper?" J.T. went into the second bedroom and pulled some paper from the printer tray.

Jack gathered up the mail and the assorted ads and flyers, put them in a neat stack, then placed them on the far end of the table. He poured two cups of coffee and set one down on the table across from him. He opened the blinds, pulled back a chair and sat down. J.T. slipped the stack of white paper to Jack and sat down opposite him.

"Okay, let's get started. Tell me exactly what happened. Don't leave out the details."

"All right. Last week I got a call from Lester Jones, the manager of the shipping yard. We were talking after a meeting a few weeks back. I told him that I was renting at this place but looking around for a place of my own. He had some land for sale, so I told him I might be interested. Maybe build a small house on it.

"Anyway, Lester called me. I thought it might be about the land, but he said he had a young guy that worked for him, a truck driver named Donnie, whose car had broken down. He said Donnie lived in a mobile home not too far from here down on Old U.S. 1. He was wondering if I might give Donnie a ride to work the next day."

"What's Donnie's last name?" Jack looked up from taking notes. He could already sense where this was going.

"It's King. Donnie King."

"Okay, go on."

"I told Lester, sure, no problem, I could give him a ride. He told me that Donnie was out on a delivery run, but he would make sure to tell him to be out front of his place in the morning. Well, next morning, I show at the mobile home where Lester told me Donnie lived. There was no one out front."

"What time did you get there?" Jack knew that the time might not be relevant, but he wanted to ensure that J.T. did not leave out any details. Asking him the time reinforced that message.

"Okay. About seven-thirty. I hear a dog barking from inside, so I figure that Donnie must know that I'm outside, so I just sit there waiting."

"The place is pretty much of a wreck. A good part of the skirting is off, and there's streaks of rust on the metal panels.

There's a screen door on the front, but no screening in it. So, the door finally opens, and I see a guy holding a huge German shepherd back by his collar and he pushes the dog back as he backs out the door. He comes out to the car and says something about 'havin' a late night' and 'sorry' he's late."

"A description would be good right about now," said Jack, cutting in. "Trying to get a mental picture of who we're dealing with."

"Oh, yeah. He's around your size but skinny. Around my age, dark hair pulled back with a small ponytail. Lots of ink. Both arms are pretty well sleeved out to the wrist."

Jack remembered when J.T., at the age of eighteen, got the spiderweb tattoo on his elbow. It was a showing of independence, and he got it against their father's wishes. If J.T.'s plan was to show his father that he was no longer under his control, then he was successful. The sad part was that J.T. had come to regret getting the tattoo, an admission that his father had been right.

J.T. was holding his coffee cup in front of him, with both elbows on the table. He set it down on the table and let out a long breath. "Donnie didn't talk much on the way in, and I got the feeling that part of that was a hangover from whatever he had been doing the night before. Anyway, I let him off in the brickyard and told him that I'd meet him at my truck at around five o'clock that afternoon.

"I park my truck in the front lot, so I can look out the window at the front of my office and see it. I looked out at around five and there is no Donnie. I continue working and checking the lot. At around twenty after five I called Lester and told him that Donnie was supposed to be at my truck at five for a ride home. Lester tells me to hold on a sec, and then comes back and says that Donnie was on a delivery run, and running late, and that he would wait there and give him a ride home.

"I knew Lester lived in the other direction from where Donnie lived. He would have given him a ride if it was on his way in, so I said, 'hey, no problem, I'll just stick here and wait on him as I've got work to do anyway.' Well, I'm waiting and waiting, and finally a little after six, I finally see Donnie walking towards the truck. He says, 'Hey, man, really sorry about bein' so late.'

"He then says something like 'the damn truck got a radiator leak,' and he had to wait around for a heavy-duty tow truck because he hadn't delivered his load yet. The tow driver took the truck to the off-load site, so they could get the bricks where they needed to go.

"He said he was really pissed off because he was supposed to meet somebody at a fast food place near the turn-off near Old U.S. 1 at five-thirty. He was going to ask me to drop him off there on the way back, but he said he would have to get with the guy later.

"Once we were outside the gatehouse and on the State road, he got out a cigarette—or what I thought was a cigarette—and lit it. I smelled it first, then turned and he had a joint in his month. He says something like, 'takes the edge off, don't it' and then asks me if I want a hit.

"I said something like, 'Donnie, you have no idea what can happen to me if I get busted for pot. Get rid of it and now!' Now I'm really pissed off. I'm guessing because I was around his age, had a ponytail, and have this stupid tatt," he stuck out his elbow, "he must have thought I got high when I was off the job.

"Donnie had just snuffed it out in the ashtray, when I saw the blue lights in the rearview. I got a sick feeling in my stomach and thought I might throw up right there. Donnie just said, 'oh shit' or something like that. He stuck the joint his mouth, and I guess he swallowed it."

"Did he say anything else?" Jack looked up from taking notes.

"Well, I really can't remember. The officer took his time coming up to the truck. I pushed all the window buttons down, hoping any smoke or smell wouldn't hang around. I don't know whether he saw me do that or not.

"I do remember the first thing the officer said when he did come up to the truck—oh yeah, I almost left out something. I had turned my head, looking over my left shoulder, as the officer was kind of in my blind spot on the left side and I couldn't really see him in the mirror. I thought Donnie moved something or got some sense that he had moved something. When I turned around he was just sitting with his arms on the center console and door armrest, with his pack in his lap."

"What pack?" Jack said, unable to mask the irritation in his voice because J.T. had not mentioned it before.

"Oh yeah, sorry I didn't tell you about that. When he came out in the morning, he had this small backpack. I kind of just looked at it and he said that he always brought his lunch to work."

"You didn't make any comment about it. He just volunteered that it was his lunch?

"Yeah."

"Okay, so you're stopped. The windows are down. You sense some movement by Donnie. He's sitting with his arms on the console and door armrest, and his pack is in his lap. Was it in his lap when he first got in the car?"

"Don't think so. I think he had put it on the floor."

"Okay. So, the officer walks up to your window. What happened next?

"He says, 'Sir, do you realize that your right brake light is out? I'm going to have to write you a citation.'"

Jack wrote down the officer's words, and then repeated them. "Those were his exact words?"

"Well, I don't know if those were his exact words, but he asked me if I knew my brake light was out and that he was going to have to write a citation."

"Okay. What did you say?"

"I said, 'no, sir' and told him I would get it fixed right away. I was feeling a little relieved, thinking, okay, we can just get out of here with an equipment citation. But then he asked me for my license and registration, and I took them out of my wallet and gave them to him. He told us to stay in the car and he would be right back.

"Not long after that another police car pulls up. I was watching through my rearview mirror. The second officer got out of the car, the two talked and then the first officer came forward and said that we needed to 'exit the vehicle.' I remember that because it sounded very formal.

"He said something about his training and experience, and he thought we had drugs in the car, that he smelled marijuana fumes, and that he was going to search the vehicle. We both got out and the other officer asked us to stand on either side of the truck by the rear taillights. Donnie was very nervous, and I could tell he knew that something was coming next. The next thing I see is the officer putting something in an evidence bag.

"Well, it turns out there was a bag of marijuana in the console. Both of us were handcuffed, read our rights, and taken down to the jail in Sanford. I had to call Aunt Gina to bail me out." J.T. stopped and stared out the window, remembering a moment in time that he would like to have forgotten.

"I could hardly make the call after what had happened at N.C. State. I had paid her back the thousand dollars she had paid for my bail on the mushroom charges with my first paycheck. I netted one thousand-fifty on the first check. I bought her flowers with the remaining fifty bucks."

J.T. stopped and put his head down in his hands, and then lifted it up again. "Donnie screwed me over. I know he put that bag in the console, but what was I going to say? It would just sound like I was trying to pin it on him, and that I knew there was pot in there. I knew enough from the last time that I just needed to keep my mouth shut."

"J.T., you did the right thing. It was found in your truck, but it was in an area that wasn't in your exclusive control or possession. What cuts against you is that the officer will testify that he smelled pot when he walked up. But let's not surrender just yet."

"Jack, I'm going to lose it all. My boss believes me, but he told me that corporate had made a big exception hiring me with my prior conviction. Another conviction and I won't stay on the job for another second. He's told them that it must have been Donnie's pot, but it won't matter. I'm out on my ass if I get convicted." J.T. hung his head down again.

"Look at me, J.T.!" Jack said with a vehemence that startled J.T. "You aren't going anywhere. We will beat this thing, and you will not lose your job. One day you just may manage that whole damn plant!" He stood up and then said casually, "That is, of course, if managing a bunch of bricks is what turns you on." He smiled and J.T. finally cracked a smile as well.

Jack looked at the paperwork that J.T. had placed in a file folder. "It says the assistant D.A. handling the case is a William Zeedow. I'm going to talk to him. If we can't work something out, and this case should go to trial, we'll look at hiring a lawyer."

A look of extreme disappointment appeared on J.T.'s face. "But Jack, I told you about all this because I was thinking you would be my lawyer. I don't trust these other lawyers. They don't care about whether I'm guilty or not. They just want you to plead guilty!"

Jack was torn. He was the team leader of a task force involved in a major counterterrorism investigation. How could he tell J.T. that he wouldn't be able to help when he was depending on him?

* * * *

WHEN Jack got back to Raleigh, he called Chuck Singer, the agent in charge of the Raleigh FBI office. He didn't want to do it, but he had no choice.

"Hello, Chuck, this is Jack Thomas from the Charlotte office."

"Hey, Jack. Heard you were operating a task force here. Guess you're calling for some assistance? Just name it, be glad to help."

"Thanks, Chuck. I had planned on calling you tomorrow

to arrange a meeting about the task force, but I'm calling now on something that has come up that's a little personal in nature."

Singer immediately responded. "Jack, whatever I can do to help."

"It's my brother, John, who lives down in Sanford. He goes by 'J.T.'. He's in some legal trouble. He gave someone from work a ride and the guy had marijuana on him. J.T. was pulled over by the police on a traffic stop and they both were arrested. I'd like to help him, but I don't know if I can with this investigation going on."

"So, you're looking for a defense counsel to handle his case," said Singer, more as a statement than a question.

"Yes, I thought that you might know somebody who has appeared for defendants in some of your drug interdiction cases. I may have to hire someone to represent J.T."

"Well, I can think of a couple of attorneys, but these are guys here in Raleigh that represent the big boys who have a lot of money. They won't be cheap."

"Not worried about the price. I'll take care of the fees. I want the best possible representation for my brother."

When J.T. was arrested on the mushroom charges, Jack had been an undergraduate at UNC. He went with J.T. and met his lawyer. Jack had to depend on a public defender who was a year out of law school to keep his brother out of jail. When he found out that J.T. had gotten probation on a plea deal he had been surprised, but then did some research and found out that the judge had graduated from West Point. He called Aunt Gina, who confessed that she had called his father against J.T.'s wishes. Jack assumed his father had somehow used "the power of the ring" to help J.T.

He had felt helpless then to help J.T. He knew that there might be other times where having a law degree would empower him to use his own judgment. Now he was an attorney and J.T. was depending on him. Jack wanted to be there for J.T., but he couldn't walk away from the mission that had been given to him. He had that feeling of helplessness again.

CHAPTER 45 – A Deal

Sanford, N.C.

District Attorney John Sinclair parked his car outside of the County Office building. He was now in his fourth term as the elected D.A. for his district, which included Sanford. He had no opposition for the last two elections, having forged a reputation as a straight-shooter, tough but fair.

The District Attorney's Office was on the second floor of the building. He had just sat down at his desk and was looking at a case file when there was a knock on the door frame. Sinclair had an open-door policy. His assistant D.A.'s could come to see him at any time and were free to call him by his first name. He only closed his door when he had someone in his office.

"Oh, good morning, Bill," Sinclair said. "C'mon in."

Bill Zeedow, carrying two case files, came in and sat down in one of the two chairs in front of Sinclair's desk. He reached forward and put one of the case files on Sinclair's desk. "John, here's the file on a case that will probably come on for hearing while I'm on my honeymoon."

Sinclair took a quick look at the file. State v. Thomas. Vehicle search. Marijuana, conspiracy to distribute and possession. "Hmmm, what's the problem? Nothing complex about this."

"It's not the Thomas case that's an issue. It's the co-defendant. We agreed to a severance as we expect each one to point the finger at the other and," he paused and held up the other case file, "the co-defendant, named Donnie King, is the subject of a federal task force investigation."

Sinclair leaned back in his chair. "My first reaction would be to just get a continuance and pick it back up when you get back. But I imagine the feds are wondering where the State charges will be going."

"That's the issue," said Zeedow. "King has a prior record, and the feds are worried that he may go to jail before he leads them to the major distributor in this part of the State. If we proceed on this case, it may well blow the federal case."

"This Thomas," said Sinclair, looking at the file, "has a prior felony conviction for dealing hallucinogenic mushrooms. Looks like a conspiracy to distribute for both. How about a plea deal where King testifies against Thomas in return for probation? Substantial assistance in prosecution. When Thomas's lawyer figures out that King has cut a deal, he'll probably want to plead out as well. He won't want to go to trial with a prior felony conviction and King testifying against him.

"Get with King's attorney first about a deal, then contact Thomas's attorney and see if he will plead out. Let his counsel know that we'll push for a lengthy sentence if he goes to trial. Second felony conviction for distribution."

"Okay, thanks John. Can't see why Thomas wouldn't take a deal. If he doesn't he'll be in Central Prison a long time." Zeedow turned and went out of the office.

CHAPTER 46 – Still Single

After Jack got back to the hotel from Sanford and spoke to Chuck Singer about a lawyer for J.T., he walked over to Mike's room. He found him watching a football game.

"Come on in," said Mike. "Grab a beer from the fridge. Your Panthers are playing."

"Thanks, Mike. Need to talk about something."

Mike saw the concerned look on Jack's face. He grabbed the remote and hit the mute button. "What's up?"

"My brother, J.T., lives in Sanford. I just came from there."

"Oh, yeah. Remember you telling me you had a brother in the area."

"He's in a little legal trouble and needs my help. I'd really like to help him myself, but with this investigation, I don't see how I'll have the time."

Mike knew what kind of stress Jack was under as the team leader. Having a family issue to deal with at the same time was the last thing he needed. "Jack, if this is a family emergency, I'll talk to headquarters about it and you can take leave to handle it."

"No, no, that's okay." Jack thought again about what oversight headquarters had on the case. "I'm going to retain counsel for him here in Raleigh. I just need to go back to Sanford in the morning to talk to someone. I want to talk to the prosecutor to get a feel for the case."

"Hey, no problem. I'll be at the hangar early and take care of the morning briefing." He knew that it must be something important—and serious—for Jack to miss giving the Monday morning briefing. "And I promise I'll be sober."

Jack smiled. "Yeah, I would hope. I've got some information to go over with you. I should be back no later than noon."

"Don't worry about it." He took a more serious tone. "Look, if there's anything I can do to help, just let me know."

"Thanks, Mike, I should be able to handle it okay." But in the back of Jack's mind, he knew that a conflict was brewing. He should be at the hangar the following morning, briefing the task force, but he couldn't just leave J.T. after he asked for his help. *Still,* thought Jack, *if headquarters wants to get in touch with me and I'm out of town on personal business . . .*

* * * *

THE following morning, Jack left early so that he would be at the D.A.'s office when it opened at 8:30 a.m. He was taking a chance that Zeedow would be in, but there was no way to call the office first.

He was wearing a tailored gray suit, white shirt, and red silk tie. He would tell the Assistant D.A. that he was representing J.T. so that he would be able to get as much information as possible. As defense counsel, he would have the right to the discovery of the evidence against J.T.

He parked at the county courthouse and went up to the

second floor. He pushed opened the door to the District Attorney's Office. The receptionist, a plump woman with a pleasant face and wearing heavy makeup, looked up from her computer screen. "Can I help you?"

"Good morning, ma'am. I'd like to speak to Mr. William Zeedow, the prosecutor in the State v. Thomas case. I don't have an appointment, but I thought I might just speak to him for a minute. I can wait."

"Mr. Zeedow is on leave. He's getting married. His cases are being handled by the other Assistant D.A.'s. Would you like to leave your card? I'll make sure the assistant who has the case gets it."

"Can you tell me who's handling the Thomas case?"

A voice from behind Jack said, "I am."

Jack knew who it was before he turned around. He thought about their last moments together. In his mind, he couldn't connect that the woman that he had loved was now prosecuting J.T.

When he did turn, he opened his mouth to say something, but before he could, Pam said, "Let's go somewhere where we can talk. Our conference room is being used, but we have additional office space on the sixth floor."

She had half-turned towards the door. He saw the silhouette that he had seen so many times before. In the morning, brushing her hair at the mirror in the bathroom as he stood in the doorway. In the kitchen, opening the cabinet to get a juice glass. Lying on the blanket at their favorite spot at the beach.

She walked into the hallway, and he followed her to the elevator, not saying a word. As they walked towards the elevator, the doors opened. Two deputy sheriffs came out.

They moved to the side to let Pam and Jack into the elevator.

"Good morning counselor," said one of the officers, as he held the door with his arm. Nice job on the Benson case."

"You made the case, Deputy Hill. I had the easy part."

She pressed number six and moved to the back of the elevator. Jack stood next to her and they looked straight ahead. Two more officers had followed Pam and Jack into the elevator.

Before the door could close, one of the deputies saw a large woman coming towards the elevator. She was holding the hands of two young children, a boy and a girl. Her eye makeup had smeared where she had wiped her eyes with the back of her hand. Her husband was going to be sentenced and taken to prison that morning.

As they entered, the deputies moved to the back, next to Pam. Two men in suits, each carrying wide briefcases, waited for the woman and her children to get on the elevator. The deputies and the large woman, still grasping a child in each hand moved back and to the side.

Jack moved to the back corner, and now Pam was so close he could feel the fabric from her suit coat on his own. He had bought the gray suit for the law school moot court competition, in no way imagining that he would be wearing it when he saw Pam for the first time in five years. He could smell her perfume. It was her favorite. He had given her a bottle on her birthday, just a month before he had enlisted.

The elevator stopped at the fourth floor. The doors opened and another man in a suit looked inside. No one was getting off. He shrugged and said, "I'll just wait for the next one." Jack and Pam turned their heads towards each other. Jack saw the trace of a smile on Pam's face and he couldn't help but smile back at her.

On the fifth floor, where the courtrooms were located, there was a mass exodus. The lawyers grabbed their briefcases and hurried off. The large woman, with children in tow, got off and began looking for the courtroom where her husband's case would be heard. The deputies also departed, off to testify in a convenience store robbery case.

Pam and Jack were alone on the elevator. Jack didn't remember how it had started, but they had always made it a point to kiss when they were alone in an elevator. *Well, guess those days are over*, thought Jack. He wondered about her and Andy Richardson. *Did they do the same . . .*

As the doors opened on the sixth floor, Jack put his hand on the side and Pam stepped out. He walked beside her down the hall to an open conference room.

She walked to the table and Jack pulled out her chair. She hesitated just an instant, thinking of all the times he had pulled out her chair and trying to remember the last time he did. She sat down. Jack went to the other side of the table and sat across from her.

"Jack, I am so sorry."

"About J.T.? He's not guilty of anything."

"No, Jack, about how I acted."

"If you mean my leaving, that wasn't about you. If anyone should be sorry, it's me."

"You did the right thing. This country was under attack. I couldn't understand how you could go. I only saw you making a choice. I could only think that if you loved me enough, you wouldn't go." Tears started to form in Pam's eyes.

"I can't tell you how many times I lay awake, wondering

how you were, whether you were okay."

"When I got back from my first tour, I did look you up. I saw that you were, uh, working at a law firm in Raleigh."

Pam tried to compose herself. "Jack, neither of us can change what happened."

* * * *

JACK remembered the conversation as if it had just happened. When he told Pam his plan to leave law school, she didn't understand. It had looked like a lifetime partnership was in the making and now he was off to join the Army for who knew how long—or if he would even return.

She made all the logical arguments to persuade Jack to stay in school. Jack listened, knowing that she would make a fine attorney. She was logical and persuasive.

"Well, J.T. has gotten back on his feet," said Jack. "He's been with the same company for almost two years. I can always come back and finish."

"Jack, this is insane! You're in your last year. Even if you feel you need to do this, why can't you just wait until after graduation?! You can be a JAG officer and not someone carrying a rifle!"

She fell into that same dark place that she went when she thought about her father. She remembered that night when he had left the house and never came home. Jack would go off to war and never come back. *He's made a choice and it's not me.*

* * * *

PAM looked down at the files in front of her on the table. "Were you trying to find out about J.T.'s case? It was one of Bill Zeedow's cases transferred to me because he's getting married."

"So, now you're the prosecutor."

"Actually, no. I saw that J.T. was the defendant. I told the D.A. that I had a, uh, personal connection and couldn't handle the case. He's going to handle it himself."

"The District Attorney is going to be the prosecutor?" Jack couldn't keep the surprise out of his voice. He knew that it was not a good turn of events for J.T. Pam nodded. "What did you tell him?"

"I told him that we had been very close." She stopped and thought about the words she would say next. "That we were going to get married." Jack said nothing for a few seconds, and the words just echoed in the room.

"Yeah, I guess we were . . . ." His voice had trailed off. He took out his agency business card and handed it to her. "I'm currently J.T.'s lawyer, but I'm looking for someone to represent him. I'm with the F.B.I. in the Charlotte office, so I may have a conflict."

Pam was visibly startled. Jack was not only out of the Army, he was a member of the N.C. Bar and living in North Carolina.

"Jack, I'm not surprised that you're a lawyer. I knew that you would finish one day. But I guess I thought you would be doing some type of corporate work. When I saw you here, I just assumed you were here for J.T. I knew you would do whatever you could to help him and that was why I went to the D.A. You would certainly be a mitigation witness—"

"Pam, I wouldn't be here in the first place if J.T. needed

mitigation testimony. In that case, J.T. would be guilty, and he never would have called me. I'm the last person in the world he would want to know about it." Jack paused. "Well, maybe not the last person."

Jack looked directly at Pam. "You can't believe that J.T. is guilty?"

"I don't know what to believe. I remember the conviction he had in college, but I knew what he had accomplished while we were in law school."

"If this case goes to trial, we'll show that it wasn't his marijuana and he didn't know it was in the truck."

She smiled and looked at Jack. He had seen that look before and it had always lifted his spirits. "Well, if anyone can convince a court on those facts, it would be you. Maybe you should find a way to represent him. I'm glad I won't be facing you in the courtroom." She paused, not sure what direction the conversation might take. She was curious and decided that the best way to find out was to let him know her situation.

She took out one of her business cards and handed it to Jack. He looked at it and Pam saw the surprise on his face. The print on the card read: Pamela Sorensen, Assistant District Attorney. "I decided that I really wanted to get into the courtroom. You know I had always wanted to be a prosecutor but the marriage, let's just say, got in the way. When I saw an opening at the D.A.'s office here in Sanford, I immediately applied."

She gathered from what Jack said about looking her up that he knew about her marriage. "The marriage didn't last long. After the divorce, I almost thought about going into family law. Those lawyers make a ton of money!"

Jack laughed. "Well, I haven't gone down the marriage

path yet, so I'll keep that in mind." Pam had the answer. *He's still single.*

* * * *

JACK drove back to the hangar with his mind in turmoil. He had always wondered what might happen if they ran into each other one day. He pictured it happening in a restaurant or a grocery store. Not across a conference table. And she's single again.

It was almost as if they had never been apart. His mind went back to the moment in the elevator. *To be that physically close to her after these years . . . and not take her in my arms.* He began to think about Kat and wondering whether he really was ready to move on.

CHAPTER 47 – The Evidence

Jack called Garrett Miller, an attorney that Chuck Singer recommended, and set up a meeting later that week at his downtown Raleigh office. At the meeting, he gave Miller a retainer to represent J.T.

* * * *

IT was late in the evening, a week after Jack had hired Miller, when Jack's phone rang.

"Hi J.T."

"Hey Jack. Just calling to let you know what the lawyer from Raleigh told me."

The previous week, J.T.'s reaction to Jack hiring an attorney had been more than disappointment. "So, you're going to desert me the same way Dad deserted Mom?"

"You know that's not the whole story! And I'm not deserting you. I'm on a task force and lives are at stake."

J.T. had been silent for a few seconds before responding, "Well, that doesn't change anything about Dad. And you can keep your money. I'll pay the lawyer myself!" J.T. had hung up before Jack could say anything else.

Now that a week had passed, he hoped that J.T. would be

a little more understanding. J.T. calling him was a good sign.

"Yes, what did the lawyer tell you?"

"Turns out this Donnie King is going to plead guilty and is going to testify against me! He's going to lie and say I was buying pot from him so that I could sell it!"

Jack had been worried that this might happen. King would agree to testify against J.T. to get a lesser sentence.

"What else did he say?"

"He said he thinks that Donnie King is getting special treatment. Probably because he is working for the feds on something else. Anyway, he thinks that we can use that somehow."

"You told the lawyer that he could talk to me about the case, right?"

"Of course, I did. Maybe you'll be able to help on the case?" There was a glimmer of hope in J.T.'s voice.

Jack thought about the best way he could say it. "J.T., I swear to you that if there is absolutely any way I can be there, I will."

* * * *

THE next day, Jack called Miller. "J.T. called me. He said King is going to plead."

"That's right. I talked to the D.A., Sinclair, yesterday. A little surprised that he's handling this. He told me that he has one assistant on leave and another that's conflicted out."

Jack thought about what Pam had told him. "Still seems a little strange to me. Why wouldn't he continue the case and let the assistant handle it when he got back from leave?"

Miller smiled. "If you ever want a trial lawyer job, call me.

Good instincts. Yes, it's a little strange and that got me thinking they need King's case resolved quickly, meaning they need him to testify in J.T.'s case as soon as possible. I have a few prior clients on the street who occasionally provide me with information—in return for some minor compensation."

"And some information got back to you."

"Uh-huh. Seems like this King is a low-level dealer in the cocaine marketplace. It may well be that he is doing something for the government on the side. We may have some leverage there on him taking the stand."

"Well, that's good news."

"True, but this case will be difficult on the facts, even if King doesn't testify." Jack waited for the bad news.

"There's a second entry on the evidence lab report. In addition to the line confirming that the leafy substance found in the console was, in fact, marijuana, the report included an entry that said that there were traces of Cannabis Sativa, with burnt edges, found in the ashtray."

Jack recalled what J.T. said King had done when the blue lights came on. He snuffed out the joint in the ashtray then swallowed it. Miller tried not to sound pessimistic, but he wasn't pulling any punches. Jack was wondering whether Miller thought that a plea deal might be in J.T.'s best interests.

"The ash tray evidence is strong circumstantial evidence tying the marijuana to J.T., if not proving his actual knowledge of its presence. The State can argue that J.T. tried the marijuana that King was selling, and it was J.T. that snuffed out the joint. With the smell of marijuana in the truck it's doubtful that a jury would believe that J.T. didn't know there was marijuana in the truck."

Jack was nodding his head as he listened. He knew things

didn't look good and he was glad that Miller was giving his honest opinion. He said, "When I found out how much pot it was, I assumed that King was a dealer. In the morning, King told J.T. that he needed to be dropped off somewhere after work."

"That's right. King said that working late had made him miss a meeting with someone—most likely the buyer. Even if a jury believes the pot was King's, the amount shows an intent to distribute. With the smell of marijuana in the truck, it looks like J.T. was the buyer—whether he intended to buy it to distribute it or not. As you know, possession is a lesser-included offense of the charge. There's enough to send J.T. to prison, even on a possession conviction."

"So, what are you recommending?" Jack was almost certain that Miller would recommend a guilty plea to possession with a reduced sentence. But he was wrong.

"Jack, you've told me about J.T. I believe he's innocent. I know what will happen if he pleads. He'll lose his job and everything that he's worked for.

"The evidence will show that it was King's boss that asked him to give King a ride to work, and J.T. didn't speak to King. Jones told J.T. where King lived. There's no showing that King even knew J.T. before this happened. Unlikely that someone would attempt to sell that much pot to a stranger."

Miller was rolling, and Jack could see why Chuck Singer had recommended him. "Sounds good."

"There's more. Why would King bring the pot to work and then sell it to J.T. after work? Why wouldn't J.T. have just gone into the trailer, tried it, and bought it right there that morning? Or gone into the trailer that night when he dropped King off? No need to bring that pot to work—unless he was going to sell it to someone else at work, or where he was being dropped off.

"If King testifies, we'll bring King's record into evidence, and ask on cross if he was promised anything for his testimony in this or any other cases. They can't bring up J.T.'s prior conviction during the trial, but I do need to ask you a question. If there is a conviction, you have some character witnesses lined up, right?"

"Yes," said Jack. "His ex-probation officer, Tom Berkshire, has already told me that he would testify on J.T.'s behalf. He would testify that there's no way J.T. would be using marijuana. They remained close even after J.T.'s probation ended years ago. He's been to J.T.'s apartment on many occasions—sometimes even dropping by without letting J.T. know he was coming. He's never seen any evidence that J.T. was using drugs."

"Well, we may need to find a way to get some type of good character evidence in front of the jury. I know you're in the middle of something. I want you to be there if possible. I'm going to prepare a motion to continue the case. I'm not sure that Sinclair will go along with it, but we'll find that out ahead of time."

"There is one other thing," said Jack. "Our father is an Army general. J.T. wouldn't want him there, but I can't help but think that if he was there, in uniform, it would have a positive effect on the jury."

"Absolutely. If you can find out his schedule, it might be a good basis for the motion for a continuance. I don't think the court would prevent someone in the military from attending his son's trial, if possible."

"Mr. Miller, I really appreciate your taking the case. I

believe that J.T. is in very good hands."

"It's Gary, and let me just ask you to do one thing for me?"

"Just name it."

"Don't let any of the defense bar know that I'm now working with an FBI agent!"

CHAPTER 48 – Attila and Mr. Clean

At the hangar, Jack stood by the printer and finished reviewing the classified document received earlier that morning. He had asked Mike, Eric, and Kat to stand by for a briefing. He brought the document to the table and sat down.

"We may have caught a break. The D.C. office had a subject under surveillance who had been identified by a confidential informant as someone to watch. He had been delivering some fiery language outside a mosque that seemed designed to incite others to violence. He was given the code name 'Attila.'

"Attila lives in the older part of Falls Church and works at a furniture store outside the Beltline. He's been seen going into the apartment of a man who lives in the District. We can't find any logical connection between the two. The interesting thing is that the person who is listed as living at the apartment is a custodian at the Sudan embassy." Jack looked down at a classified summary of the current assessment of terrorist activity in Sudan that he had asked Eric to print out prior to the meeting.

"Sudan has a long history as a state sponsor of terrorism.

They've been harboring terrorist groups, including al Qaeda. When Osama bin Laden left Saudi Arabia in 1991 and moved to Khartoum, he was protected by the Sudanese. While he was there, al Qaeda bombed two hotels in Yemen, targeting U.S. troops that were heading to Somalia. Sudan was placed on the State Sponsor of Terrorism list in 1993.

"In 1996, the agency linked two Sudanese diplomats to a terrorist cell that was planning to bomb the U.N. building. Two years later, it was believed that al Qaeda operatives based in Sudan were involved in the bombings of U.S. embassies in Kenya and Tanzania. After 1999, Sudan seemed to be willing to cooperate in the war against terrorism. It appeared to have been ridding itself of al Qaeda bases but it's still on the State Sponsor of Terrorism list.

"The CIA doesn't believe that Sudan is harboring al Qaeda terrorists at this point but isn't sure of what other assistance it may be providing al Qaeda. It's possible that there is some lone wolf operating without the knowledge of the Sudan government, who is using his diplomatic status to assist al Qaeda.

"This embassy employee, given the codename 'Mr. Clean,' was also put under surveillance. We were able to get a wiretap on Attila's phone based on his inciting others to violence and the unusual hours of visitation to Mr. Clean, who is an employee of a country on the State Sponsor of Terrorism list.

"We have photographs showing Mr. Clean removing a small carry bag from his trunk when he returned to his apartment after work last week. That same morning, prior to leaving for work, he got into his car with nothing in his hands. He didn't open the trunk."

"So," said Mike, "he picked up something at the embassy. Probably came in a diplomatic pouch."

Jack nodded. "Yes, and then last Sunday, Mr. Clean left his apartment with a black backpack and a walking stick. We didn't have a tail on him, so we don't know where he went or whether he might have met someone.

"He showed back up at the apartment a few hours later, with the same backpack." Jack paused, and then said "Or so we thought at the time. A call came in to Attila not long after Mr. Clean got back. Attila answered the phone, and someone speaking English with an accent said, 'It is done.' Only Mr. Clean had been seen coming in or out of his apartment."

"A backpack switch," said Kat.

"Apparently," Jack said. "After the call, a full tail was authorized on Mr. Clean and Attila. A little after ten p.m. that night, Mr. Clean put a large plastic garbage bag in his trunk.

"He drove to a supermarket on 17th Street and before going in, he pulled up to the side of the market, got the plastic bag out of the trunk, and threw it in the dumpster at the back of the store. He then pulled around front and went inside.

"Another agent was called in to tail Mr. Clean after he left the store. The original team went dumpster diving and got the bag back to our lab. Inside the bag was a bunch of garbage and a black backpack."

"And there was blank paper inside?" Mike said.

"No," said Jack, "but that is what would normally be expected. There were T-shirts inside. There was an exchange of bags. A transferor with a bag, briefcase, or other container, with something needed, maybe money, and a transferee with an identical container, with filler of some kind. The switch takes place and then the transferor gets rid of the container."

Kat interjected. "Why would someone put T-shirts in the backpack? Seems like some type of evidence could be gained from clothing."

Jack said, "Exactly. Our transferee must be a novice or thought T-shirts couldn't provide any evidence. Not well-trained in any event."

"Perhaps the T-shirts will yield some DNA evidence," said Eric.

"Nothing on the T-shirts," said Jack. "They had been recently laundered but there were some strands of hair that were found in one of the strap buckles on the backpack. Again, assuming this was a new purchase, not a borrowed bag that someone else had used, the hair would belong to whoever packed the T-shirts."

Eric said, "If nuclear DNA material is found, it would allow us to directly identify the subject if he, or she, has a DNA sample on file. It would also allow us to identify the subject's paternal line. If we can only identify mitochondrial DNA, we may still be able to identify the subject's siblings and maternally-related family with the same sequence."

Jack said, "It's the backpack itself that may yield something. It looks brand-new, and a brand carried by only one of the big box discount stores, the S-marts, or 'Smart' stores as they're called."

"Anything else found inside?" asked Mike.

"Nothing but the T-shirts. The T-shirts were plain white with no imprints, team names, or any other writing. We can make some assumptions. The person who owned these is probably short and slender. They were all adult, small size.

"These are white T-shirts worn under another shirt—not as an outer garment. They were not torn, no threads, no worn spots, and not stretched out. There were no sweat stains or stains of any kind. The person can afford to replace them on a regular basis—likely a professional person. The outer shirt is usually a shirt that has buttons and a collar. A white-collar type. Perhaps someone who wears a tie. We could be looking for anyone from a car salesman to an attorney."

"Both held by the public at the same level of esteem," said Mike.

"Now that hurt," said Kat, giving Mike a side-long glance.

"Student," said Eric. "Maybe a grad student."

"Based on?" said Jack.

"Two things," said Eric. "First, I would fit that profile. When I was getting my undergrad degree at UVA, I wore T-shirts with a button-down shirt. No tie though. I liked the pocket on the front of the shirt, and those classrooms are air-conditioned, so a T-shirt alone wouldn't work. Plus," he paused for a moment, then said "my brother wouldn't let me wear just a T-shirt anyway." Eric had a sheepish look on his face. "I was only fifteen at the time."

Eric continued, "Second, when I was getting my Ph.D., I did notice some of the students wore T-shirts and a button-down shirt. Most of these students were international, from places like India, Singapore, and Egypt. In many places, students are required to wear a uniform of sorts—including private schools. Students get used to the idea of not having to worry about what they are going to wear every day."

"Okay, let's get to work," said Jack. "Eric, we need records from all S-Mart stores in the Mid-Atlantic region for sales of this type of backpack for the last 3 months. Hopefully, the inventory identifier will include the color. If we can get the date and time of sales, we can review video from their store cameras to see who made the purchases. We may be able to follow them on the outdoor parking cameras and get visuals on their license plates. In the meantime, let's hope the lab comes up with something."

* * * *

TWO days later Jack called the team over to the conference table. "The lab was only able to get mitochondrial DNA from the hair sample, which gives us information on the mother's side. We were hoping to get nuclear DNA that has information on both parents. It may have helped on whether we were looking for an Arab-named suspect—paternity information that could be linked to an Arab region.

"The information that we did get is that the suspect's mother is Anglo-Saxon. Doesn't mean that his father wasn't from an Arab region, and it could narrow the search if we are looking for a home-grown terrorist. They generally let their views be known. When a person of Arab-descent speaks of jihad, people take notice. If a non-Arab starts talking like a jihadi, people will definitely remember it."

CHAPTER 49 – Rental Truck

Cal Hendricks dropped off Johnny Lee down the street from the truck rental center in Charlottesville. He was wearing a University of Virginia sweatshirt, jeans, and running shoes, much like hundreds of other students. He also wore a plain baseball cap pulled low. The rental center was busy. Cal had called in and reserved the truck a week before.

"Can I help you?" said the young man at the counter, a student who had just been fortunate enough to land a part-time job at the rental center.

"Yep. Name's Haislip. Reserved a truck. H-A-I-S-L-I-P."

"Sure, one sec." The young man had a white plastic name tag that said "Tim." He keyed the name on the beige keyboard. "Robert Alan Haislip. A fifteen-footer."

"That's the one."

"And this is a one-way," he said, still reading from the screen. "Two-week rental. Drop in Los Angeles."

"Yep." Johnny Lee's instructions were to only answer questions.

Tim hit some keys and a form printed out on the counter behind the front desk. He picked up a clipboard from beneath the counter, pressed down the silver clip on top, stuck the form under it and then let the clip down. "I'll need to see your driver's license and a credit card."

Johnny Lee pulled out Haislip's wallet. It now contained only the driver's license in a pocket with a plastic front and the credit card. He pulled out the credit card and laid it down on the counter, next to the open wallet. The plastic pane in front of the license had slightly yellowed, making it somewhat difficult to see the picture clearly. Tim's focus was not on the picture.

"The license has a different address than the reservation sheet." When Cal called in the reservation, he gave the address in Pacoima that was on the scrap of paper in Haislip's wallet.

Johnny Lee began to get nervous. He hadn't been briefed on what to do if there was a problem with the license. "Uh, I'm movin' out to my sister's place."

"Oh, that's okay. I just need to ask someone if I should be putting a different address from your license on the reservation. You aren't a resident there yet. I'll be right back. Okay to take the license out?"

Johnny Lee just nodded. Tim took the license out, stuck it under the clip, and took the clipboard to the back office.

Johnny Lee was now extremely nervous. Only knowing that his father expected him to stay there and get the truck kept him from running out of the center and leaving the card and license behind.

What if Haislip was reported missing? I know that no one has found the body. But if Haislip was reported missing, maybe the police were looking for him. Maybe everyone who rented a truck was put in a computer to see if they were wanted for any traffic tickets. Maybe they were checking the name for traffic tickets and the name came up. Maybe the police had been alerted that someone was using his license to rent a truck—

"Okay, no problem," Tim said as he came out. "I'm new and wasn't sure how to handle this. We make a copy of the license and just leave the new address as the forwarding address." He had made a photocopy of the license and swiped the credit card through the credit card reader. He handed the cards back to Johnny Lee, who stuffed them back into the wallet.

Tim slid the clipboard around to Johnny Lee and showed him where he needed to initial. Cal had told him to go ahead and check the insurance block. He signed Haislip's name on the bottom. He had been practicing for hours. Tim didn't even look at it. He grabbed a set of keys hanging off the board on the wall behind him.

"It's parked out back. Just match the bumper number to this one." He pointed to the number on Johnny Lee's copy of the contract and handed him the keys. Johnny mumbled "Thanks," turned and hurried for the door.

Tim said, "Hope you like it out there," to Johnny Lee's back as he was going out. Johnny Lee didn't turn around; he just raised one hand and went out the door.

CHAPTER 50 – Harley

Southwest Virginia.

This was their third trip into Virginia and the third different fertilizer supply company. Cal had already accumulated fifty bags by purchasing them at his usual supplier in Person County. He told the supplier that he was buying it off-season because he was taking his family overseas to live with his wife's family for a year. The fertilizer would be stored and used by the men he hired to work the farm the following Spring. When the supplier heard that Cal was going to live with his in-laws for a year, all he could say was "Good luck with that!"

The supplier hadn't been surprised when he was handed hundred-dollar bills for the fertilizer. Cal always paid in cash. In his mind, the Jews had woven themselves into the country's banking and monetary system. He was convinced that the interest charged by the credit card companies and the banks was part of the money that they contributed to Israel. Although he would not have paid any interest by paying off the card each month, he knew that a percentage of every sale went to those companies and their banks.

He believed that buying all of what they needed at one place might be suspicious and trigger a report to the FBI. He told Frankie and Johnny Lee that they needed to finish buying with the card that day. Someone would begin missing Robert Alan Haislip.

Frankie backed the truck up to the loading dock, then went around to the back of the truck. He pulled up on the door handle and the door slid up and into the truck. Johnny Lee came around the corner of the brick building with a yellow receipt. He showed it to the heavy-set man who came out of the shadows of the warehouse.

The man had a crew cut and wore jeans and cowboy boots. His khaki shirt bulged out over his belt. The name "Harley" was stitched in red thread inside a white oval piece of cloth over his breast pocket.

Harley looked at the receipt that Johnny Lee showed him and motioned for him to come through the large open door into the warehouse. The warehouse was large, almost half the size of a football field, with a concrete floor. Light filtered through the dirty glass windows that ran across the top of the back wall. Dust was everywhere. It coated the floors, the metal shelves that lined the walls, and lay thick on the plastic wrapped around the stacks of bags on pallets lined up on the warehouse floor.

"Okay, here's your load." He pointed to two stacks of bagged fertilizer. "I can get these over to the edge of the dock, but you'll have to load them into the truck." By then, Frankie had joined them. He took one look at Frankie and said, "Shouldn't be a problem. They're 'round fifty pounds per bag."

Harley hadn't seen these boys before, but he knew the farms were hiring all kinds these days. *Can't understand why anyone would want to wear those hippie beards and long hair,* thought Harley.

Harley got up on a forklift, speared one of the pallets, lifted it a foot off the floor, and took it over to the edge of the loading dock. He let it down onto the dock floor near the back of the truck, backed up the forklift, then went back for the other pallet. Frankie and Johnny Lee removed the plastic wrap covering the stacked bags and began loading the ammonium nitrate into the truck.

CHAPTER 51 – Secret Entry

Obtaining the explosives to detonate the bomb had taken a little more planning and preparation. This was a military-style operation, and Cal Hendricks took some satisfaction in planning it. His first step was to don camouflage and do a night reconnaissance of the Forest Service storage area.

The storage building's back wall faced the steep incline of a hill. The building was heavily secured, but there were no round-the-clock guards. The fence with razor wire would not be a problem. Neither would the heavy padlocks on the double metal steel door, the video camera, or the alarm connected to the door.

A crushed gravel drive ran through the woods, by a Forest Ranger cabin, and then for another quarter-mile until it reached the fence gate in front of the storage area. There would be no way to drive by the cabin without being observed, and the drive was the only way to approach the storage area by vehicle. He went back to the farm and spent the next week planning.

At the new moon, the three men drove into the woods around midnight. The closest road was approximately two miles away from the storage area. They wore camouflage clothing and face paint. Their tools were in a single backpack.

The two other backpacks they brought were empty.

Using his compass, contour map and small flashlight with a red-light filter, Cal led his sons through the woods to the crest of the hill on the backside of the storage area. Frankie stayed at the crest with night vision infrared binoculars. He had line of sight on the Forest Ranger cabin. The light on the porch lit up his view of the cabin like a spotlight. He would be able to see any movement from the cabin and notify Cal by radio.

Cal and Johnny Lee tied on climbing harnesses, put on full-finger climbing gloves, then fast-roped down the side of the hill. When they reached the bottom, they were at the fence at the back of the storage area. Cal used a bolt cutter to cut the chain-link, then peeled it back far enough so that he and Johnny Lee could squeeze through. The storage building was made of concrete block, which is a misnomer since the blocks are not solid concrete. The typical block used for walls has two hollow chambers.

Cal took out a small sledge hammer and a cold chisel from the backpack and went to work at the bottom of the back wall. The hillside was at his back, and the Forest Ranger cabin was a quarter of a mile away on the other side of the storage building. The thud of the hammer on the thick plastic top of the chisel was barely audible on the other side of the storage building.

In less than ten minutes Cal created a hole large enough to crawl through. He was confident that the storage building did not have motion detectors inside because there were no windows and the only door was heavily secured. The door might have a motion-detector mounted nearby, but that wouldn't be a problem since they wouldn't be going near the front of the building.

The storage lockers inside were as he expected. The government had a huge contract with a specific lock manufacturer. The same locks hung on every storage cage, in every government supply room.

Cal found what he was looking for and cut the padlock. He filled both backpacks and passed them out to Johnny Lee. He closed the locker, put the matching government padlock he had brought with him on the hasp, and locked it.

He found a cardboard box with camping supplies, pushed it over to his entry hole, and drew the knife from the scabbard strapped to his calf. After cutting a small hole in the bottom of one side of the box, he went out through the block wall feet first. Cal then reached back through it, grasping the box using the hole that he had cut into it. He pulled the box up against the inside of the wall, completely covering the entry hole.

At the top of the hill, Frankie attached a pulley to the base of a tree. He threaded his end of Johnny Lee's rope through it and pulled as Johnny Lee climbed to the top. He repeated the process for Cal. They moved quickly back through the woods, put their packs in the back of the truck, and headed back to Person County.

It would be three weeks before a forest ranger tried to open the explosives cabinet to conduct a monthly inventory. After trying every key on his ring, he cut the padlock off with a bolt cutter. He swung open the door and saw nothing but empty shelves where the water-gel explosives had been stored.

CHAPTER 52 – A Birthday Missed

The FBI might never have gotten a lead on the Hendricks if not for a birthday. Sheila Haislip's birthday was two weeks after her brother got into the Hendricks' truck.

Haislip hadn't seen his sister in several years, but never missed sending her a card and calling on her birthday. She did the same on his birthday. He would call her and sing "Happy Birthday" to her on the phone. But not this year. And that worried her.

She called him and got his voice mail message. She first was calm and left a message to please call her. But when the day wore on and she still hadn't heard from him, the messages became more frantic. She thought that maybe he got tied up on something and had forgotten her birthday.

It was a Sunday and the restaurant where he worked wasn't open. She would have to wait until early morning to call him. He had a key because he was the breakfast cook and had to be in the kitchen at five a.m., getting things ready for the six o'clock opening.

Sheila couldn't sleep. She watched the clock until it was 2 a.m. She dialed the restaurant. It was 5:00 a.m. on the East Coast and Bobby would be making biscuits for the truck drivers who headed out early on the road. The phone rang four times, five times, six times. No answer. She waited five minutes and tried again. No answer. She kept dialing.

Finally, at 2:30 a.m. her time, the phone was picked up and a female voice, sounding elderly and out of breath, said, "Sorry, been havin' trouble with my car batt'ry—"

"Hello? Who is this?"

"Oh, sorry, thinkin' you were Mister Hardison. Name's Loretta. He been checkin' up on me." Bert Hardison was Haislip's landlord and the restaurant's owner. Sheila's first thought was that Bobby had been fired.

"Do you know Bobby Haislip?"

"He usta' work here. He be gone now."

"This is his sister. I'm trying to get in touch with him."

"Alls I know is what Mister Hardison told me. He lef' 'bout two weeks back. Goin' to Cal-I-fornya. Mister Hardison jus' shook his head. Said the boy was goin' to thumb it out there. His car was broke down."

"He told you that Bobby was going to hitchhike to California?"

"Yup. Sorry, ma'am, I needs to get these biscuts goin'. "

"Oh, okay, sorry. Thanks." She set down the phone, fearing the worst. *Gone two weeks. He should have been here by now. Probably going to surprise me and sing Happy Birthday in person this year. If he was safe and had stopped somewhere along the way, he would have made it a point to call yesterday.* She pictured him hit by a car, maybe in a hospital somewhere. Tears began rolling down her cheeks. She picked up the phone and called the California Highway Patrol.

The dispatcher at the CHP, Delores Hunnicut, tried to calm Sheila. She told her that people on the road sometimes stop to work and pick up a little money before they head back on the road.

"Yes, he was coming to California and wouldn't miss your birthday, but people also lose track of the dates when traveling."

"Yes, I can understand that your brother would never forget to call you on your birthday."

"Yes, ma'am, we'll file a missing person report. It's been more than seventy-two hours since anyone has seen or had contact with your brother."

As the dispatcher disconnected the call, she wondered what she would do if her daughter in Missoula hadn't called her on her birthday and no one had seen her for two weeks. When Hunnicut got off her graveyard shift at seven a.m., she went over to one of the troopers in the investigations division. "Hey Marvin, put your coffee cup down for a second. I need your help on something."

Marvin put down his cup. "Delores, I'm really busy this morning."

"Yeah, that's why you're reading a gun & ammo magazine and drinking a cup of coffee. I know you're off-shift and don't leave until eight o'clock to meet your buddies from the sheriff's office for breakfast."

"Okay, busted. What's up?"

Delores explained the situation. Marvin contacted the Virginia State Police and requested a run on the DMV computer database listing inquiries on Robert Alan Haislip's driver's license number. In less than a minute, the Virginia trooper came back on the line and said they had a hit. Ten days ago, Haislip had rented a truck in Charlottesville. The inquiry on his record came in from the dealer.

Marvin and Delores looked at each other with the same

expression. Not likely that a guy hitchhiking to California from Culpeper would end up days later in Charlottesville, only an hour away, and rent a truck big enough to move a two-bedroom apartment.

Marvin sent the missing person report to the Virginia State Police. The VSP ran the standard protocol on a missing person case. Credit card purchases by Haislip were checked from the date he left the boarding house, as provided by his employer, Bert Hardison.

The VSP found a large payment, as well as a rental truck and three purchases on the credit card. All the purchases were made at large agricultural supply stores for nitrogen fertilizer, specifically, ammonium nitrate. A rental truck. Large amounts of ammonium nitrate. The State Police contacted the FBI.

CHAPTER 53 – A Deadly Formula

Jack was running late. He had gone to an early appointment with Garrett Miller that morning. The previous night, he had been doing research on J.T.'s case and saw something in the North Carolina statutes that he wanted to discuss with Miller. He had called Mike and asked him to cover for him.

When Jack got in, the team was sitting around the conference table in the hangar. Mike had a sheet of paper in his hand. It looked like he was about to brief the others. He handed him the message from the D.C. office and waited while Jack read it.

Mike said, "I called over to the Raleigh office. Kat was over there to get some information. I told her you'd probably want to do a briefing. I contacted the State Bureau of Investigation here and asked them to send a liaison. They coordinate directly with the Virginia State Police. I also called in the State Highway Patrol and the other law enforcement reps."

"Thanks, Mike. I really appreciate your stepping in for me this morning. I'll explain later what's going on with my brother." Jack couldn't help thinking, *he did everything that I should have been doing.*

"Don't worry about it. We're a team."

Jack reviewed the VSP reports and contacted the FBI field office in Richmond. The Richmond office was now involved with the investigation and a liaison was assigned to the task force. Jack told the Special Agent in Charge that members of the task force would be traveling to Virginia, and he would keep their office informed.

Eric briefed him on all the information he had obtained that morning. After he spoke with Eric, Jack called the Charlotte office and spoke to Childs.

* * * *

ONCE all the task force members arrived, Jack began the briefing. "The Virginia State Police received a missing person report from the California Highway Patrol this morning. The name of the missing person is Robert Alan Haislip. In doing the investigation, the VSP discovered that a Mr. Robert Alan Haislip—or someone using his identity—rented a large truck in Charlottesville capable of carrying over a six-thousand-pound load. We were notified because in addition to renting the truck, Mr. Haislip purchased enough ammonium nitrate to take down a multi-story building.

"Haislip's sister reported him as missing. He left Culpeper, Virginia, two weeks ago. His sister says that he has never missed calling her on her birthday. Except yesterday. There has been no activity on Haislip's cell phone since he left Culpeper, and the NSA has been unable to locate the phone. We don't know where Haislip is, but we do have evidence of identity theft. Eric, what did you find?"

Eric had the print-out showing all the credits and debits

on Haislip's account. "Haislip's account was paid in full by a cashier's check, not long after he left his job. The truck rental place entry on the account was a pending charge in case the truck wasn't returned on time. There's no way to leave a cash deposit, so whoever rented the truck had to use a credit card."

"Any evidence that this Haislip is part of an anti-government group?" asked Kat.

Jack said, "Agents have spoken with Haislip's landlord." He looked down at a report. "A Mr. Bert Hardison, who was also his boss at the restaurant where he worked. He said that Haislip was a big supporter of the military. Hardison said that if he was involved with any gang members or other white-supremacy groups, he would have known it."

Eric said, "This Robert Haislip doesn't have any of the markers for the type of profile we would expect. We have a 28-year-old cook with limited education, no known affiliation with any gangs, and no history of travel out of the country who rents a truck in his own name, and then uses his own credit card to buy enough ammonium nitrate to fertilize an extremely large area of pasture land—or build a very large bomb.

"The normal profiles show that these hate groups generally use force to assemble materials, either by break-ins or other types of robberies. The evidence presents the profile of an anti-government or other hate group assembling materials for a bomb but showing a much greater degree of sophistication than in previous cases, so this is where the profile begins to differ from the run-of-the-mill white supremacy hate group profile."

Kat said, "Stealing a truck, which certainly doesn't require cash, leads to quicker law enforcement involvement and investigation. If time is needed, then stealing a vehicle shortens the timeline of the operation. Whoever is behind this needs time, without arousing suspicion, to get what they need."

"We can't assume anything," said Jack. "Someone could be driving a bomb up to a target as we speak, but the last purchase of ammonium nitrate was just yesterday morning. It will take some time to put the materials together. We do have some information on the individuals involved. We know that there were two men that loaded the ammonium nitrate into the truck."

Mike said, "There's a specific formula for the mixture of ammonium nitrate, nitromethane, and diesel fuel. Diesel fuel is easy to get. I've been scanning for reports on theft of explosives and fusing. Nothing yet, but that doesn't mean it hasn't already been obtained in a way that wouldn't show up. They'll need some type of detonating explosive. Could have stolen some water-gel explosives from a road construction company and it hasn't been detected yet."

Eric nodded his head up and down as Mike was explaining the formula. "Yes, yes. Based on the purchase of the ammonium nitrate, an immediate inquiry was transmitted to all bulk distributors of nitromethane, in the southwest Virginia, northwest North Carolina area. Nitromethane is primarily used as a fuel in drag racing. There were several sales, but there were large purchases at two different distributors.

"These purchases were also unusual," said Eric. "Generally, bulk purchasers have an account and are billed for their purchases. Purchases by a non-account holder in these amounts at two different distributors is entirely consistent with the developing profile of our terrorists."

Jack said, "Special Agents Childs and Adeniyi have been detailed to the task force. They're already on their way to talk to the distributors. We can't assume that the nitromethane purchases are connected to this investigation. But if we can confirm that the rental truck was used, or the same two men that bought the ammonium nitrate bought the nitromethane, then we have our connection.

"We have some partial descriptions. The person renting the truck was a white male with a beard and long hair, which is consistent with the photo on Haislip's license. He wore dark sunglasses, so we have a sketch that is basically Haislip with dark sunglasses on. The clerk said that he did seem a little nervous and didn't say much. We'll go there tomorrow and interview him in person.

"They will probably hide the truck until they are ready to use it. Haislip has disappeared and they know that sooner or later his disappearance will be discovered. They won't be driving a truck with the license plate on the one rented using Haislip's credit card. If a plate from another truck is put on the rental, and it will look like a thousand other rental trucks on the road."

*   *   *   *

AFTER the briefing, Jack told Kat that he was heading up to Virginia the following morning and she was welcome to join him. He had struggled over asking her. *Does she really need to go?*

"We'll go to the fertilizer warehouses with charges that showed up on Haislip's account, then we'll head to Charlottesville and talk to the clerk at the truck rental place."

"Sure," said Kat. "I'd like to help in any way that I can." She had wondered where Jack had been that morning but assumed that he would tell her if he wanted her to know. *This will give us a chance to talk . . .*

"I'm pretty certain they rented the truck in Charlottesville, a short distance from Culpeper, to not raise suspicion," said Jack. "Makes sense to do it in a large city not too far from where he lives."

"I think you're right," said Kat. "I checked this morning when the report came in. There's only one truck rental place in Culpeper and the employees might know Haislip. He could have gone to the same high school."

Jack was impressed. Kat was a definite asset to the investigation; it settled any question in his mind. "There's a meeting in two days at FBI headquarters. We'll head there after the interviews tomorrow, so bring a suitcase. The lab folks will be giving us everything they've been able to put together.

"Mike and Eric will be staying here, and we'll conference them in. Childs and Adeniyi will be meeting us up there. And before I forget—don't be surprised by anything Agent Childs may say. He is a great agent but has what I would call an unusual sense of humor."

CHAPTER 54 – The Shop

Cal decided not to use the rental truck for the mission. They could change its appearance, but the truck's size and type would create difficulties in accessing a secure area. He told Mahmoud that he would look for the vehicle after he had found a place to store it.

Mahmoud asked him how much it would cost. "I thought we were going to just use the rental truck and told my contact that the money we received would be sufficient."

Cal said, "It was smart to use a rental truck tied to someone else to pick up materials." Now, we need to make sure that we get in where we need to go without being questioned. Don't worry about the money."

Before Cal left, Banafsha trimmed his hair and beard and darkened both with hair dye. He bought four burner phones. In an emergency he would use a phone and immediately ditch it.

He left early in the morning in the blue pickup truck, drove east on I-85, exited onto I-95 heading north, and arrived early in the afternoon. All the listings were within one mile of the target. After seeing the first two locations he found exactly what he was looking for in an industrial park just off the interstate. He drove to the leasing agent's office.

The building had housed an auto interior and trim shop. There was a large roll-up door at the back to bring vehicles, including big trucks, into the work area. The floor was concrete slab and there was space to work on six vehicles. Work benches lined the twelve-foot high, concrete block side walls. A large ventilation fan was built high up into the back wall. The fan had been installed to help clear the glue fumes and other vapors from the materials used to replace head liners, upholstery, and other trim.

When Cal arrived at the leasing office, he wore a suit, hat and glasses. He told the leasing agent that his company did vehicle restorations, including touch-up body and paint work. It would take two months to retrofit the interior, so the front office of the shop would be closed until then.

He gave the leasing agent a cashier's check for a month's rent and the deposit, telling him that they wanted to move in immediately. He explained that he had arranged, on a C.O.D. basis, for an air compressor and six infrared paint curing lamps to be delivered to the shop the next day. When asked for a contact phone number, he gave him the number of one of the burner phones.

Cal drove to the shop and parked in front. He took a new door lockset out of his truck and replaced the door knob on the front door that opened to the small office area. He then went to the back of the building, removed the padlock on the roll-up door, and replaced it with the one that he had brought.

He pulled out the burner phone with the number he had given to the leasing agent. He created a voicemail message for the caller to leave their name and number and he would call them back. He then destroyed the phone so that it couldn't be traced.

Back at the truck he took five one-hundred dollar bills out of the lockbox welded under the backseat and drove back to I-95 for his next appointment. The location was only a few minutes away. He exited the interstate, drove past several streets and turned into the graveled parking area.

It was a short walk and he found the man, who was wearing a blue windbreaker, waiting on a nearby bench. After a quick inspection, Cal handed him the cash, shook hands and went back to his truck. *Always have an exit plan,* thought Cal.

CHAPTER 55 – Anonymous

Cal returned from his trip up north. He went into Durham, purchased the Sunday editions of both the Raleigh and Charlotte newspapers, and began searching for a vehicle to use in place of the rental truck. He found what he was looking for in a listing from a small dealership near Boone and planned a trip to the bank the next day.

The next morning, a storm suddenly blew in from the west, bringing torrential rain. Lightning raced across the sky and the rolling thunder sounded to Cal like a distant artillery barrage. He put on a hooded raincoat, grabbed a small duffel bag, and went out to his truck.

He took his time as he drove the twenty miles to reach the small bank branch on the north side of Durham. The blue lights of a deputy sheriff's car suddenly appeared in his rear-view mirror and he took his foot off the accelerator. The deputy's car swerved around him and quickly sped away.

As Cal crested a hill, he saw ahead through the rain that a vehicle had left the road and plunged into a swollen creek. The front end was submerged, and the rear of the vehicle jutted up at an angle back toward the road. Cal wondered whether the driver had failed to plan for the weather and was rushing to get to work on time.

At the bank, Cal signed the register and a banker escorted him into the vault. Once he had the safety deposit box in a private room, he opened the lid. Bundles of one-hundred-dollar bills, ten-thousand dollars in each bundle, were lined up in stacks inside. He removed three bundles, unzipped the small duffel bag, and put them inside. He closed the box lid, left the room, and returned the box to its place in the vault.

When he left the bank, he saw that the sky had resumed its famous shade of "Carolina blue," the storm having moved on as quickly as it had arrived. In the street, streams of water gushed into the gutter drains, trapping paper and debris on top of the grill. The damp concrete, absorbing the sun's intense rays, gave off its familiar smell. *All things change in good time,* thought Cal.

* * * *

IT was dark at 6:15 p.m. in the small town in the northwest North Carolina mountains. The leaves were past peak, and it was no longer high season. The crowds of tourists that had flocked to the town to enjoy the fall colors had quickly thinned out as the trees shed their leaves. The streets were now as bare as the poplar trees on the sides of the mountains surrounding the town.

Down past the last of the stores on main street, where the road name changed back to a state road number, Bill Hammonds headed out the front door of the small log building he used for his office. It was set off the road, next to a large patch of crush and run gravel. The used car lot had provided enough income to pay off his two-bedroom house up on the hill behind the lot and had sent his daughter to Appalachian State University.

Hammonds was getting close to sixty-five years old, and his gout was acting up. He had begun wondering how long he would be able to get up the hill to the house. Maybe he should just sell the lot and start drawing Social Security. He could just sit at the small general store down the road in the mornings with his buddies. Drinking coffee and telling lies.

Hammonds had just turned around from locking the front door when a tall man came out of the darkness. He was startled at first, but then looked past the man and saw a fully restored '66 Mustang GT on the side of the road. There were two men sitting in the car. Puffs of white smoke were coming from the dual exhausts, the heated gases contacting the cool mountain air.

Hammonds said, "Nice looking Mustang. Might be interested in buying it. Don't see many like that 'round here." He saw that the man was wearing work jeans, boots, and a cap with a tractor company logo. He had a beard and it looked like his hair was in a ponytail.

The man said, "Thanks, but I'm not selling."

Hammonds got nervous again. He had been robbed two years before by some ex-cons from Tennessee. They had stuck a gun in his face and took what cash he had. He almost sold the lot right after that, but he needed income then because he was helping his daughter after her divorce.

"I'd like to buy that Ford you've got over there." He had pointed to a Ford E450 that was on the front corner of the lot. "I don't like to dicker over price. I'll give you what you're asking."

Hammonds was wondering whether it was a trick. He got the Ford for a steal and had put a high price on it. He had placed ads in all the used car and truck magazines, and even in the big city newspapers. He never expected to get the asking price. He had put in the ad that it was low mileage and in excellent condition—then put the price almost three thousand dollars over book value. Most dealers expect lower offers, and most buyers expect dealers to ask more than they will take.

Maybe they were there to steal it. *Nope, no one would steal a vehicle like that,* he thought—*but no one that looked like this old farmer would likely buy it either.*

The tall man came up on the porch. "Sorry to be getting here so late, but we had to travel a' ways." Cal had easily moved back into using the accent he had grown up with. Hammonds stuck out his hand and said, "William Hammonds. But call me Bill."

The man shook his hand and said, "Nice meeting you, Bill. Tell you why I'm here after that Ford." As Hammonds let go of his hand he realized that he still didn't know the man's name.

"My family made a lot of money in the land and timber business. My daddy always tried to do right by people and believed in giving to charity. Before he left this earth, he told me that he expected me to do the same. I've been lucky enough to continue the family business and we've done pretty good over the years."

Hammonds could tell that this farmer wasn't telling him the whole story. He knew that some of these farmers were multi-millionaires, but you'd never know it by looking at them. They lived in the modest homes they grew up in. Hammonds knew that the Mustang out by the road cost a pretty penny. It would be the kind of thing that one of these good ol' boy millionaires would buy.

The man pulled a wallet out of the side pocket of his overalls. It had a metal ring sewn into one corner and was attached by a chain to one of his belt loops. He opened it up and pulled out a folded check. He handed it to Hammonds.

Hammonds opened it and tried to make sure his face didn't reflect his excitement. It was just like the man had said. A cashier's check for the full amount that he had advertised, made out to the dealership.

He took a close look—as Cal had expected and the reason they had come up earlier in the day. He knew that the check would need to be drawn from a local bank. A car dealer in a small town would be very familiar with the local bank.

Hammonds was satisfied that it was the real thing. The check was drawn on their local bank and even had Eileen Carswell's signature on it. Eileen was his wife's cousin and had been at the bank for thirty years. He wondered what she must have been thinking when this old farmer handed her that much cash. He'd have to call her in the morning. With what he had paid at auction, he would make enough money to buy that new truck he had seen at the Chevrolet dealership in Boone. He knew the dealership owner as he bought some of their beat-up trade-ins to resell on his lot. He'd get it at dealer cost.

He wanted this stranger to know he would be fair. He might be a repeat customer. "Well this is mighty generous, as you know I'd a' probably taken a little less."

"I'm buying it to give to a good cause. They need a vehicle like this in a small town near where we're from. Just thought I'd give it to 'em."

"That's a nice thing to do," said Hammonds. "Guess you can at least get a nice tax deduction."

"Well, that's another thing. Just sign over the title and leave the buyer name blank. I don't want any credit. Just going to leave it with the title and a note."

Hammonds had heard of people giving things without leaving their name. Somebody had even paid off everyone's Christmas layaway down at the new S-Mart store on the highway. But that was only a little over five thousand dollars.

"Well, let's go in and I'll get the title and keys. It's ready to go."

After the man had left in the Ford E450, with the Mustang following, Hammonds called his wife. "Be right up the hill, honey. Sorry I'm late, but you're not going to believe this. You know that Ford E450 that I put out all those ads on. I just sold it—at full asking price!"

* * * *

THE next day Hammonds called his cousin Eileen at the bank. He asked her what she thought when that old man gave her that much cash. She said it wasn't an old man that had given her the cash. It was a young guy who had handed her his driver's license. "His name was Robert Haislip."

"Musta' been his son that was in there. Don't let on that the man bought that ambulance from me. He wants to give it away anon'mus.

CHAPTER 56 – A Makeover

Frankie opened the barn door, and Mahmoud, Cal, and Johnny Lee went in. Frankie followed and closed the door behind him.

Once inside, Cal told Mahmoud about his trip up north and his purchase of the ambulance. After giving Hammonds the check, Cal had driven the ambulance from the lot and pulled off onto a side road near the car lot. Frankie and Johnny Lee had followed in the Mustang. They switched vehicles and Frankie and Johnny Lee drove the ambulance north through the night.

They arrived at the shop before dawn, locked the ambulance inside, and then took a fifteen-minute cab ride to the train station. They purchased their tickets with cash and had arrived in Durham later that same afternoon.

*   *   *   *

WHEN Frankie and Johnny Lee were in their teens, Cal bought a beaten-up '66 Ford Mustang GT convertible and had it towed to the farm. Since Muslim teens don't date, whenever the boys weren't doing farm work, they were working on the car.

Johnny Lee was an excellent mechanic and maintained all the farm equipment. While he rebuilt the Mustang's engine, Frankie did the body and paint work. Frankie's paint finishes were first class and rivaled the work done at the custom paint shops in Durham.

When Mahmoud came out to the farm and entered the barn he saw that plastic sheeting had been hung from the rafters. Frankie went over and lifted one corner of the plastic so that Mahmoud could see his latest paint job.

The green rental truck from Charlottesville was now a white box van with a hydraulic lift on the back bumper. The lift could be lowered to the ground, heavy items placed on it, and then lifted to the level of the truck bed for loading directly into the truck. Johnny Lee had welded racks to hold several barrels inside the truck.

Mahmoud walked around to the side of the truck. On the cab door, in script, was the name of a heating and air conditioning company. "Has the same colors and lettering as the company uses," said Frankie.

Cal said, "We'll pull a plate off a vehicle in long-term parking at the airport."

Frankie and Johnny Lee had already brought over several barrels and the scales. The barrels with diesel fuel were ready. They began measuring and mixing the ammonium nitrate with the nitromethane and then loaded the barrels into the truck.

CHAPTER 57 – Road Trip

Jack drove to the hangar and parked his car next to the Mercedes. Kat had volunteered to drive to the interviews in Virginia so that Jack could review notes and make calls.

He took out his overnight bag and waited as Kat walked out towards the car. She opened the trunk and Jack put his overnight bag next to her suitcase. At the top of the trunk were two HK 416 assault rifles in a rack bolted to the floor. "I guess those are some of the heightened security measures the prior owner added," said Jack.

Kat just smiled. "I had those installed."

"Nice choice."

When he closed the trunk, Jack thought, *guess this is what it would look like if we were going somewhere for the weekend.* He turned around and Kat was smiling, as if she was thinking the same thing.

As she started the car, Jack said, "There's no ejection seat on this thing, is there?"

Kat laughed. "I'll make sure the sunroof is open."

They headed out to the interstate and took the exit for the state road heading north to Charlottesville. "We'll stop first at the supplier that showed up yesterday on the account," Jack said. "There may be a day or even two before a charge appears on an account, so they may have bought the fertilizer a few days ago. We got lucky that they acted so quickly in contacting the Virginia State Patrol.

"Unfortunately, the chances of finding Haislip alive are slim. In a theft case, the victim would have reported it right away, so this identity theft looks like an armed robbery and homicide. It's not likely they're holding him hostage."

Haislip's sister worrying about her brother reminded Jack of J.T. and his situation. "I can definitely understand his sister's concern. I have a brother here in North Carolina who's in some legal trouble."

So, Kat thought, *that must be the reason he wasn't here for the morning briefing.* "Something you're helping him with?" Jack hesitated. He told himself that she was there as the HS liaison. He felt that he could confide in her. He wanted to . . .

"Well, I don't really have the time. I'm having to hire someone to help him."

Kat sensed something in his voice. She could imagine what it might be like to have a family member that needed your help—and having to say you didn't have the time. "I'm sorry," said Kat, "it's a personal matter—"

"No, that's okay. My brother, J.T., was arrested. He was giving a ride to a guy that works where he works. The police stopped him for an equipment problem and did a search."

Kat glanced over at Jack, and then back to the roadway. "How did they have probable cause to search? Did your brother just consent?"

Jack let out a long breath. "Unfortunately, J.T.'s passenger lit a joint before J.T. got pulled over. J.T. had yelled at him to put it out but that's when the blue lights came on. The officer smelled the odor and searched the truck. Turns out the guy had a bag of pot in his backpack and stuck it in the console before the search."

"Whoa, that is really an unfortunate set of circumstances. So, what are you going to do?"

"I've hired an attorney to represent him, but I'm hoping I can help him after we've made some arrests in this case—if his case hasn't been heard. He's always depended on me in the past and I feel like I'm letting him down."

Kat sensed there was something more but, again, decided that Jack would tell her if he wanted to. "Is there anything I can do to help? You know, I've already confessed that I used to be a criminal lawyer," she said with a smile.

Jack didn't miss the genuine concern in her voice. Her offer of support was something he hadn't heard from a woman since he and Pam had parted.

"Thanks, Kat. I hope you'll leave the offer open. I just may need some help down the line."

"Just let me know."

Jack decided to change the subject. "So, what about you? Any brothers or sisters?"

"Nope. Just me. Guess that might lead you to believe I'm the spoiled princess type."

"No, wouldn't guess that at all. You wouldn't have gotten where you are if that were the case."

"My dad's loss of an arm didn't stop him from achieving his goals. When I was growing up he made sure that I understood that he didn't consider himself handicapped in any way. He taught me that it was about hard work. Giving him a bunch of excuses as to why I couldn't do something was not going to work with him."

Jack said, "So if I'm late to one of our meetings, I guess the overslept excuse won't work."

Kat almost laughed out loud. "Jack, I doubt you've overslept a day in your life. You were in the Army."

"Yeah, something that I never thought I would say—that I was in the Army."

"You didn't think you would join the military?"

"Nope. My Dad is a career officer." Jack paused and again wondered again how much of his personal life he was ready to divulge.

"My father was, I guess you would say, an absentee Dad due to his military career. I never thought that I might follow in his footsteps. My mother died when I was young—"

Kat looked over to Jack when he suddenly stopped speaking. He was gazing out through the windshield. He turned, leaned to his left, looking at the dash. "How are we doing on gas?"

"Could use some. I'll stop at the next exit."

CHAPTER 58 – Scarface

Kat pulled up to the fertilizer supplier that made the last sale of ammonium nitrate on Haislip's credit card. It was in a small town just outside of Danville. Jack left some files in the car, so he checked the door handle after they got out to make sure it was locked.

Kat noticed and said, "This car has a great feature. When there's less than seventy pounds of pressure on any of the seats, the doors lock. Even with the key inside."

Jack said, "Now I'm thinking you weren't joking about the ejection seat."

"Even a locksmith would have a difficult time opening this car. It has to be opened by a remote signal. The worst part is that if you call in to get it opened, your name goes up on an 'honor roll' list back at HS headquarters. Very embarrassing."

"I guess it would be more embarrassing if you left it unlocked and the rifles in the trunk came up missing. I'd rather have my name on the honor roll."

They went in and showed their badges and credentials to the man behind the desk. The manager wasn't in, so he told them that they could use his office to talk to the employee.

He lifted a hinged portion of the desk and they walked

through the counter area to the manager's office. As they did, the man leaned down and pushed a button at the base of a microphone on a short metal stand. They heard, "Harley, you are wanted in the manager's office" echoing down the hall from the box speaker mounted above the door to the warehouse area.

In less than a minute, Harley came in. He was wearing the same too tight jeans and boots that he had worn when the Hendricks had picked up the ammonium nitrate. When his wife found out that he was going to talk to the FBI that morning, she made sure he put on a clean work shirt.

Kat and Jack shook hands with Harley and they sat at the round table in the corner of the manager's office. The table had been wiped clean, although it looked like all the catalogs, folders, and other papers that had been on the table were now plopped onto the middle of the manager's desk.

"Mr. Pearson, thank you for meeting with us," said Jack.

"You can call me 'Harley,' I mean, if that's okay and wouldn't be breaking any rules or anything."

"No, no, that's fine, Harley. We appreciate your help. We're investigating a case of identity theft and understand that you helped two gentlemen the other day on a fertilizer pick-up."

"Yep, that was me. I used the lift to put two loads on the dock by their truck. I didn't help them load it. I hurt my back a few years ago, so I don't do any heavy liftin'."

"Well, that's something right there," said Kat. They didn't have any problem picking up these bags?"

"If you mean whether they were lightweights, no, ma'am, these were big boys. One was, I'd say, more n' six-three, and the other maybe an inch shorter. Both plenty able to pick up those bags. The bigger one picked up off the pallets and the other was in the truck and loaded 'em inside. Put 'em over the rear axle. They knew what they was doin'."

"Were you able to see into the truck?"

"Oh, yeah. Nothin' in it—well, maybe I did see a hand-truck in there. But might just be thinkin' that because it was a rental truck. You know, since I saw it was a rental, I might just be thinkin' about see n' a hand truck inside another one sometime—"

"But you didn't see any other bags, or anything else?" asked Kat.

"No ma'am."

"So, these guys looked like they were farm help?" asked Jack.

"Well, yeah, they looked like farm boys, except their hair. They had long hair, parted in the middle, and had it in pony tails, both of them. The big one was kinda' foreign lookin'. Dark hair and dark beard. The smaller one—who was still big as I was sayin'—had kind of light brown hair, close to blond."

"The one you said was foreign looking. What country do you think he might have come from? Or maybe he was American Indian?"

"Naw, he weren't no Indian. I got a cousin who's Eastern Band of Cherokee, lives in Carolina."

"So maybe he was an Arab?"

Harley hesitated. "You know, this kinda' sounds strange, but I thought that first. I said to myself 'hey, maybe he's an Arab,' and maybe they're goin' to make a bomb."

Kat and Jack consciously avoided an exchange of glances. The last thing they wanted to do was to start a rumor spreading through the community.

Harley continued, "But then I thought about it. Why only buy this amount? And then the more I looked at him, the more I could place him. Not an Arab. He looked like the guy who plays the Godfather—well, you know, the son who then gets to be the Godfather later."

Kat said, "You mean Al Pacino?"

"Yeah, that's the guy. Played that drug dealer in 'Scarface' too, right? Thelma—that's my wife—me and her like to watch movies. Got a DVD player and rent them over at the grocery store. They got a rental place near the drink section. Not too much else happenin' 'round here. Anyway, from what I heard 'em say—weren't much—but they weren't no terrorists. I could tell by what they said."

"By what they said?" asked Kat.

"Well, not really what, but how. Those boys were from Carolina. Could tell by the accent and if they'd been from anywhere 'round here, would have seen 'em before. I would've asked 'em what happened to their truck."

"Why would you have asked them about their truck?" asked Jack.

"It was a rental. No farmer 'round here would rent a truck to pick up fertilizer. They'd have their own flatbed or send a couple guys in pickups. I figger' these boys come from somewhere not too far away and their reg'lar supplier was out and maybe they had a truck out for maintenance.

"Wasn't gonna' pry in their business, though. Jacob up front can tell you if the suppliers south of here were out. Might be, 'cause it's kinda' late in the season to be puttin' out straight nitrogen on pasture so I'm figgerin' this was for some kinda' early fall vegetable plantin'. Most use nitrogen as side dressin'. Pour it straight down the sides of the plant rows, then water it in. Gives you good leaves."

He stopped, then said, "Then it hit me." He had a knowing look on his face. He lowered his voice, and said, "I figgered out why the FBI was lookin' into it."

Kat and Jack did look at each other this time, wondering whether Harley might have important information.

Harley said, "Marijuana. These boys are growin' crops all right. Don't want to be tracked. Rented a truck, using some guy's ID they stole." He smiled as if he had just cracked the case.

"Well, Harley," said Jack in his most official tone, "we can neither confirm nor deny anything about this investigation." They continued to get as much descriptive information on the two men as they could get. They thanked him for his time, and Jack gave him his card and told him to call them if he thought of anything else.

Jack and Kat continued to the other suppliers and received information similar to what Harley had provided. The further north they went, they received corroboration that the men were from North Carolina.

At one location the clerk told them that he had a discussion with one of the men about crop yield rates. The clerk was certain that the guy wasn't just buying fertilizer for someone else. He was sure that the man worked on a farm.

They spoke to Tim at the truck rental center in Charlottesville. He hadn't noticed anything unusual about the person renting the truck, other than they had a different address on the license than what was on the reservation. His description of the man, as to size, hair color, and beard, fit the same description of the smaller of the two men who had purchased the fertilizer.

They got back in the car and headed towards Georgetown where Jack had reserved rooms for the night. Childs and Adeniyi would be staying at the same hotel and he hoped to meet with them after dinner.

*   *   *   *

THAT night, when Harley got home, Thelma asked him how it went. Harley told her that some longhairs were planting and harvesting marijuana, and he was the one that put the FBI on to them. "Don't be surprised if there's some helicopters buzzin' 'round south of here tomorrow."

CHAPTER 59 – Hotel Rooms

The hotel was located in Georgetown and wasn't far from FBI headquarters. Kat lived in Falls Church but decided to stay in town when Jack told her about the late meeting. They would be sharing notes and working on a briefing for the next morning.

The hotel had valet parking, but agents parked their own vehicles in the dedicated lot. Kat pulled up to the front entrance of the hotel. Jack got out and unloaded their bags from the trunk. While Kat was parking the car, Jack took Kat's suitcase and his own bag into the lobby and waited for her at the hotel desk.

He had reserved a room for Kat under his name. When he got their key cards, Jack noticed that the room numbers on the cards were both even and sequential, 618 and 620. When she came into the lobby and he handed her one of the key cards, he couldn't resist smiling. When Kat decided to stay in D.C. that night, Jack had not considered the appearance of their getting into an elevator, getting off on the same floor, and walking down the hotel corridor together.

"Wonder if you're thinking what I'm thinking," said Kat.

Jack looked at her and smiled. "Now I am convinced you're a mind-reader."

The hallway on their floor was thickly carpeted and the

walls had dark wood wainscoting. Crystal sconces provided lighting and there was a textured fabric covering on the top portion of the walls.

"Nice place," said Kat, only to break the silence as they walked toward their rooms. She had a strong feeling that Jack felt the same way she did, but that there was something other than his being the task force leader that was holding him back.

They got to Kat's room, 618, and she stopped to take out the plastic key card out of the small folder. Jack continued down the hall to his room still carrying Kat's bag. Kat said, "Jack, I'll need my suitcase." Jack's mind was somewhere else. *Kat in the room next door . . .*

He quickly turned around and started back towards her—hoping that the flush he felt in his face had faded quickly. Was she thinking that he had them both in the same room on his mind?

"You must be thinking about the case," she said, smiling in a way that meant that she didn't think that at all.

"Guess I'm not much of a bellman," said Jack. "Shall I open your door for you?"

"I think I have that," said Kat. Jack had turned and was about to open his door when Kat said, as she was entering her room, "but I'll call you if I need anything."

Jack was about to reply when the door to 622 opened. Out came Adeniyi.

"Well, about time you guys got here." Adeniyi had stepped out in the hall and Childs was not far behind him.

"Kat, this is Special Agent Kalu Adeniyi and Special Agent Steve Childs. Gentlemen, this is Special Agent Kat Morris, with Homeland Security." He looked at Childs. "I believe I mentioned that Kat was joining the task force to you on the phone." They said their hellos, and then Childs couldn't resist.

"Yes, Kat, I have heard so much about you. We're really glad to have you on the team and I know that you will enjoy working, uh, closely with Jack." He smiled and then said, "I guess the agency would frown on doubling you two up in the same room, even though it would save some taxpayer money."

"Uh, let's not go there," said Jack.

Kat decided to play along. "Yeah, I checked with your headquarters and they said no, since I was from Homeland Security. Something about the two agencies not getting in bed together."

Childs' jaw dropped. Jack just laughed, and said, "Okay, let's get settled and meet downstairs at seven for dinner."

* * * *

AFTER dinner they met in the small conference room that Jack had reserved. A speaker phone sat in the middle of the table. Mike called in from the hangar and Eric was also on the line. Childs and Adeniyi briefed the team on their interviews with the nitromethane suppliers.

Childs said, "Each of the suppliers said that a guy called and said he needed some nitromethane for a drag racing team. He said he was in a hurry and asked if they could just have it ready at their warehouse.

"The place in Martinsville, by the Speedway, told him they could have the nitromethane shipped over from their supply warehouse in Virginia Beach, but it would take two days. The guy gave them the credit card number over the phone. He called back two days later, and when they told him it was in, he said he was coming right away to pick it up."

Jack said, "Tell me they have a record of when he called and when he picked it up."

Adeniyi said, "No written record of when he called, but the clerk specifically remembered he was about to clock out at noon for lunch when the call came in. The purchase time is on the supplier's copy of the credit card receipt and we verified the accuracy of the time-stamp. The clerk said it took about ten minutes to load the barrels. The slip shows a time of 1:43 p.m."

Eric's voice came out of the speaker. "At an average speed of fifty miles per hour on the roads in that area, with a deviation factor for slowdown due to lunch hour traffic, offset by a reasonable assumption that the purchaser was driving an average of five miles per hour faster than the speed limit, a radius of approximately seventy-five miles around the supplier's location near Martinsville is obtained. Seventy-four-point-seven miles to be exact."

Jack said, "And I'm guessing you already have a map prepared?"

"Yes. It's been scanned and sent by secure mail to your agency email address. After reviewing it, if you would like to include it in your briefing tomorrow, just reply 'yes' and I'll transmit it to headquarters."

"Thanks, Eric. Great work." He opened his email on his laptop and looked at the map. "There's a couple of major caveats on this, as far as locating the two men. First, we're assuming the two men in the truck are from North Carolina, and second, that the call came from wherever these two guys are based."

"Three men," said Childs. "I hadn't gotten to that yet.

The supplier described the two of the guys that showed up. The description matches the guys buying the fertilizer but there was somebody else in the truck."

CHAPTER 60 – On Video

"There was no description of the third person. Only that he backed the truck up to the loading dock," Childs said. "He didn't get out of the vehicle. For that matter, we can't be sure it was a guy. Could have been a female."

"According to the man that was on the loading dock, the two guys put the barrels into racks inside the truck. He said he was a little surprised to see the racks inside a rental truck but figured they had just rigged it up since their regular truck had broken down."

"Okay," said Jack, "we have an approximate distance of seventy-five miles to Martinsville from the home base. We're looking for someone who probably has a farm. The men knew about farming and a farm would be a good place to hide a truck, in some outbuilding or barn.

"Eric, if we included Virginia in our seventy-five-mile calculation, how big a search area are we talking about?"

Back at the hangar, Eric stared into space. "That would be seventeen thousand six-hundred sixty-two and one-half square miles."

"What part of the circle is in North Carolina?" asked Kat.

Eric said, "Just about the bottom half of the circle, or eight thousand eight hundred thirty-one square miles."

Jack said, "On the assumption that the truck drove the entire time at the calculated speed, then the starting location would be about sixty to seventy-five miles from Martinsville. Somewhere inside a fifteen-mile wide arc inside North Carolina."

Eric added, "And we can exclude all areas in the arc that are covered by water and other non-residential areas, such as state or national park lands."

Kat looked up from her laptop screen, where she had pulled up a topographic map. "What about creating a list of all farms that are registered with the State Department of Agriculture that fall in that geographic area? If it is a working farm, they will be registered with the State."

Eric said, "Yes, I can do a quick algorithm using both geo-spatial data and some of the State's closed data. I'll get with the SBI here to get us into the databases."

Jack looked down at the map on his screen. "Let's use a band that has an inner boundary of sixty miles from Martinsville, and an outer boundary that's ninety miles from Martinsville. Just in case the truck went faster or slower than the initial assumptions. With a listing of names filed with the Department of Agriculture, we might get a hit on a common name from another case file or other government records. We can get that arranged in the morning."

Jack looked toward the speaker-phone on the conference table. "Okay, Mike, what do you have for us?"

"I've been saving the best for last," said Mike. "We went through all of the S-Mart backpack sales in Virginia and North Carolina over the last three months. There were twenty-three sold during that time period.

"Most are in North Carolina, but there were three in

Eastern Virginia. Of those, sixteen were paid for with a credit card. We checked those out and only two purchasers don't have the backpack. They were given as gifts to children for school bags. We were able to confirm that the children who received them still had them.

"We were able to get video on all of the remaining seven cash purchases. One sale was in Annandale, Virginia, which was the closest store to Mr. Clean's apartment. Sure enough, there was Mr. Clean, buying our backpack. So, we now have video evidence tying him to the purchase of the bag, and that he threw it in the dumpster with other trash."

"Okay, Mike, so what is the 'best' news?"

"Of the remaining six with video, we had three purchases by females. We tracked them on the parking lot cameras and got license plate numbers. We interviewed them. They were buying backpacks for their sons. Guess black is the color choice for boys.

"The other three buyers were males, or more specifically, one young boy, who looked about ten years old, one teenager, and one young man. The boy put his backpack on and got on his bicycle. This was in a more rural area in central North Carolina, and there is only one elementary, one middle, and one high school in the town. We were able to locate his school and the student in the video. We verified that he still had the backpack.

"The teenager was black, and rather tall and heavyset. This store was in the Fayetteville area. We couldn't get a plate, but he was driving a pick-up truck with a high school decal. We found his picture in the school yearbook and contacted him. His hair profile wouldn't match and there was no way he would be wearing a men's small T-shirt, but we talked to him anyway, just to be sure he wasn't buying it for someone else. He wasn't, and he still had it."

Jack looked at the list of S-Mart stores in North Carolina. "Let me guess. The last sale was in Durham and occurred close to the exchange date. The young man purchasing the backpack was small and looked like he was from an Arab country. Perhaps looking around in a nervous manner as he bought the backpack?"

"Pretty much nailed it, Jack, except that the sale was in Raleigh and not Durham. Which leads us here to believe that we're on the right track. And indicates that the man buying the backpack may live in a different area than the others.

"Now, the interesting part of the Raleigh sale. It was dark, but on the parking lot video we were able to make the vehicle the buyer drove off the parking lot. It was a dark 2006 or 2007 Ford Escape or Mazda Tribute. We couldn't get a plate number. But we were able to make out a decal for N.C. State University in the rear window."

Jack said, "Seems like Eric may have been correct. A student or grad student."

"Right," said Mike, "and Eric has already read and memorized a list of all current students who applied for an on-campus parking permit listing a vehicle that matches our description. The University provided us with the commencement pamphlets for the last three years that lists all the graduates' names. Eric's already memorized those names as well.

"He's looking for any match with names in the DMV records. We just received the video a couple of hours ago. We are running those makes and models on the North Carolina DMV records."

"It's possible that he's not a student or graduate. He might just be an N.C. State fan," said Kat.

"True," said Jack, "but this is a good lead. We have something of consequence to brief to the division chief tomorrow. It's been awhile since the last fertilizer purchase. I'm worried that a truck bomb may be ready now."

CHAPTER 61 – Failure

Jack's concern was prophetic. At one a.m. the next morning his cell phone rang. It was Mike. "They found our truck." Jack was immediately wide awake.

"About forty minutes ago, there was a bombing at the new mall in North Raleigh. I had asked someone I know at the SBI to contact me immediately if anything happened, anywhere in the State."

"Casualties?" Jack's heart sunk. They were too late.

"Two. A security guard and a janitor. The blast took out all four levels of the parking deck and most of one side of the large department store next to the deck. The guard was about a hundred feet in front of the department store. He was cut down by the flying glass and concrete from the explosion. The janitor was inside the department store and was buried under a wall that collapsed.

Jack's worst fears had been realized. He thought about the victims' families. They might have wives and children that they had left that night before going to work. They would never come home. *It's on me,* he thought. *What could I have done differently?* He knew that he needed to be detached and analyze the facts. Maybe this was some completely unrelated act.

"How can we be sure it's our truck? I'm guessing it was pretty much demolished?"

"The responding officers found the truck's rear axle near the road, over two hundred yards away. They found the VIN stamped on the rear axle housing. It's ours." Jack's mind whirred. Why blow up the truck at a mall? In the middle of the night?

Mike then added, "Another strange thing. Based on the description I got of the damage, the truck could not have been loaded up. We have phony purchases in amounts that exceed what Timothy McVeigh used to take down a third of a nine-story building and left a crater that was thirty feet wide and eight feet deep. The McVeigh bomb registered about three on the Richter scale at Norman, sixteen miles away. If the Oklahoma bombing was a shotgun, this was a water pistol."

"Get Eric up and run all this by him. See if he can equate it to any other files he's reviewed on terrorist attacks in the last thirty years and what we should be looking for now. And have him call me as soon as he does."

Eric called him at two a.m. Since Mike had called, Jack had been turning things over in his mind. The blast, the victims. He turned on the lamp at the side of the bed and put the phone on speaker mode. He got a legal pad from his briefcase.

Eric said, "I've come up with two very close matches in the past thirty-eight years of terrorist activities around the world, both involving the Red Army. These were homegrown terrorists acting with the help of a foreign government. One or more of the homegrown terrorists were graduate students at a nearby university, which may be why there was more sophistication and planning than usual.

"Both involved explosives, and technical expertise was apparent in both creating and detonating them. In both cases, an isolated area was used to prepare two bombs, and the initial detonation was used to ensure that the bomb would detonate. The specific purpose was to gauge the potential explosive capability."

Jack said, "So, based on these cases, what other factors should we be looking for?"

Eric said, "What's missing is an indicator for the target. If the blast at the mall was not the target, and we don't think it was, then we can assume that the bombers were testing the explosive capability of the bomb on a structure like the mall. Perhaps an office building like the first World Trade Tower explosion in 1993, when a rental truck with a twelve-hundred-pound bomb blew up in the underground garage of the North Tower. This bomb could have been detonated during a busy time at the mall, so the motivation was not to spare civilians."

"What do you think is most likely?" asked Jack.

"Based on the test explosions conducted in the other cases, it looks like they wanted a test run with no risk of discovery. They conducted the test when the risks of detection were minimal. There would be many reasons that a large truck couldn't get into the right position during rush hour at the mall, including traffic jams. They could have detonated it in an open field, the way McVeigh tested his bomb, if they just wanted to see if the bomb would work."

"What do the comparable files suggest is the target, or type of target?"

"The military," said Eric. In both cases, the bombers struck a military target or a building containing military personnel. It could be the Pentagon but it's unlikely that a truck could get near the Pentagon without a complete inspection.

A building with large numbers of military personnel would be at the top of a potential target list. This would include every military installation in the country. A review of all potential locations in the geographic area results in Fort Bragg having the highest statistical probability as the target. It houses more troops than any military post in the country and—utilizing secondary roads—it is only 75.4 miles from Raleigh. It is unlikely that a terrorist would drive a truck bomb great distances to reach a target."

"Thanks, Eric. Let's send out a warning notice to the Department of Defense. The DOD may want to raise the DEFCON alert level for all military installations in the mid-East region. I also want you to find out what you can about the Raleigh blast victims and how to contact their families. Everything you can. I want to know the final arrangements."

* * * *

LATER that evening, Attila picked up his phone. It was Mr. Clean, and he wasn't happy. The agent on wiretap duty sat up straight.

"We trusted you with a large sum of money and the college student blows up an empty department store! This will get back to those supporting you. Someone will pay for this!"

"Do not worry. This explosion was only a test. It was done in preparation for what will come. Our friend is working with others. You will soon see a mighty blow struck against America."

CHAPTER 62 – In the Shower

After Jack spoke to Eric, he laid back on his bed. There was nothing he could do until morning, so he set his watch alarm for 5:15 a.m. and closed his eyes. He woke up at 5:10 a.m., showered and dressed.

When he went out into the hallway, he noticed light coming from under Kat's door. He paused for a second, then decided to let her know what had happened that night.

He knocked gently. There was no response. *She might be in the shower,* thought Jack, and he turned to go to the elevator. He had taken a step when he heard "Who is it?" coming from the other side of the door. He turned back.

"It's Jack. You up?" The door had cracked open.

"I'm just getting ready. Did you want to"—she hesitated, searching for the right word.

Jack knew that he needed to say something before she said another word. Did she think I knocked to get her to invite me into her room? What if she does?

"Was going to let you know that a truck bomb went off in Raleigh. It was the rental truck."

"Oh my gosh!" said Kat. The door was now open wide enough that Jack could see that he was right. Her hair was wet and tousled, and she had a bathrobe on. The top of the robe was opened, and he could see the swell of her breasts.

He hesitated. This was a woman unlike any he had met since he had left Pam. But the deaths that had just occurred weighed on his mind. Involvement with a subordinate was strictly prohibited in the military and he knew what it could do to a unit's cohesion—potentially affecting their mission. And now, after seeing Pam again, she still lingered in the back of his mind . . .

"Let's meet down in the dining room. I'll fill you in then. I was just going to knock on Childs and Adeniyi's door to let them know."

"Okay, see you then." She closed the door and leaned back against it. Jack had been going toward the elevator when she had cracked open the door. The other agents' room was in the other direction.

*   *   *   *

THEY had just finished breakfast when a call came in on Jack's cell phone. It was a brief conversation, with Jack mainly answering "yes" and "this week" and "okay." After he disconnected he turned to the others at the table.

"The division chief has cancelled the briefing. He wants us to investigate the bombing and then report back. We need to find this group *now*. Eric thinks that this may just be a warm-up for a much larger explosion. Let's get our stuff together and hit the road. I'll tell Mike that we'll meet at the hangar as soon as we get in."

Kat left the Mercedes in D.C. for maintenance, so they took a flight from Dulles to Raleigh-Durham. They arrived back at the hangar later that afternoon.

Assembled around the conference table, Jack asked, "Any ID on the backpack purchaser?"

"Nothing specific," Eric answered, "but I now know the names of all students currently attending N.C. State. The University gave us the list but can't provide us with any detailed information without a warrant."

"I imagine any judge would say having a decal on the car is insufficient. The term 'fishing expedition' comes to mind, but if we can sufficiently identify a student by the picture or other evidence, we'll give it a shot."

"I hate to be a spoiler," said Mike, "but there's always the chance that the person was a student and dropped out."

"True," said Eric, "and it is also possible that he bought the car with the sticker already on it. I'm also compiling a list from the North Carolina Division of Motor Vehicles of all registered owners of 2006 and 2007 Ford Escapes and Mazda Tributes. As soon as the list is complete I'll be able to determine if there are any matches with a student and the subject vehicle."

"It's possible that the car is registered out of state," said Jack, "but we've got to start somewhere. The campus police are combing all university parking areas for our subject vehicle. If it does have an out-of-state plate, we'll run the tag in that state." Jack looked over at Mike. "See if you can get some idea about the explosive capability based on what may have been used at the mall, and what they actually had on hand after the third buy.

"They might also have had more ammonium nitrate than there are charge receipts for, but they probably won't be using a much larger vehicle than the rental truck. The selection of that size vehicle was probably for a reason. Larger trucks might not fit into where they want to go or might be more easily detected."

CHAPTER 63 – Load Up

Frankie and Johnny Lee helped Cal load the bomb materials into one of their farm vehicles, a surplus M809 Army five-ton truck with a front winch. Cal had bought the vehicle years before to haul large loads and pull out other vehicles that occasionally got stuck in the field ditches.

They had built a wood box on the back to replace the canvas covering. The back doors opened from the middle and were located just above the rear tailgate. When closed, sliding metal bars could be locked into the tailgate. A padlock secured the tailgate to the truck body.

Johnny Lee installed steel plates against the box's interior wall surfaces. Clips were also attached to the front wall to hold three AR-15's. Cal had purchased a Remington 700 sniper rifle with a scope and carrying case. He secured the case to one of the truck's side walls.

After loading the M809, Frankie and Johnny Lee drove north in the '66 Mustang. They would use the Mustang as their primary vehicle coming and going to the shop. It was a perfect restoration and consistent with the business that Cal had told the leasing agent would be operating out of the shop.

As soon as they arrived at the shop, Johnny Lee went to work on the ambulance. The box was twelve-and-a-half feet long and, in normal configuration, had numerous metal cabinets for medical equipment and supply storage. It took him several hours, but when he was finished the ambulance box had been gutted. All the built-in cabinets were removed, including the cabinets accessed by opening exterior panel doors which now were welded shut from the inside. He attached racks on each side above the ambulance's axles to double-stack barrels. The interior space of the box was now equal to the fourteen-foot box on the rental truck.

The ambulance model had a walk-through between the cab and the box, allowing the driver to move into the box portion and set the fuses. By the time Cal drove the M809 through the rear opening into the shop, the ambulance was ready to load.

CHAPTER 64 – Staubach

Jack knew that he had to make the call, whether J.T. would want him to or not. He had already confirmed with Aunt Gina that his father was at the Special Warfare Center at Fort Bragg. He walked outside the hangar and dialed the number on his cell phone.

* * * *

HE had been bitter, in the same way as J.T., when he had been in college. They had talked on occasion but there was still the memory of his mother dying in the bedroom without his father. It was only after 9/11 that he began to understand.

Jack had called when he enlisted. He was told that Colonel Thomas was "not available" and wouldn't be for some time. It was the code phrase for deployment on a classified mission somewhere in the world. When asked if it was an emergency, he said "no" and disconnected without leaving a message.

When he arrived at Fort Benning for OCS after basic training, there was a message waiting for him. He wished Jack well—but if he really wanted a military career, he "might regret not having gone to West Point." His message had noted that it would be difficult to attain general officer rank with an OCS commission, but he would help him in any way that he could. The last thing Jack wanted was help from his father, who was now the commander of a Special Forces Group. Jack hoped he would not try to influence anyone in his chain of command. He decided the best thing he could do was not to contact him.

He did regret that he didn't call his father when he was in the hospital. When he became an officer, he began to see how much alike they were. Lives depended on decisions that he had to make. There was a loyalty between him and the men under his command. They were fighting for each other and knew that they depended on each other for their own survival. They both had left someone they loved because of the duty they felt towards their country. They both had been responsible for leading men in combat. And they both had seen some of those men die.

When Jack graduated from law school he called his father. It was a strained conversation. He didn't know about Jack's combat injuries. Jack just told him that he left the service to finish law school. He could hear the disappointment in his father's voice. He had wanted to talk to him about his mother but couldn't find the right words. He hadn't talked to him since.

* * * *

"JFK Special Warfare Center and School, Captain Avery speaking, sir." The voice was hoarse and had the sound of sleeplessness. Captain Avery was the Staff Duty Officer, coming off a long night shift as officer-in-charge of the Center overnight.

"Good morning, Captain Avery. This is Jack Thomas. I

need to get in touch with General Thomas. It's important. I'm his son." Captain Avery was immediately as alert as when he had started his shift.

"Yes, sir. What number should he call?" Jack gave him his number, hit the off button on his phone, and waited.

Two minutes later, Jack's phone rang. Jack spoke first.

"Hello Dad."

"Hello Jack. It's really great to hear your voice."

"Yeah, Dad, I guess I should have called you some time ago. Guess I don't have a good excuse."

"Jack, I know you needed some time. I, uh, found out that you were hospitalized with combat injuries. I know what that can do to someone."

"I'm now with the FBI. I'm on a counterterrorism task force working here in North Carolina."

"Well, congratulations! That's great, Jack. You know that I was always proud of your accomplishments. There's probably nothing more important now for homeland security than rooting out terrorism. Glad to hear it Jack." He paused. "I've really missed you. And I know a lot of this had to do with what happened with your mother." Jack heard something that he never recalled hearing before.

"Jack," said Max, "I'm so sorry. I wanted to be there for the whole time . . . your mother would have none of it . . . but I should've been there—"

"Dad, I understand what you probably went through—times you had to be away. I resented it for many years and carried it with me. But I've been where you've been and now can understand. I guess the person who sacrificed the most was Mom. But she did what she had to do. It was a call of duty for her." He stopped and decided that they would continue the discussion the next time he saw his father. "Dad, let me tell you what's happening now. Something you can help me with—actually, it would be helping J.T."

"Anything," said Max. "Just tell me what it is."

Jack went through the whole situation with J.T. His hard work in getting his degree and his rise in position with the brick company. The night when J.T. was arrested.

Jack and Max discussed what Jack wanted him to do, which was to be in the courtroom, in his uniform. It would show his support for his son and, as cynical as it might sound, it might help with the jury.

"Absolutely, Jack. Only have one trip planned for the next few weeks. They're having some of us old-timers out on the field at half-time at the Army-Navy game. If I need to cancel to be at the trial, no problem."

"I don't expect anything this month, so it shouldn't interfere with your plans. I'll tune in to the game if I can."

"Great. If I see Staubach, I'll get you an autograph."

Jack laughed. "Thanks, Dad. Appreciate that and I'll talk to you soon." Without thinking, the words came out. "Love you, Dad."

"Love you too, Jack."

CHAPTER 65 – A Name

Eric was missing the next morning and there was no message from him. It was late morning and just when Jack was about to launch a search, Eric walked in. Before Jack could say anything, Eric said, "We have a name."

It hadn't looked like there would be a pay-off for Eric's memorization of the current student list, the graduating students' names for the last three years, and the list of registered owners of 2006 or 2007 Ford Escapes or Mazda Tributes. Jack had hoped that his memorization would have saved time as opposed to manually creating a database. But after reading all the data, Eric immediately said that there were no matches. The campus police had also looked in all the lots on campus. They failed to identify a vehicle matching the description with the same decal in the same place as the one on the video.

Eric had contacted the Raleigh Police Department the night before on a hunch. Could they give him a copy of all tickets written on specific models of vehicles over the past year? No, unless he had a warrant. But they could let him view copies of all forty thousand four hundred and thirty-three tickets, which were public record, and "he could look for himself." Eric believed that he only needed to view each ticket for one second. It would take him less time than it would to obtain a warrant. A Raleigh police officer assigned to the task force would pick him up.

He went to the station at 7 a.m. and sat before a computer as tickets flashed by on the screen, one per second. He was focused on the task at hand and it never entered his mind to notify anyone of his whereabouts. Three hours later, he stopped the sequence. A ticket for a 2006 Mazda Tribute. The ticket had been for a parking violation in downtown Raleigh nine months ago.

"The owner's name is Peter Mahmoud." He had instantly recalled the name from the current student list he had memorized. "He's a junior at N.C. State. The DNA profile on the hair found in the backpack indicated Anglo-Saxon heritage on the mother's side. His last name is Arabic, but his first name isn't, which is consistent with his mother being Anglo."

"The car is licensed in Ohio, so that's why it wasn't on the DMV registry here." He pressed a button on his key board. An Ohio driver's license appeared on the large screen that had been affixed to the wall. Peter Mahmoud's picture took up a large part of the screen. It was clearly Mahmoud in the video buying the backpack. "He lives in an apartment in Cameron Village, not far from the University."

"Great work—again," said Jack. He thought how fortunate they were that Mike had arranged for Eric to join the team. "Let's get Childs and Adeniyi to the address. If his car is out front, we can just sit and watch it. If he comes out, we'll tail him."

Jack pulled out the report from the lab showing the DNA profile. "We have Mr. Clean and Mahmoud buying the same backpack at about the same time and then Mr. Clean discarding his in the trash. We have the T-shirts but need to get a sample of Mahmoud's DNA to tie him to the backpack.

"We didn't arrest Mr. Clean or Attila based on their discussion of the department store bombing because it wouldn't produce any lead on the actual bombers and the target. Neither would have talked, and we'd lose any chance to find out more specific information from the wiretap.

"Kat and I will get an affidavit together for a search warrant at Mahmoud's apartment. Today is a trial day, so there should be a judge or magistrate available at the courthouse."

* * * *

AS Jack and Kat were preparing to go to the federal courthouse, Cal, Frankie, and Johnny Lee were weighing ammonium nitrate and combining it with nitromethane. In seventy-two hours the ambulance would be rolling out the door to its final destination.

CHAPTER 66 – Like The Towers

In mid-November, two weeks before they loaded the ambulance with explosives, the Hendricks and Mahmoud went to Lincoln Financial Field for the Philadelphia Eagles game against the N.Y. Giants. Cal's sons had never been to a football game, but they didn't spend any time in the seats that Mahmoud had purchased. They mingled with the fans who were jamming the areas around the concession stands.

It was a night game, and the temperature was forty-three degrees. The Hendricks were wearing heavy work coats and knit watch caps with their hair tucked underneath. Mahmoud hadn't brought a hat, so he bought a black, green, and white striped knit cap with the Philadelphia Eagles logo at the airport souvenir shop.

Cal studied the openings at the ends of the stadium that allowed wheeled vehicles to access the concrete floored concourse on the first level. Between game days, small delivery and supply trucks entered through gated openings. In an emergency, fans could be cleared so that an ambulance could pull up to the narrower passageways leading into the stadium seating areas. A fan with a medical emergency could be placed on a stretcher and loaded directly into the ambulance on the concourse.

Mahmoud studied the structure of the grandstands and the placement of the supporting columns. He took pictures with a Canon EOS camera he had purchased with some of the backpack money. He also took pictures from different angles of one of the ambulances that was parked close to the stadium in a specially designated area.

After going to the stadium, the four men went back to the shop. Mahmoud set up his laptop computer on a workbench and transferred the images from the camera to the laptop.

He explained to the others how the explosives would work. "The previous stadium here was demolished in 2004 by many small charges, exploding in sequence around the interior columns of the stadium. This was done to ensure that all the structure fell towards the field. The stadium collapsed under its own weight when the supports were destroyed. So, that was an implosion.

"The explosion of this ambulance will dwarf the amount of explosive power used to implode the stadium that was here before. It will be even greater than what was used to destroy the federal building in Oklahoma City. The Oklahoma bomb also destroyed or damaged over three hundred buildings in a sixteen-block radius."

"And where will the ambulance need to be placed?" Cal was concerned that it would be difficult to get the ambulance to the location needed to achieve the maximum effect.

"See this area here," said Mahmoud, pointing at the computer screen. It displayed a picture that was taken looking down the length of the concourse. His finger was on a spot midway down, approximately in-line with the fifty-yard line on the field. "There are openings to the stadium seating areas on either side of the concession stand."

He switched the images on the screen, back and forth between the passageways and the concession stand. "Right here," and he pointed to the screen, "is one of the main support columns. It should be placed anywhere near this column, across from the concession stand. With the flashing lights on, the stadium security will move people out of the way. You can then set the fuse just before you get out."

"The kick-off is at two-thirty," said Cal. "Johnny Lee will drive it in just after kick-off and will set the timer." He looked again at the screen and pointed to the restroom that was adjacent to the concession stand. "Johnny Lee, you can take off the scrubs in this bathroom. It will be a five-minute time fuse. If you are in position by two-forty, then the blast should be about two-forty-five."

Banafsha had taken a set of medical scrubs and opened all the seams. She then sewed quick-opening fasteners on the edges of the panels that formed the uniform. Johnny Lee would be able to completely remove the scrubs in seconds.

Mahmoud said, "After removing the scrubs, you should have at least four minutes to get out of the ambulance and as far through the parking lot as you can. The explosives are shaped to blast towards the field, but as this side collapses, significant debris will be hurtling into the parking areas."

Cal turned toward Johnny Lee. "As soon as your watch timer goes off, hit the ground. You should get behind the nearest vehicle if you are still in the lot."

Mahmoud pointed at the screen. "The blast will demolish the first tier, and certainly most of the second. The top tier will pancake down onto the second tier, or it may just lift and flip over.

"The amount of blast debris that will be generated from

the exploding bleachers on this side," he said, and pointed to the side where the ambulance would be parked, "will act like the discharge of a massive shotgun. Thousands of pounds of concrete, metal railings, and pieces of seats will be a gigantic wall of shrapnel that will slam into the other side of the stadium. Some of the blocks of concrete will be very large.

"As the other side is impacted by the blast and the debris, the tiers will shift and the columns supporting it will buckle. The tiers will collapse on top of each other, much like the floors of the towers in New York."

CHAPTER 67 – A Receipt

Mahmoud lived on the second floor of a two-story apartment building near the campus. Childs circled the block, parked down from the apartment building, and called Jack.

"Not sure he's inside," said Childs. I don't see a vehicle matching our description. He may have parked somewhere nearby and walked, or he could just be out somewhere." Childs had made a call to the college and told them that there was an emergency and they needed to contact Mahmoud. They said they could give him the Engineering department administrative office to see if he was in class today. Childs was able to find out that Mahmoud had been in class the day before but had missed his engineering class that morning.

Jack asked, "Can you get to a spot around a corner and keep eyes on the apartment? He may go by on a side street and see you guys waiting out front."

"Can do."

"Okay, we're on our way to the federal courthouse. If you see him park and go in, just standby. If he leaves again before we get there, follow him."

"Okay, we're pulling out to reposition."

"I've already called our Raleigh office," said Jack. "The local law enforcement liaison is lining up traffic control. The map shows a grocery store across from the apartment building. Eric and Mike are on the way in the van and will set up in that lot."

* * * *

JACK and Kat found a magistrate in her office. After reviewing the affidavit, the magistrate signed the warrant. Kat contacted Childs and he told her that there had been no movement in or out of the apartment.

As Jack pulled into the grocery store lot, he saw that police were preparing to block traffic on both ends of the street. Mike had already put on his Kevlar vest and had secured a battering ram to open the door. Jack and Kat put on their vests.

Mahmoud's picture from his driver's license was being widely circulated. There were agents sitting in the vehicles at each end of the street. City police officers on bicycle patrol duty near the campus were circling the area. Childs and Adeniyi pulled around to the back of the apartment building to cover any rear exit from the building.

There were stairs on each end of the building. Mike went up on one end, and Kat and Jack went up the other. As they approached Mahmoud's door, Jack and Kat crouched beneath the living room window at the front of the apartment. On the other side, Mike, flattened against the wall, reached around, knocked and announced, "FBI! Open the door! We have a search warrant!"

There was no response. Jack gave him the signal. Mike

quickly checked the door knob, found it was locked, then swung the battering ram. It landed squarely on the deadbolt lockset above the door knob. It caved in and a crack appeared where the door met the frame. The second blow caused the door to burst open and it slammed against the interior wall.

Jack, Kat, and then Mike entered with guns pointed and spread through the apartment. It was empty.

Jack spoke into his headset microphone, giving the "all clear" signal for technicians to begin evidence collection. They began dusting for prints and collecting any hair strands they could find, hoping for evidence of other conspirators having been in the apartment.

Jack and Kat waited outside the front door as the technicians went through Mahmoud's apartment. They heard a voice coming from the interior.

"Okay to come in. Something in here you might want to see." It was the agent in the bedroom. They entered and noticed that the closet doors had been slid to one side. Hanging inside were some empty hangars, a few pair of pants, and some button-down shirts.

The agent was standing by the bed. He had on surgical gloves and was holding a crumpled piece of paper with tweezers. "Here's something I thought you might like to know about right away. I found it in the bottom of a pants' pocket. Looks like he stuck it in his pocket, then pushed down on it with his wallet, or maybe a cell phone." The technician carefully pulled open the piece of paper and placed it on the top of a plastic bag that was on the bed spread. He took a close-up photo, and then backed away.

Jack bent over and read the faint lettering on the slip of paper. It was a sales receipt for an Eagles knit cap purchased at the Philadelphia airport gift shop two weeks earlier.

"Philadelphia," said Jack. "Maybe he was doing recon on the target. We should be able to trace his movements. He had to use a credit card for plane tickets. Maybe a rental car."

Kat said, "Plenty of buildings there that might be targeted. First one that comes to mind would be something historic, like Independence Hall. The Declaration of Independence and the Constitution were both adopted there."

Mike said, "They could be making a statement. One of al Qaeda's goals is to dominate the world through an Islamic caliphate. They would be destroying the symbols of a government by the people. Also, softer targets than buildings in D.C."

"Eric said a military target," said Jack, "where soldiers might be quartered. The Army War College is in Carlisle, Pennsylvania. Officers from all service branches who are being groomed to be general officers attend the course. There are also civilians from the DOD, the National Security Agency, and foreign country officers. If he went there, then there's going to be some paper trail."

Jack called Eric. "The warrant includes all financial records. Let's hope that we find a charge on his credit card for a rental car or motel, or both. See if he bought any plane tickets, then contact airport security and check the departing flight lists for Mahmoud's name. He may have paid with cash. Ask them to check for the Mazda in the inventory of vehicles in the parking garage. If it's not there, see if it can be located in their long-term parking lot."

He gave Eric the date from the receipt. "He may be at the same hotel he stayed at when he went to Pennsylvania the last time. Let's hope he didn't pay with cash."

Jack opened the top dresser drawer. He told the technician to take the T-shirts as evidence and to ask the lab if there was a way to match any residual laundry soaps or chemicals found in the material with the T-shirts that were in the backpack found in the dumpster. He noted that the brand on the label and the size were a match to the backpack T-shirts.

The other technician came out of the bathroom holding a clear plastic bag. In it were strands of hair. "Bingo," said Mike.

CHAPTER 68 – Mustang GT

Airport security called Eric and confirmed that Mahmoud had taken an early morning flight to Philadelphia. The plane had landed at just about the time Mike used the battering ram on his front door.

Jack and Kat joined Eric in the command van across from Mahmoud's apartment. Eric said, "The Mazda was parked in the airport's long-term parking lot. It has the N.C. State logo in the rear window. We've got technicians heading there now to search and fingerprint it. It may have prints of others that could be involved."

Eric looked up from the list of passenger manifests for all flights leaving Philadelphia for the next six hours. "Mahmoud had no checked luggage and he's not listed on any flights out of Philadelphia. It is possible he remained in the terminal waiting for someone else's flight to arrive but that is speculation. We've sent his photo to airport security, and they are searching the terminals now. I also have remote access to the airport's video system that covers the curbside areas. If he's already gone, we might be able to pick up video of the vehicle that picked him up. We're checking all the cab companies and car rental agencies now."

Jack said, "If a cab did pick him up, the others would have told Mahmoud to go to a prearranged location. They would pick him up after making sure he wasn't followed."

"I will let you know if anything comes in."

"Thanks, Eric."

*   *   *   *

THE team returned to the hangar and within thirty minutes a technician arrived with several clear evidence bags. Three receipts had been found in the Mazda's console.

Two of the receipts were for gas at a station in Durham and one was from an ATM withdrawal. The time on the receipts were prior to noon or in the early afternoon, and the ATM was at a bank near where the gas was purchased.

The dates were several months old and spaced apart by weeks. Eric immediately said, "The dates for all three of these fell on a Friday." In addition to his other abilities, Eric could tell what day of the week any given date fell on—whether the date was in a past or future century.

Mike said, "All on Fridays. That's the day a Muslim would go to a mosque and all the times are around noon—a special mid-day prayer time. Mahmoud must have been going to the mosque in Durham. He had to have some reason to go there. He could have gone to the one in Raleigh. It's only a few miles from his apartment."

"Sounds like he was meeting someone at the mosque, or maybe more than one person," said Kat.

Jack immediately contacted Chuck Singer. The Raleigh office also covered Durham County. He told him about the Durham connection and listened for a minute.

"Thanks, Chuck. I'll be right here and will wait for your call."

Jack disconnected the call on the command van's communication panel and turned to the others. "Chuck has somewhat of a special relationship with the imam at the Durham mosque. He will contact him and tell him that someone that goes to his mosque is missing.

"If he talks to others at the mosque, he'll tell them that the police are trying to locate any of the missing person's friends who might have information that could help them find him, which happens to be true. We do have cases where Muslim men have been attacked and we have initiated hate crime investigations."

Mike said, "So, it makes sense that a victim's friends may have information about when the victim was last seen, or places they normally go."

"Right," said Jack, "so this is a good cover for the imam, just in case it comes out that he might have knowingly helped the FBI. There are extremists out there that might not appreciate the imam providing us with information.

"Chuck will send Mahmoud's photo to the imam and remind him that he is from Raleigh. They don't always know names, but with a picture and knowing that the person hadn't been coming there a long time, he might remember Mahmoud and whether he had any friends at the mosque."

Fifteen minutes later the call came in. Jack picked up, listened for a minute, and then said, "Thanks, Chuck, that is a tremendous help."

Jack turned to the others. "The imam said that he has only been at that mosque for about a year, but that yes, there was a young man who fits Mahmoud's description that came to the mosque some three or four months ago. He said that he did remember him talking with two other men, around the same time.

"He came sporadically since that first time, but the imam can't recall seeing him speak with the same two men on those later occasions. The interesting thing is that he can identify those men."

Mike said, "Strange that the imam would remember him talking to two men three or four months ago and can identify them."

Jack said, "Not when the men have long hair, beards, and are Americans who came to the mosque regularly. He also said that he happened to see them when they went to the parking lot. The imam loves classic American cars. He had remarked to his wife about the beautiful '66 Ford Mustang GT that the men drove."

CHAPTER 69 – House Call

Eric immediately contacted the DMV for the names of all registered owners of 1966 Ford Mustang GT's in North Carolina. The GT model had a V-8 engine, and either the 225 HP or 271 HP high performance engine. This meant that the letter "A" or "K" would be in the vehicle identification number sequence in the space designated for engine size.

He immediately focused on the list of results that showed owners in Durham or surrounding counties. He expected that the number would be small, and there were only four. A classic car broker in Durham. A professor who lived in Orange County, outside of Chapel Hill. A furniture store owner in Burlington. And the fourth was owned by a farmer in Person County named Calvin Hendricks.

Eric spent several minutes initiating database searches. He requested driver's license photos for Hendricks and any other licensees with the same rural route address as Hendricks. He sent an urgent request to the FBI records division for anything it had on Hendricks. He ran a query on NICS, the National Instant Criminal Background System. The system is used whenever there is a transfer of a firearm from a federally registered firearm dealer to determine if a prospective purchaser is disqualified from receiving the firearm.

In minutes the photos of Calvin Hendricks, and his two sons, Francis Rosetti Hendricks and Johnny Lee Hendricks were displayed on the wall-mounted screens. Jack said, "The descriptions we have match Francis and Johnny Lee. They reside at the same location, the rural route address. Eric, contact Chuck Singer and tell him we need assistance on getting arrest warrants on these three."

"There are NICS inquiries for Calvin Hendricks for the purchase of three AR-15 semi-automatic rifles," said Eric. The AR-15 was sometimes called an assault rifle because the same model, designated the M16, was the standard issue rifle for U.S. Army infantry soldiers. The M16 could be fired in automatic mode. There were legal after-market parts that could be attached to the AR-15 that allowed it to be fired at the same rate as an automatic.

"We'll have to assume that the rifles have been modified," said Jack.

"This is very interesting." Eric was looking at the screen where he had just pulled up an enlarged photo of a military ID card. On the card appeared a much younger Calvin Hendricks. He was clean-shaven and only stubble adorned his head. "This Calvin Hendricks is a Viet Nam veteran. He was Airborne and Ranger qualified but left the service in the 70's. There's also a government file relating to him that is highly restricted.

"The file has the same type of markings and restrictions as my file." Eric stopped to consider the security clearances of those in the room. Satisfied, he continued. "In the early 1980's the CIA hired contractors to work secretly in Afghanistan aiding the mujahideen. Based on his age and his military background, it is very possible that this Calvin Hendricks was involved on the ground in Afghanistan."

Jack asked, "Can you get into his file?"

"No. That is not possible."

"You sound pretty certain about that."

"I am certain. I designed the security protocols and the CIA made sure there was an additional variable designed into it that was out of my control. In case I went rogue."

"Well, we'll need to go through channels then to get access, ASAP. Since you're involved maybe they'll speed up the process. Make sure they know that any delay could result in the loss of life."

After reviewing the photographs, Mike said, "Well, guess Francis is Al Pacino and Johnny Lee is Robert Haislip."

"Looks that way," Jack said. "Calvin Hendricks was probably driving the truck at that last nitromethane pickup."

Jack looked over to Mike and said, "There's a chance that Haislip is being held hostage on the farm and we know they have the AR-15's. There could also be explosives ready. How long would it take the enhanced SWAT team from D.C. to get here?"

Mike looked at his watch. "An hour to marshal at the airfield and about forty-five minutes flight time here. If the National Guard has a chopper ready, they can be on the target site in around two hours."

Jack said, "Eric, get with the local law enforcement liaison. We need the city police SWAT team for backup. Also, an EOD team ready to roll. We need to get out there now. We'll call for the HRT if we can't handle it ourselves."

Eric pulled up a satellite image of the Hendricks farm on the computer screen and they made their entry plan. Childs and Adeniyi would work their way around the sides of the house and cover the back. Jack and Mike would also come up each side of the house and then angle in, staying out of the direct line of fire from the upper windows.

They put on Kevlar vests and helmets and took MP5's and HK's from the racks in the van. Childs grabbed some flash-bang grenades and Adeniyi took several tear gas canisters.

The drive took forty minutes and the sun had set by the time they arrived at the farm. They drove past the farm house, saw that lights were on and parked off the road. "Not sure the men are home," said Jack, "but knowing Hendricks' background, there may be hidden obstacles, even mines. Eric says that Calvin Hendricks was married to an Afghani and both sons had registered marriage certificates, so there may be women on the site."

They were assembling when Eric came out of the van. "Warrants have been issued."

"Thanks, Eric. Don't need them in an emergency situation, but good to have them issued now. Get the warrant information out to all field offices on the East Coast." He looked at his watch. "I'd like to wait for the local SWAT team, but I think we need to move in now."

Kat had been looking at the long approach to the house. She turned to Jack and said, "How about letting me approach directly. Could be the women are armed. They might hesitate if they know it's a woman coming in."

"Maybe," said Jack, "but I wouldn't count on it." Jack hesitated. Kat had been in some danger when they entered Mahmoud's apartment. This was different. She would be directly in harm's way. The point person, without a weapon drawn and walking up to the front door.

"What's your plan?"

"I'll drive right up to the front door." She grabbed her FBI windbreaker, turned it inside out and put it on over her Kevlar vest. "I'm a woman, alone. Could be lost and looking for directions. They'll see me drive up, and I'll walk up to the door and knock. If someone opens, I'll move in and you follow. Childs and Adeniyi come through the back. You and Mike just be on either side of me, out of sight. I'll have my .45 in my hand, in my pocket."

Jack hesitated. *I'll be putting her in danger. But this could be the best way of getting in now. We could end up with a hostage situation. If I say no, I'll be putting my personal feelings ahead of the mission.* He nodded. "Okay. Just wait until we're in position."

* * * *

JACK and Mike came up through the woods on either side of the house. When everyone was in position, Kat drove up to the house. She got out, walked up the steps and knocked on the door.

Banafsha looked out the window, saw Kat, and opened the door. Kat drew her weapon and announced "FBI!" She told Banafsha to take a step back and raise her hands over her head. They heard the door slam in the back as Childs and Adeniyi rammed it open. Jack and Mike came through the door behind Kat and fanned out, rifles directed toward the stairway. They heard Childs yell "Clear!" from the back of the house.

Jack said, "Is there anyone else here?'

"Just the wives of my sons. They are upstairs."

"Ask them to come down with their hands over their heads. We'll still need to search the house."

After they searched the house, the barn, and the nearby outbuildings, Jack asked the three women to step outside to the drive. "We have warrants signed by a federal magistrate for the arrest of Calvin Hendricks, Francis Rosetti Hendricks, and Johnny Lee Hendricks. They are fugitives from justice. If you know where they are, you need to tell me now."

The women remained silent, as they had been instructed to do if the police ever came to the house.

Jack continued, "Since you are intentionally refusing to provide information as to their whereabouts, you are under arrest for harboring fugitives. There is evidence that a weapon of mass destruction was being assembled on this property. You are also arrested for conspiracy to commit acts of terrorism." Their rights were read to them. They remained silent.

Several sheriff's deputies had arrived with a prisoner transport van. The women were led into the van and taken to Raleigh to appear before a federal magistrate.

CHAPTER 70 – A Rivalry

Cal knew that every year there was a gathering of the top military leaders of America. One bomb could eliminate them, and perhaps even the President, their Commander, who sometimes attended the event. He relayed the new plan back to Omar through Banafsha's brother, who was now living in Falls Church.

The message from Atal to Omar was that the gathering of soldiers included the ones who would be leading the Americans to kill the Taliban in their own country. In much the same way as the attack on 9/11, the attack would occur on live television.

* * * *

THE football teams from West Point and the Naval Academy first met in 1890. The teams played the following years until 1894. There was a short break, and the series resumed in 1899, meeting every year since, except for a handful of times.

The annual game is an intense rivalry. In addition to the student bodies from each academy, it draws numerous alumni, including the top generals and admirals in their respective services. The game had been played for many years in

Veterans Stadium in Philadelphia. In 2004, Veterans Stadium was demolished by explosives in just over one minute and a new stadium had been built.

*   *   *   *

IT was late. Jack and Mike were back at the hotel packing for the next day's flight to Washington to brief the Division Chief. They would head to Philadelphia immediately after the briefing.

Jack finished packing and walked over to Mike's room. He could hear the sounds of the Monday night football game coming from the room.

Mike opened the door and Jack walked in. "Who's winning?"

"Tied in the fourth quarter."

A commercial came on, then a network promotion for the game being televised the following Saturday. It was the Army-Navy game.

In the back of Jack's mind, the dots connected. Soldiers gathered in large numbers in Philadelphia. It wasn't a building that was the target. It was a stadium—and his father would be there.

CHAPTER 71 – Game On

Tuesday, 0915 hours.

Jack immediately contacted headquarters and designated the stadium as the expected target. The FBI set up the conference call for the following morning. Philadelphia city officials, including the mayor and city manager would be on the call, as well as the superintendents of West Point and the Naval Academy.

Jack and the rest of the team sat at the conference table in the hangar. He had wanted to brief the officials in person, but time was short.

After introductions, Jack began the meeting. "We have a suspect, a young man of Jordanian descent, named Mahmoud, who has spent a significant amount of time visiting family in Jordan where he could have become radicalized. We believe that he traveled from North Carolina to Washington D.C. and received a backpack from a man who works in the Sudan embassy, who is a suspected al Qaeda operative."

The West Point superintendent said, "This is General Peter Karlson. I'm assuming there has been ongoing surveillance of this embassy employee?"

"That's correct, sir. We linked Mahmoud to a backpack that the embassy employee discarded. Mahmoud attended a mosque in Raleigh but was observed at a Durham mosque with two brothers, Francis and Johnny Lee Hendricks, who live in a rural area in a nearby county. The brothers match the description of the men who used a missing person's identity to rent a truck and to purchase bomb making materials.

"We were able to access highly classified documents early this morning. I am only authorized to tell you that the father of the two brothers, a man named Calvin Hendricks, is a highly-experienced soldier, a Viet Nam veteran, who fought with the mujahideen in Afghanistan and is married to an Afghani woman. We believe he is the ringleader of the terror cell.

"Johnny Lee Hendricks matches the description of the man who rented the truck that exploded at a North Carolina mall parking deck and killed two people. We believe that the truck explosion was a trial run.

"The parking deck next to the mall was similar in construction to the stadium. I said that it was similar because the deck was leveled, as was most of the adjoining three-story department store—and the size of the blast indicates that the truck wasn't fully loaded with explosives. Mahmoud is an engineering student and we believe that they used the mall location as a test site because its construction approximates the stadium's lower levels.

"Mahmoud traveled to Philadelphia in early November. He was there at the same time as an Eagles game was played at the stadium. He bought a Philadelphia Eagles cap at the airport. We believe he was doing recon on the stadium, reviewing how the stadium was constructed to determine the best location to place the explosives. The stadium's security video is only kept for a week, so we don't have a way of confirming the suspects were at the stadium.

"When we identified Mahmoud we immediately went to his apartment. We just missed him. He had boarded a flight to Philadelphia that same morning."

"This is Mayor Thompkins. Sounds a little circumstantial to me. Couldn't there be other targets they're after? What about Independence Hall? Seems like we'd being putting all our eggs in one basket, so to speak, if we just focused on the stadium. Do we have anything specific to the stadium, other than a parking deck?"

Jack was irritated but kept his voice even-keeled. "No, sir, we don't, but we believe that we should prioritize based on the evidence that we do have. The stadium is what we would call a target-rich environment due to the large number of military leaders and future leaders at one location." *This is exactly the type of target someone with Hendricks' military experience would pick,* thought Jack. *The leadership.*

The mayor frowned. He was in his first term and this was the first public safety challenge he had encountered. The game was a major tourist event. "Do you have any evidence about where Calvin Hendricks and his sons are now? Do we know whether another truck was stolen?"

"No," said Jack, "we raided the farm where they live, and they're gone. We discovered through interviews that Hendricks owns an Army truck. The model that he owns could carry the same explosive load as the rental truck. It's also gone."

Bob Hastings, the city manager and an Army veteran, had been in his position for fifteen years. He had previous experience in reacting to bomb threats to public buildings. "It sounds to me like we should put our emergency security and response plans into effect." Jack detected a note of annoyance in his voice, and he imagined that he was looking at the Mayor when he was speaking. "Starting with a sweep of the stadium."

"This is Special Agent Katherine Morris, Department of Homeland Security. We already have bomb-sniffing dogs from four different agencies going over the stadium now. We're inspecting all vehicles currently on the grounds and any vehicle entering the stadium."

General Karlson said, "If a specific threat on the stadium had been made, we wouldn't postpone the game. We'd be doing what we're doing now. Conducting a massive search and taking every precaution to prevent an attack. The same threat exists for any number of potential targets." He looked over to his Naval Academy counterpart, Vice Admiral Jacob Densler. "I don't know about you, Jake, but I don't see postponing this game."

"I'm with you on that, Pete," said the admiral.

The outcome of the meeting was now clear to Jack and Mike. Jack said, "The task force will establish check points on all streets leading to the stadium."

Mike looked over to Jack and nodded. "This is Special Agent Mike Bronson, FBI. Our enhanced SWAT team will be stationed there and ready to deploy as a reaction force wherever an attack might occur."

The game would go on.

CHAPTER 72 – The Hunt

Tuesday, 1125 hours.

Banafsha called her brother, Romal "Attila" Abdullah, from the holding room in the courthouse. Banafsha told him about her arrest and that the FBI was looking for Cal and the boys.

As soon as Attila finished talking to his sister, he called Mahmoud. A trace was attempted but the line was only open long enough to trace it to a general location in Philadelphia. Before the call ended, the words "and the world shall again see the might of al Qaeda on Saturday," were recorded.

* * * *

THE team took a flight to Washington to give the briefing and to plan for the operation in Philadelphia. They were at the headquarters by two p.m.

Jack closed the file after briefing MacCauley. "Hendricks is a military tactician. He has been ahead of us every step. It was Mahmoud that led us to him. And the good fortune that an imam admired collectible cars. But the point is that he knows that if you are outmanned and outgunned, you better have the element of surprise. If he believes that the site can still be hit, then he is still in the area.

"It is very likely that he either rented a warehouse or other closed area where they could assemble the truck bomb. He wouldn't have prepared the bomb in North Carolina and driven it all the way to Philadelphia. The vapors in the cans would start compressing with the constant moving and jostling. He could have ended up blowing out a section of I-95 on the way up."

MacCauley had closed his briefing file. "So, you think they have another truck ready to go?"

"I think so," said Jack. "The M809 can be outfitted with a large box on the back bed and stacked with the same amount of explosives that could have fit in the rental truck. He might paint it to match a National Guard vehicle. Put a Pennsylvania Guard unit number on the bumper. His sons may have cut their hair and beards and could wear military uniforms bought at a surplus store. Hendricks will do whatever is necessary to accomplish the mission, even if shaving their beards goes against their normal religious principles.

"We're also looking for the '66 Mustang and at least four people. Keeping two vehicles hidden from view for any length of time would take a warehouse of some kind. We don't have any record of Mahmoud staying at any motel, as he did when he went up earlier in the month. He left without knowing we had identified him, so he would have no reason to use an alias and pay with cash. It's likely that Hendricks has created a base where they are staying until after the attack. He would want to avoid a lot of coming and going to his location."

McCauley looked around the conference table. "The bottom line is that we have four terrorists with a truck that may look like a hundred other trucks. If it isn't the M809, then it is another box truck that could have any number of company logos painted on the side."

Jack said, "We need to control street access to any possible target. They could change their target if they don't think they can breach the stadium security. We know that a truck is going to be used. Unless we can find it before Saturday, we need to put checkpoints at all thoroughfares leading to Independence Hall, the Liberty Bell, and other public attractions."

Prior to the meeting, MacCauley had called Mike for an appraisal of Jack as the task force leader. He knew about the situation with Jack's brother. He had a decision to make and Mike's report confirmed his own assessment.

MacCauley looked directly at Jack and said, "I'm going to send all available SWAT assets from the region to Philadelphia. As task force leader, you deploy them as you see fit. You have full authority as commander on the scene."

"Thanks, Mack."

Eric had flown directly to Philadelphia from Durham. The Mercedes was back from maintenance. Kat, Jack, and Mike left the meeting and got in the Mercedes. They were in Philadelphia faster than if they had waited to catch the next flight out from D.C.

CHAPTER 73 – A Change of Plans

Wednesday.

While Jack was briefing the division chief, the Hendricks and Mahmoud were loading barrels into the ambulance. Frankie's paint and detail work were perfect. The ambulance was identical to the one that Mahmoud had photographed at the stadium.

Mahmoud told Hendricks about the call from Abdullah. The women were under arrest and Cal expressed his concern about the success of the operation. "I just drove by the stadium. There was a lot of activity that I could see from the interstate. They may have determined the target by now. Every vehicle will be stopped and searched before it can get into the stadium."

Mahmoud knew the importance of the mission as designed and was willing to sacrifice anything to accomplish it. He suggested a change in the plan to Cal.

"If you can create the emergency ahead of time, I'll drive the ambulance. I'll set the fuse when I am close and then drive it into the stadium. I will be coming fast with flashing lights, for a real emergency or not. If I don't get out of the ambulance in time, then it is His Will."

Hendricks considered the proposal and then agreed. He came up with a plan that would ensure that there was an emergency inside the stadium that would require a response from multiple ambulances. "The guards will let the ambulance pass."

CHAPTER 74 – Not a Charity

Thursday.

The federal Bank Secrecy Act requires financial institutions to report any suspicious activity that might indicate money laundering or tax evasion. Records must be kept of cash purchases of negotiable instruments, including a cashier's check in an amount over ten thousand dollars. A currency transaction report must also be made to the federal government.

Jack had asked the Treasury Department to run an inquiry on the data base containing reported transactions as part of the Haislip investigation. If the terrorists had cash to pay off Haislip's card, perhaps they had used cash for other purchases. Even though Jack had asked for an expedited report, his request didn't get processed until the previous day.

"You will be very interested in this," said Eric. He handed the paper to Jack that he had pulled off the printer. The report listed the purchase of a cashier's check at a bank in West Jefferson, a small town in northwest North Carolina.

Jack immediately called the bank that had reported the transaction. He was told that Eileen Carswell, the person who had reported the transaction, was on break. He left the office and extension number and told the receptionist that it was extremely urgent that Ms. Carswell call him.

Eileen Carswell was on a smoke break behind the bank. "Call for you, Eileen," said the receptionist who had gone to the back of the bank to find her. "A man says he's with the FBI and needs to talk to you. Says it's urgent. I left the number on your desk."

Eileen snuffed out her cigarette on the special receptacle for cigarette butts and dropped it in. "Oh well, no rest for the weary." She walked back to her office. Before calling, she checked the number to make sure it was the FBI. *Never know these days with all the fraud and identity theft going on*, she thought as she dialed the number.

"Special Agent Thomas speaking."

"Yes, this is Eileen Carswell. How can I help you?"

"Ms. Carswell, I'm part of an investigation into criminal activity that may involve the identity theft of a Mr. Robert Haislip. I'm calling about the purchase of a cashier's check for over twenty-two thousand dollars."

"Yes, that was very unusual. This Mr. Haislip giving me so much cash, especially from someone who's not from around here. But," and she hesitated for just a second, "I did find out what that was about."

"Really?"

"Yes, it turns out that his father, or we're thinking the man was his father, wanted to donate to charity."

"His father? Was his father with him? And how do you know about some donation?"

"Well, I've got a cousin, his name is Bill, and he did tell me that the man we think was his father gave him the check later that evening."

"Your cousin runs a charity?"

Eileen Carswell broke out laughing. "I'm so sorry, but I just couldn't hold that back. Lord, no, Bill don't run a charity! He sells used cars. A man bought one with a check and said he was donating it. Bill told me that the man didn't want to give his name. Wanted it to be anonymous."

Jack had been furiously writing notes. He motioned for Kat to come over and he put the phone on speaker.

"So, this man bought a used car from your cousin Bill with a cashier's check. Did he tell you what kind of car it was?"

"Yes, he told me, except that it wasn't a car. It was an ambulance." She paused. "Will Bill have to give the money back?"

CHAPTER 75 – A Prayer

Thursday, 1910 hours.

Cal got out of the cab in Wilmington, Delaware. It had been a forty-five-minute ride and the cabbie appreciated the big tip. Cal walked around the corner toward the car dealership in the suit, hat, and glasses he had worn when he had leased the trim shop. It was dark outside but the pole lights on the lot provided enough light for the salesmen to see him walking toward the entrance.

A short swarthy man in an electric blue suit smiled at the other salesman on duty. *Yes! My turn up and this could be a sale!* He jumped up and hustled over to the front door. Cal had stopped at the front entrance area began looking at one of the vehicles parked out front. He had not planned on entering the dealership. He assumed that they would come to him.

"Good evening, sir!" The salesman stuck out his hand. "My name is Ras Salazar. Nice vehicle you're looking at. We're very motivated and this model is on sale."

Cal shook his hand. "Nice to meet you. Yes, I have been looking for an SUV. My wife and I are giving it as a gift to our son." He walked around the new SUV parked in front of the dealership, looking it over. "I think he would like this model."

Salazar was ecstatic. He had a slow month in November and was under pressure to meet his sales quota for the quarter.

"Your son will be very safe in it. It has side airbags and a five-star side impact rating. Anti-lock brakes. It also has an excellent rating for quality. Great resale value. If your son ever decides to trade up to a new one in a few years, we could do very well on a trade-in. Would you like to drive it?"

"Well, my wife dropped me off and will be back in a little while to pick me up. She doesn't like shopping for cars." Cal had been walking around the vehicle so that no one inside had a clear view of him. He stayed on the passenger side of the vehicle.

"May I just ride with you in one that you have for sale. I plan on surprising him. If I like it, I will bring him by on Monday. Would it be all ready for delivery by then?"

"Oh, of course! No problem! We'll have everything ready. Do we need to start a financing agreement tonight?"

"No, that won't be necessary. We will have a cashier's check for the amount we agree on."

"Absolutely. Did you have a color preference? We have several on site. If we don't have the color you want, we can have it transferred here."

"How about this white one?"

"Certainly! This also has many extra features. It is a Limited model with a V6 engine and four-wheel drive. The gas mileage is very good for this size vehicle." Salazar could not believe his luck. Not only a sale, but one with a huge mark-up because of the options. *This will be a nice commission check!*

"I'll get the key and a tag. Be right back." He went into the dealership and told Larry, the other salesman, "Be back in a while. Going to make a big sale!"

He went back out to the vehicle, where Cal was waiting. He pushed the remote entry button that unlocked the doors and stuck the magnet with the dealer plate on the back of the white 4Runner. Cal got in the front passenger seat and they left the lot.

As they were turning onto the highway, Cal said, "Do you think we could head over to the Brandywine Park? I'd like to see how the four-wheel drive works. I know an area over there where we can check it out. My son likes to hunt, and he told me that if he ever got a vehicle it would have to do well off-road."

Salazar hadn't had a request to check out the four-wheel drive. Most drivers never went off-road. They would use the four-wheel drive in the snow. "Well, I guess we can do that." He headed for the park, and they were there in fifteen minutes.

As they drove up to the entrance, he was relieved to see that the park was closed. Cal said, "Just turn left here. I know a road where the maintenance trucks go in that's not paved."

Salazar was now apprehensive. It was dark and there were no vehicles in the area. When he turned towards Cal to tell him that they needed to go back he saw the gun pointing at him. He froze in terror.

"Just do what I say, and you won't get hurt. All I want is this car. Drive down this road and turn right on the State road."

Salazar did what he was told. The State road was on the back boundary of the park and skirted the southern side of a farm. Cal looked for an access road for farm equipment.

"Slow down. Turn onto that dirt road up ahead." The road had deep, water-filled ruts from trucks that had entered and exited at the turn-in. "Stop. Put it in low four-wheel drive and turn the lights to the parking light setting." Salazar's hands shook as he complied.

They drove in until they were in an isolated location. Cal had his combat knife and decided that he would use it instead of firing a gunshot.

"Stop here and turn it off." Cal took the keys and told Salazar to put his hands on the steering wheel. Once Salazar's hands were gripping the steering wheel, Cal pulled out handcuffs and snapped them on Salazar's wrists.

Cal got out. He went around to the driver's door and opened it. He grabbed Salazar's collar and started to pull him out of the car. Salazar had gripped the wheel tightly and hung on. His knuckles were white from the pressure. Cal took the butt of his gun and slammed it down on Salazar's fingers. He screamed in pain and released the wheel. Cal pulled him out by his wrists and Salazar fell to the ground.

"Get up." Salazar struggled to his feet.

As Cal pushed him into the woods, Salazar whimpered, *"Please, please! I have a wife and children. Please don't kill me!"* He began to cry and stumbled as Cal pushed him further into the woods. He tripped and fell face first into the wet leaves.

Salazar knew he was about to die. He had never been a religious man, but now, as he struggled for breath and the panic was overwhelming, he turned and looked up at Cal, who now had his combat knife in his hand. "Will you let me pray?" Cal paused for a moment, then nodded.

Salazar slowly rolled over and pushed back on the ground until he was on his knees. He did not think he could stand so he turned slightly to a direction he thought was the East, put his handcuffed hands flat on the ground, then bowed his head towards the ground until his forehead was flat against it. He prayed as he had done in years past.

When he was finished, Cal said, "Where are you from?"

Salazar had feared that this American would kill him as soon as he saw that he was a Muslim. But he was now calm. He said, "My parents brought me here from the Philippines when I was a boy."

"What is your name?"

"My full name is Rashid Mohammed Salazar." He saw that Cal had put away his knife.

"Get up." Salazar struggled to his feet.

Cal pulled out a ring with a small key and opened one handcuff. He motioned Salazar over to a nearby tree and Salazar stumbled over to it.

"Get down on your knees and put your hands around it." Salazar was trembling as he reached around the tree. Cal took the loose handcuff and reattached it to Salazar's wrist.

"No one will hear you from here, but a call will be made in the morning to the place where you work. They will be told where to find you. Allahu Akbar." Cal went back to the 4Runner and left.

Chapter 76 – An Unknown Vehicle

Friday, 0830 hours.

The task force was looking for at least three vehicles. The M809, the Mustang, and the ambulance, which they believed would be the bomb vehicle. It was possible more than one vehicle would be loaded with explosives.

Jack and Kat were at the Philadelphia FBI field office. Mike had taken charge of the enhanced SWAT team and was at the stadium.

Jack said, "The evidence list from the barn in Person County includes parts typically used with an acetylene torch, but the torch is missing as well as other metal working equipment. They were using the M809 to transport the bomb materials, so the ambulance must be here in Philadelphia. An empty ambulance box is about the same size as the rental truck box. They would have needed the torch and equipment to modify the ambulance to hold the explosives."

Kat had pulled up a photo of a Philadelphia ambulance. "We're pretty sure that they'll be painting the ambulance to match a Philadelphia ambulance, right?"

"That's right. There was also evidence that the barn had been used as a paint booth. A neighboring farmer said that one of the boys was a real wizard doing paint and body work. He had talked to them about the paint job on the Mustang."

Jack was standing in front of a map of the city. It had been enlarged and covered a five-foot by eight-foot section of one of the walls in the conference room. Areas that had been searched that contained any type of warehouse were marked off in red.

"We had a report that a restored Mustang has been seen in the vicinity of the stadium, but that's it. No specific model or other information to connect it to the Hendricks."

"They were probably leaving the truck and the ambulance hidden and using the Mustang for transportation," said Kat. "Now that they know we have been at the farm and that we're looking for the Mustang, they probably will keep it hidden also. They must be using an unknown vehicle."

CHAPTER 77 – In Position

Saturday. Fifteen minutes before kick-off.

Johnny Lee had cut his hair and trimmed his beard. He had not wanted to do it, but his father said it was required.

He pulled the M809 over into the break-down lane. The truck had been painted solid white, the winch had been removed, and the bumpers had been replaced. The box on the back had a company logo painted on the sides. Other than the number of wheels, it didn't resemble a military vehicle.

The interstate bordered the southern side of the stadium. Johnny Lee had pulled over just southeast of the stadium, adjacent to the parking area to the east of the stadium below. The truck had been heading west on the interstate, with the stadium to its right, so there was nothing between it and the guardrails closest to the parking lot below.

He got out and put orange traffic cones at an angle trailing behind the truck. He pulled out a tarp and spread it on the ground underneath the rear end of the truck then grabbed a tool box that had been on the floor boards and placed it on the ground by the tarp. He took out a rusted universal joint that he bought at a junkyard and put it next to the tool box. He opened the box and laid out some tools.

Cal was sitting on a stool inside the box on the back of

the M809. He swung inward the square of wood that had been cut out of the sidewall of the box. It had been hinged so that it could be opened. The exterior of the piece was black and had been part of the underline under the name on the side of the box. From a distance, the opening in the side of the truck was indistinguishable from black paint surrounding it.

He opened the case to his sniper rifle and took out the rifle. He attached the scope, adjusted the sights, and waited.

CHAPTER 78 – Man Down!

The stadium had been searched from top to bottom. Every vehicle. Every supply room, storage room, ticket office, mechanical room, locker room, and trashcan. If someone was going to explode a bomb, they would have to bring it in because there were none in the stadium.

All the normal supply and delivery trucks had already come and gone. Mike's enhanced SWAT team was in position. Teams with dogs would stop and search all trucks.

Jack set up a command post by the stadium in one of the FBI vans that contained computer and communications equipment. Inside the van, Eric sat at a computer screen showing eight different video feeds in real time of the area around the stadium.

The stadium security office was monitoring all internal cameras, as well as the cameras located at the top of the stadium for TV play-by-play. Jack had arranged for direct communication between the network televising the game, the stadium security office, and the command van. Eric was patched into the television producer's communication network and could transmit directly to the camera operators.

The shot rang out just as jets flew over at the end of the national anthem. Cal had singled out a group of three sailors walking quickly through the east-side parking lot. They had driven from Newport, Rhode Island, and were late due to traffic.

Cal followed them with his scope as they moved away from him towards the stadium. The instant before he squeezed the trigger he had a flashback to the mountains of Afghanistan. These were the enemy of his people and it was kill or be killed.

The first round slammed into the trailing sailor's shoulder. He spun around and dropped to the asphalt. His buddies instinctively ducked. When they saw that their friend was hit, they began moving back toward where he was lying on the pavement. Hendricks aimed for center body mass of another sailor, fired the second round, and a dark circle of red appeared in the middle of his uniform.

The shots had been lost in the roar of the jets. A security officer at the east lot saw the sailors go down and screamed "shot out!" and "man down!" into his microphone. "Get an ambulance to the east lot!"

Jack yelled, "Eric!"

Eric scanned the screen views. He saw nothing in the east lot. He got to the upper right section. "White box truck. Southeast of stadium. Stationary on the interstate."

While Eric was reading the screen, a report came in from the police officers on the north side of the stadium. Two ambulances with lights and sirens were approaching. Over the speaker, they heard, "The second one! About fifty yards behind the first one! It's the one!"

"Okay," Jack said, "Let the first one through and make sure you stop that second one!"

All gates had been equipped with stop sticks to spread across the roadway. The driver would be targeted as well as the vehicle tires. All necessary force was to be used to bring the ambulance to a halt. If an explosion occurred at the checkpoint distance it would not demolish the stadium, but it would still kill many people—including those with the duty to stop it.

*   *   *   *

AS the ambulances sped towards the stadium, police officers were blocking off the east and west bound lanes of the interstate. A SWAT team began maneuvering between parked cars in the parking lot towards the white truck above on the interstate.

Rounds fired by Cal from the truck smashed through the windows of the cars where the officers were taking cover. After the last vehicles on the highway cleared the truck, the SWAT team opened fire. The rounds fired by the SWAT team penetrated the wood box walls but flattened on hitting the hardened steel plates fastened to the interior of the walls.

A police car sped up the on ramp and onto the interstate toward the truck. Cal had moved to the back of the truck and cracked open the back doors. As the police car came closer, he fired several rounds between the back doors. The rounds smashed through the police car's windshield. The car swerved, hit the guardrail, flipped and tumbled down into the parking lot below, landing on its top. The tank ruptured, and flames leapt up the sides of the car as the officers scrambled out the window openings.

*   *   *   *

AT the north gate, the guards let the first ambulance through then threw out the stop sticks across the gate opening. The sticks did their job. The ambulance stopped rolling three hundred feet from the stadium. It sat silent in the middle of the road to the parking areas. Mike had immediately sprinted towards the approaching ambulance when he heard the call. As he approached, he looked through the front windshield. No one in the cab.

Mike ducked low and approached the driver's side door and yelled, "I'll give you three seconds to come out or you're a dead man!" From inside the cab, rounds started bursting through the sheet metal in the door. One of the rounds hit Mike's Kevlar helmet and knocked it off his head. Another round hit Mike, just outside his vest's coverage, and ripped through his side. He hit the ground, blood darkening the side of his uniform.

The rounds stopped and with all his strength, Mike grabbed the door handle. He pulled himself up and shoved the MP5 over his head and through the broken glass jutting up from the door sill. He opened fire and rounds sprayed through the ambulance cab. He yanked the door open and saw Mahmoud on the opposite side. His body was riddled with gunshot wounds and had sunk down onto the passenger side floor. His head was resting back on the seat cushion, mouth open and eyes staring at the ceiling of the cab.

Mike put a foot on the running board, grabbed the door frame and swung into the cab. He looked through the opening between the cab and the box. He saw the detonator, a bundle of water-gel explosives that had been tightly-bound to a timer, and duct-taped to a barrel. He ripped the detonator off the barrel, jumped out of the cab, and heaved it as far as he could into the sea of empty cars in the parking lot. It skittered off the top of a Honda Civic and landed between two rows of cars. A second later, the cars on either side of the explosion rocked back like the parting of the Red Sea. The glass in cars within a fifty-foot radius shattered. Car alarms blared.

* * * *

JACK and Kat grabbed their MP5's and got into the Mercedes parked nearby. Kat sped towards the nearest entry ramp to the interstate. As they entered onto the interstate the car was already doing eighty miles per hour.

Just as they merged onto the interstate, there was a massive explosion a quarter-mile ahead. Kat braked hard and the tail end of the car swerved around. Shrapnel from the exploding truck pelted the side of the car, and spider web cracks appeared in the bullet proof windows. The truck's tailgate flew by, narrowly missing the Mercedes, and slid down the highway.

* * * *

TWENTY seconds before the explosion, Eric was agitated and had struggled with how to tell the camera operator at the top of the stadium what he wanted him to do. He finally shouted into his headset, "I would like to see the other side of the white truck on the interstate!"

The operator quickly swung the camera around. Eric now had a view of the roadway, which was otherwise deserted, and caught sight of two men dashing across the east-bound lane and then jumping over the railing to the embankment. Just as the men cleared the railing and dropped to the embankment below, the truck exploded and obscured the picture.

He shouted again into the headset, "Move the picture to the road on the other side of the interstate!" As the smoke cleared, Eric caught sight of a white Toyota 4Runner. "Keep the picture showing that white Toyota 4Runner! " He calmed down and said, "It is this year's model."

"Jack, are you there?"

"We're here, Eric. Did you see the truck explode?"

"Yes, but two men got out before the explosion and jumped over the side railing. They are in a new white Toyota 4Runner. I just lost visual contact."

CHAPTER 79 – Escape Route

Cal had bought airline tickets for Banafsha and their daughters-in-law weeks before. They were all U.S. citizens, free to travel to Pakistan. Cal, Frankie, and Johnny Lee would go to Pakistan first, and then Afghanistan. Cal told them that they would "fight alongside the Taliban against the invaders."

After leasing the shop, Cal had contacted a charter boat captain. "Yes, the fifty-five-foot Ocean Sport Fisherman could be booked for a forty-eight-hour fishing trip. Great idea to spend time out with your sons. Has three staterooms, three heads, and a full galley. Five-hundred dollars will hold it for that day, but I'll need the balance at the time of departure."

The escape out of the U.S. had been arranged with al Qaeda's help. A cargo ship was departing from Jersey City to the United Arab Emirates three days after the bombing. The shipmaster would receive identity papers for three Americans, and they would be brought on as crew members. Al Qaeda affiliates in the U.A.E. would arrange for transportation of the Hendricks to Pakistan, where they would meet up with Banafsha and the other women.

When they were in the inter-coastal waterway, Cal would "convince" the captain by gunpoint that it was in his best interest to take them to the Jersey City port. Once they reached the port, they would kill the captain and dispose of his body overboard. Even if the FBI discovered that the three were alive and could connect them to the missing captain, they would be long gone.

The arrest of Banafsha had complicated things. But Cal had told his sons that she had plenty of cash, and he had retained a good lawyer. They couldn't prove that she knew where they were when she was asked. They couldn't prove that she knew what they were doing in the barn. They would have to release the women.

CHAPTER 80 – The Docks

"They must be going to the docks," said Jack. "Hendricks would expect that we'd be looking for a car or truck."

Kat swung the car towards the riverfront. "If they get out in a boat, we may lose them. There are hundreds of boats on the water. It's a short trip across the river to New Jersey. No way the Coast Guard can stop and search every one of them."

"Eric, this is Jack. Call over to the New Jersey State Police. Tell them that the suspects may be crossing over the river to the New Jersey side by boat. They must have a vehicle over there waiting on them."

Kat turned down South Columbus Boulevard, which ran along the waterfront. As they passed each street they looked down its length towards the river.

"Wait, go back!" Jack said. "I think I saw a 4Runner go down that last one." Kat slammed the car into reverse, racing backwards and turned the wheel so the nose of the car pointed down the street towards the water. She shifted back into drive and sped toward the docks.

A vehicle backing up from a parking space didn't see the Mercedes. Kat braked hard and tried to steer around the tail end of the vehicle. She didn't make it. The Mercedes clipped the car's left rear bumper and spun it around. The Mercedes skidded to its right and stopped with its right side toward the 4Runner.

Rounds started smashing into the side of the car and windows. Enough rounds were hitting the bulletproof glass that it weakened, and bullets began penetrating into the car.

Kat and Jack ducked down as rounds ripped into the upholstery. They slid out of the car on Kat's side with their MP5's. Kat crouched low and using the Mercedes as cover, dropped back into the row of parked cars behind them. She motioned to Jack that she was moving down the row of cars to get a better firing angle on the 4Runner. Jack understood and gave her the go sign.

Jack stayed by the left front tire of the Mercedes, putting the car and its engine block between him and the incoming fire. He leaned around the front of the Mercedes to give Kat covering fire, shooting out the 4Runner's windows and rear tires.

He heard a fishing yacht's engines and saw a man with a white boat captain's hat untying the rope that held the boat to the dock. A tall man with graying hair and a beard was holding a gun on the back of the captain's head.

"It's over Hendricks," Jack yelled. "Throw down your gun! Think of your wife. She would want you to live."

Johnny Lee sprang from behind the 4Runner and ran towards the boat. Jack popped up from behind the Mercedes, resting his rifle on its hood. He quickly aimed and fired a three-round burst, striking Johnny Lee. He stumbled and sprawled on the dock, with his head jammed against a post and showing no signs of life.

Rounds began hitting the hood of the Mercedes and Jack

ducked low behind the fender. Another burst of fire came from his right where Kat had maneuvered to a position on the other side of the 4Runner. Frankie had been firing from the rear end of the 4Runner. The rounds Kat fired had torn away a large portion of his forehead. He fell against the rear bumper and crumpled to the ground.

When Jack looked up, he saw the boat moving quickly away from the dock with no sign of either Hendricks or the boat captain. Jack slowly raised up from his position, not realizing that Cal had left the boat.

Jack yelled out, "Kat, you okay?!"

Cal had circled around Jack. He was now behind the car that Kat had clipped with the Mercedes. Jack heard Kat scream "Jack!" almost simultaneously with a burst of automatic weapon fire.

Cal Hendricks, standing ten feet behind Jack, was hit center mass by several rounds. He hadn't seen Kat who had moved back to a position behind Jack. Hendricks' backward motion, caused by the rounds slamming into his chest, raised his rifle just enough so that the round that he managed to fire flew inches over Jack's head.

Jack turned and saw Cal sprawled in the parking lot gravel. His war had ended.

CHAPTER 81 – An Offer

The next day, Jack and Kat visited Mike in his hospital room. An ambulance had taken Mike to the hospital immediately after the explosion in the parking lot. The round that deflected off the door went through the outer portion of Mike's hip, but there would be no permanent damage.

"You're sure I can't sue the government?"

"Mike, you know that wearing any of that protective equipment doesn't guarantee that you won't get shot," said Jack. "Besides, you're too big a target to miss."

"Very funny." He looked over at Kat. "You're a lawyer too. How about a second opinion?"

"I would agree with Jack. You are too big a target to miss."

"Okay, guess I'll just be glad the round didn't mess up any of my tatts. Tough to touch those up."

Mike paused and in a serious tone said, "Kat, that was quick thinking on your part about the ambulance. Don't know if we would have been able to stop the attack if you hadn't come up with that plan."

* * * *

AFTER Jack got off the phone with Eileen Carswell, who had

said that her cousin Bill had sold an ambulance to Hendricks, Kat had turned to Jack and said, "They're going to paint it to look like a Philadelphia ambulance. We need to change the odds on finding this ambulance before they strike the target.

"How about we contact the New York field office and tell them we need to do an ambulance exchange. I checked and the ambulances in each city are different enough, in pattern and color scheme, that you can tell them apart without even reading the name on the side. Any Philly ambulances not sent to New York should be grounded."

When the New York fire departments and law enforcement agencies learned why the request was being made, there was more than just agreement. The fire department was willing to send rescue vehicles, with off-duty volunteers, to work the day in Philadelphia. Off-duty law enforcement officers volunteered to assist in site security under state assistance agreements already in place. New York offered firetrucks, off-duty SWAT team members, bomb squads, and whatever else Philadelphia needed. The vehicles would be on the road that afternoon and arrive after sunset.

On Saturday morning, all Philadelphia ambulances that remained in the city had been grounded. Word had gone out that any moving Philadelphia ambulance would be stopped using any force necessary.

* * * *

AS Jack and Kat were leaving Mike's hospital room, Jack said, "Get well soon and come down and visit us in the sticks."

Mike first looked at Kat and then over at Jack. "I hate to tell you this, but it looks like you're going to make it back to civilization—if that's what you want."

"Meaning?"

"Headquarters asked me about someone to fill in for me as head of the enhanced SWAT team here in D.C. while I get back to full speed. I have a feeling the job may be more permanent. There was talk of transferring me to the Academy as Special Agent in Charge."

"And you recommended me?"

"Yeah, but your call. If you want to stay in the boonies, they'll go with someone else." Jack looked at Kat and saw a trace of a smile.

CHAPTER 82 – Foolish Pride

The D.C. office had arrested Banafsha's brother, Romal Abdullah, and the Sudan embassy custodian, Mohammed Alazhari. Alazhari had no diplomatic immunity and with numerous charges under the federal anti-terrorism act, both he and Abdullah would be spending the rest of their lives in a maximum security federal prison.

After Cal had purchased the airline tickets for the women, he gave a large cash retainer to a prominent Raleigh criminal defense attorney, Jamison Dell. He explained to Dell that he wanted to have an attorney who could be contacted on short notice for representation.

Dell accepted the fifty thousand dollars in cash that Hendricks had given him and held it in a trust account. Hendricks had documentation that it had been received tax-free, and Dell was satisfied that it had been lawfully obtained. Attorneys had been indicted for federal money laundering by accepting ill-gotten gains in return for services. He gave Hendricks his business card with his personal cell phone number on the back. Hendricks gave it to Banafsha before he left with instructions on what to do if law enforcement came to the farm.

The government disclosed to Dell the evidence that it had

against the women. After speaking to Banafsha at the jail, Dell called Daniel Baxter, the Assistant U.S. Attorney handling the case.

"Hey, Dan, this is Jim Dell."

"Jim Dell. And why do I have the pleasure of getting his call?"

"I represent the Hendricks on this supposed conspiracy to violate anti-terrorism laws."

Baxter had litigated against Dell in the past. He was good and was not one for boasting when he thought the government had a weak case—unless it did.

"Okay, Jim, lay it out for me."

"First, the government has no evidence that shows that these women took any steps at all to aid or abet the commission of any offense or even knew what was happening in the barn. The call from Banafsha Hendricks to her brother was to be expected. Of course, she would call her brother and tell him that she had been arrested and that the FBI was looking for her husband and sons. Her brother was her only relative in the United States and would be the person she would turn to if arrested."

Baxter had assumed Dell would be angling for a favorable plea deal. "Come on, Jim. So, it's pure coincidence that her brother, an al Qaeda agent, is conspiring with her husband, and she calls him immediately after she is arrested, and she tells him that they are looking for her husband and sons." Baxter paused, waiting for the expected response.

"You know that this kind of circumstantial evidence isn't sufficient to show a definite step to aid or abet her husband in a conspiracy. Further, if the government could prove, and I'm not saying it can, that the women knew where their husbands were, the most that she or any of the women could be found guilty of would be harboring a fugitive."

Baxter thought about it. *He wants to deal. Guilty to harboring and drop the other charges. He hasn't run it by his clients yet.*

"Jim, I understand what you are saying. I'll see if there's any interest in offering a deal. Perhaps your clients have information about other terrorists. But if your clients want to go to trial, we're willing to roll the dice."

Dell said he would get back to him. He went back to the jail the next day to speak to the women. He told them that the government would throw the book at them and it was possible that at least one or more of the charges would stick. It was always a risk going to a jury, and in the climate now about terrorism in the United States, they could be looking at very long prison terms—even if convicted of lesser charges.

The next day, Dell called Baxter.

"Hello, Dan."

"Hi Jim. What's up?

"On the Hendricks case. We're concerned that a jury would find it difficult to follow the court's instructions, due to the circumstances. To avoid a conviction where emotions might prevail, and my clients are found guilty of something they didn't do, they might plead guilty to the right offer."

"Okay, what's the right offer?"

"The government probably has sufficient evidence to show harboring a fugitive. They'll plea to that with a major fine. They would agree to relinquishing their citizenship, deportation and permanent bar from entering the United States."

"And?"

"That's it. You get convictions—which aren't a given in

this case. Of course, the farm will be forfeited to the government. They pay a major fine and are deported. We can show that the Muslim culture in general, and in this case, is a male-dominated one. Women aren't involved in decision making. They are required to worship separately. Do you really think that a jury is going to believe these passive women were involved in this plot?"

"Look, Jim, you know we can't let this go without prison terms. We've also got a charge of failing to report treason—these were American citizens helping those who are killing Americans overseas. They are at war with us. That's a seven-year prison sentence. We're going to need them to serve some time."

"Well, run our harboring plea up the flagpole and let's see what the U.S. Attorney says. I don't know that I could recommend a deal that puts them in prison when the government has a shaky case anyway."

The next day, Baxter called Dell. "Okay, here's what we will do. They plead to the harboring charge. They pay a fine of two hundred thousand dollars. We know they have it since we got into Hendricks' safe deposit box with a court order. They renounce their U.S. citizenship, do a year in a minimum security federal country club—excuse me, I meant a federal penitentiary—deportation and lifetime ban on entry into the U.S."

"Okay, I'll have to talk to my clients, but I doubt that they'll be interested in prison terms. I'll call down to the jail to see if I can meet with them this afternoon."

* * * *

LATER that afternoon at the jail, Banafsha told Dell something that he thought might be very helpful. It was close to 5:30 p.m., and Dell caught Baxter as he was leaving his office.

"Okay, Dan. Here's what I am authorized to tell you. The deal is fine, except for the prison time. We want to make a counter-offer. One of my clients, and I can't tell you which one, has told me that she might have information on the whereabouts of Robert Alan Haislip. She did not tell me what the information might be. She says that if the government is willing to delete the confinement, then they would all go for the deal that you proposed. Otherwise, no information, and they would go to trial."

Ten years before, Dell had been involved in a similar situation when he was a State prosecutor. He learned then that the whereabouts of a missing person, almost always the body, was a powerful incentive to the government to resolve a case. The victim's family would be consulted first. If the State, or in this case the federal government, could bring closure for the victim's family, they were usually willing to give a better deal.

There was silence for a moment from Dan Baxter's end of the line. "Just so I understand this. Same deal we just gave, less confinement, and your client tells us where to find Robert Haislip."

"That's my understanding."

"I'll check and get back to you." Baxter hung up and pushed the speed dial button for the U.S. Attorney for the Eastern District.

* * * *

IT had been on the night that Frankie and Johnny Lee had taken the pickup truck and were gone for several hours. Their wives were worried. Cal said that they had to go pick up something and to go to sleep. They would be back later that night.

It was close to ten p.m. when Banafsha woke up. She lay in bed with her eyes closed but heard the truck drive around the back of the house on the gravel driveway. Cal had put on his overalls and boots and headed out the back door.

Banafsha got up out of bed and stood back from the dark upper back windows of the farm house so she couldn't be seen. She saw Cal get on his backhoe and start the engine. The pickup truck was parked on the garden side of the barn. Cal dug a trench behind the back edge of the garden where the produce had already been picked. Frankie and Johnny Lee put a tarp in the trench and Cal covered it up.

The next day, Cal used the tractor to rake out a large area on top of and surrounding where he had dug the night before. He spread a quick-growing grass seed. He fertilized the area and put straw on top. The grass had come up and now there was no difference between the newly sown area and the surrounding yard.

Banafsha had read the federal charges about the use of a man's credit card and drivers' license. The date of the first use was several days after the night that she saw Cal dig the trench by the garden.

The day after Dell told Baxter that they had information on Haislip, Dell got a call from Baxter. "Tell your clients that we have a deal if we find Haislip. If not, no deal."

* * * *

A WEEK later, in a small cemetery outside of Culpeper, Virginia, Bobby Haislip was buried next to his mother. Jack, Mike, Kat, and Eric were there.

Sheila Haislip had come from California. She stood by the grave and a gray and shriveled old man sat in a wheelchair at her side. He breathed with the help of oxygen running through clear plastic tubing from a tank. Tears rolled down his face. He had been estranged from his son for many years. The last words they had spoken to each other had been words of anger. *Oh Lord! Oh foolish pride!*

CHAPTER 83 – Change Of Heart

Jack was on administrative leave. It was standard practice to do a line of duty investigation when a suspect was killed during an investigation. He had come back to Fayetteville and had received authorization to act as co-counsel in the upcoming hearing in J.T.'s case.

Aunt Gina said, "Oh, it is so good that I can cook for both of you! It's been a long time. Too long."

Jack said, "Aunt Gina, all you have to do is ask us to dinner, and we'll come! No one can cook like you."

J.T. said, "Yeah, Aunt Gina, you know that I'll come to Fayetteville in a heartbeat to eat here. I'm ready to make up for lost time."

As they were finishing dinner, Aunt Gina set down her glass of wine. "Boys, there is something that I need to say. You are both grown men and maybe I should have said this a long time ago." Jack and J.T. stopped eating and put down their silverware.

"It's about your mother, bless her soul. She was a very strong woman, especially towards the end." Both Jack's and J.T.'s eyes began to moisten. "She was strong because she had to be—for both you boys and for your father.

"He was caught up in the war and your mother knew that there was nothing that he could do for her here. No one knew how long your mother would live. It could have been six months, or even several years.

"She told me that he had wanted to stay here with her. Give up his military career. Your mother would have none of it. She knew that your father would probably save the lives of other men by his decisions, so they could come home to their families.

"The end came much quicker than anyone thought it would. When your father was told that she had perhaps three months to live, he made sure that he would be back in two weeks. But it was only three days after he left when your mother took a turn for the worse. We got word to him right away and he headed back." Aunt Gina began to cry and wiped her eyes with her napkin.

"He flew to Germany, and then to the U.S. He was still in his field uniform when he came in that same afternoon, only hours after your mother had passed.

"She had told me the day before that she didn't think that she had much time left. She told me to tell your father, if she couldn't, that she loved him and that he should have no regrets that he might not be here when the time came. She knew that she was always in his thoughts, and in his heart." She stopped and looked from one to the other.

"She knew that you might resent him not being here during the many times when you were young, and at the end. But she hoped as you grew, you would come to understand his sacrifice—not being the father and husband that he could have been because of the call of duty for his country."

J.T. began to see what Jack had learned from his own

experience. Their father's career in the military, and his willingness to sacrifice what others might take for granted, wasn't done out of selfishness. His father's service to the country was for his own family's protection. But it was also something bigger. It was part of the combined effort by all that serve to ensure freedom for all Americans.

EPILOGUE

Jack parked in the courthouse parking lot. Kat got out on the passenger side. She was also on administrative leave and told Jack she wanted to stay in North Carolina for the hearing, if that was okay with him. Jack had smiled and said, "I couldn't think of anyone better to be there. You did tell me that you were 'a criminal lawyer,' right? I may need your help."

"I seriously doubt that. From what we've discussed, I think you would make a great trial lawyer."

When Mike had told Jack about the job in D.C., he was almost relieved. Now he would have to decide. Kat was no longer detailed to the task force. And yet, Pam was in North Carolina. He decided that he would focus on J.T.'s case and put the D.C. job offer on hold.

He grabbed his brief case and they headed up the walk. He saw Mike in the lobby area, standing next to a tall, attractive woman. It wasn't until he got closer and they both turned towards him that he recognized the woman.

Jack looked at Mike and said, "Well, I guess Hell has officially frozen over. Sarah, don't say I didn't warn you about this guy."

"I would have to admit that there was full disclosure," said Sarah with a grin.

"We're headed to Myrtle Beach later to do a little investigation of the shore line," said Mike. "We thought we'd stop by to see you in action. I'd say good luck, but I don't think you need it."

"Well, thanks for the moral support. See you later." Jack opened one of the large doors to the courtroom and they went inside.

The courtroom was crowded. All the Assistant D.A.'s had cleared their schedules for this one. The Honorable John Sinclair, the duly elected District Attorney, was in the courtroom.

General Maxwell Thomas sat in the first row on the defendant's side of the courtroom. On the left side of his uniform dress coat were eight rows of multi-colored ribbons, including the one representing two awards of the Purple Heart. He wore the Combat Infantry Badge, the Airborne, Ranger, and Special Forces tabs, and an overseas combat patch. The uniform bore the evidence of a life of sacrifice for his country. He had just received his third star and Lieutenant General Thomas would soon be stationed at the Pentagon.

Aunt Gina sat next to Max. She wore a simple dress with no jewelry. Her hair was now snow white. She helped as a teacher's assistant at the elementary school on post and still prepared meals for Max, who complained that her Italian cooking would be the end of his physical conditioning program. Tom Berkshire, J.T.'s probation officer from his case in Raleigh, sat next to Aunt Gina. Jack went up to Aunt Gina and they hugged. He shook hands with his father and Tom Berkshire, and then went to the defendant's table. J.T. was sitting next to Garrett Miller.

Jack had told J.T. that now would be a good time to get a

haircut and wear a suit. J.T. had grudgingly agreed. He looked like a mid-level manager of a large manufacturing company—which he was.

Jack sat next to J.T. and looked over to Miller with some uncertainty. "You're sure I should be handling this motion?"

"Absolutely. When you called me with the argument, based on the statute, I was very impressed. Who better to argue it?"

"Well," Jack said with a smile, "I'll wait to thank you for continuing the case until after the judge rules."

Jack knew that the judges rotated among the districts to hear cases. It was possible that Judge Ackerman, who had given J.T. probation on his felony conviction would be the trial judge. He knew that would not bode well for J.T.

Judge Ackerman was not the assigned judge, but he was in the courtroom. He had a standing order with the Court Clerk's office to notify him if anyone he had sentenced to probation was ever re-arrested. In this instance, he thought it was possible that another West Point graduate, who happened to play football for the Academy, would be in the courtroom. He told JoAnn Burnett to clear his calendar on the date of the hearing.

"I have someone I have to meet in Sanford, and I'll also be having lunch with Judge Flynn to discuss the presentation at the judicial conference."

"Okay, judge," said JoAnn with a smile, fully realizing why he was going to Sanford. "Please say hello to General Thomas for me—if you should just happen to run into him while you're there."

* * * *

JUDGE Claiborne Flynn had graduated near the top of his class at Harvard Law. He had been born in Sanford and went to Duke University on a full scholarship. He graduated with a 4.0 average, and a double major in English and History. He had written two books. One was on the changing English lexicon in America's courtrooms since the 1700's, and the other was on the use and description of courtroom proceedings in nineteenth-century American fiction.

Judge Flynn looked down at D.A. Sinclair at the prosecutor's table and at Jack and Miller at the defendant's table. "Counsel, are you ready to proceed?"

After getting affirmation from both counsel that they were ready, Judge Flynn continued, "We'll hear the defendant's Motion to Suppress, Mr. Thomas. It is my understanding that there are no disputed facts? We will not need any fact witnesses?"

Jack stood. "Yes, your Honor, that's correct. I have a Stipulation of Fact that I would request be admitted as our Exhibit 1."

D.A. Sinclair said, "we have so stipulated, Your Honor."

"You may approach."

Sinclair already had his copy. Jack walked it to the clerk, who stamped it, marked it as Defendant's Exhibit Number One and handed it up to the Judge. Jack returned to his seat.

The judge took a minute to review the exhibit. "The stipulation before me is that the State has agreed that Officer Dearborn approached the defendant's vehicle, said, 'Sir, do you realize that your right brake light is out? I am going to have to write a citation.' That nothing else was said, and that no other reason was given for stopping the vehicle. Is that correct?"

Jack responded, "That's correct, Your Honor."

The judge nodded and said, "You may proceed."

"Your Honor, the defendant seeks the suppression of the evidence in this case, both the marijuana that was obtained from the console, as well as the trace evidence found in the ashtray, based on an absence of probable cause for the stop of the vehicle.

"Simply stated, your Honor, the controlling statute is not ambiguous. A single 'brake lamp' is all the statute requires. This can be distinguished from the statute's requirement that a vehicle have rear 'lamps.' Although rear lamps or taillights are required, only one brake lamp, or light, is required.

"Because the defendant was operating his vehicle fully within the law, Officer Dearborn stopped the defendant's truck without any legal basis. This was an unlawful seizure of both the defendant and vehicle.

"Absent an unlawful stop, he would not have had any cause to search the vehicle. The evidence in this case is the 'fruit of the poisonous tree.' It is evidence obtained after an illegal seizure. Under case precedent, which is binding on this court, it is inadmissible. The defendant respectfully requests that the Motion to Suppress be granted."

Miller had worked with Jack on the motion to suppress. He told Jack not to recite his entire motion. He had done some background research on the judge, and knew that he would have read the motion, would understand it, and probably would not appreciate a long repetitive presentation by counsel. If the judge had any questions, he would ask them.

Judge Flynn had no questions. He nodded to Sinclair. The District Attorney was nonplussed. If he was concerned about the motion, he didn't show it. He appeared confident as he began his argument to the court.

"Your Honor, Officer Dearborn is charged with the safety of the public, in this case on the roadways. The lack of an operating brake light could have disastrous consequences. Operating brake lights on both sides of the back of a vehicle help drivers to know—from any angle—that they must slow down or stop to avoid a collision. Clearly, Officer Dearborn observed something that he considered unsafe—"

"Objection!" Jack stood up.

Judge Flynn looked over to where Jack was standing. "On what basis, counsel?"

"Counsel for the State is speculating on what the Officer was thinking. The stipulation only states what he said to the defendant, not what he was thinking."

Judge Flynn smiled. He knew that Jack had limited experience in the courtroom but was impressed.

"Counsel," said the judge, looking at D.A. Sinclair, "the only evidence before the court is that Officer Dearborn asked the defendant whether he knew his brake light was out, and he was going to write a citation. I've already concluded that he believed that having only one operating brake light is a violation of the state's statute on required vehicular equipment. Objection sustained."

While the judge was speaking, Miller leaned over towards Jack and whispered, "Nice job, Jack. Looks like I'm going to have to raise that starting salary offer."

If Sinclair was upset by the ruling, he didn't show it. "Your Honor, regardless of whether the officer had grounds under the statute, he believed that he did. His mistake was an objectively reasonable one. He believed that a vehicle running with only one brake light was a violation of the statute. The

Fourth Amendment only requires a "reasonable" suspicion to justify a seizure.

"As noted by the court just a minute ago, we can logically infer that Officer Dearborn believed the statute required two brake lights, not one. Because Officer Dearborn's suspicion was reasonable, there was no constitutional violation, and the evidence must be admitted. The State respectfully requests that the Motion to Suppress be denied." Sinclair sat down.

Judge Flynn looked down at his notes, and then looked at both counsel tables. "If there is nothing else from the parties," he paused and waited several seconds, "I'm going to call a recess to deliberate." He smiled and said, "Don't go away." He banged the gavel. "This court is in recess."

Jack sensed Kat before she lightly put her hand on his shoulder. "You did a fantastic job, Jack. This is a major policy decision that could really end up in the Supreme Court one day."

Jack turned and said, "Thanks, Kat. He thought back to the docks in Philadelphia. "I wouldn't be here at all if it weren't for you."

She smiled. "I never told you, but I only fired that model one time before that day. I was just lucky I didn't hit you instead of Hendricks."

Ten minutes went by and Jack saw the bailiff about to call the court into Session. They all moved to their seats and stood while the court was called back into session.

Judge Flynn looked to both Jack and to Sinclair. "I would like to congratulate both counsel for their representation of their respective clients. This is an extremely complicated area of the law." He looked down at his desk, and then up again.

"Initially, I must tell you I find it fascinating that the term 'brake lamp' is still used in one of our statutes. I may just have to write a book about that." Several of the attorneys in the courtroom who knew of the judge's publications, and his wry sense of humor, almost laughed out loud but quickly caught themselves.

"Mr. Thomas, your brief points out some case precedent which strongly supports your argument. Unless there is some ambiguity on the face of a statute, then it must be read in its entirety and gain its context from the plain meaning of the words utilized.

"The same statute speaks of the requirement of taillights, in the plural. Logic supports your argument," he said, looking at Jack. "If that great legislative body that sits up the road in Raleigh had wanted 'brake lamps' to be in the statute, it would have put an 's' on the end of the word.

"Further, it is well-established law that any ambiguity in a criminal law is construed against the drafter, in this case, the State. A criminal defendant is protected against any attempt to rescue an ambiguity through artful construction by the State. In this case, I find the language unambiguous. A brake lamp means a single brake lamp, or light as we currently use the term."

Jack knew that even though the court had found that only one working brake light was required, he could still rule that the search, based on a mistake of law, wasn't unreasonable.

The judge continued, "However, the State makes a good point. There is another legal issue involved. If the officer believed that the statute required two brake lights, then is it unreasonable for him to have stopped the defendant's truck when only one was working?

"The problem I'm having with the State's position is this:

How do we objectively determine whether the officer truly made a mistake of law? What if a car is going forty-five miles per hour, the speed limit, and the officer wants to stop a vehicle based on any number of factors which may not provide probable cause, such as the appearance of the driver, the license plate, certain bumper stickers. He stops the car and there is evidence of unlawful activity. He later says that he 'thought' the speed limit was forty miles per hour."

As soon as the judge said, "The problem I'm having with the State's position," the lawyers and most others knew which way he was going to rule. "Based on the evidence before the court, and hearing the arguments of the respective parties, I find that Officer Dearborn did not know what the law required. He believed that the defendant had violated a statute, and that an offense was committed. I find further that the defendant was operating his vehicle fully within the requirements of the law.

"However, because the court finds that a 'mistake of law' cannot provide the reasonable suspicion required under the Fourth Amendment and doing so would ultimately undermine the protections afforded by the Constitution, the court concludes that the defendant's constitutional rights against search and seizure were violated. Of course, an appellate court may, at some point, create a different rule—but this court will not do so."

The judge paused and looked to the prosecutor's table, where Sinclair was taking notes. He then turned to the defendant's table and continued, "Evidence received as a direct result of such a violation is the fruit from the poisonous tree, as the defendant has alleged, and is inadmissible.

"The motion to suppress is granted. The bag of

marijuana and the trace of marijuana found in the ashtray may not be considered by the court in any trial on these charges."

The judge looked over to where Sinclair had been writing. Sinclair looked up. "Mr. District Attorney, would the State like to enter a dismissal at this time?"

Sinclair slowly stood up, determined not to show any disappointment in the court's decision. "Yes, Your Honor. In light of the court's ruling, in the absence of any admissible evidence of criminal activity, the State dismisses the charges in State v. Thomas."

"The case having been dismissed and there being no further matters for hearing, the court is adjourned." He banged the gavel, the bailiff said, "All rise," and the judge then exited out the side door into the adjoining chambers.

J.T. came forward and embraced Jack. "Thanks for being here for me, Jack." He turned to his father. He had thought about what Aunt Gina had said at dinner. "And thanks, Dad, for being here too."

Max hugged J.T. and looked at Jack over J.T.'s shoulder. "Thanks, Jack, for all you have done. I couldn't be prouder of you—and J.T."

John Sinclair came over and shook hands with Jack. "Good job, counselor. Guess you are off to a good start. Understand this was your first time in the courtroom. Glad it worked out for you."

"Thank you, sir. I know the State had evidence that my brother may have committed an offense. I think you would have found from all that know him that J.T. was innocent."

"Well, we are only seeking justice, and the court has ruled. As far as I can tell, justice has been done." He paused a second, then said, "I was very impressed today. I have an opening in my office for an assistant D.A. With your criminal investigative background and experience, I would be able to start you at a salary level that is probably comparable to what you're making with the FBI. You have my number. Think about it and give me a call."

Jack thanked him—then remembered that Pam had told Sinclair about their background together when she told him that she couldn't take the case. *She knew about the opening and suggested to Sinclair that I might be interested in the position.*

* * * *

MAX, Aunt Gina, and J.T. walked toward Max's car. Aunt Gina said, "I knew everything was going to be all right. I've got a big lunch planned to celebrate!" She looked at Jack and smiled. She then turned toward Kat, took one of her hands in both of her hands, and said, "Now Jack, you will be bringing this lovely lady with you to the lunch, won't you?"

"Absolutely, Aunt Gina. There is no way I would deprive her of one of your home-cooked meals! We'll meet you at the house."

Just then, they heard a voice behind them call out, "General Thomas." Max turned around. Walking briskly toward him was an impeccably dressed man in a gray pinstriped suit, white shirt, and purple tie. He stopped in front of Max and stuck out his hand. "General Thomas, I'm Sam Ackerman, West Point graduate. I'm sorry I didn't get to see you play in person, but I just wanted to shake your hand."

"Well, thank you, Sam," said Max, and he shook hands. Suddenly, Max remembered the name. "Aren't you Judge Ackerman, from Raleigh?" He realized that this was the judge who had sentenced J.T. to probation on his felony charge.

"Yes, General, one and the same. Something told me that your son here," nodding towards J.T., "was no real criminal that needed to go to prison. He just needed a wake-up call so that he didn't head down a path that could ruin his life. I spoke to Tom Berkshire before the hearing. If he tells me that 'no way' was it your son's marijuana—and that's what he told me—then I believe it."

Max looked over to J.T. "Well, my sincere appreciation for giving him the chance to show that he could make something of himself after his bonehead mistake at age nineteen. How about the next time I am up your way, we get some lunch together?"

"Sounds great, General. Anytime. Just call my assistant, JoAnn—who, by the way, sends her regards."

As Judge Ackerman turned and walked away, Max caught a glimpse of someone at the front entrance that he thought he knew.

"Uh, Jack, is that who I think it is over there, talking to the prosecutor?"

Jack followed his father's gaze and looked over to the front entrance. Kat also looked over to where a very attractive blonde-haired woman was talking to D.A. Sinclair.

"I think so."

Max said, "We'll go on ahead. See you at the house." Aunt Gina and J.T. got into the car. Kat had noticed a sudden change in Jack's demeanor.

"That's Pam Sorensen," said Jack, nodding in Pam's direction. We dated when we were in law school." Kat immediately sensed that Jack and Pam had been in more than a dating relationship.

The others were already leaving, and Jack wouldn't leave Kat by herself in the parking lot. "Mind if I go say hello? I'll introduce you."

Kat had sensed an initial hesitation in his invitation to meet Pam but then she thought it might just have been her imagination. "Not at all. I'd love to meet her."

When they got to the top steps, Pam immediately stepped forward and gave Jack a hug. "Great job in there, Jack."

Jack had a surreal moment when he hugged Pam. It was as if they hadn't been apart. He flashed back to when he had come out of a moot court competition and Pam had been there to congratulate him.

"Thanks. Pam, this is Special Agent Katherine Morris, with Homeland Security. We've been working together on a case."

"Nice to meet you Pam," said Kat. "And please call me Kat. Jack was telling me that you two met in law school."

Pam could see that there was something between Kat and Jack but wasn't quite sure what it was. *She is a beautiful woman.* "Yes, we were together for two years before Jack went into the Army. It's been great to see him again. I was really glad when I ran into him here last month." She could see from Kat's expression that Jack hadn't told her about their meeting. *A good sign.*

"Yes," said Jack, "I was surprised when I found out that Pam might be representing the State in J.T.'s case. Glad I didn't have to face her in the courtroom."

Kat now thought that there still might be something between Jack and Pam. *He met her here last month and here she is today.* "It's great that Jack got to see you again before he heads to D.C."

"Oh, you're moving?" Pam looked at Jack.

"I've been offered a position in the D.C. office."

He didn't say "yes" that he's moving, thought Pam, *and he didn't say that he had accepted the job. Another good sign.*

"Well, good luck on whatever you decide to do," said Pam. "Been great seeing you again." She stepped forward, gave him another hug and whispered "call me" into his ear away from Kat. She looked over at Kat. "Nice meeting you, Ms. Morris—I mean Kat," then turned and went into the building.

Jack and Kat walked back to Jack's car. "Hmmm. 'Together' for two years in law school. A meeting last month. And she just happened to be here today?"

A smile crossed Jack's face. "Well, she is an Assistant D.A. here." He was silent for a moment. He started the SUV, left it in park, and turned toward her. "Would you like to have dinner with me?"

AUTHOR'S NOTE

A case that would ultimately be heard by the United States Supreme Court began with a traffic stop on Interstate 77 in North Carolina.

In 2009, a police officer following a vehicle noticed that when the vehicle slowed, one of the brake lights was inoperable. The officer turned on his blue lights, believing that operating a vehicle with only one working brake light was a violation of North Carolina's traffic laws.

During the stop, the officer began to suspect that there were illicit drugs in the car. Nicholas Heien said he "didn't care" if the officer searched the car. The officer found cocaine and Heien was convicted of drug trafficking.

Heien moved to suppress the evidence at trial, arguing that because the traffic law only required one brake lamp, the stop was without probable cause. The trial court denied the motion.

Heien appealed to the N.C. Court of Appeals, which reversed the trial court's ruling and held that the stop violated the Fourth Amendment. The court stated that "an officer's mistaken belief that a defendant has committed a traffic violation is not an objectively reasonable justification for a traffic stop."

The State appealed to the North Carolina Supreme Court. The N.C. Supreme Court agreed with one of the federal circuit courts that an officer may make a mistake of law, but still act reasonably in making a stop. It held that the officer had acted reasonably and reversed the lower court's ruling that had suppressed the evidence.

The Supreme Court of the United States agreed to hear Heien's appeal. In 2014, the Court, over one dissenting vote, affirmed the ruling by the North Carolina Supreme Court. The Court held that a police officer's reasonable mistake of law can provide the suspicion required by the Fourth Amendment to justify a traffic stop based upon that understanding.

In reaction to the extended litigation, North Carolina amended its traffic laws. As of October 15, 2015, *two* working brake lights are required by statute.

ABOUT THE AUTHOR

HOWARD ALAN PELL received his B.A. in English and his law degree from the University of Florida. He retired from the Army with the rank of Colonel after a thirty-year career, active duty and reserve. He retired as an attorney with the State of North Carolina after a twenty-five-year career.

In the Judge Advocate General's Corps, he served as a prosecutor; defense appellate attorney; administrative law officer; commissioner (law clerk) for the Army's appellate court; and was the designated legal counsel to a Special Forces Group commander and a Major General commanding a Reserve division. He is a graduate of the Command and General Staff College and his awards include the Legion of Merit.

Mr. Pell was a Special Deputy Attorney General with the North Carolina Department of Justice, representing the State in criminal appellate litigation in State and federal courts, including oral argument before the N.C. Supreme Court. After ten years with the NCDOJ, he went to the N.C. General Assembly and served as a committee counsel for House and Senate Judiciary committees. He also drafted criminal law statutes and provided legal counsel to legislators on criminal justice issues. From 2000 to 2008, he was an Adjunct Professor of Law at the College of Law, University of North Carolina at Chapel Hill.

Mr. Pell has publications in several legal journals and periodicals, including the Florida Bar Journal and the Natural Resources Journal. *The War Within* is his first novel. Visit his website at http://www.howardpell.com.

Made in the USA
Coppell, TX
23 May 2020